The ... of Glass

A Gilded Gothic Romance

Brenna Lauren

GENTRY HOUSE PRESS

The Memory of Glass

1st Edition September 2023.

brennalaurenbooks.com

Published by Gentry House Press

Savannah, GA

Cover Artwork by Maple Projects, LLC

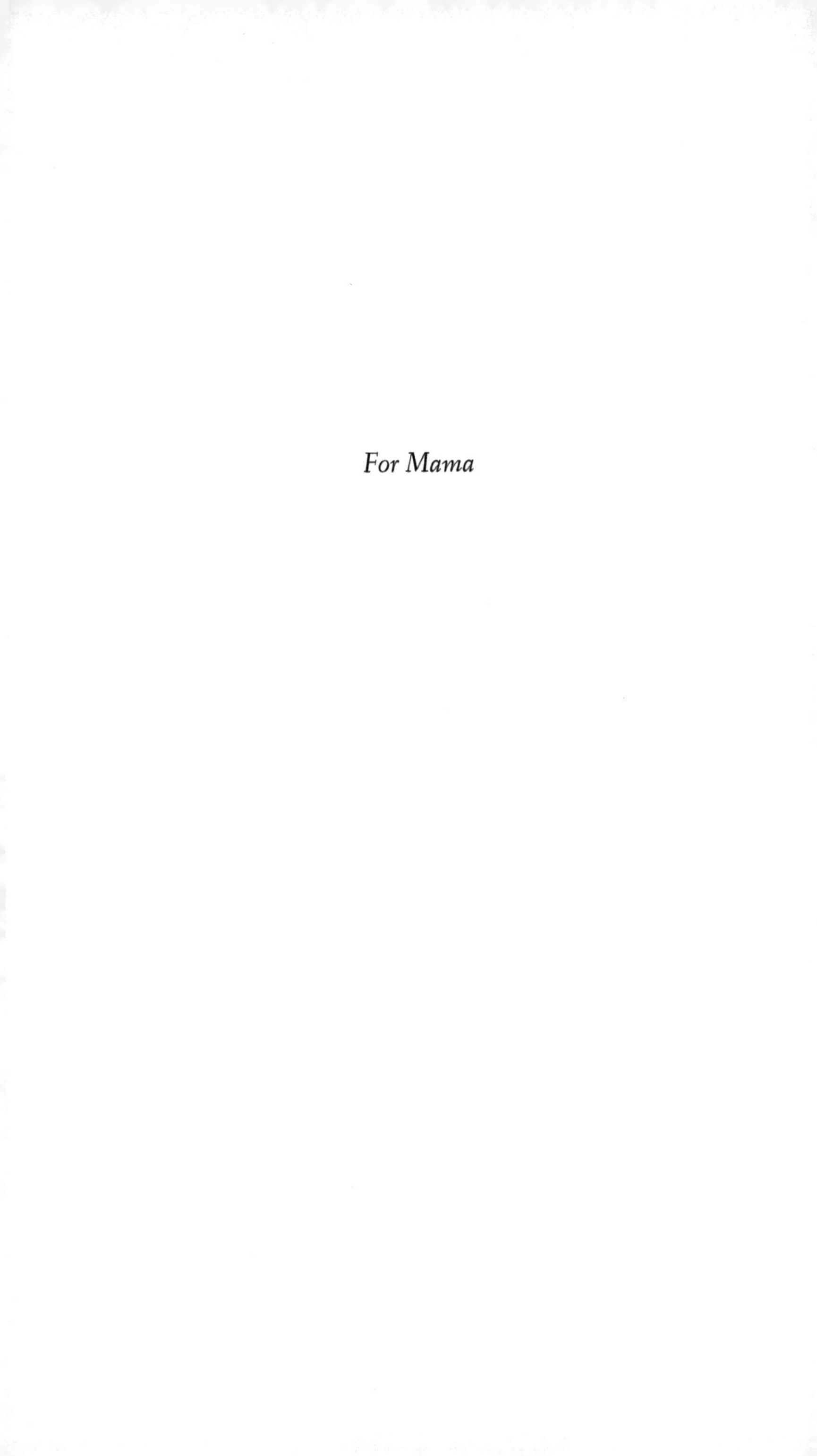

For Mama

Prologue

William Darling | 1933

"*Bury it.*
Six feet under the house.
Never you touch it again.
Move it, and the blessing falls to curse.
Move it, and he'll come after you."

My mind chanted the warning, over and over, twisting it through my brain.

I squeezed the vial of grave dirt in my trouser pocket.

For Julia. My Julia.

My boot slid across a mound of black pluff mud, sending a cascade of small ivory crabs scattering, vile and angry, in all directions.

I clenched my jaw.

Some claimed the Lowcountry was a magical place. Earth so lovely and wild, that the ocean made love with the shore, and the marsh was born. Beauty from chaos.

Solomon sent me here. Insisting on the old marsh magic.

And now I was beholden to it.

The root doctor had looked at me with kind eyes, wise and understanding. But he'd been deathly serious. Once the vial was buried beneath the house, it would protect my family from the penalty for what I'd done. But once buried, the vial could never be moved, never lifted from the ground beneath Darling House, or its protection would be voided, and all manner of hell let loose.

I looked back over my shoulder, impatience lengthening my stride. The root doctor's palmetto-flanked house sat not half a mile behind, perched on a hammock of land that stood sentinel amid a wide sea of spartina grass. Rolling black clouds sailed across the grey sky like schooners on a smooth ocean.

The tide would be in soon.

My gaze tracked several steps ahead.

Horace had told me once about seeing a man dragged from the grassy edge of a river. The alligator had moved like lightning, nearly wrenching the man's arm clear from his shoulder before he twisted with him into the dark water, never to be seen again.

My pulse leapt and I picked up my pace.

I should've brought a gun.

A gun.

A fresh shot of rage coursed through my bloodstream, but I shoved last night's bloody scene from mind. The white gown. The secret. The door at the bottom of the stairs.

The glass would remember. That was enough.

The glass remembered everything.

My fingers flexed and curled. The warmth and quiet of my glassblowing cottage. That's what I needed. The familiar ebb and flow of energy as the glass moved from molten shapelessness to solid, cool beauty. My heart ached for it. The simplicity.

Chaos to order.

That's what the glass had given me.

Julia.

A life.

Obnoxious wealth.

A miracle, really, having been born on the streets of Edinburg to a woman who'd never once told me her name, let alone given me one.

But for a time, she had called me Darling.

I'd grown up hard. And fast. My days and nights spent on cold, grey streets and hunkered down in alleys, waiting for morning markets to open, where I'd weave in and out of crowds like an ebony-haired mouse, fingers flying into purses and pockets.

Ever undetected.

Until that golden morning.

I'd reached past silky, rose-colored purse strings, only to find my wrist caught in the grip of a calloused hand, faster than my own.

"That would be my daughter's purse," a bear of a man said.

"Pardon, sir. Please. I meant no harm."

The man was slow to shake his large, silver-maned head, "I suppose you did not." He turned his attention to his daughter, "Julia, what should we do with this? Should we report him?"

The angel stepped out from behind her father. Golden curls fell over her shoulders and her hazel eyes glowed with sly curiosity. "How old are you, boy?"

"Fourteen, miss."

"Your name?"

"Darling."

"Darling?" She giggled. "That's a ridiculous name for a pickpocket."

"My mother called me that."

Her gaze softened.

Something passed between us. Gentle, like a hot mug on a frozen day. Quiet and mesmerizing. Simple.

We stood still, studying one another, the way you might study the map of a place you're only seeing the first time.

"We should bring him home. Give him a meal," Julia said.

"Let's off, then." Her father already turned to walk down the lane. "Follow, boy."

"Come along, Darling." Julia smiled. The most graceful, lovely smile I'd ever seen.

In that moment I'd known.

For the rest of my days, I'd follow her. Anywhere.

Do anything. Anything for her.

My mind snapped from the memory as I neared my automobile on the riverbank.

The gun. The blood. The diamond.

Julia.

The vial of grave dirt pressed against my palm.

This would protect us from what I'd done.

For Julia.

Chapter One

Whitney Darling | 2023

If I returned to Savannah, to Darling House, I would die there.

Either the curse I'd accidentally unleashed on my family would finally catch up with me, or I'd flatline at the sight of Ephraim Callaghan.

Charmed.

That's what they used to say.

About the Darlings and our glass.

We couldn't be sure what it was that allowed us to speak with it, or why the glass chose to communicate with us at all. What we did know was that William Darling seemed to be the first. And the glass had stayed with us, generation upon generation, whispering into the ears of its chosen Darlings, telling us everything it wished to be.

And as we gave the glass its form, it grew our fortune.

Charmed.

That's what they called us.

Before the curse.

I chewed my lip and gripped the steering wheel harder. Somber grey sky and endless, golden marsh stretched on either side of me. I couldn't remember a colder, rainier autumn.

Almost there.

My pulse kicked up a notch.

When Seth, my twin, died, he took my heart right along with him. He'd been the curse's first victim two years ago. And in many ways, I had been its second.

It had seemed clear to me at the time that since I'd awakened the curse, it would not only haunt me, but continue to put those dear to me in danger. So, I'd packed up my grief, and left behind my loved ones and my ancestral home, headed for the next best place I knew, Charleston, South Carolina.

But despite my absence, my family suffered.

Out of guilt and misplaced precaution, I hadn't come back for my brother-in-law, Caleb's funeral, or when Aunt Rose had her stroke, or when Daddy took an opportunity in Paris and finally left Mama alone for good.

But this time I had no choice.

I couldn't miss another funeral.

Not this one.

Even if it meant the end of me.

Not that my life had turned out anything like I'd imagined.

Turning thirty this month had been interesting. Curses aside, the milestone had served as a line between the doe-eyed, self-aware young woman I'd once been, and the neurotic, superstitious, workaholic I'd grown into. If life had gone to plan, the way twenty-one-year-old Whitney had daydreamed, I'd be a renowned glassblower by now. A crafter of fine crystal chandeliers. On the board of *Darling & Potter*. I'd be a wife and mother, with time to spare for Savannah social things like coffee at Clary's, bridge club games on Gaston Street, and volunteering at my children's school.

I swallowed hard.

And at the center of it all, I would've been married to Ephraim.

His handsome, brooding scowl flashed across my mind.

I turned my car onto an unassuming road, and followed what quickly became a badly paved winding path over narrow, tree-scattered hammocks of land in a sea of water-logged spartina grass.

Anyone who didn't know better might get this far and think they'd made a wrong turn, headed down a path to nowhere. Little would they imagine the small secluded island or the house that waited, a bit farther, tucked out of sight.

People used to ask Granddaddy how it was he could keep our glassblowing studio so near the ocean.

"What if a storm comes? You could lose everything."

He would smile, nod and say, *"Of course, you're right."*

But he never did move it.

An imposing iron gate came into view. It opened automatically as my car approached; the sensor clipped to my sun visor still in working order. I drove beyond the sprawling, intricate ironwork and over a private bridge that connected our island to the mainland.

I cruised down paved brick, past rows of budding camellia trees and dormant azaleas, finally rolling to a stop in the circular front drive of an elegant Greek Revival mansion.

Darling House.

The house my family had called home for a century.

Despite its stately melancholy, the white four-story structure gleamed in the morning sunshine, presiding over manicured grounds and gardens that gave way to wild marsh on three sides, and the mouth of the Atlantic Ocean to the East. Two massive live oaks, their branches gnarled and dripping with grey Spanish moss stood like ancient sentinels on either side of the columned front porch.

A humid, salty breeze tossed my ponytail as I stepped out of my car and pulled my luggage from the back seat. Time slowed. My gaze drifted wistfully over the place I'd dreamed of every night since I'd left.

The past two years had been unkind. Darling House looked like the centerpiece of a gothic film. A layer of soft green moss crept up the footers of the towering columns, and the front steps were worn, in need of a pressure wash and fresh paint. The array of white Kehoe iron railings and cornices that adorned the house, peeled in the corners. No flowers graced the giant black urns flanking the steps. No boxwood topiaries. No wreaths hung on the front doors. A lone rusty rake rested at the end of the porch, propped care-lessly against a cracked pane of original poured glass in one of the parlor windows.

The house was silent. The island still.

No sound of frogs. No cicadas. No crooning marsh birds.

Just silence.

And the macabre sensation of being watched.

I stepped toward the porch.

I'd half expected the entire family to be waiting on the front steps when I arrived, but I was running early, and no one appeared any the wiser.

Good.

I wasn't prepared to greet the whole Darling clan at once.

"Who goes there?" A squeaky voice brought me up

short, and I turned on my heel to see a tuft of bright red curls peeking up from behind a plastic Jack-o-lantern mask. A blue and white striped beach towel flapped down the tiny boy's back like a cape, secured around his neck with a hair clip. Vine-green chinos hugged his spindly seven-year-old legs.

I lowered my sunglasses and stared down at my crimson-haired nephew, Percy.

Even with the Halloween costume, I knew my sister's son was a perfect likeness to his lost father, his hair a flaming reminder of the brawny man brought to a sudden and senseless end by a curse he'd inherited only by marriage.

The thought made my heart squeeze. "Hello, Percy."

His courage spent, the little boy ran away. He bounded up the front steps and threw open the tall doors with a flourish of his cape. "She's here!"

So much for a quiet entry.

My lips quirked at the squeaky bellow, and I steeled myself for the outpouring of relatives from the house in a flurry of linen pants, grey hair, and gardenia-scented perfume.

I stood, waiting.

Long seconds passed.

Wind rustled the live oaks and camellias lining the driveway at my back.

No one came.

I stared at the pair of black doors swung wide in gloomy invitation.

Nothing.

I walked to the base of the front steps, peering above for signs of life in the upper windows, when a movement caught my eye.

A flash of white.

The drawn, pale face of a woman gazed down at me, blonde ringlets of hair spilling over her thin shoulders.

My toe jammed on a step, and I stumbled forward, the weight of my luggage throwing me off balance. I managed to right myself and looked back up at the window.

But she was gone.

A familiar chill tickled the back of my neck, but I forced it away.

It was well-known that Savannah, Georgia was the most haunted location in the South, if not the country. *The City Built on Its Dead*, they called it. A title intriguing enough to have visitors the world-over flock here each October for a ghost tour and a jaunt around one of the timeworn cemeteries. But the Historic District had nothing on Darling House.

Shaking my head, I crossed the porch and stepped inside.

The sophisticated interior was as I'd left it.

Sort of.

The scents of coffee and bacon, beeswax, and age mingled on the air. A dried cinnamon broom sat propped beside the front doors, recalling memories of cozy autumns past. Ivory walls covered in antique picture frame moldings rose fifteen feet to the ceiling, crowned with more molding, and dotted with crystal-laden sconces and a mixture of antiques and moody oil paintings. Black walnut floors ran from the foyer, into the double parlor, and beyond. An imposing white marble staircase, adorned with cast-iron railing, climbed elegantly up to the second floor, then wound higher to the third and fourth floors. Hazy light spilled through a Darling chandelier above my head, bathing the entryway in pale, dancing prisms.

"Welcome home, Whitney Darling," it whispered, it's

voice delicate and ephemeral inside my head. I smiled up at it in greeting, as though it were a familiar friend.

When I'd been a little girl, Granddaddy had convinced me the shower of kaleidoscope lights the chandelier reflected was the end of a beautiful rainbow that only we could see. Many of the Darlings, he'd said, could see and hear things that others couldn't. Most outsiders conceded only that our family was at worst, a little odd, and at best, a little eccentric. As for the true Lowcountry natives who knew a thing or two about the mystical roots of the area, they were content to accept about us what they didn't understand.

My mother was the first to hurry down the steps. Her matching ivory cashmere top and pants draped elegantly on her lithe body, complimented by her signature strand of pearls around her neck, and small gold hoops on her ears. Even in grief, she was the epitome of coastal chic. Her blonde bob, more silver now, was perfectly coifed. Her full lips were a pleasant shade of nude, and though I could tell she'd taken extra care with her makeup that morning, there was no denying the circles under her eyes, or the pink, chapped skin above her upper lip, rubbed raw from tissues.

She pulled me into her arms with a dulcet sigh. "I worried you might not come. I almost can't believe it." Her soft voice and the cozy scent of her vanilla almond lotion wrapped around me.

"Here I am."

Mama stepped back, surveying me at arm's length for a moment. Was she seeing Seth's face when she looked at me, his chestnut hair, his wide, handsome eyes? Did it break her heart, the way it did mine when I looked in the mirror?

"I'm glad you're here," she said, her composure cracking. "A broken neck. Can you imagine? After everything your grandfather was battling with his health, to die so."

"It's about time you were home," Aunt Adele quipped from over my shoulder, and I turned to see her appear from the front parlor, effortlessly on-brand in a monogrammed smock and an oversized gardening hat. She rushed forward and pulled me into a fierce hug, then studied my face as if expecting a lifetime of change etched there.

Her twin sister, Aunt Rose, wheeled her chair close and pressed an approving kiss to the back of my hand, her cotton ball hair shining translucent in the sunlight. She looked strong, despite her recent stroke, and she mooned up at me with sparkling eyes. "I knew you'd come, Whitney Darling. I dreamed it."

I leaned down to embrace her, overcome with guilt that it had been so long.

A tap on my shoulder made me turn.

"I'm so glad you're here." My older sister, Addison, stared joyfully back at me. My heart leapt. She looked so much like Seth it nearly took my breath away. Only Addie took after our mother's pale coloring. Her pert nose was more delicate, and her eyes shone blue, contrasting the honey blonde hair that tumbled in soft curls over her shoulders. She was grace incarnate. Inside and out. And how I'd missed her.

She pulled me close.

Stunned, I stepped back to stare down at the caftan-draped swell of her belly, words failing me.

"I was going to tell you," she said.

Adele crossed her arms. "She's not exactly a walk in the park to be around these days."

Rose wheeled over and grabbed my hand again. "The baby will be a girl. Girls are easy."

Adele snorted, "*You* were easy."

"Addie," I said. "You should have called me, at least. How far along are you? You're huge."

She rolled her eyes, "Thanks, you look great, too."

"I only meant –"

"She knows what you meant," Adele quipped.

"She's eight months, today," Rose said.

Overwhelmed, and in desperate need of a glass of water, I motioned toward the kitchen. "Would it be alright if –"

"Lord, the girl's asking for permission to use her own kitchen." Adele walked past, motioning for everyone to follow. "We've got pastries and coffee at the ready."

Addison wrapped an arm around my shoulders. "I know what you meant, Whit," she said. "I'm glad you're back."

"It's only for a couple of days," I said.

Addison's grip on me tightened, but she didn't say anything more.

* * *

Several hours later I stood in my bedroom doorway. Late afternoon sun bathed the room in gold. The scent of vanilla and Jasmine clung to the air.

Ivory plaster walls covered in picture molding boasted large, ornately framed paintings of flowers and the ocean and the sky. A pale wool rug cozied up the original heart pine floors. White and blue chinoiserie drapes hung in the windows, matching the canopy over my antique bed.

Addison sat there on a quilt, staring at me. Days away from giving birth, my sister looked as stunning and comfortable with herself as I'd ever seen her. Only, there was something quieter about her now. More measured, as though life had tripped her up enough to make her watch her step. I supposed losing a husband could do that to a person.

"The baby isn't Caleb's," she said, flatly.

"Okay. Who's then?" I asked, doing math in my head. Caleb passed away last December. A fall while hanging Christmas lights on the back of the house. My stomach twisted at the thought. What a cruel way to die. "You're eight months, so that would mean –"

"Francis."

I bit back a gasp. I'd been gone too long. "Caleb's best friend, Francis?"

"Don't say it like that," she blushed. "It's complicated."

I crossed to the bed to sit next to her. "Apparently."

"He never left my side after Caleb's accident," Addison said. "He came bursting in the front door the night it happened, walked straight through the house to where I sat on the terrace. He took me in his arms and cradled me to his chest. I cried so hard I thought I'd die. But Francis held me together." Her eyes glistened. "He's been with me since."

"I'm glad," I whispered, my opinion immediately softening. Francis had been here when my sister needed someone most. And that was more than I could say.

"Percy loves him," she continued earnestly. "He's a vet, so Percy's always bringing him some injured animal or another. He's so gentle. And kind. Francis – " Her voice caught.

I lowered my gaze, unable to stop the slow trickle of a tear down my cheek.

"I never blamed you," Addison said. "For not coming to Caleb's funeral. It was too soon after Seth. I knew you couldn't handle it."

Her words, though intended to be compassionate, stung.

I'd lost my twin to the curse. But she'd lost a brother. And then a husband.

I clasped her hand.

A thud sounded from outside the door, startling both of us. I got up and looked into the hallway. One of several gilded frames, each displaying family wedding portraits, had fallen to the floor. I knelt and carefully turned it over, my eyes tracing a tiny crack that splintered the center of the protective glass. William and Julia Darling stared back at me from an old black and white photo, looking every bit like the Lowcountry socialites they had been, beautiful and still.

Mama walked up, then paused, as if the sight of me back at home still took her by surprise. "Oh, that frame keeps falling." She took the heavy piece from my hands and rested it gently against the wall. "I'll have Francis rewire the back of it. It's getting old." She stepped inside my room, motioning for me to follow as she made her way to the bed and pulled one of Addison's swollen ankles onto her lap, massaging it with practiced fingers. "You packed quite a bag for a two-day trip."

I shrugged. "I brought a bit of everything. You know how fickle the weather can be this time of year."

The ivory clock on the mantle ticked.

I perched on the edge of the mattress next to them, the feel of my old quilt unsettling beneath my fingertips. I motioned to my sister's belly. "Are there any more surprises I should be aware of?"

Percy vaulted into the bedroom, still wearing the Halloween mask and beach towel cape. He glanced at me shyly before focusing his attention on his mama. "Francis says dinner's ready. He's setting the table."

Addison placed a well-aimed kiss on top of Percy's little

head, careful not to disturb the mask, "Thank you, sir. Tell him we'll be right along."

My nephew nodded and flew back out of the room.

"He's gotten big," I said.

"You never can take for granted how quickly the time goes." Mama's lips pursed and she pulled me into a little hug before stepping toward the door, "Come on, Addie, give your sister time to freshen up for the meal," she looked at me pointedly. "Adele likes everyone seated promptly at five."

"I remember," I said.

Addison paused as they stepped into the hallway. "There's one more thing you should know. About Ephraim."

I held up my hand and gave her a pleading look. "Please. Not yet."

She smiled gently and nodded, "See you downstairs."

I collapsed back onto the pillows as I listened to their retreating footsteps, and squeezed my eyes shut.

Ephraim.

My whole body sparked to life at the sound of his name. I tried to focus past the tightening at my core, the memory of his deep voice, thick with barely restrained emotion. We'd only just given in. To the yearning. The obsession. He'd kissed me in the garden, hours after I'd found the vial of grave dirt and been stupid enough to lift it from the ground. And then Seth had died.

I pictured his face, the green-eyed man who had almost been mine.

My fingers trembled. Ephraim hated me now.

For leaving at the height of our pain.

And the worst of it was, he had been right. I couldn't outrun the Darlings, or the curse that snapped at our heels.

"*Promise you won't follow me.*"

"*I won't do that,*" he growled, his voice raw.

"*Ephraim, please.*" I gripped his hand, unable to look up at his face. "*Please.*"

"*I won't let you leave.*" He towered over me, broken, and devastatingly beautiful. His fingers squeezed my arms, holding me in place, as if he could force me to stand there with him forever. He smelled like the ocean, and the cruel river, and the salty, spicy air I'd breathed in and out all my life. His emerald gaze bore into me, expectant. Waiting for me to comply. To give in to him.

But I was shattered. Despite how stubbornly he tried to hold me together.

"*I can't lose you too. I won't let you die because of me.*"

His grip tightened. "*I'll protect you. We'll figure this out.*"

I stood on my tiptoes and pressed a soft kiss to his lips, my throat convulsing with unshed sobs, the taste of my tears sharp and salty on my tongue.

"*Whitney.*" His voice was gravel.

I didn't look him in the eye as I pulled from his grasp and walked away.

Chapter Two

Whitney Darling

The dining room was meant to be impressive. At the time of Darling House's construction, my Great-Great-Grandfather William, wasn't your classic nouveau rich businessman. He'd been an artist, eager to prove himself among the restricted echelons of society. He must've come to realize quickly that here in the South, presentation was everything. Because he'd spared no expense.

With this room being one of the primary spaces for entertaining, extra attention had gone into every facet of the space. The domed ceiling was vaulted – floating a full twenty feet above the floor, gleaming white, and adorned with alabaster moldings. Picture molding on the ivory walls separated out twelve intricately painted murals – each one an ode to Savannah culture and folklore. Among them were sweeping depictions of the marsh, the glittering Forsyth Park fountain, and a painting of an alligator tipping a fishing boat, its jaws open wide, like a hungry sea monster.

My stomach twisted. The scene conjured morbid thoughts of Seth and his last, terrified moments in the water.

As kids, he and I loved that painting the most.

It was so like the Darlings to leave it there for history's sake, despite everything.

I hadn't unpacked yet. I could still change my mind and head back to Charleston and my chic little Meeting Street apartment. That would certainly please James. He'd begged me to join him for a latte at Harken Café this morning before I hit the road. Friends since our time together ten years ago at the College of Charleston, we'd bonded over our mutual love of the southern coastal art scene. He'd offered me a job writing and marketing remotely for his Lowcountry lifestyle brand, *Coterie*, the day I'd let him know I'd moved back to the area. Now, after having worked with him, I knew James' feelings for me had deepened. He would miss me while I was in Savannah.

But as with everyone else, I kept James at a safe distance.

He didn't know that caring too much for me was dangerous.

Bustling noises came from the kitchen, separated from the dining room by a butler's pantry.

I took a steady breath. If I could make it through dinner without anything strange or dramatic happening, I could excuse myself early and go to bed.

Attend the funeral.

Get back to Charleston.

Easy as that.

Striding in my direction from the foyer, tall and assured, came easily one of the most handsome men I'd ever seen.

Francis.

His wavy blonde hair was carelessly tousled. A black linen button down covered a broad chest and tapered waist. His jaw was square and firm, his cheekbones high and sculpted. He studied me with icy blue eyes as he approached and held out a hand.

"Good to see you again, Whitney," he said, his Lowcountry accent riding a deep, sophisticated tenor. "You've been missed."

I'd met Francis before on one or two occasions. Never had I imagined he'd end up my brother-in-law. I shook his hand, happy to find his palms rough with callouses. The sort of Savannah boy who didn't have calloused hands wasn't the right kind of Savannah boy. That's what Granddaddy used to say.

"Thank you," I said. "Addison's been singing your praises since I arrived."

"Ill-deserved, I'm sure." His full lips lifted into an easy smile that displayed well-defined dimples on both cheeks. The kind of smile that made you feel safe and seen. In an instant, I understood the spell he'd cast over my sister. He motioned to the long table, then pulled out an upholstered dining chair, "We've got about two minutes before Adele starts shuttling platters of food in here."

I took a seat, smiling a little as he pushed the chair in for me.

On cue, Adele shimmied through the butler's pantry, a silver platter balanced on one hip, and a breadbasket on the other. A burst of delicious aroma followed close on her heels, making my stomach growl. "I hope everyone has a good appetite," she said. "These Carolina grits are laden with bacon grease, and the shrimp's fresh off the boat."

Aunt Rose, looking pretty in a pink dress and pearls wheeled herself into the room, trailed closely by Percy, a Halloween mask in the shape of a kindly-looking ghost bouncing atop his head. Mama and Addison brought up the rear.

"We're here!" Percy proclaimed, running over to Adele wrapping his little arms around her wide, apron-clad hips.

"Hello, sweet Darling," Adele said, patting his ruddy hair. "Oh, I've forgotten the serving spoons."

"You ladies take your seats," Francis said, "I'll grab them." He was already passing through the butler's pantry before Adele could protest.

I gave Addison an approving grin. "Francis is nice."

"You have no idea," Adele crooned. "He and Ephraim are the only reason we've been able to keep this place running. Well, and Monica, too. Until she abandoned us with the studio."

"Auntie, please," Addison said.

"When will Ephraim be here?" Percy bounced in his chair.

I stiffened, feeling the blood drain from my face.

Mama cut a glance in my direction. "Ephraim won't be joining us tonight, sweetie. We'll see him tomorrow."

"At the funeral?" Percy looked positively disappointed.

"Yes," Mama said, her voice cracking a little.

Francis strode back through the door and planted the serving spoons into the platter of shrimp and grits, before ladling a sizable portion into the china bowl in front of me.

I smiled up at him and lay my napkin in my lap.

"We've got to bless it first!" Percy squealed.

"Of course, forgive me," I said.

Percy bowed his little head, pressed his palms together, and squeezed his eyes shut. "God our Father, we thank you for our many blessings. Amen."

"Amen," the table repeated after him.

"Now, don't let it get cold," he said. "The ghosts will steal it."

Squelching a laugh, I lifted a bite to my lips. The heady

aroma of heavy cream, bacon, and chives made my mouth water.

The doorbell chimed.

"Who could that be?" Adele began to stand.

Francis held up a hand. "I'll get it."

The table went silent as we each listened for the sound of voices at the door.

"Of course. Come in, sir." Francis' enthusiastic welcome rumbled from the foyer.

The answering melodic timber, one I hadn't heard in a long time, made me put down my spoon. My reflex was to look over at Seth's chair, to smile at him excitedly.

But Seth wasn't there.

Instead, I stood, turning politely as Francis appeared alongside a man who I hadn't let myself remember existed.

He'd been one of the treasured ones, so hard to leave behind.

The years had been kind to Solomon Potter, though his black skin boasted deepened wrinkles, and his shoulders looked thinner than I remembered. He smiled when he saw me, and his eyes glowed with the same light that had made me love him as a child.

He'd been Granddaddy's best friend in the world, not to mention the other half of *Darling & Potter*, the luxury sunglass company jointly founded by our two families a century ago.

Mr. Solomon was always grinning, and he smelled so wonderful, like the ocean after the rain, and pipe tobacco and warm, coastal spices all at once. A necklace of threaded bone hung from neck. He'd always told Seth and I that they were the bones of his wife's ring finger – he'd taken it after she'd died so he could continue to be, *wrapped around it.*

He'd said it so solemnly, and so often, we never could tell if he was teasing.

Solomon knew all about the mysterious things, wild things I was too afraid to ask about. Granddaddy Alistair said Solomon's culture was an old one – sacred, and nothing less. The magic that lived on the marsh wasn't the same as what you read about in fairy stories, or even like the strange relationship concerning the Darlings and our glass.

No, the marsh magic was different – ripe with curses and blessings, and sometimes things in between. Like our vial of grave dirt.

"Solomon," I stepped close, and he pulled me into a warm hug. He was wet with rain, but I didn't care.

My throat tightened and my eyes stung.

"I've brought you something, Whitney Darling," he whispered in my ear.

I pointed to the necklace of woven bone at his neck. "Tell me true. Is that your wife's ring finger?"

His eyes twinkled, but sadness flashed there too. And I wondered if it was because I'd mentioned his wife, or because he'd just lost Granddaddy. Maybe it was both.

He pressed a prickly bundle into my hand, and I curled my fingers around it, recognizing the texture and heady scent of bundled sage and cedar without having to look. A ubiquitous protection charm here in the Lowcountry that went all the way back to early indigenous tribes. And it worked.

"We hold onto the ones we love the best we can," he said.

I nodded and leaned forward to give him another squeeze as a boom of thunder shook the house.

A cold breeze tickled the back of my neck.

The lights flickered once. Twice.

And then they went out, plunging the room into darkness.

"No one move. I'll have a candle lit faster than you can catch a grasshopper," Adele said calmly.

My eyes strained to adjust as I listened to the sound of my aunt's feet shuffle toward the sideboard.

"I'll tell you what," Solomon said, his voice a deep rumble. "This stormy weather is something else. I can't remember a colder, rainier start to Autumn."

"It's certainly not your traditional Lowcountry fall," Mama chimed.

Suddenly, the light of a cell phone illuminated the room.

Adele cast Francis an appraising stare, as if determining the severity of which she'd been insulted. "No phones in the dining room," was all she said. But the way her eyes crinkled up at the edges told me she'd been glad for the assistance.

"Yes, ma'am," Francis gave the room a sheepish grin. He stood from his chair and moved to Adele's side, lighting her path. A few moments later, two antique candelabras sparkled with the light of various tapered candles.

Rain poured in heavy sheets outside the windows. The little bridge that connected the island to the mainland was certainly flooding.

I turned to Solomon. "Looks like you're stuck here a while. Care for some dinner?"

"I've got a fresh pot of coffee on the stove that'll be ready any minute," said Adele. "Have a seat, Solomon."

"Yes, ma'am," the old man said, and slid into the chair across from me.

Seth's chair.

I looked down at my lap and squeezed the tightly

bundled sage and cedar Solomon had pressed into my palm. Freshly made. It smelled like marsh magic. Like the wild.

"Nora, come help me in the kitchen, will you?"

"Of course." Mama cast Solomon a sweet smile as she followed Adele.

"How've you been, Mr. Solomon?" Addison asked from her chair beside Francis.

"Oh, I've been fine, young lady. That child will make his appearance soon, yeah?"

Addison rested a gentle hand on her belly. "Next month, believe it or not."

"I figured as much," Solomon reached into his jacket and pulled out another bundle, a small velvet pouch, and passed it to Addison. "I brought this especially for you and that sweet babe. Supposed to help with a safe delivery. Never seen it not work before." He gave Addison a wide grin. "I've seen more babies born than I can count, and that's saying something. You put that under your pillow, and you'll be right fine, you understand?"

"Yes, sir," Addison nodded. "Thank you."

"My good friend, Alistair, would have loved to meet that child. He told me himself. Would have loved to meet that child."

The room fell silent.

My heart pounded. If Solomon started crying, I'd lose control of my tears too.

"Mama, Grandma's in the kitchen," Percy whispered conspiratorially. "Can I tell Whitney the secret now?"

"Secret?" Solomon perked up.

"There was an angel outside Aunt Whitney's room," Percy explained matter-of-factly. "I saw her."

"Percy that's enough. That's no talk for the dinner table."

"An angel?" The memory of the woman I'd seen upon my arrival flashed across my mind, the woman in white looking down at me from my bedroom window.

"A pretty lady," Percy said. "She smiled at me."

Solomon mumbled indiscernibly.

My sister sighed and lolled her head back to look up at the ceiling. "Francis."

"Percy, your Mama asked you not to say anything. It upsets your grandmother."

"Why would it upset her?" I asked.

Addison slid annoyed eyes over to me, "Because our mother doesn't have the tolerance for much these days. Least of all, talk of ghosts. Or curses. It's been worse since Daddy went to Paris."

Addison said that last part so low, I almost didn't hear it.

I'd held off wondering if my father would make an appearance at the funeral tomorrow. Surely, I wasn't the only one. But I hadn't thought enough about what my father's abandonment was doing to Mama, especially now. I didn't blame her for not wanting to hear about the curse, or the ghosts it had left in its wake. Real or otherwise.

Solomon's stare bore into me across the table.

"Thank you, Percy," I squeezed the bundle of sage and cedar again. "I like the idea of angels watching over us."

"Me too," he whispered.

I met his tender gaze. He'd lost so much in his short little life. Mine had been a childhood of safety. Percy's was marked by curses and loss. It made me want to pull him onto my lap and hug him tight, and whisper that I was sorry for being away.

It made me want to make him safe.

Adele and Mama returned, carrying a tray filled with mugs, cookies, and steaming pots of coffee.

"Here we are, Mr. Solomon," Mama placed a mug in front of him.

"Thank you, kindly, Ms. Nora."

I looked again at Percy. He appeared perfectly content now that he'd gotten to share his secret. "Tomorrow you and I should go for a walk outside. You can show me your favorite places to find shells."

Addison shook her head. "I doubt there'll be time. With the funeral."

Thunder boomed again, making the windows tremble and moan.

"God's rearranging the furniture," Solomon said, his deep, steady voice strangely comforting, like a candle's glow in darkness. "Miss Whitney, I wonder if I might have a word with you in Alistair's study?"

I straightened in surprise, "Of course."

He stood abruptly, shaking the glasses on the table.

"You mean, now?"

Adele motioned to the steaming pot on the table. "Your coffee will get cold."

"Not to worry," Solomon held up a hand. "This won't take long, and I feel a pressing need to have it done."

He took hold of a gleaming candlestick and strode out of the room.

"Well, this is odd," Mama said. "Whitney, do you know what this is about?"

"Of course, not." I rose from my chair and followed Solomon, the heavy weight of curious eyes on me as I left the room.

The darkness of the hallway beyond the foyer was consuming, all but suffocating the flickering light of Solomon's candle. He walked several paces ahead, before disappearing into the study, the room Granddaddy Alistair had guarded above all others.

There were family secrets in that room.

History. Records of valor and tragedy, all tucked quietly away in the pages of books that lined the walls.

I hurried to catch up, then hesitated at the door, crossing my arms tightly in front of me.

Solomon stood beside Granddaddy's desk when I entered, the candlelight carving peculiar angles on his face. He stared back at me with midnight eyes. "The night he died Alistair asked me to deliver a letter to you. He made me promise no one else would see it. Not a lawyer. Not a friend. Not your sweet mama." He fished inside the lapel of his jacket and pulled out a small cream-colored envelope.

"For me?" My voice sounded strange.

"There are forces at work here, Miss Whitney, that your Granddaddy spent the last of his days trying to decipher." He held the letter out to me.

I crossed the room and took it with shaky fingers.

Solomon nodded and let out a quiet breath, as though he'd been holding it a long time. "A final wish, granted." He straightened his jacket and stepped toward one of the glass doors to the terrace. "If you'll convey my apologies to your family. I'd better be going."

I looked up at him in surprise. "But the bridge. It won't be passable for hours. Not until the tide goes out. There's been too much rain."

"Don't worry about me." He winked and pressed a kiss to my forehead. Then, without another word, he slipped outside into the sodden, inky darkness.

I stared after him a long time, listening to the storm and feeling as though I'd fallen into a dream.

Only yesterday I had been sitting in my office in

Charleston, surrounded by the bustle of the city, what felt like a million miles away.

I moved close to the candelabra, where the dancing light was enough to illuminate the script on the envelope.

My Whitney

I swallowed and turned it over. A blood-red seal graced the center, Alistair's personal monogram etched in raised bubbling wax. I slipped a finger beneath the top fold and broke it, then unfolded the letter inside with slow, mechanical movements. I narrowed my eyes at the achingly familiar, graceful handwriting and began to read.

My Whitney,

You can't hide your true feelings from me, my love, because I have known you best of all.

To get right to it, I'm afraid it's incumbent on you, my dear, to carry the burdens of all Darlings - past and present - on your shoulders.

There's a darkness hiding at Darling House, and until we root it out, this curse on our family will continue to follow you, no matter how far or long you run.

Since the day you found the mojo charm, that fickle dirt-filled vial, since the day we lost our Seth, I've searched for answers.

Old diaries, photographs, epitaphs – they've been my constant companions in my search to free us. But I'm old. My hands and my mind are tired. I know there are logical connections I will never see.

But you, Whitney. If you continue where I leave

off - if you listen to the whisper of the glass, there can still be salvation for our family, and for our marvelous home.

Break the curse, before it breaks you.

Much more will be revealed to you in time.

I pray you'll forgive me for what I'm forced to do. I see no other choice.

Be kind to Ephraim. He loves you desperately.

I love you as well, my Darling.

Listen to the glass. The glass remembers.

Watch for the chandelier.

And remember, P is for persistence.

I will miss you.

Your devoted Grandfather,

Alistair Napoleon Darling

I stared down at the letter for a long time, tracing the dancing script with my eyes until the letters blurred and the words jumbled. A pulsing tapped in my right temple, and I massaged it away, squeezing my eyes closed.

When I opened them, my gaze sought the line that made my legs go weak.

Be kind to Ephraim. He loves you desperately.

Seconds passed into minutes. I read the note over and over, a tumult of emotions culminating in a cocktail of frustrated confusion. My throat went dry. My heart beat hard.

I swallowed.

"I'm sorry, Granddaddy."

I stretched out my arm and dangled the letter above the open flame of the candle, watching as the paper began to smoke, steeling myself against the desire to snatch it back, to study the way he'd written my name, sprawled in ink for the last time.

But I couldn't give in to the sentimental part of me.

Granddaddy didn't know what he was asking.

I was cursed, and I cursed those I loved around me. It was too dangerous for me to stay at Darling House.

My heart ached as the letter ignited. I dropped it into a copper bowl on the desk, watching through tears as it flamed and writhed to blackened embers.

Granddaddy didn't understand.

I wasn't the person he thought I was.

That had been Seth. The glass had loved him best. And my brother was a long way from here.

Tomorrow, after the funeral, I was going back to Charleston.

A flash of lightning illuminated the sky outside the veranda doors, drawing my gaze to the outline of a figure in the inky distance, walking along the marsh.

Solomon?

Lightning flashed again.

No, this man didn't move like him.

He moved like -

I narrowed my eyes, straining to see the shadowy figure past the swaying of moss-laden live oaks and angry torrents of rain.

Another flash.

Thunder boomed.

And he was gone.

Chapter Three

Whitney Darling

The mossy earth was green and black, soft with morning dew.

Thick fog, a delicate swirling mist, cradled Bonaventure Cemetery in a hushed, ethereal embrace. Live oaks, their branches heavy with resurrection fern, stood alongside matronly magnolia trees and regal camellias, each of them bone-still, as if paying respect to the silent sea of marble and granite below.

My family and I sat in the first of five rows of white chairs, all situated near the base of the marble mausoleum at the center of the Darling plot. A melancholy sculpture of a beautiful weeping angel draped itself in mourning over the tomb of William and Julia Darling. The first roots of our heritage lay concealed together, their bones entwined for eternity. Surrounding their tomb smaller headstones dotted the ground, marking the resting places of Alastair's parents, and beside them, his older brother, who'd passed away young. Great aunts and uncles I had never met. Cousins long lost to dust. Altogether, there had to be twenty or so stones.

But it wasn't the quiet presence of my fallen ancestry that had me pinned to my chair, the sound of my own heartbeat thundering in my ears. Neither was it the hearse that sat parked at a respectable distance, or the stately black casket that waited, suspended above a fresh grave. I was strangely numb to all those things. A self-defense mechanism that I hoped would hold out until I could escape somewhere to be alone with my grief.

I twisted my fingers in my lap.

No.

This distress was of a different kind.

The most dangerous kind.

A familiar silhouette moved toward me through the mist, his progress marked by the silent gazes of stone angels as he strode past the crypts and obelisks of mighty men long turned to dust.

A black, tailored coat clung to his broad shoulders. The crisp white of his shirt glowed in the half light. I could almost make out the strong set of his jaw, the way his black, wavy hair brushed his collar.

My breath came fast as he neared, his every step nicking some invisible, vibrating cord between us. My mouth went dry.

Of course, I'd known Ephraim Callaghan would be here. I'd tried to prepare myself for it, the way I had for seeing the grave, or the coffin, or Seth's headstone that looked too aged, and too settled in the soft ground.

But my pulse beat like a cornered rabbit's.

Ephraim was devastating.

Somehow more handsome, more striking than I remembered.

He slowed as he approached, his eyes trained on me, steady and forbidding.

His lips curled into a cold smile, and he looked down at me as if I were a fly in his ambrosia. "Whitney."

His voice was whiskey down my throat, splashing deep, and sparking something dead back to life.

I lowered my sunglasses and tried to match his cool appraisal. "Ephraim."

His gaze flicked to my lips.

My red lipstick was in stark contrast to the ghostly pallor of my skin – but without the color I had looked dead. I fought the urge to squirm.

Ephraim looked away from me and nodded to my mother, Adele, Rose, and Addison beside me. And then he stepped around my chair to stand next to Francis, behind me.

The muscles in my neck tensed with the effort to compose myself, and I straightened, releasing a long, silent breath as I counted to ten in my head.

I understood why he hated me.

It wasn't only because I'd left.

He thought I blamed him for Seth's death. For not reaching my brother in time before the river and the wild things could swallow him up forever.

But it was my fault. If I hadn't found that vial. If I hadn't unleashed the curse, none of this would have happened.

It was nearly two years to the day since the Darlings had laid my twin to rest. Or at least pretended to, all of us huddled over Seth's ornate stone marker jutting up from the mossy ground.

His body wasn't there, of course. In the grave. He was with the wild things. Torn away from us by twisting, thrashing jaws, then swept away down the river's dark, unforgiving current.

Ephraim had stood close to me that day, wrapped his steel arms around my shoulders as if he could absorb some of the pain that threatened to send me to my knees. But it hadn't worked. Try as he might, Ephraim couldn't save the Darlings from our curse.

I squeezed my eyes closed and tried to push away the vision of the tiny vial in the center of Seth's calloused palm. He'd been so captivated by it. By the proof that the legend Alistair had told us all our lives, of the good luck graveyard dirt at the heart of our family's easy prosperity, had been proven true. But we'd realized too late. The moment the vial left its resting place beneath the house, uprooted by time, an unsuspecting landscape artist, and then lifted from the ground by me, our luck had died, and given way to a curse.

None of us knew the curse's origin.

How to stop it? Good question.

The irony was rich.

But that day, Seth's death day, the way he'd stared down at that dusty, old bottle - it was as if he'd known. Something was coming.

We couldn't have imagined how quickly.

How cruelly.

But the glass had known.

It had tried to tell me. Only I hadn't understood.

I straightened in my chair.

Only a few hours from now and I could leave. Get back to Charleston and James and figure things out from a safer distance. I would be fine. I could keep my emotions at bay, if I avoided Ephraim.

I watched, silent, as they laid Granddaddy deep, far beneath the ground. So near to where Seth would have lain, if we'd been able to find his body, that they might've reached out and held hands in the dark. As it was, their lives were both marked now by neighboring marble headstones, artfully sculpted in the old style that matched the Darlings who'd come and gone before.

There would never be another quite like Alistair Darling. A scruffy gentleman, he'd grown up unafraid and brawny. But he'd also given the best hugs, and tender forehead kisses, and he'd written poetry while he sipped coffee beside the marsh. He'd had the most beautiful handwriting. And he'd always told the truth. Always. Even when it cost him.

"I'm going to miss you." I mouthed the words, but no sound came. I dropped my chin and pressed my fingertips to my lips, thankful for my sunglasses, and wide-brimmed hat. I stared down at the pointed toes of my shoes.

I wouldn't let tears come.

If they did, I might not be able to stop them.

A graceful, masculine hand reached around me and slipped something into mine.

I straightened. A handkerchief. The initials, *E.C.* embroidered in strong black letters, winked up at me from a crisp edge.

"Thank you," I whispered, and dabbed my cheek.

Refusing to look back at him, I lifted my chin and trained my eyes on a random tiny stone at the corner of the family plot, desperate for a momentary distraction. Anything to keep from crying.

The marker almost looked like a footstone, but it wasn't positioned as such, tucked at a distance and behind the rest of the headstones. I narrowed my gaze and tried to make out the inscription etched into the soft marble, but decades of humid, salty air had done their work. Whatever might have been written there was almost entirely worn away.

The pastor began a prayer, reclaiming my attention.

We sang *Amazing Grace.*

And then it was over.

Just like that.

A procession of family and distant friends dropped red and white roses over the lowered casket. Someone handed me a rose, but I held it tight. I couldn't bring myself to stand, to drop it in the earth where it would wither and die beneath the weight of dirt and darkness.

I stared at the grave, until the last of the watchers finally turned and strode away. I sat there, alone, long after Mama and the rest kissed my cheeks and left for Darling House. Only Francis waited to drive me back.

Well, Francis and Ephraim, who still loomed behind me, like an angry specter intent on cruel torment.

All the others had dropped their roses and gone.

They didn't realize.

Once you walked away from a grave, that first time, it was final.

Francis whispered something, followed by the soft unintelligible rumble of Ephraim's reply.

"Come, Whitney." A hand squeezed my shoulder, and I turned to see the men staring down at me, their eyes grim, and solemn, and something else.

I started to argue, but their troubled gazes made my stomach drop.

Something bad had happened. Something worse than the obvious.

"Your mother needs you," Francis said. "I'm afraid there's been an incident."

* * *

"What do you mean the house was broken into?" my mother's tenor could've peeled paint from a wall.

"Someone forced an entering, ma'am."

I didn't think the officer was trying to be sarcastic, but Mama certainly wasn't going to give him the benefit of the doubt.

"Don't take that tone with me, young man. I know your father."

The officer's cheeks turned a little red and his chin dropped a couple of notches. "Yes, ma'am. We're simply responding to an alert from your security company. We need to ask you a few questions. I understand this is a challenging time."

"You think?" My mother motioned over her shoulder to the long line of black SUVs and cars that crossed over the marsh bridge and onto our little island. Darling House would be host to Alistair's funeral reception, and no expense had been spared in making the affair fitting for someone of his stature in the Savannah community. "Can you at least have your partner turn off those tacky squad car lights and park that thing somewhere less conspicuous than the front lawn? For Heaven's sake."

"Yes, ma'am," the officer, whose name tag said Evans, nodded and radioed my mother's wishes.

"Thank you," Mama said, her expression a little too saccharine. "Now, if you wouldn't mind explaining what's happened. Was anything taken?"

"We don't believe so. We need to get a full account from you, of course. But there are many portable valuables left in plain sight. It looks to me like someone was searching for something."

"What would they be looking for?" Ephraim's voice rumbled over my shoulder.

"Your guess is as good as mine, sir. We imagine it had something to do with Mr. Alistair. May he rest in peace." Officer Evans crossed himself clumsily, and I wondered if he was Catholic, or if he made the gesture because he thought we might be. "The majority of the mess was left in the study," he said. "There's papers strewn all over the floor and books pulled off the shelves. It's a disaster in there."

Mama started to cry, her frail shoulders shuddering and heaving the way they had back at the cemetery.

Officer Evans' cheeks darkened again, and he looked to me, his eyes pleading. "Maybe you should be the one to look things over, Miss Darling."

"We'll both have a look," Ephraim said.

"Excuse me?" I glared at him, effectively breaking my vow to ignore him completely.

Ephraim's expression brooked no refusal. "Who do you think's been running Darling House since you left? I know more about what to look for in that office than you do."

"Both of you come," Officer Evans said. "Then y'all can get back to your reception. It won't take long." He nodded to my mother.

"Oh, dear," Rose chimed.

I patted Mama on the arm and motioned for Adele to come and escort her to the foyer where guests would be filing into the house momentarily. "I'll take care of this. You go see to things."

"Thank you," she sighed, linking elbows with Adele and dabbing her nose with a pressed handkerchief. "I'll never understand the nerve of people. Who would break into a house on the day of a funeral? It's bad home training."

I bit the inside of my cheek to keep from rolling my eyes. Mama had a way of bringing every little thing back to etiquette.

Officer Evans led Ephraim and I to the study.

"We've taken photos and swabbed for prints. The space is clear to be tidied. But I figured it'd be a good idea for someone accustomed with the room to take a look before we head out." Officer Evans placed his hands on his hips. "See anything out of place? Other than the obvious?"

Ephraim scanned the room, and I watched with a mixture of annoyance and jealousy. Both because he appraised the study as if it were his own, and also because he'd been one hundred percent correct regarding being more familiar with it. I had my memories. But Ephraim was the one who'd been here the past two years.

"Just a moment," he crossed the room to where several high shelves of books sat undisturbed. He pulled a volume from its place and thumbed gently through it, then hesitated, peering up into the slot the book occupied before sliding it back.

Was something hidden on the shelf? I made a mental note to check it out later.

Ephraim turned to Officer Evans. "Everything seems alright. The more expensive volumes are intact, and the safe in the closet looks marked up, but still locked. Whatever they were looking for, I think they ran out of time before they found it."

Officer Evans nodded, "Well, if y'all find anything missing, give us a call."

"Of course," Ephraim said.

Officer Evans paused as we reached the door that led to the yard where the squad car waited. "I'm sorry for your loss, Miss Darling. Mr. Alistair was a fine man."

"Thank you," I said. "We'll be in touch."

He tipped his hat and turned away.

"Just a moment," I called after him. "The house alarm is

silent when no one's home, isn't it? What do you think made the intruder leave?"

Officer Evans rubbed his chin, his gaze darting up to the shadowed upper windows, and I wondered what he might do if he caught sight of a ghost looking back at him. He shrugged, "Something must've spooked 'em off."

* * *

The funeral reception was a blur of black ties, finger sandwiches, tissues and dank-smelling lilies. Aunt Adele had taught me once, during one of our family picnics at the Darling plot in Bonaventure Cemetery, that lilies were used at funerals because their robust scent overpowered the stale fragrance of death.

Seth's funeral reception had been covered with them.

Granddaddy Alistair's was too.

I hated lilies.

I lost count of the number of elderly Savannahians who pulled me into frail, gardenia-scented hugs and told me how sorry they were for my loss.

There was a reason I didn't attend funerals.

I couldn't bear to wallow. I couldn't stand the in-between, to be caught in the current that carried you from the end of someone else's life to the beginning of your own without them.

Baskets of flowers arrived at the house in steady, colorful procession. One of the largest arrangements from my father, who hadn't made it back to Georgia in time for the funeral. He claimed his flight had been cancelled. Which was true, I checked. His arrangement was an ostentatious riot of yellow daisies, white roses, and pink carnations. Blatantly cheery. A passive aggressive masterpiece.

Beside my father's offering was another bouquet, this one a spray of bright lilies, bursting in all directions like morbid, fragrant stars. I leaned close to read the accompanying card.

> We are, each of us, our family's legacies incarnate. It was an honor to work under such an artist. I hope to rejoin Darling Glass soon. I'm so sorry for how I left. - Monica

My brows drew together. No one had mentioned our studio manager leaving, though Adele had brought up Monica last night at dinner. Granted, my family had stopped sharing details about that sort of thing with me a while ago, content to leave our conversations to how my life was going in Charleston. Monica had been with us for so long, her whole life, really. She was only a couple of years older than me and had trained alongside Seth and I from the time we were old enough to hold a blowpipe. She'd been a staple member of Darling Glass as head studio assistant, just as her mother, and her grandmother had before her.

I couldn't imagine her ever leaving. Unless, of course, it had all gotten to be too much. Had the curse come for her too?

I looked over my shoulder at Mama. The one who stayed, no matter what. She stood regal in her tailored black sheath dress, a picture of southern refinement.

So many times, I'd approached her today, intending to let her know that I needed to get back to Charleston. I was expected at the office in the morning. But each time I tried I couldn't bring myself to say the words. Instead, I offered to get her something, or to sit with her a while, or deliver a message to Aunt Adele, who was busy coordinating the comings and goings of the kitchen and the needs of Savannah's most notable.

"Whitney Darling, you are a vision of grace," the compliment drifted over my shoulder in saccharin, dulcet rhythm.

I turned, expecting to see someone I recognized, a friend of Mama's or one of my aunts. But a woman I'd never seen before stared down at me from super-model heights, her siren eyes dripping with carefully curated sympathy. She extended a delicate hand. "You may not remember me. I'm Evangeline Walker. I was acquaintances with your late brother, Seth. He and I went on a few dates together."

I shook her hand, struggling to flip through my mental files of women Seth had dated over the years. He'd been a romantic with the swagger of a southern gentleman. There had never been a shortage of beautiful women around Seth Darling.

"Yes, I recall," I lied. "It's kind of you to pay your respects to my grandfather after all this time."

She smiled a perfect smile, and I wondered for a moment if her teeth were all real.

"Well, Ephraim was so close to Alistair. The least I can do is offer him my support."

I smiled back at her, hoping my cheeks weren't blooming red. "Ephraim?"

She patted my shoulder, gently, as though I was a small, confused child and she a beautiful, patronizing pre-school teacher. "Oh, I'm sorry. Ephraim and I are together now. I keep forgetting you've been in Charleston and out of the loop all this time."

I swallowed, my gaze drifting over her lithe form, her long, chestnut hair, the perfect, delicate pout of her lips. At just under five feet and four inches, I was squarely in the petite category, with rounded curves and a waist so short my ribs were intimately acquainted with my hip bones. Grief and loneliness had done nothing for my waistline, and while I usually didn't obsess over it, this moment brought all my insecurities swiftly to the surface. I had a pretty face, but there was no denying the past two years had been unkind. They had aged me, battered me, left me looking gaunt and hollowed out. And I got the distinct impression Evangeline Walker wanted me to take note of how great the contrast between she and I had become.

I rolled my shoulders back. "I've not been too out of the loop, really. It's only, I could've sworn Mama recently told me Ephraim was seeing someone named Ashley. She must've been mistaken."

Evangeline's eyes went a degree cooler, and I bit my cheek, accepting a glass of champagne a waiter handed me as he passed. I wasn't one to lie. But this situation was bringing out the worst in me.

"Did I hear my name?"

Ephraim's voice rumbled beside me as I took a sip of champagne. I choked, half-inhaling the drink, and was instantly rewarded with the sting of bubbles up the back of my nose.

Evangeline smirked as I sputtered and gasped for air. "Whitney and I were getting reacquainted." She slipped her arm possessively through the crook of Ephraim's elbow before placing a kiss on his cheek.

I stiffened. I wanted to rip her hands from him, to yell at her that she had no idea what she was doing, or who Ephraim truly was, or who I was, or what the two of us had been to each other.

The passion. The years of yearning, and hoping, only to

have the destiny we deserved ripped away by a curse that took no prisoners.

She didn't know. She couldn't know.

The only reason he and I weren't together was because I had left to keep him safe.

She stood there, looking down at me as if ours had been a passing fling.

But I'd been his first love.

And he had been mine.

Tears pricked my eyes, and I struggled to swallow.

Aware of how bad I was at hiding my true emotions, I downed another swig of champagne and motioned across the room toward Aunt Adele and a gaggle of taffeta and silk-adorned ladies.

"Excuse me. I think I'm needed." I stepped to the side, studiously avoiding Ephraim's pitying gaze, when a feminine hand grabbed my arm from behind, pulling me to a stop.

"Whitney!"

I twirled around, "Oh, Isla!" I exclaimed, a little too enthusiastically. "I've been searching for you!"

My friend pulled me into a willowy embrace. She was glowing, a blonde, natural beauty who made an effortless practice of looking like she'd leapt from an American prep catalogue. Isla was genuine and kind and represented everything I'd taken for granted about the easy days of my old Savannah upbringing.

"I've been making the rounds," she drawled. "You know how it is."

I did, in fact, know what she meant. Isla was the sort of person who was greeted by everyone at an event like this. She seemed to know every Savannahian by name, and in turn, they adored her. I'd bet it had taken her twenty minutes of friendly greetings to make it from the front lawn to the foyer.

She smiled politely at Ephraim and Evangeline. "It's a pleasure to see you two, as well. I swear, Ephraim, if I hear about one more Callaghan party that I'm not invited to, I'll go pea green."

Ephraim grinned charmingly. "An oversight that won't be repeated."

"Good," Isla said, pulling me tight to her side. "Meanwhile, Asher sends his regards."

Ephraim nodded. "How's your brother?"

"As glued to his businesses as you are. The pub's keeping him extra busy these days. Who would've imagined our little city of Savannah would become an international tourist destination?"

"People appreciate true beauty where they can find it." His eyes darted to mine a moment, before focusing on someone over my shoulder.

"Whitney."

I turned to find a prim young woman staring earnestly back at me, her brown hair pulled into a sleek, high pony-tail. She smiled hesitantly and held her hands clasped tightly in front of her. She wore a black Lilly Pulitzer shift dress and a short strand of pearls around her neck. Aside from her obvious grief, she looked as polished as I'd ever seen her.

"Monica!" I said, genuinely surprised.

"It's good to see you," she said, her eyes red and brimming with unshed tears. "I'm so sorry about your grandfather. I loved Alistair like –"

Her face crumpled and I rushed forward, pulling her into a tight embrace, "He loved you, too," I said. "I'm glad you're here."

She stepped back, wiping at her cheeks with an ivory handkerchief. "I almost didn't come. After the way I left, I didn't want to cause your family any more drama. But I couldn't keep away. I had to see for myself," she paused, taking two long sips of air, "that he was gone."

"I understand," I said. "Whatever happened before, I'm sure everyone understands. It'll get worked out. I promise."

She nodded, and a demure smile graced her porcelain face. The friendly look of it took me back to when we'd been small, and our biggest worry at Darling House had been whether the rain would spoil a summer afternoon.

"Y'all, excuse us," Isla cleared her throat. "Whitney's Aunt Adele seems to be motioning her over." She squeezed my hand, indicating I should go along with her. "We'll catch up with y'all in a bit."

"Of course," Monica said, stepping to the side. "See you soon."

"We need to be making the rounds as well." Ephraim placed a hand on the small of Evangeline's waist and motioned to a group of men gathered near the grand piano in the corner. "It was lovely to see you, Isla. Tell Asher I said hello."

Ephraim nodded tightly at Monica, then didn't so much as glance at me as he and Evangeline stepped away into the crowd.

Seconds later, Isla had me halfway across the room. "Sorry to whisk you away like that, but I figured two more minutes of standing in that pressure cooker, and you might spontaneously combust." She skirted us closer to where Aunt Adele stood. "Did your mother tell you what Monica did on the day she quit the studio?"

I looked at her in confusion, feeling suddenly tired.

Isla shook her head. "No, of course she didn't. She

wouldn't have wanted to upset you." She squeezed my arm and slowed our pace. "It was a few days after your grandfather had his fall. Monica had a breakdown. She smashed several orders waiting to ship out. Then she stormed into the house and demanded someone investigate further what had happened to Alistair. She insisted he'd been pushed, not fallen down the studio steps. She screamed at your mother that she didn't feel safe on the island, and that someone was skulking around the property watching her work. Before your mother could offer up a solution, Monica quit." Isla pursed her lips, looking sad. "It was hard on your mother. The only reason I know any of this is because Ephraim told my brother what happened, and that he's been trying to convince your mother to install security cameras."

"But she won't," I said. "She doesn't trust they're truly private."

"Exactly," Isla said. "We all know how the Darlings are about their famous need for privacy. But everyone was hoping that if you came home, you'd be able to talk some sense into her."

I sighed, "I'm afraid I'm the worst person to give Mama advice. She acts like I'm made of glass, one more crack and I'll shatter."

Isla's gaze softened. "I can understand that. We've all been worried for you, Whitney. It's good that you're back."

"It's only for the weekend," I said, steeling myself against the disappointment on her face. Isla knew about the curse. She knew why I stayed away. But the knowledge didn't make things any easier. "I need to get back to Charleston."

* * *

For all its angst and memory, Granddaddy's funeral reception ended as abruptly as it began.

As if heeding the tenants of some unspoken society rule, the collective mourners departed our little island as one, driving over the bridge and back to their lives in town. I released a long breath as Evangeline and Isla climbed into their respective cars and pulled into the procession. Isla had promised to make a weekend trip to see me as soon as she could manage. It had been so good to see her that I hadn't been able to refuse.

"Mama," I said, as she and I stood on the columned front porch, shrouded by Live Oaks and Spanish moss, waving politely as the last of the guests drove out of sight. "I'm afraid I need to get back."

She shook her head, then reached out and clasped my hand in her own, not saying anything.

"Mama, please."

"Not yet, Whitney Darling," she turned red-rimmed eyes to mine. "We're not done with today."

As if he'd heard her, Ephraim stepped outside. "The executor's ready, Nora," he said. "I'll escort you ladies to the study."

"Thank you, Ephraim," Mama took his outstretched arm. "Come on, Whitney. Not a word of argument."

I nodded and resigned myself to a late-night drive. Mama looked so exhausted. The least I could do was be here for her a little longer and pray the curse wouldn't punish us all for the kindness.

I followed them, unable to keep from studying the way Ephraim walked, straight and strong, or the way his black suit jacket hugged his body, as though it had been custom-made for him. No doubt, it had. His hair was brushed into submission, so unlike the way it looked after he'd spent the day out on the marsh, on a boat with Seth, windswept, shaggy and wild. He towered over my mother, but there was a gentleness in his presence, a protectiveness that tempted me to walk closer, to reach out and wrap my fingers with his and rest my head against his big shoulder. But we continued in polite distance. Silent. Solemn.

We turned the corner into Alistair's study. The rest of the family already waited there. Someone had gathered the miscellany of loose papers and files into neat stacks to be sorted and put away. It was impossible tell the room had been recently ransacked.

Golden evening sunlight streamed in through the wall of windows behind Alistair's desk, where my attention settled on a short, unassuming man wearing a well-tailored striped suit, complete with tasteful gold cufflinks. He smiled pleasantly at the room.

Addison and Francis sat in two velvet salon chairs near the door, Percy at their feet working on a crossword puzzle. Adele and Rose sat nearby, and motioned for us to come in.

"Thank you all for attending. I'm Mr. Allen, the executor of Mr. Darling's will. I know this has been a trying day. However, Mr. Darling was quite adamant that not a single family member, or Mr. Callaghan," he said, looking pointedly over at Ephraim, "were to leave Darling House before his final wishes could be imparted."

"Let's get to it," Aunt Adele said, as Ephraim and I took our seats near Alistair's desk. "As you said, it's been a long day. And I need to see about dinner."

"I'll help you," Addison chimed.

"We all will," Mama said.

"Do y'all have any idea how many casseroles are in the fridge after today?" piped Rose.

"Yes, alright." Mr. Allen cleared his throat. "First thing's first. There have been endowments set aside for Miss Addison and her children, as well as for Adele and Rose, and of course, Mr. Darling's daughter, Nora. Should the rest of the will be disregarded, some of the proceeds from the sale of Darling House will go toward a home in the Savannah Historic District large enough to house the ladies together. As they live now.

"Sale of Darling House?" My mother shot to her feet, her face ashen.

Mr. Allen gave her a sympathetic look and motioned for her to sit. "Please, Mrs. Darling, there's more."

Mama sank back to her chair, and Aunt Adele placed a comforting hand on her shoulder, not managing to keep the worry from her own face.

"As for the matter of Darling House, and the subsequent Darling Glass Company, both of which were owned in full and whole by Mr. Darling . . ." Mr. Allen cleared his throat again.

"May I get you some water?" Aunt Adele asked.

"No thank you, ma'am. Well," he pulled out a handkerchief and dabbed his forehead, "maybe after we're done here. I'm sorry, this is highly irregular." He cut a nervous expression over to Ephraim before leveling his gaze on me.

"Irregular?" Adele asked.

"Yes. That is, currently. That is to say, it's perfectly legal – I checked. Several times."

"What is it?" Francis' impatient, masculine tone bolted through the room, nearly startling me from my chair.

My heart thumped in my chest. A strange feeling swelled there. One I'd had before, a long time ago. Before we'd found the vial, and everything had changed. Something was about to happen and there was nothing I could do to stop it.

"I'm sorry," Mr. Allen said. He looked pointedly at the paper in his hands, then began to read. "Mr. Ephraim Callaghan and Miss Whitney Darling are to be married," his voice squeaked on the word married, "for the span of at least one year, and together run Darling Glass as partners. Or not at all."

Chapter Four

Whitney Darling

"What did you say?" I leaned forward in my chair pressing my fists hard against my lap to still them from shaking. "I don't understand."

Mr. Allen's face took on a fuchsia tone. "It means that if you and Mr. Callaghan don't get married and run things together, then no one will be running Darling Glass. At all. Mr. Darling stipulated that if you refused, the whole place would be sold for a reasonable amount to the state of Georgia," he pressed his handkerchief to his glistening forehead, "to be run as a nature preserve and a hotel. Similar to Jekyll Island."

I laughed, a shrill, hysterical sound. "Jekyll Island. Like Jekyll Island? Darling House?" I laughed again. "Did y'all hear that? Jekyll Island."

My gaze darted to Ephraim.

He stared at me coolly from his chair across the parlor, completely unaffected. Except for the slight ticking of his jaw, he could've just heard the weather report for all the emotion on his face. He'd always been like that. Composed and controlled no matter what. Even the way he sat now, with one ankle crossed over the opposite knee, shoulders relaxed against the firm, tufted leather at his back. A picture of control.

"When was the will updated?" I rubbed a familiar spasm at the base of my throat, trying desperately to calm my nervous system. I thought back to a technique I'd picked up in therapy and started taking an accounting of the colors in the room. Blue. Red. Green. Brown. Jekyll Island. Married.

"These amendments were added quite recently. After Mr. Alistair Darling learned the nature of his declining health."

Another brief silence. Percy giggled from across the room.

"How long do they have to make their decision?" Mama asked from over my shoulder, a tone in her voice that I couldn't place.

"Midnight this evening."

"If they marry for a year," Francis said, "they're free to divorce after?"

Mr. Allen nodded.

"This gets more interesting by the minute," Rose said.

"Now's not the time, Rose," Adele snapped.

"Both of you, please." My mother reached forward and rested a hand on my knee. "Whitney, I had no idea about any of this."

My blood pounded in my ears, and I studied the intricate swirling lines of the Aubusson carpet beneath my feet. I couldn't look at Ephraim again, though I felt his steady gaze boring into me.

"Ephraim and I need the room." I spun around in my chair, facing my family, whose expressions ranged from surprised to amused. "We need the room," I said again. "Alone."

My mother stood and motioned for everyone else to follow her through the door and out into the hall.

Mr. Allen stood as well, tucking his notebook firmly under his arm. He nodded at Ephraim and I with an awkward jerk of his chin. "I'll wait in the front parlor."

"Thank you," Ephraim said, finally deigning to speak.

The door clicked shut behind them, and I shot from my chair. "Did you do this?"

His eyes sparked with anger, but his jaw dropped a little in a satisfying display of emotion. "What are you inferring?"

"You know perfectly well what I mean. Did you talk Alistair into this?"

Ephraim stood and closed the distance between us, all six feet of muscle tight with indignance. "You forget, I already carry the weight of one successful corporation, and over one-thousand employees, who demand a good deal of my time. Getting a piece of an artisanal glass business has hardly been high on my priority list."

"Don't be a snob, Ephraim Callaghan."

"I want what's best for this place."

"And what do you think is best? When have you had a say in what should or shouldn't be done here? You're not a member of this family." I regretted the words immediately.

He arched an angry brow. "Despite your contempt, the Darlings are the closest thing I have to family." His gaze narrowed. "Regardless, Alistair had been concerned about the future of this place since you left. He couldn't count on you."

"And he trusted you to run things?"

"Running things is what I do."

My knees wilted and I sank back into my chair.

Ephraim sighed, as if all of this was hardly a revelation. "He didn't write you out. He bequeathed you half. Run all of it yourself, for all I care. We're only committed for a year."

"You never answered my question. Was this your idea?"

"I'm not a masochist," he sneered. "What's here for me? Tragedy? Obligation? You and I aren't so different, Whitney. You're not special in your pain. The difference is I think of others beyond myself."

His words hit their target. But I squeezed my fists, focusing instead on the sting of my fingernails against my palms.

"I'm stronger than you," Ephraim said, lightly. "Alistair knew that. He also knew it would take both of us, you under some sort of legal responsibility, to see this place attended to. At least in the beginning, until we can get a real infrastructure established. Alistair was a proud man. He wouldn't want to see his legacy fall apart. I'll establish a trust for the property. You'll help me find the right people who can live up to the vision, minus the creepy whispering glass stuff. We'll market the whole thing as though it was all by choice. After the agreed upon year, you and I will part ways."

The tick of the grandfather clock was the only sound.

"That's what's going to happen, Whitney." He came to stand in front of my chair, towering over me.

"Ephraim, I –

"It's a yes or no answer, Whitney. It's my way, or I walk. You know all about how easy that would be."

But he was wrong.

It hadn't been easy for me to leave. Not Darling House. Not my family or the glass.

Not him.

It had been the hardest to leave him.

But I *had* left. He'd asked me to stay. Begged me. And I'd left.

He was under no obligation to help me or the Darlings now. And yet, here he was, taking charge.

I could refuse.

But he knew I wouldn't.

I thought of the note Granddaddy had left for me and his mysterious apology for forcing my hand.

This. This was why he'd apologized.

I'd imagined that by putting distance between this place and myself I could protect the ones I loved, and somehow live like the horrible memories, like the curse itself had never happened. But that wasn't how curses worked. That wasn't how any of this worked.

I swallowed hard, embracing the inevitable truth. If I was going to escape Darling House and its ghosts, I had to figure out what was going on. And I had to stop it. Before anyone else got hurt.

"We don't have all night, Whitney. What do you want?"

I looked up at him with disdain. "You've no right to speak to me like this."

He took a step back, taking on a more casual demeanor as he poured a shot of whiskey into a cut crystal tumbler. "I won't go down memory lane with you. I've done more than well for myself over the years." He tilted his head back and drained the whiskey in one swallow. "Trust me, I haven't been lonely." He set the glass down on the table and his eyes scanned me from navel to nose. "I doubt you've been lonely either."

A vision of Evangeline in Ephraim's arms flashed across my mind, and I stood, my breath coming in shallow little bursts. "How dare you!"

"Whitney," he smiled wickedly, "there you are."

"I hate you," I spat, wanting nothing more than to wipe the conceit off his face.

"You forget, this isn't about us." His emerald eyes bore into me so intently I almost looked away.

Almost.

"Do you know the last thing your grandfather said to me?"

I shook my head, angry tears threatening.

His hand flexed at his side. "He told me that love is the antidote to chaos."

Silence settled between us, an endless chasm, burdened with the weight of what might have been.

"One year," I whispered. "One year. And then you'll never see my face again."

Ephraim strode past me across the carpet and swung open the heavy walnut door, looking not the least surprised to see my aunts, mother, and Addison crowded close, as though they'd had their ears pressed to the wood. "Mr. Allen!"

"Yes, sir." The executor peeped immediately from around the corner, his cheeks a little red.

"We have an agreement. Miss Darling and I will see to the marriage license tomorrow."

"Thank you," Mr. Allen stammered. "That would be fine."

"Excellent." Ephraim nodded politely to our audience. "I'll spend the night in town. Good evening."

And without so much as a glance back in my direction, he strode from the room, leaving Darling House behind.

Chapter Five

William Darling | 1922 | Scotland

Julia's hair was golden. Like the sun. She wore it in a pretty braid that fell over her shoulder. And she walked in that gentle, self-assured way that girls of high means are born with. There was fire in her eyes and life on her tongue.

I'd been a worker on her father's estate four years now.

Not long after I'd arrived, she'd decided to call me William because it had been the name of her cat, and also a beloved uncle. And because Darling was not a sensible first name for a young man. But she still called me Darling when she wasn't thinking about it. And I liked the sound.

"Darling," she said to me one day, "I think it's time for you to learn the etiquette of a proper dinner table. I'll teach you when you're not in the stable, and then maybe, Papa will invite you to join us at mealtimes."

I nodded, knowing it wouldn't happen. But I never turned down the chance to have her attention. She was always wiping dirt from my cheeks with her handkerchief, or straightening my collar, as though it mattered how I looked. I rarely left my work with the horses.

I was a man's man now.

My arms were strong, my back broad and muscled. I knew how to use my hands. How to solve a riddle. How to offer not only my body to a task, but my mind as well.

I was born for labor. For callouses and dusty hair.

But there had been mornings, since the one Julia and her father plucked me off the streets and set me in their horse barn, when I'd felt a calling.

A voice.

Soft, and kind, like Julia's.

And it beckoned me always to the workshop where her father plied his wares.

The man blew glass. Swinging the stuff around his head like a grand magician. I would crouch on the ground and peer between the cracks in the doors or the windows and watch him turn the glowing, golden substance to hardened sculptures blue as ice.

The glass spoke to me. And I could often tell what it would be long before it began to take shape. The magic had become my obsession.

The glass. And my Julia.

"I would settle for the glassblowing bench rather than the dining table. To be near the glass would be enough."

Without a word, Julia took me by the hand and pulled me behind her, stalking across the courtyard and up the stone steps that led to her father's well-appointed workshop.

Her father turned, his eyes darting to the hand Julia wrapped around mine.

I broke free from her grasp and crossed my wrists at my back, giving a quick bow of my head to the man who stood between my position here and life on the street.

Julia's father had plans for her. And they didn't include me.

My chest squeezed at the thought. A thought that hollowed me out. One day another man would come. A fine, fair-haired gentleman. And he would take Julia away from me.

"Papa," Julia chimed. "We've come to ask of your need for an assistant. William has served you well in the stables. And we wonder if –

Her father held up a hand, bringing her words to a halt. He turned his gaze to mine. "William's a man full grown. Let him inquire for himself."

I hadn't been prepared for the abrupt exchange. I'd played it out in my mind often enough, but now here I was. "I am thankful for my position in your home, sir. I'm content with the horses."

Julia cast me an annoyed expression that I felt more than saw out of the corner of my eye.

"If you're content, then why are you standing here, interrupting my work?"

"I – I would like to learn about the glass, sir. To assist you. If you'll have me."

"Why?"

I drew in a deep breath. A silent energy hummed around me, like how the air quivers before a rainfall. "Because it calls to me," I whispered.

"What was that?"

"It beckons to me, sir," I said, more steadily this time, remembering what Julia had told me once about a man's word being his honor.

He nodded. "Yes, I know that."

"Sir?"

"Don't you think I'm privy to all the stolen minutes you've spent watching me? I know a man with destiny in his eyes when I see him. You've only needed to ask. And now that you have – you will have it."

Julia threw her arms around my neck. "You see, William? You will be apprenticed! You will have a profession, real and true."

"You'll be here before the sun rises in the morning," her father said.

"Yes, sir. Thank you."

"That's enough grinning, the both of you." His eyes weren't so harsh as his tone. "Julia, you have piano lessons waiting."

"Yes, Papa."

Julia grabbed for my hand again as soon as we were out of sight.

"Am I dreaming?" I grinned.

"You'll become a man of resources now, William." She glowed like an angel, making it hard for me to concentrate. "Do you know what that means?"

I didn't speak, the implications of what had happened only beginning to sink in.

She led me around one of the garden sheds, looking up at me with shimmering eyes. "It means we have a future. Darling, we can be together. For always."

She stood up on her toes and braced her delicate hands on my chest, and then she leaned forward and gave me the purest, sweetest kiss in the history of women giving kisses. Her lips tasted like springtime honey, and it was all I could do to not tangle my fingers in her hair and pull her closer.

She lowered back to her heels and looked up at me with a face so bright scarlet, my heart swelled.

"For always," she said again.

And then she turned and ran toward the house.

* * *

I'd been across town buying supplies the day trouble came to our door. The selection of goods had been as meager as my purchasing power. While riots and unrest had largely calmed, many still struggled severely in the aftermath of The Great War. Julia's father languished, both in his finances, due to a series of bad investments, as well as in health. But I'd learned my new trade quickly, excelling beyond mine or my mentor's wildest expectations. After only a few months of apprenticeship, I'd taken over the glassblowing studio's primary responsibilities. In time, if I worked hard and listened to the glass, I'd restore Julia's household to its former glory.

Exhausted, I turned the corner onto our street.

The scent of smoke and the sound of raised voices brought me up short.

A fissure of dread crept down my spine.

I shrugged my bag from my shoulder and ran.

Julia.

She stood in the street, frozen, gaping up at our burning home. Flames licked across the roof and spread like water to the glass studio, cracking and popping with fury.

"Julia, where's your father?"

She shook her head, her eyes wide with fear.

I took her by the shoulders. "Where is he?"

"Dead," a woman snapped from over my shoulder. "She says thieves killed him. Stuck him like a pig."

The world went red. "Is this true?"

"He wouldn't give them what they wanted," Julia choked. "He wouldn't tell them where to find our money. They stabbed him and set the house on fire." She shivered violently.

"Did they touch you?"

"I tried to hide, but they found me. The things they threatened — "

Her chin trembled, but she didn't cry. "I gave them everything. They took all we had left. Darling, they killed my father."

The fire brigade arrived. Men ran back and forth as they worked to extinguish the blaze, mostly in an effort to spare the nearby houses. Our home was beyond saving.

I held Julia tight against me.

We watched the house smolder all through the night, until it fell to glowing embers, and all that remained of it and the glass studio were bits of charred wood and twisted metal.

I gazed down at Julia. She hadn't made a sound all night. Hadn't said a word. She'd barely moved, only trembled and watched, knowing as well as I that everything she'd had was gone. The life we'd shared here was over.

All the while, the glass whispered to me. Strange and beautiful things.

Find me across the sea. Look to the chandeliers.

I pressed a kiss to the top of Julia's head. "Cry," I whispered. "The hurt will get trapped, and one day it will kill you if you don't cry."

"You would know that, wouldn't you, Darling?" Her breath hitched, then came in short little pants, until her thin shoulders heaved, and a whole ocean of tears welled up and spilled from her eyes. She cried and cried. And then, finally, she stopped. "We'll be together," she said.

"For always."

* * *

It didn't take long to settle our affairs. The money Julia's father had left in the bank was used to see him buried, as well as Julia and I lodged, clothed, and fed in the few weeks following the fire. Her father's death was under investigation, but there was little to go on. Violent thieves were no rarity.

I'd told Julia what the glass had said, that I should find it across the sea.

We'd hoped to purchase tickets aboard the steam liner *Constance* headed for America. But when we got to the docks, we were shy more than a few pounds.

"William, the ship leaves in an hour. There's no way we can raise the money in time." She pulled a long strand of pearls from beneath her dress, the only piece of home she'd been able to save. "I can sell these. Perhaps to another waiting passenger."

"Put those away. If someone sees, they'll try to steal them. You're not selling the last thing you have in this world." I glanced around the docks, searching for some kind of inspiration to leap out at me. "There's always a way with these things."

"We could stow away."

I scowled. "Not worth the risk."

"And the alternative?"

"There are plenty," I said. "We're not stowing away."

She sighed, and I noticed the circles under her eyes.

"Have a sit down on one of those trunks." I pointed to a pile of luggage waiting to be loaded on the ship. "I'll get us tickets aboard. You don't move from this spot."

"William, you're terribly bossy."

"All I need is to lose you. Wait here and I'll be back before you know it. Swear to me."

"Fine." She rolled her eyes and set her jaw in that way that said she wouldn't be speaking to me the rest of the day. I kissed her on the cheek and disappeared into the crowd.

I was good at disappearing into crowds.

At least I had been once.

My hands were quick when I needed them to be.

* * *

We boarded the ship moments before it made way, under the name of Mr. and Mrs. Chevalier. Who the real Chevaliers were? We would never know. But we thanked them in our prayers for months to come. The contributions of their boarding passes, as well as a lovely knapsack of dried beef and boiled potatoes were the catalyst for our lives in a new world.

"William, I won't ask you how you managed this, if you promise you'll never do it again."

"I'll keep you safe. That's the only vow you'll get from me."

She wrinkled her nose and fell backwards onto the bed. "It's so soft," she sighed. "I could close my eyes and sleep until we reach America."

I stared down at her, my gaze caressing the length of her neck, her chest, her waist. She was so pretty. And she was brave. And she was smart. And kind.

"I love you," I whispered.

"You'll have to speak louder."

"Marry me," I said.

Her eyes shot open.

"What?"

"Be my wife."

Julia smiled. "I love you too, William Darling."

An old pastor, whose name I would never remember, married us two hours later. The three of us, and his elderly wife, huddled on the deck, the scent of saltwater and freedom stinging our noses and making our eyes water as we spoke our vows. Julia wore her pearls.

The ship was quiet and the little room we occupied was barely big enough to stretch our arms out. But it had the soft bed, and that was the only detail Julia and I were concerned with.

She blushed the first time I saw her naked. And then she blushed more once I was naked too.

"You don't know what your eyes do to me." I traced a finger along her pretty jaw. "You see straight to my soul."

She nodded. "From the first."

She rose and pressed her lips to mine. And then she took me to heaven.

We disembarked two weeks later on a cold Wednesday morning. Rain fell in fat, splattering droplets from the sky, soaking our clothes and hair. Poor Julia crouched in a soggy heap. We needed food. We needed shelter. We needed a moment free of this blasted wetness.

My gaze drifted over the grey lane, over carts, automobiles, and horses as tired of the rain as we.

Julia raised wide, searching eyes to mine. I saw fear there. And worry. Exhaustion.

She had been so confident and dear. So assured and secure.

I turned and kicked the wall of the shipping office at our backs.

"William, don't. We can't let our emotions sweep us

away." She stood and placed a steadying hand on my arm, her frozen fingers trembling against the thin cotton of my shirt.

I gathered up her small hands into the warmth of my own and raised them to my lips, "I'll offer to help unload the carts off the liner. It may take some time, but I can earn enough for a night's shelter."

"I'll come too. We'll have twice as much."

"They would never allow it, love. Even if you weren't a woman, you're far too scrawny."

"Am I supposed to sit aside and do nothing?"

"For now." I motioned to an officer who looked to be in charge of unloading the ship's hull. "I'll talk to him and explain our plight. You wait in the warmth of the shipping office while I work."

"But William –"

"Don't argue." I squeezed her hands. "There's no time. I'll make a way for us. A day of labor and I'll turn it into a lifetime of profit. I promise you."

"But –"

"I promise."

She nodded. Her eyes brimmed with tears. "I'm so cold."

"I know, love. After today you'll never be cold again."

"My mother's pearls."

"We'll never part with them. One day you will wear them with a beautiful gown, inside your beautiful mansion by the sea, at a beautiful party with beautiful people, and I will dance with you. Only you. And I will tell you how lovely you look in your pearls."

A tear traced a slow path down her cheek, and I swiped it away, replacing it with a kiss.

"Go to the ship's office and sit by the fire." The muscles in my arms and legs trembled violently as I watched her walk away from me. I kept my eyes on her until I knew she was safe inside, and then I turned and made my way to the docks.

It had been a long time since I'd been a boy on the streets. But not so long that I didn't remember the way of things. I knew how to find the distracted ones. The stupid ones. The ones that carried a purse too loosely.

Within an hour I'd amassed enough money to see us secure for a full week of lodging. Plenty of time to search out the glass artists and factories where I could return to my craft. The glass would see us safe.

I was halfway back to Julia when a firm grip hauled me backward by the shoulder. "Easy there, son. We've had an eye on you for a time now." And then the cruel cold of a metal cuff closed around my wrist.

The jail house walls were old. And damp. The smell of must and unwashed bodies mingled on the air. A fire crackled in the belly of a cast-iron fireplace in the corner, the only source of heat.

An untouched plate of bread and carrots sat on the end of the wooden bench I stretched out on. I stared at the ceiling, thinking of all the ways I could make this right. And if Julia would bother forgiving me if I managed to.

That was, if I could find her. I squeezed my eyes shut with a curse, pushing away for the thousandth time all the horrible images of what could be happening to her.

A door creaked open on old hinges and the sound of soft

footsteps came quickly down the hall, followed by vulgar catcalls and whistles from nearby cells.

I sat up.

"Julia, what are you doing here?"

Her eyes were red and swollen, as was her bottom lip, as if she'd been chewing it with nerves. Her golden hair glowed in the dim lamp light. She wore a new dress. Leagues beyond what we could afford.

"I've come to get you out." Her voice quaked, breathless.

"I'm afraid it's a bit more complicated than that, sweet."

"Not this time. Someone's paid for your release. He convinced the injured parties to drop their grievances since there was no lasting harm done."

I leapt to my feet. "Julia, you've not sold your pearls?"

She shook her head. "A man. We met him once before. Or at least I did. On the ship. He was traveling with his sister. I saw them on the street after you didn't come back. He helped me find you."

"Does this man have a name?"

"Horace. Leroux." Her voice broke on the words. God, she looked so tired.

Guilt washed over me anew. "He sounds quite accommodating."

"He is. He was," she said. "He wants to meet you."

"Why?"

"He's a patron of the arts. He's headed home to Savannah and he and his sister want us to go with them."

"Julia, things like this don't happen."

"I know. But if it will get you out, then we do it, and we figure out the rest later."

"You're not telling me everything."

"I'm telling you what matters, Darling. You're free."

A stout officer ambled down the hall and plunged his key into the lock next to Julia's hip. The door swung open with a creak and I stepped out.

"Are you alright?" I pulled her into my arms.

"I am now. Let's get out of here."

Chapter Six

Whitney Darling

I stared at the canopy above my bed, my eyes tracing the chinoiserie fabric, wondering who I should call first, James at the office, or my therapist. I had to let each of them know I wouldn't be back to Charleston as soon as I'd thought.

I wouldn't tell them I was getting married.

Because I was not, in fact, going through with it.

I didn't care what I'd agreed to. I could certainly argue duress.

I chewed my bottom lip, picturing James' face if I told him the truth. Would pain flash behind his eyes? Loss? In the many late-night conversations that he and I'd shared at the *Coterie* offices, I had always insisted marriage wasn't for me. I'd seen hints of his frustration. James had been playing the long game with me. Trying to win me over. And we both knew it.

What would he say now? Would he argue? Would I send him a wedding invitation? I squeezed my eyes shut with a sigh.

After Ephraim's departure earlier that evening, I'd been

wrapped in a kind of familial cloud. A chattering of details and assurances. Gentle hands on my shoulders and kisses to my cheeks. Mama had watched me closest of all. As though I were an injured animal, not to be prematurely spooked back to the wild.

Aunt Adele and Aunt Rose had launched immediately into a diatribe on how the truth of the matter must remain top secret, and the engagement reported to the papers as soon as possible. A grand wedding would be held on the lawn beside the river, with a reception to follow in the ballroom. I would wear Julia Darling's opera pearls, a favorite tradition among Darling brides.

But I wasn't a bride.

Not really.

This reality I'd tumbled into was nothing like the long-ago dreams I'd once hoped to build my life around.

Trust me. I haven't been lonely.

I swallowed hard at the memory of Ephraim's cutting words, the way his lips curled into a sneer when he'd said them.

He'd kissed me with those lips.

My first kiss.

But now, in this current situation, I was under no illusions.

It wasn't me Ephraim was helping by agreeing to the terms left in Granddaddy's will. He hadn't been able to save his family all those years ago, or the loved ones in mine. But he could save Darling House. Our heritage. The heritage that had welcomed him, and fed him, and offered him a home and a place to belong when he'd lost everything.

After all this time, and all that happened, he was tethered here.

Just as surely as I.

A stab of guilt made me catch my breath.

My mind raced with the implications of sticking to the agreement. What would happen to my apartment in Charleston? I loved my apartment. My job, the career and reputation I'd forged for myself in The Holy City was something I was immensely proud of. My friendship with James. The co-workers and interns who had stepped in and made my life bearable in the aftermath of so much tragedy. My life in Charleston had become my shell. The refuge I'd grown attached to.

And this agreement, this foolishness put all that in jeopardy.

What had Granddaddy been thinking?

It was enough to ask me to help solve the mystery behind the curse. I understood that request. I'd consider accepting it.

And the glass. I was happy to oversee the management of the *Darling & Potter* sunglass facility on River Street downtown and our team of boutique glassblowers stationed there. I could entertain embracing my responsibility as resident glass whisperer. I could come back to manage the traditional glassblowing here on the island, where our famous chandeliers and bespoke pieces were still assembled. I could understand his deep desire for all of that.

But marrying Ephraim? Why was that necessary? Did Granddaddy think he could rebuild my old life from beyond the grave, like some wizened spectral puppeteer, pulling strings and writing his own version of my happily ever after?

My chest tightened. It wasn't that simple.

As far as I knew, there weren't any stipulations in the will regarding what marriage to Ephraim had to look like. This was more formality than anything. A contract.

And that was the loophole I would hold to.

It wasn't real.

There'd be no living together.

No intimacy.

No sex. An image flashed across my mind, Ephraim's powerful form, his hands, his lips caressing my cheek, my neck, my –

I gasped and sat up, swinging my feet over the edge of the bed. I willed my heartbeat to slow and glanced at the little brass clock on the bedside table. After midnight. Most of the family had turned in around ten. It would be empty downstairs. Quiet.

My stomach growled and I pressed a hand to my belly.

I hadn't been able to eat earlier. Even when Aunt Adele had offered me a fresh slice of creamed cheese danish and tea. My favorite.

Daddy had texted me shortly thereafter, a clipped, *"Sorry for your loss, honey."* That had done away with the final remnants of my appetite.

I sighed. Lying awake in bed, replaying my horrible day was a practice in misery, and I refused to wallow.

Minutes later, wrapped in a white silk nightgown and a pair of velvet house shoes, I opened the door and stepped silently from my room.

The air was colder in the hallway. Markedly so. Rows of doors lined the long corridor. Most led to other bedrooms, one to an old service stairwell, and another to a playroom. Addison, Seth, and I had spent many hours in there when we were little. Isla too. And Monica, during the years she and her mother had lived here on the island.

Percy used it now. And soon the new baby. The days running up and down this hallway, from room to room, laughing and imagining we were all manner of fantastical things, seemed like a lifetime ago, no longer in technicolor, but faded, the memories pieced haltingly together like stop photography.

A ruffling sound, the crush of satin fluttered behind me. Forgetting my old discipline of ignoring bumps in the night, I glanced over my shoulder.

There was nothing there.

Not that I could see. But the sensation of being watched sent a cold sliver of alarm to my fingers and toes. Was this Percy's angel?

We learned young here, not only at Darling House, but, I'd found, in these old southern places in general – you don't let the dead know you sense them. Don't let them know you know they're there. It only encourages them.

The ghosts here weren't dangerous. At least we didn't think so. Mostly responsible for mysterious sounds in the night, or during the day, for that matter, they'd rearrange furniture, change the channel on the television, or hum a tune. But nothing nefarious had ever happened. They were content to watch from a distance, only making their presence known from time to time. Aunt Rose always said we couldn't blame them. She wouldn't want to be forgotten either.

I stepped fast down the hallway, meaning to make quick work of the staircase that waited not five paces ahead of me, when my slipper caught the ornate golden frame Mama had leaned against the wall. It fell forward onto the floor with a thud. I squatted down and lifted it upright again.

The air around me went from cold to frigid. William and Julia Darling stared back at me from their wedding photo, and I fleetingly wished I could ask one of them to hop out and walk with me. My eyes narrowed on a bit of linen, now hanging loose from the back. Fingers numb, I did my best to press the fabric back into place. My finger brushed the edge of something sturdy, a folded piece of paper. Gently, I pulled it from the frame.

A sigh sounded over my shoulder.

My eyes widened as I unfolded the delicate material.

It was a letter. From William Darling to Julia.

> My Julia,
> No words can undo the grave happenings that have befallen our household. What we've lost – I cannot write it. The pain is too great.
> I would not undo what I did. These hands alone will bear the responsibility. I didn't protect you as I should have, my love. For that, I am eternally sorry.
> You are the center of my world, and we will persevere in the face of this chaos. I have seen to it that a quiet and blessed life will make up the days ahead, for us, and for the generations to come here at Darling House.
> Forgive me, my love.
> To new and charmed beginnings,
>
> Your Darling William

A cold breath caressed the back of my neck. Rising, I tucked the letter clumsily into my robe pocket, curled my trembling fingers into fists, and strode measuredly to the stairs, the sensation of eyes on me never waning until I reached the bottom.

What had William done? And why was an apology letter of all things secured behind his and Julia's portrait?

I walked faster, desperate for the coziness of the kitchen.

A thud from Alistair's office brought me up short.

I bit my lip. I should stick to my mission for a snack.

Another thud, louder this time.

I stepped toward the study.

What if it was the burglar? So much had happened today, the memory of this morning's break-in had slipped from my mind. A fresh dart of adrenaline shot through me, and I veered to where a slender marble statue perched on a pedestal. I took the small sculpture in my hand, embracing the solid weight. If there was an intruder in that room, at least I'd have the benefit of surprise.

I hesitated outside the study door. I should get Francis.

I pushed the thought away.

No doubt, he'd tell Ephraim. And if it turned out to be nothing but a ghost, it was the sort of fodder Ephraim would relish using against me. My fearfulness. My inability to handle things.

The room was shadowed when I peeked inside.

The air sparked, as if the energy Ephraim and I had spent there still hung in the atmosphere. I scanned the room, my gaze drifting beyond a blue silk-upholstered sofa and cane-backed salon chairs. The leather club chairs were empty. No one stood near any of the floor-to-ceiling windows, or the glass doors that led out to the terrace. Alistair's mahogany desk faced me, vacant.

Had the sound come from here at all?

I turned to leave, but as I stepped into the hall, another thump, like something small and dense hitting the floor, broke the silence. I whirled around and reached inside the door, clicking on a lamp. The room flooded with warm light.

Still, there was nothing.

Almost nothing.

Two books lay in the center of the rug.

Squaring my shoulders, I crossed the room and picked up a volume, setting the marble sculpture at my feet.

"The Phantom of the Opera," I whispered. "Funny."

Satisfied my observer was of the spiritual persuasion, I relaxed a bit, only half-wishing I'd brought along Solomon's gift of sage and cedar.

I knelt to pick up the other book. This one was a good bit older. An antique. I examined the flaking leather spine.

The Odyssey.

I opened the book to a page crumpled in the fall. I worked my fingers over the tender paper, studying the line of text at the top. A quote by Penelope, her name underlined in faded black ink.

How I wish chaste Artemis would give me a death so soft, and now, so I would not go on in grieving all my life . . .

"Penelope, you have no idea."

I snapped the book closed, scanning the bookcase for where it belonged. A space big enough for both the fallen books winked at me near the top shelf and I stood on my tiptoes to slide *The Odyssey* back in place. The hollow sound of glass, like a small bottle tipping over, made me stop. Something was in the way. I set the books on the ground, shimmied one of the club chairs over, and climbed up to see.

A delicate, narrow bottle the length of my hand lay tipped on its side, a black rubber stopper at its mouth.

My heart skipped, and I reached for it, recognizing it at once.

I stepped down from the chair and opened my hand.

The glass vial was filled to its neck with dirt.

Grave dirt.

The mojo.

The protective charm I'd rendered null and void the

moment I'd plucked it from a hydrangea bed at the base of Darling House.

Such a small thing.

A movement caught the corner of my eye. I whirled to see a woman in white outside the glass doors on the veranda, her back to me. Only this time she didn't disappear. This time she leaned forward, her elbows perched on the iron railing that overlooked the marsh and the river beyond.

I released a long breath as recognition dawned. Aunt Adele. The folds of her cotton nightgown fluttered in the salty breeze and a woven afghan draped around her shoulders. Her pale grey hair was tied neatly in a bun at her nape.

Slipping the vial into my robe pocket next to William's letter, I opened the delicate glass doors, and stepped outside to stand beside her.

"Can't sleep?" I asked.

She smiled a greeting. "Never could sleep well after a funeral, knowing my day isn't far off."

"Don't say that. You have a lot of time."

"That's easy for you to say. You're not pushing eighty."

I swallowed a laugh. She had a point.

It was at the tip of my tongue to tell Adele about the letter tucked tight against the vile of grave dirt in my pocket, but this day had already held enough revelation.

"What are we looking at?" I propped my arms on the rail and stared out at the marsh like she did, my eyes adjusting to the darkness. It was hard to tell where the marsh began, and the black sky ended. It was after midnight, the wild hour, when the night animals stretched their legs and filled their bellies. The time when the marsh belonged to the bats, and the frogs, and the sharks.

Adele pointed, her long, trim finger, bone white against the dark.

I followed her direction and after a moment my eyes trained on a silhouette striding down the boat dock, barely visible.

"Is that?"

"Sure is."

Evidently, the night also belonged to Ephraim.

He crossed the length of the dock, then stepped onto the fishing boat in the far slip. It was his shadow I'd seen the other night when Solomon had slipped away into the storm.

"I thought Ephraim was spending the night in town."

"Guess your fiancé changed his mind."

"Please don't call him that. You know he's not my fiancé."

"You're going to marry him, aren't you?"

"Not like that."

"Like what?"

"Like a real marriage. That's not what we're doing, and you know it."

"I don't know any such thing."

I rolled my eyes. "What's he up to?"

"Walking down the boat dock in the dark."

"You're being obtuse on purpose."

"I see. You spend a few years in Charleston and come back too serious for a sense of humor."

"Are you going to tell me what he's doing, or not?"

Adele's lips drew into a straight line. "He's done this since you left."

"Done what?"

"I don't think he'll ever stop searching," Adele said. "For exactly what, at this point, I don't know." She shook her head. "He searched endlessly for your brother when Seth disappeared. Your father tried, but we couldn't bring him in. He didn't sleep for days."

"And now he does this every night?"

"Not every night, no." Adele's pale eyes trained on the marsh, though the outline of the boat was barely visible now, save for the single light on the hull, ducking in and out of view in the winking moonlight. "He goes out when the tide is with him. I think he does it mostly when he's missing Seth. Or his parents." She turned and looked at me. "Or you. He's missed you very much."

I looked away, not willing to process her words. Adele was mistaken. Ephraim hated me. "And you let him go? You let him take out the boat this time of night? It's dangerous."

"Honey, Ephraim is a grown man. He doesn't need me pointing out what's safe and what isn't."

"Seth was grown too."

"Yes. He was."

I groaned and stared down at my slippers. Long moments passed as I listened to the night sounds on the marsh. "Will we ever move past this?"

My aunt cleared her throat, but it was a while before she spoke. "You know, I don't believe you do get past these things. You learn to carry them. And that makes you stronger. And kinder."

I straightened. "And what if it's too much to carry? What if I'm tired?"

"Then you rest." Adele reached out and squeezed my hand, the way she had when I was little. "Or you go for a boat ride in the dark."

I wrapped my arm around her thin shoulders. "When will he be back?"

She chuckled. "It's best to go to sleep and let men be men."

I nodded, not one hundred percent sure I agreed.

A thump, like the sound of another book hitting the floor, sounded from the office behind us. Adele didn't seem to notice.

"Have you heard any strange noises from Alistair's study lately?" I asked.

"Darling girl, the real question is when have I *not* heard strange noises from that study?" She patted my cheek. "Welcome home, Whitney Darling. Now, get yourself off to bed."

My stomach growled.

Adele smiled. "Best stop by the kitchen on your way. Enjoy the cheese danish."

* * *

The glass woke me long before the sunrise, when night still cleaved like ink to the sky. And after two years of faithful disregard, I decided it was time to finally answer.

Silver moonlight spilled through the open windows of the studio, dancing its way over ancient, ocean-scented rafters, and shelves and shelves of gleaming blown glass, then swept soft over my sweat-dusted skin.

I still wore my white silk nightgown, and my hair twisted in a messy bun atop my head, though I'd stripped off the green field jacket I'd donned for the chilly trek from the house.

Heat glowed in the furnace in front of me, like some wise and hungry monster, warming the salty air until it was thick enough to taste.

Sweat dripped between my breasts and trickled down the small of my back. I focused past the ache in my arms and shoulders, my gaze trained on the soft, orange glob at the end of my blow pipe.

Waiting for the glass to whisper.

Waiting for it to prove what Granddaddy had written in his letter was true. That if I listened hard, the glass would help me.

And if I could make that happen fast enough, maybe I could break the curse without having to marry Ephraim Callaghan.

Unfortunately, the glass had always seemed to enjoy mocking me – especially when I most wanted to understand it. Oh, it called to me the way it had to Seth, and to Granddaddy, and to all the select Darlings who could hear it before. But unlike with them, to me the glass only ever spoke in riddles. Frustrating, indiscernible, stupid riddles.

"Listen, I don't like you all that much either. But I'm all that's left. So talk to me, or hush altogether. Got it?" I twisted the pipe, counting down from ten in my head. If the glass didn't speak clearly by the time I reached zero, that was it. I was going back to bed. I'd try again tomorrow.

Three.

Two.

One.

I lowered the pipe, my patience spent.

Broken.

I gritted my teeth. "No more puzzles. If you want me to stay and figure out what's going on, then cooperate. Help me."

Broken. Broken. Broken.

I narrowed my eyes, caught in the throes of full-blown annoyance. "That's it. I'm done. I'm leaving."

I let my blowpipe clatter to the floor near the polishing bench and turned for the door.

A single, shrill note chimed, high and abbreviated. I glanced over my shoulder at Granddaddy's old baby grand that sat buried beneath glass pieces and half-filled sketchbooks. The piano had been one of many alternate creative outlets Alistair indulged on days the glass hadn't spoken. The pale wood of the old instrument made it unlike any I'd ever seen. Rugged, and wizened, and as full of secret history as the glass studio itself. I'd forgotten about the piano, and the invisible ghost who liked to play it.

I stepped again toward the door, reaching for my jacket.

Another shrill, angry note chimed, and the air around me tingled, charged, as if lightning were about to strike.

I held my breath.

"Broken." The word was whispered beside my ear, in a voice so soft I almost didn't hear it. Rivulets of ice shot straight to my fingertips. The hair on my arms stood on end, and out of the corner of my eye, I glimpsed her.

The pale hair, white gown. It was the woman from the upstairs window.

I lurched back, turning on my ankle, then tripped and bumped hard into a polishing bench. My arms flew out for purchase, knocking over a trio of blue vases. They hit the ground and shattered, as I joined them there, landing hard on my tailbone.

Afraid of who or what I might see, I kept my eyes trained on the floor, inspecting the sparkling cerulean mess with detached acceptance.

Glass teardrops on the massive chandelier above *tink-tinked.*

Broken.

I looked up. The chandelier had a name. *William Darling's Pride.* It had hung in the grand conservatory of

Darling House for a time, a glimmering, eight-hundred-pound, priceless centerpiece.

In the little stone glass-blowing studio, it was almost ridiculous.

I'd asked Granddaddy once, why the heavy, elegant piece hung here now and not the house. He'd smiled charmingly and said the chandelier had always told him that it had a destiny here.

"You and me, both," I grumbled, bracing myself to stand.

But I paused when my fingertip grazed a small engraving in the flagstone - a single letter *P*. I hesitated, tracing the rough carving. Like the resident ghost, none of us knew where the etching came from or what it meant. We supposed it was a stone mason's mark. But as a little girl, and a young woman training in the studio, Alistair had used the errant script as an opportunity to remind me of certain words that started with the letter.

"*P is for perfection – there's no such thing,*" he would say. Or "*P is for persistence. Or P is for passion. P is for purpose.*"

I closed my eyes for a moment, my heartbeat beginning to slow.

"P is for passion," I whispered.

Two of the teardrops *tinked* again.

"We have an errand to run, Miss Darling."

I screamed, almost coming out of my skin, and whirled around at the husky voice.

Ephraim straightened, pushing a broad shoulder away from the doorframe where he'd been watching me for who-knew-how-long. His dark, emerald gaze danced with amusement.

Disheveled, black waves fell carelessly over his forehead, and a days' worth of scruff grew along his square jaw. He wore a crisp white button-down, the sleeves rolled to his elbows, revealing tan, muscular forearms, and a pair of pale jeans.

I stood on shaky legs, well aware I looked like death warmed over.

"You weren't in your room," he said, taking a measured step toward me. "I admit, this is the last place I expected to find you. My money was on you being halfway back to Charleston."

"You went to my room?" I hated how my voice shook.

"Come with me, Whitney."

I blanched, frozen for a moment before motioning to the blowpipe, "I'm in the middle of something."

"I'm afraid nervous breakdowns don't count. Let's go."

"Where?"

His lips curled into an amused smile. "I think you know. I prefer to get this matter between us settled."

I lifted my chin, bracing against my pounding heart. "And if I've changed my mind?"

A motion by the window, a flicker of white skirts, almost made me look.

His eyes darkened, "It's too late for that."

I tried to swallow, but my mouth had gone dry. "Grand-daddy's lawyer never should've amended the will. There must be another way."

Ephraim smiled sardonically. "Actually, you can put about anything you'd like into a will. Believe me, I checked. Several times. As did my lawyers."

"Adele and Rose are planning a big wedding," I said, hating the tremor in my voice. "No one would approve of us taking off in the night."

"Seeing as how I'm the one making the larger sacrifice,

we're going to do this my way. Refuse, and it's the Darlings you'll let down again, not me." He took another step closer.

My fingers moved to the familiar little palpitations at the base of my throat, a warning of a coming panic. "I haven't had any coffee yet."

He chuckled, a deep, menacing sound. "I'll get you a latte after. Is your Starbucks order still five minutes long?"

He was close now.

I caught the scent of him. Saltwater and wild.

My pulse leapt. I motioned to my white silk nightgown and canvas boat shoes. "I'm a sweaty mess."

"Somehow, I find that all the more appropriate." He moved fast. Too fast. In one fluid motion, he gripped me by the hips and swung me over his shoulder.

Mortified, I pounded my fists against his back, struggling for equilibrium. "Ephraim, stop. Put me down. Now!"

His arm tightened, a steely vice around my legs, as he stalked for the door.

"What will you do, carry me kicking and screaming into the courthouse?"

"Of course not." He swatted me on the butt with his free hand. "We'll do this at my townhouse. We're not animals."

I pummeled his back again, but he didn't flinch.

I tried not to focus on my nightgown riding up my thighs, or how his fingers pressed into my bare skin. "You've lost it. Everyone on this island has lost it."

"You should feel right at home then." He marched outside the studio and down the steps.

The frigid air stole my breath. "We left my coat. Ephraim, it's freezing."

"It'll be warm in the car."

The moon had passed behind a cloud, casting the night

pitch-black. Only a faint flicker of light filtered out through the studio's shutters, enough for me to spy the outline of an SUV parked on the riverbank.

"Are you actually kidnapping me?"

"Is it possible to kidnap your wife?"

"I'm not your wife," I punched him in the back again. "And yes, I believe it *is* possible. I'll confirm with the police."

His fingers dug into my skin. "Conveniently for you, my old friend the police chief is our witness for the ceremony."

"You're not serious."

"Oh, my sweet Whitney." He slid me down his muscled body, my nightgown bunching at my thighs as I went. He held me tight against him as he swung open the passenger door. "I'm always serious."

Chapter Seven

Whitney Darling

Ephraim Callaghan was many things, but a liar wasn't one of them.

True to his word, his black BMW pulled in front of his Jones Street townhouse as sunlight kissed the sky. The stately nineteenth-century mansion was built entirely of Savannah grey brick, its foundation taking up at least twice the space of its neighbors.

Imposing man. Imposing house.

The ride into town had been silent. Oh, I'd had plenty to say. But I knew this man. When it came to a battle of wills, he was a warrior, an expert in discourse. It was what made him so successful in business, allowed him to acquire companies and properties and all manner of assets in a carefully curated menagerie of accomplishments. He was cunning. Cutting. Linguistically lethal.

Nothing would have fueled him like a good banter.

And so, despite my fury, I'd refused him the satisfaction.

Now we stood opposite one another in front of the ornate marble fireplace in his formal parlor, both of us radiating contempt. The composed, elegant Ephraim from my past was nowhere to be seen.

A priest, who I vaguely recognized, stood in a white robe to our left. And over Ephraim's shoulder was the chief of police, an amused smile on his round face.

My heart pounded. I focused on looking as dignified as I could in my crumpled satin nightgown. Rage swelled in my chest, and it took all my willpower not to grind my teeth and not to openly glare at the smug man standing across from me.

Angry as I was, I understood why he was doing this.

It was his revenge.

For leaving him behind two years ago, when he'd all but begged me to stay.

I straightened, ignoring a fresh and unwelcome pang of guilt at the memory.

Fine. I'd allow him to think he was in control. For now.

But if Ephraim thought he could embarrass me, he was sorely mistaken. I wouldn't give him the satisfaction of seeing me lose my composure.

Let him enjoy what vengeance he could muster.

"Ready to proceed?" The priest's voice made my heart sink.

Ephraim nodded, his gaze steel. "The abbreviated version, please."

I dug my fingernails into my palms.

"Dearly beloved, — "

"Abbreviate harder," Ephraim snapped.

The priest cleared his throat, his eyes darting to mine before focusing back on the Bible in his hands. "The rings?"

Ephraim shook his head, "We're not that formal."

"Right." The priest's brows grazed his hairline, and he took a steadying breath, "Do you, Ephraim Callaghan, take Miss Whitney Darling to be your lawfully wedded wife?"

"I do."

"And do you, Miss Whitney Darling, take Mr. Ephraim Callaghan to be your lawfully wedded husband?"

"Evidently," I said.

Ephraim shot me a warning glare.

"I'm afraid it's a yes or no answer, Miss Darling."

"Yes, then."

"I pronounce you husband and wife," the priest said, with a deadpan matter-of-factness that almost made me laugh. "You may now kiss the bride."

I stiffened, bracing myself for the contact.

Only, Ephraim quite pointedly did not kiss his bride, but instead spun on his heel away from me. "Gentlemen, thank you again for your assistance. Chief, I'll see you at the benefit next Wednesday. Father, your secret remains safe with me."

Both the men nodded and strode stiffly from the room without another glance in my direction.

I blanched, reeling at the speed of the exchange. "What the hell was that?"

Ephraim glanced over at me casually, as though he'd forgotten I was there. "Your wedding. Was it everything you dreamed?"

"You know what I'm talking about."

He scratched at the scruff along his jaw. "You're no stranger to how things work in Savannah, Whitney."

"Excuse me?"

"The good old boys club." He smiled sardonically. "Your father's a card-carrying member, absent as he may be."

I tried not to flinch. It was true. I'd grown up witnessing

my share of closed-door deals over the years. In an old city like Savannah, there were the politics you could see, and then there were the politics that got things done. Nothing was ever the way it appeared on the surface.

"I'm a person, not a business deal on the golf course."

He smirked and motioned toward the adjoining front parlor, "Follow me."

I stood still, fuming, as I breathed past a sudden wave of panic.

"It wasn't a request, Whitney," Ephraim clipped. "Come in here, please."

I stomped after him, "Why this way?" I snarled. "You're so angry with me, that you thought you'd try to humiliate me?"

He turned on his heel, his eyes snapping, "I wasn't about to let you sneak off in the middle of the night and destroy Darling House and what's left of your family. We're good and married now, Whitney Callaghan. And come hell or high water, we'll stay that way for the next year."

I swallowed hard. There was nothing I could say to that.

He was exactly right.

I had been thinking about leaving, and he knew me well enough to guess as much.

And once again, he'd been the one to put the good of my family above everything.

"What if I say no?"

"It's too late for that."

"As if you gave me a choice."

"There's always a choice, Whitney," his words dripped with contempt.

"How will Evangeline feel about all this?" I blushed, my breath coming faster now. "She doesn't strike me as the forgiving kind."

"You leave her out of this."

"It's a valid question."

His jaw ticked. "That's between Evangeline and I."

Did he have feelings for her? Real ones?

My knees weakened, and I perched on the edge of a pale blue sofa.

Ephraim leaned his shoulder against the doorframe, and for the first time I noticed a black satin bag dangling from his fingers. "Tell me," he said, holding it out to me. "Do you have any idea why Alistair would have asked me to give you this?"

I realized he had no intention of walking over to me, and so after a moment I rose stiffly to my feet, each step toward my new husband driven solely by pure curiosity.

Not meeting Ephraim's gaze, I took the bag and tilted it upside down, until a small, cool item tumbled onto my palm. A circular gold pendant attached to a delicate chain winked up at me. I turned the pendant over. What looked like pale thread was woven in an intricate swirling design in the shape of a flower in the center, all of it kept safe under a smooth dome of glass. Almost like a locket.

"I've never seen this."

"Mourning jewelry," Ephraim said matter-of-factly. "That flower's made of human hair."

I shuddered and set the necklace on the marble coffee table, "Whose?"

"I was hoping you'd be able to tell me." Ephraim took a seat on the sofa, stretching his long legs out in front of him. "Your grandfather gave that to me about a week before his fall. He warned me you'd be coming home soon, and that I should give it to you."

"I can't begin to imagine why." I swallowed hard, hesitant to ask the question that had been on my mind. "Was Granddaddy alright when he died?"

Ephraim quirked a brow. "Well, no, he wasn't. I'm afraid that's why he didn't make it."

"I didn't mean – "

"I know what you meant. He and I had a clever, lively conversation days before his fall."

I sighed, ignoring the pang of grief in my chest. "I don't know what to make of any of this. He's left me a cryptic letter, antique mourning jewelry, and orchestrated what amounts to an arranged marriage. I can't be the only one who finds this all ridiculous."

"What letter?"

"What?"

"You said he left you a letter."

My cheeks warmed. Aunt Adele had always teased me as a child that if someone wanted to start some gossip, they should tell me a secret.

"I won't ask you to betray your grandfather's trust," Ephraim straightened. "But I will ask you this – and only once. Is anyone in danger?"

"I don't think so. I mean, I'm not sure. I can hardly tell what's real anymore and what isn't." The familiar *tap tap* of a spasm in my throat started up again and I rubbed at it reflexively.

Ephraim's eyes narrowed at the movement. "Here's what we do know," he said. "Your Grandfather passed away, and Darling House was broken into almost immediately. Nothing was taken. In the meantime, he's left you a cryptic letter and a dead person's hair. So, the question stands. What's going on? And, more importantly, why are you in the middle of it?"

"How am I in the middle?"

"This obviously has to do with the glass."

"Why the glass?"

"Because you're the only one the glass will speak to."

I'd already come to the same conclusion, but I wasn't about to admit that. "A coincidence."

He narrowed his eyes at me, "I've seen through my obligation. That creepy necklace is no longer my responsibility. Consider it my wedding gift."

I studied the necklace on the table.

I'd learned about mourning jewelry in college. The trend had caught on during the Victorian era, when deaths from things like cholera and tuberculosis were so common families lived in perpetual states of bereavement. Death was a part of the culture, and so wearing the hair of your deceased loved one was seen more as a romantic memento than macabre.

I picked up the pendant, smoothing my thumb over the weathered glass.

Would I have kept a lock of Seth's hair if I'd had the chance?

"There's something else," Ephraim said, pulling a black envelope from inside his jacket. He dropped it on the table.

My name was scrawled across the front in gold lettering, Granddaddy Alistair's distinct script instantly recognizable.

I stiffened.

I didn't want to know what it said.

I thought of the first letter. The one Solomon had pressed into my hands the night before the funeral. Granddaddy had told me more information was coming.

How many of these letters would there be?

"You going to open it?" Ephraim prodded.

Despite reservations of logic, my fingers itched to pick

up the envelope and break the seal, if only to hear from my Granddaddy one more time. But too much had already happened this morning, I wasn't prepared to look at something so tender and personal when I still felt so angry.

I drew in a breath and narrowed my gaze.

"You're serious?"

"I am."

"You're not going to read it?"

"No."

"I'd like you to read it."

"Well, then I'm definitely not going to."

Ephraim chuckled and leaned forward, a storm of frustration brewing in his eyes. "I'm as tied to all of this as you are, Whitney. I'd like to know what's going on."

I picked up the envelope, ran my finger along a smooth edge, then set it on the cushion beside me. "I promise to share any pertinent information." I lifted my chin. "Also, keep in mind we're married by name only. You have no other rights to me. No ground to try and tell me what to do, or how to do it. I'll run Darling Glass as I choose. I'll come and go as I choose, when I choose, and with whom."

He scowled. "As will I."

"Good."

"Good." Ephraim reached for the mourning necklace on the table, his tan fingers wrapping gently around the long chain. He lowered it back into the black satin bag and held it out to me. "I need to grab some things upstairs," he said. "We should head back to Darling House. I was informed Adele's making my favorite for brunch today."

"Fried chicken and waffles." I smiled a little at the familiar memory.

He stared at me for a moment, then nodded. "Make yourself comfortable."

"Ephraim."

"What now?"

I bit my lip, "Do you believe in ghosts?"

"I've never seen one, if that's what you mean."

"Not even at Darling House?"

He turned and strode from the room, his deep voice stern from over his shoulder. "As far as I'm concerned, Whitney, the dead are a long way from here."

Chapter Eight

Whitney Darling

cool breeze off the ocean whipped my hair around my head and I crumpled Alistair's letter against my chest.

My Darling Whitney,

Here you are, my love. If you're reading this, it means you've not taken off back to Charleston. You're home, at Darling House, where you belong. And what a beautiful bride you'll be.

I apologize for forcing your hand. It wasn't so much my intention, as it was necessity. There are things conspiring at Darling House that you don't yet understand.

I fear revenants of our past.

Upon my death, our beloved glass is not the only thing in danger. Our family name is in jeopardy. And perhaps our very family itself.

Someone has been watching us. Closely, I believe, for quite some time.

I suspect it's tied to the curse, and somehow, William and Julia Darling.

Things have not always gone easy on our little island. There are things that happened – long ago. Terrible things I don't dare write here.

The ghosts of Darling House are on the move. They're trying to warn us. And you would be wise to listen.

I know for certain that you and Ephraim together will have both the wits and the strength to face whatever revelations arise in the coming days and weeks, and to set to rights all that threatens to undo our legacy.

I wish I could be there for your wedding day, to see you dressed in white, Julia's beautiful pearls draped around your neck like all the Darling brides before you.

Look to the pearls. Watch the chandelier. P is for persistence.

I love you.

Your Granddaddy Alistair Darling

I stood alone, my back to the wide, sprawling marsh and one hundred million wild things, all of them vibrant and quiet and secret beneath the surface. Hermit crabs, turtles, and dolphins, and all manner of life teeming and diving and glancing up high, past the river. Salty wind off the easterly ocean set my linen shirt billowing like a flag of surrender.

Darling House, in all its splendor stared back at me, pearly white and stately, the glass walls of the grand, four-story conservatory sparkling in the morning light.

I'd walked down to the marsh beach at daybreak, more

out of muscle memory than from desire. I'd walked until the Spartina grass gave way to sand, and the earth and the greedy river released themselves to the sea, determined to finally read Granddaddy's letter.

And now I wished I hadn't, because in true Darling fashion, things only continued to grow more mysterious. More tragic. More complicated.

Revenants from our past? Someone watching the family?

I thought of the break-in the morning of the funeral.

I massaged away the too-familiar spasm at the base of my neck and forced myself to take deep, steady breaths.

Why did Granddaddy believe I was the one to decipher this mystery? Because the glass spoke to me?

Sometimes, I hated the glass. I resented it the way I resented the river, and this house, and this whole damned island. What was the point in speaking to glass, to having it tell you what it could be, what was to come, if it wasn't going to warn you against unleashing old curses, or loved ones drowning, or the host of pain and loss we'd been forced to endure over the last two years?

And why in the world would Granddaddy add insult to injury by tying me to the one person, the one man who could break my heart open in the midst of it?

After bringing me back here from our impromptu wedding ceremony, Ephraim had stuck around for brunch. We'd stopped on the way, of course, for me to buy fresh clothes since I couldn't walk in the front door wearing a rumpled nightgown, and then mutually we'd agreed that neither of us would breathe a word about what had happened. As tempting as it was to have the distasteful event behind us, there was no chance Mama, or my aunts would take lightly the news of a shotgun wedding. For now, as far as anyone else was concerned, Ephraim and I were simply engaged, not yet man and wife.

Adele had met us in the foyer where she'd readily bought our explanation that Ephraim had picked me up early to discuss our business arrangement over lattes at a little café near the island, at which point she'd ushered us into the breakfast room where the rest of the family sat gathered around an array of post-funeral casseroles, an assortment of pastries, and a fresh carafe of steaming coffee.

Mama's eyes had glowed at the sight of Ephraim and I together, effectively rekindling the rage I'd tempered on the car ride home.

Apparently taking mine and Ephraim's feeble congeniality toward one another as consent, Mama and the aunts had spiraled almost immediately into talk of wedding plans. As it happened, a heritage invitation design had been waiting in the wings since before the day I was born, usually updated only with a different featured flower for each new Darling bride, a detail we would overlook in this instance as there was no time for that kind of customization. There was discussion over menu items, a live orchestral band, and enough debate about potential tablecloth colors to leave me grinding my teeth.

But despite my reticent mumbling of the occasional opinion, Ephraim was decidedly jovial. He'd played the future groom perfectly. It was an attempt, I knew, to get as far under my skin as possible.

And mostly, I supposed, a show of the deep respect and love he held for my family.

But that had been two days ago, and I hadn't seen him since.

Not up close, anyway.

I'd spied him from the veranda the last two nights, his

dark silhouette in the moonlight as he'd disappeared down the boat dock and out onto the river beyond.

Mama told me once that wild things were like that. There one moment, and gone the next, like the ghosts that walked the hallways of our sprawling Darling House.

Our island and the whole wide marsh belonged to the wild things.

And we belonged to them.

I shivered and tilted my chin up to the pale sky.

Seth, Ephraim, and I had stood here on this beach fifteen years ago, when Mama had come down from the house to find us, her cheeks white, her eyes red and swollen.

She'd strode right past Seth and me, and pulled a stunned Ephraim into her trembling embrace. Her voice had been measured, steady and tender, a stoic melody of grief and strength as she reached up and took his handsome, young face in her hands and told him the news that would change him forever. His parents' helicopter had gone down over the marsh after leaving their private retreat on Ophelia Island. No one on board survived.

We'd all stood still, breathless, quiet, and then Mama had wrapped Ephraim in her arms again, as if he were one of her own, and she didn't let him go for a long, long time. And after Ephraim's strength was spent, he collapsed to the salty, sandy ground, and let out a sound I'd never heard before, like a wail, and a scream, and a sigh all at once. Mama whispered softly to all of us, as if we were still young children, that sometimes things happened and there wasn't a reason. Sometimes flying things fell out of the sky.

There had been no living with Ephraim after the accident. Pain took up residence behind his green eyes. And anger. He grew hard, and somehow older, as if he'd caught a glimpse of a gloomy secret not meant for him. And while he found himself always welcomed at Darling House; every other facet of his life was eternally altered. At seventeen, he was suddenly under the guardianship of his aunt and uncle, who were nothing like the romantic, adventurous people his parents had been. The sole heir to a Savannah dynasty of real estate and myriad businesses, Ephraim carried a firm weight on his shoulders. And he took it out on the world around him by being as disagreeable as possible.

But Seth, though two years younger than Ephraim, had a steadying effect on him. They'd been best friends for years. And it always seemed that at Darling House, Ephraim was able to recapture a taste of life the way it had been before. As if escaping here had offered the illusion that life was safe and normal again, as if his parents were back at home on Jones Street, waiting to hear if he'd be back in time for dinner.

He'd worn his tailored brown school trousers here one grey afternoon to go crabbing with Seth, and soon black marsh mud splashed up clear to his knees.

I pointed at the mess. "I hope those stains come out."

"That's my housekeeper's problem."

Shocked, I clenched a piece of driftwood I held in my hand. I knew he hadn't meant it. He wasn't like that, not really. But he'd said it anyway. And brave, good men, the kind of man I knew he truly was, never said things they didn't mean. "You're a snobby ass, Ephraim Callaghan."

He flashed me a sardonic smile.

"Ignore her." Seth said, glaring at me with the same disappointed look he did when I cheated at board games. "She's so emotional lately. No one's asked her to the debutant ball, and she's sore about it."

My cheeks burned, but I didn't break my gaze with Ephraim.

I wanted to wrap myself around him and cry together. The way we had standing in Bonaventure Cemetery after his parents' funeral, when the last of the photographers and business associates and church deacons had finally left, and it had been just the three of us. The three of us and a sea of elegant tombstones, two that represented all Ephraim had lost.

I wanted to fall into his arms.

But I threw the driftwood stick at him instead. Aimed straight for his beautiful, too-big head.

He dodged it, his emerald eyes widening enough to satisfy my need for a reaction.

Tears sprang to my eyes. I hopped up, turned on my heel, and sprinted toward the marsh and the ocean beyond, feet pounding into the hard, grey sand.

I could have raced across the beach like that forever.

But as fast as I ran, I could feel him behind me.

Running close.

Both of us wild things.

I half-laughed, half-screamed when he grabbed my arms, and our bodies tangled and twisted. He spun me around and fell back onto the sand, knocking the air from my lungs when I landed square on his lean chest. We wrestled and rolled until he'd pinned my wrists down on either side of my head.

Cold earth tickled the back of my neck.

"Whitney." He whispered my name, like it was the answer to a question.

And then his lips brushed against mine.

A kiss.

My first kiss.

"I was always going to take you to the ball, Whitney Darling."

I closed my eyes.

"Whitney."

The way he'd said my name. Like it was the answer to a question.

"Whitney!"

Startled, I turned on my heel.

"Mama."

She didn't answer right away, but stood watching me, a steaming mug of coffee in hand. There was something vulnerable in her expression that reminded me of a little child. She started to speak, but hesitated, as if trying to find the words. "I watched my father my whole life, like he was some kind of magical, handsome mystery."

I swallowed, steeling myself against a sudden pang of emotion.

"Eventually I realized that though I couldn't blow a piece of glass to save my life, and though I'd never share that magic with him, I still shared his dream, and still felt this pull at my heart for the glass and what he'd made for us here, what he'd done for our family." She took a slow sip of coffee. "When Monica found me, and took me to where he lay, at the bottom of the glass studio steps, it wasn't only Daddy I thought we'd lost."

"The glass," I whispered.

"Yes, the glass." Mama stared at me hard, a tempest of unspoken words raging behind her eyes.

What did she want me to say? That I was sorry for leaving? That now, after everything, and despite the curse, I would step into Granddaddy's shoes?

I was the only one the glass spoke to, now.

But Granddaddy's final wish was the only reason I was here for the listening.

And everyone knew it.

Mama straightened and looked pointedly at her watch. "I came down here to get you. We've got an appointment at Beau's in an hour."

"Beau's?" I ran through my mental files, trying to remember why that name sounded so familiar. The color drained from my face as it hit me. "The bridal boutique next to Clary's?"

"That's the one," she smiled, a sudden glint in her eye daring me to argue. "I've had this scheduled since the day after Daddy's funeral, and we can't miss it. We'll lose our place in line, and then you'll never have a gown in time for the wedding."

"It's supposed to be a small family ceremony. I don't need a gown for that. A white church dress from somewhere on Broughton Street will do fine."

She gasped over-dramatically. "The youngest Darling daughter is marrying Ephraim Callaghan. That is not an occasion for a simple dress. The invitations have already been sent. And in a distasteful hurry, too. Everyone will assume you're pregnant." She pointed toward the house in a silent command for me to get moving. "If we finish in a reasonable time at Beau's, we'll have time for tea."

I pursed my lips. I wanted to tell her I was absolutely not participating in a pretentious circus of a wedding for the sake of Darling pride and the entertainment of the Savannah elite.

But something held me back, and it wasn't only how nice it felt to see Mama excited again.

I sighed. "The best I can give you is an evening gown. Banish all ideas of me in anything resembling a princess dress."

Mama beamed. "I'll take it."

Chapter Nine

Whitney Darling

To an outsider, the storefront nestled in the garden level of the Jones Street Georgian-style mansion might have appeared unassuming. Even dated. But to the true Savannahians who called Historic Savannah home, *Beau's Wedding Belles* was a family tradition.

"Hold your arms out to the sides. Yes, that's it." Beauregard Gordon, proprietor of the famed bridal establishment, stood beside me wearing a smartly tailored jacket and fitted chinos, holding a pale blue measuring tape. "Don't worry, I never share the measurements of any of my clients."

I forced a laugh.

Ephraim had driven Mama, the aunts, and I to the Historic District, in a twenty-minute adventure I would need a strong cup of coffee before repeating on the way home. He'd helped Rose into her wheelchair and escorted us into the shop, then excused himself to a business meeting across town.

Isla had been available to meet us shortly after we arrived, which was fortunate, because the idea that today I had to find a dress, and off the rack, to Mama's shame, made my head spin.

"How have you been, Beau?" Mama asked from a pretty antique chair alongside a row of gowns. "How's your mother?"

"Fine. All fine," Beau said. "Mama's finally agreed to move back into town from Isle of Hope. Sweet thing's blind as a bat, and twice as cranky. I told her a woman going on eighty-five with her history of sleep walking has no business living alone in a big house right next to the water."

He shook his head as he let the tape measure unroll from my bust to the floor. "She could get eaten by an alligator for heaven's sake. It happened again the other day to a poor lady out walking her little white dog by a pond. A real tragedy."

"Life on the water comes with its risks," Mama said.

Did she think of Seth? If so, her pretty face never gave it away, which was either because of Botox or a lifetime of hiding her feelings. Regardless, she'd mastered the kind of charm and self-control for which southern ladies were famous.

"Where's your mother now?" I asked.

"Upstairs. She'll be living with Phillip and I from now on. Which, I admit, I'm loving. Her weekly canasta club meets in the yellow parlor, and I tell you those gals are stocked on medicinal marijuana."

Mama's eyes widened, and I stifled a laugh.

The next hour was a flurry of gossip, satin, and chenille.

With each new gown I tried on, there was an ongoing accounting of life in Savannah, described in a way only a local like Beauregard could relate.

That was until I came out wearing a tailored gown of

white satin. Understated and refined. The lines of the dress hugged my curves tastefully, before fanning out in a train.

"I think we may have found the one," Beau said, coming to stand behind me. He bundled the train in his arms and demonstrated how to bustle it for the reception. "You'll want this out of the way for dancing and such. Judging by the way that fiancé of yours enjoys a good party, you'll be doing a lot of that."

"Parties? Ephraim?" I laughed.

Beau paused, a hand on his chest, "Don't tell me you've not attended one of his Jones Street affairs. Oh, honey, there's no telling how many nights Phillip and I have been staggering back home from karaoke at McDonough's, only to see all the lights on in Ephraim's house and dozens of people slopping out onto the sidewalk. He's a regular Jim Williams. Well, you know what I mean. The parties bit."

The bewildered look I gave him must have made him uncomfortable, because he went on talking, like a reflex, the words spilling out at an incredible pace.

"We had no idea he was involved in such a serious relationship with you. It's the best-kept secret in Savannah. Although, I suppose if anyone has the resources to maintain a long-distance affair, it would be Ephraim Callaghan. Would you consider Charleston long distance, though? Phillip and I drive up there to meet friends for brunch at Magnolia's, so I guess it's reasonable."

"No," Mama said abruptly, a fake smile plastered to her face. "Charleston would not be considered long-distance, no. And as you can see, Whitney and Ephraim have managed fine."

"Of course." Beau said, looking relieved. "In any case, I'm glad he's not with that Evangeline anymore. We were all convinced he'd end up marrying her, the number of events she spent hanging on his arm. She's not hard to look at, but she's not the friendliest, let me tell you. Hardly ever smiles back when she passes you on the street. Why live in the South if you're not going to smile at people?" He motioned to my reflection in the mirror. "So, is this the dress, Miss Darling?"

I stared at myself for what felt a long time, my mind reeling.

Visions of Ephraim and Evangeline together danced across my mind's eye, Ephraim holding her hand, kissing her, making love to her.

And it hit me, the emotion that clawed at the pit of my belly.

Jealousy.

I was jealous of Evangeline.

I rolled my shoulders back and drew in a long breath. By fate or by folly, I was the one wearing the wedding gown. A gorgeous one.

"Yes." I smoothed a trembling hand over my waist. "This one's perfect. Thank you, Beau."

"Wonderful. It hardly needs altering. Like it was made for you." He started right in on fresh measurements, making notes on a little pink pad of paper.

Isla hopped up from her seat, snapping photos with her phone. "You look exquisite, Whit. Ephraim's not going to know what hit him when he sees you in this."

I smiled back at her in the mirror, at a loss for words.

What would Ephraim think of it?

Would he care?

I held my breath, willing my heart rate to slow as Beau finished measuring my hem. "I think I'll hurry and change. I don't know about all of you, but I'm starving."

"Dress hunting will do that to a girl," Rose said. "Just watch your head back there."

I nodded, not quite sure what she meant by that, but too overwhelmed to ask.

"I'll help you with the laces," Isla said, following me around the corner to the little dressing room.

She shut the door behind us as she set to work loosening the gown. "I can tell you're having a lot of feelings. I say we order mimosas instead of tea at lunch."

I stared ahead at my reflection. "How did I end up here?"

"Are you looking for the chronological answer, or the philosophical one?"

I groaned.

"I've missed you, Whit," Isla said. "I know you've felt like you had to stay away." She bit her lip, her eyes studying my expression. "I understand. Really, I do. But it doesn't seem," she paused, "staying away doesn't seem to have helped. Don't you think you might as well be home? With the people who know you and love you?"

"What I think is immaterial," I said. "What I want, or what I might have chosen to do on my own doesn't matter anymore. Granddaddy saw to that."

Isla smiled gently, "You know he loved you. Of all the Darlings, you were the sparkle in his eye. I don't believe he ever would've done anything to hurt you."

"Of course. I know."

She loosened the last of the laces, then squeezed my arms. "Then allow that knowledge to carry you. He must've had his reasons. And, besides, there are far worse fates than marrying Ephraim Callaghan. He's perfection walking."

"Don't let him hear you say that. His head's already too big for his shoulders."

Isla shook her head patiently, "Hardly. Is he too serious? Yes. Brooding? Yes. Haunted by the ghosts of his past? Obviously. But conceited? I don't buy it."

I pursed my lips. She was right, if not a little generous.

Ephraim wasn't a snob. He was too complicated for that. He'd been born to wealth and power. It wasn't something he'd come into the world asking for. And I knew he felt the weight of duty his unique privileges afforded him. He took his obligations seriously, not only with his parents' company and the employees it supported, but also toward the legacy of involvement and philanthropy they left behind. He thrived on the responsibility, even as it made him solemn.

But there was tenderness to him as well. A sentimentality that drove him. Not unlike how it had been between Granddaddy Alistair and the glass.

"I know this situation isn't what y'all would've asked for," Isla said. "But I think if you trust the process, trust what your grandfather believed would help, you'll be surprised. The curse strikes even when you're not here. The ones you love are in danger either way, and none of us are going anywhere. So, you might as well stay."

I blinked back a tear. "Thank you, Isla."

She reached over and squeezed my hand. "Like I said, I'm glad you're home."

"Don't speak too soon," I scoffed.

"I've made it this long," she said. "I'm not afraid."

I pulled her into a hug, the scent of her perfume taking me back years, to before all of this had happened.

"I'll leave you to change," she said, as she slipped from the dressing room. "But hurry. I'm getting hungry."

I listened to the melodic chatter between my mother and aunts, each of them hurriedly talking over one another about wedding details and how pretty the gown was as I wiggled out of it, feeling as though I was in a dream.

My wedding gown.

I stared at it for several moments, then hung it on a nearby hook. I pulled on my black turtleneck and bent down to retrieve my ivory trousers that lay in a messy pile on the floor.

The room went cold.

I gasped at the abrupt change in temperature, and my eyes widened at the puff of mist my breath left on the mirror, which was now covered in a glistening frost.

A feminine sigh at the back of my ear, sent a shot of adrenaline down my spine.

I straightened, banging my head hard on the dressing room door handle.

I squeezed my eyes closed, bracing against the sudden, throbbing pain.

The temperature continued to plummet, accompanied now by the distinct smell of gunpowder. And something else. Something earthy and metallic, so strong I could almost taste it.

Blood.

My mouth moved, but no words would form. I couldn't breathe. I couldn't move. I was no longer alone, and someone, who I strongly suspected was Julia, wanted me to know it.

But why? Why like this?

The feather-soft touch of fingertips stroking my hair jolted me into wild, frantic motion.

I screamed, flailing for the door handle, my gaze catching the impression of a pale-haired woman, her eyes black and hollow, her red lips open as though she tried to say something to me.

In an instant I spilled out into the hallway, gulping for air, my heart in the back of my throat.

Beau and my mother darted around the corner.

Beau, spotting my lacy pink underwear and bare thighs, stopped short and spun on his heel to face the other direction. "Miss Darling?" his voice was a few octaves higher than usual.

My mother stared openly in horror. "Whitney, explain yourself!"

I could only blink back at her, partially in shock, partially at a loss for how, or if, I should describe what I'd seen. "A spider," I finally choked out. "A huge one. Scared me half to death."

Beau shuddered. "How big is big?"

"The size of my palm, at least. I think it's one of those wolf spiders."

My mother pursed her lips, seeing right past my lie, but visibly hesitating to call me on it.

"You get dressed, Miss Darling," Beau rushed stiffly back to the main shop area. "I'll text Phillip and tell him if he doesn't come find it, we'll burn the house down."

I sighed, sorry for the goose chase I'd set poor Phillip on.

Still trembling, I stepped into my trousers and smiled shakily at my mother. "Ready to get out of here and have some tea?"

She looked past me into the dressing room, as if she'd discover the answer to her questions there. "I'm thinking a mimosa might be more appropriate."

"You're not the first person to tell me that this morning."

She narrowed her eyes.

I forced a laugh. "I'm sure that spider's halfway to Charleston by now."

"Right." She turned on her heel. "Let's get out of here before our reputation is officially beyond saving."

I nodded in agreement and followed her back down the hallway, bracing against the sensation of Julia's steady, pleading gaze behind me.

* * *

Following our group's awkward departure from Beau's, we made our way to a fancy little teahouse at the corner of Bull and Jones, where we were quickly seated at a long table with a gleaming white tablecloth situated beneath an antique Tiffany chandelier.

"Well, if this isn't the most nostalgic afternoon," Rose said. "Makes me think of the day I picked out my wedding gown."

"Rose, you never married," Adele said.

"I know. But I still picked out a wedding gown."

A handsome young man wielding a shining carafe approached the table. "How are you ladies today?"

"We're well," Mama said, "And you?"

"Just fine, Mrs. Darling." He filled our empty water glasses and took our orders for high tea.

"I don't know what it is about a dapper man serving me tea," Rose said, "but it makes me – " Her words cut short and a strange look crossed over her face, as if she were about to fall asleep, only her eyes fixated on the chandelier above our heads.

"Rose?" Mama started to reach for her hand, but Adele motioned for her to stay back.

"She's having her one of her episodes," Adele said. "Give her a moment, it'll pass."

Mama flopped back in her chair, looking annoyed. "Of

course. Our first normal afternoon out in forever and Madame Fortune is joining us at the table."

Rose's jaw slackened, and her hands curled into tight little fists. "Whitney," she whispered.

I leaned close to her, hoping no one at the neighboring tables had noticed her strange behavior. It'd been years since I'd seen her do this.

"Whitney."

"I'm here," I said, my hand on her shoulder.

"The chandelier remembers. The chandelier knows."

I nodded, tongue-tied at the sound of the familiar phrase.

"This chandelier?" Adele motioned to the light fixture above our heads, her brows drawn in annoyed confusion. "Rose we're in a tearoom."

"The chandelier remembers," she whispered, almost too softly to hear, and then Rose's eyes fluttered closed. She slumped in her wheelchair.

Ice shot through my bloodstream.

I shook her arm.

A moment passed.

Then another.

Rose sucked in a deep breath and sat up straight, her eyes clear as day. "I hope the scones are out soon. I'm starved."

I let out a relieved sigh.

"What the hell?" Adele pinched the bridge of her nose.

"What's wrong?" Rose asked, "Getting a headache?"

"More like a pain in my ass."

My gut tightened at the thought of Alistair's letters. *Look to the chandelier.*

"Let's all try to relax and have a nice a time," Mama soothed. "This is Whitney's day."

I started to object to that when I spied Ephraim striding in through the open front doors.

Great.

"Here comes handsome," Rose said.

Ephraim approached us with an amused smile. "If it isn't the loveliest group of ladies Savannah's ever seen." He paused beside my mother's chair, kneeling to pick something up off the floor. "You dropped your napkin, Mrs. Darling."

"Thank you, Ephraim." Mama placed the linen back in her lap, then motioned to the empty chair across from me. "Please, have a seat."

Ephraim shook his head. "I've only brought the photos of my parents you requested for the wedding reception."

Mama took the yellow envelope Ephraim held in his long, tan fingers. "You'll be happy to hear Whitney's found a stunning gown. She's going to be the prettiest bride Savannah's seen since Addison married Caleb."

I stiffened at the mention of my sister's fallen husband as Ephraim's gaze caught mine.

The handsome server approached with a cart of tea and pastries and set to work placing them on the table. He placed a teapot of hibiscus tea in front of me, which I absent-mindedly poured into my teacup without waiting for the hourglass timer to run out.

I lifted my hair over my shoulder. "Beau had a bit to say about the city since I've been gone. Sounds like Jones Street has turned into quite a social scene. Something about wild parties. And a lot of mention about Evangeline." I took a sip of steaming liquid, my gaze never leaving Ephraim's.

He didn't smile, but his eyes crinkled at the edges. "Jealousy isn't your color, w -," he stopped himself from almost calling me wife, "Whitney."

"What does she have to be jealous about?" Mama asked. "Soon enough she won't only be attending the parties on Jones Street but hosting them."

I sucked in a breath, inhaling more than a modest amount of the bright pink tea. I collapsed at once into a fit of coughing.

Mama patted me on the back. "Honey, honestly, try to control yourself."

Ephraim's eyes twinkled as I half choked to death. "I'm afraid as soon as the police figure out what's been going on around Darling House, I'll be spending most of my time back in New York. Which means my wife will be the one running things here. I doubt she'll have much time for parties."

"Exactly," I wheezed.

Mama shook her head and smiled, looking like a cat sipping cream. "Whatever the two of you say. In the meantime, I'm going to enjoy the hullaballoo."

"Maybe I'll change my mind," I bristled. "And all this hullabaloo, as you call it, will come to an end."

Ephraim chuckled, a deep sound that wound its way around my core.

Suddenly, a man's familiar, almost frantic voice crashed through the tearoom. I leaned to the side to peer past Ephraim, who had already turned to survey the commotion.

My breath caught and a rush of heat spilled onto my cheeks and down my neck.

"Whitney Darling!" The handsome man stumbled past the hostess stand.

My mouth went dry.

James Steele. He never abandoned the *Coterie* offices on a weekday. Oh, Lord. What was he doing here?

He rushed toward our table, the hostess following close on his heels.

"Miss Darling," the hostess squeaked, "this man says he was looking for you. Should I get a manager?" The young woman looked genuinely concerned, and I didn't blame her. James was irritated and haggard, with tiny beads of sweat peppering his forehead.

I held up my hand. "It's alright, thank you."

"Is there some emergency?" Ephraim drawled, standing casually behind Mama's chair.

James didn't answer him. Instead, his gaze bore into mine. "Whitney, I heard what's going on. This is ridiculous."

I lifted my chin, grasping internally for some small shred of dignity. "Mama, everyone, this is James. My boss from Charleston." I looked up at him with obvious irritation. "What are you doing here?"

He shook his head. "You came back for a funeral. And now you're getting married?" He glanced at Ephraim before leveling a concerned gaze on me. "Let's go. Whitney, I'll take you away right now, no questions asked."

"Like hell you will," Ephraim's tone was almost polite, but his steely glare was anything but.

I held up a hand, motioning for him to stand down.

"James, I'm not sure what you've heard. But I'm alright. I promise."

He ran a hand through his hair. "We talked about this. Neither one of us wanted to get married. We agreed on so much."

"What did y'all agree on?" Ephraim asked, casually.

I glared at him.

"How did you find me here?" I asked.

"I was wondering the same thing," Ephraim said.

"I went to Darling House. To see you. I felt guilty for not offering to drive you down for the funeral."

Ephraim's eyes shot daggers now.

"When I got there," James continued, "your sister told me you'd come into town to look at wedding dresses at that Beau's place, which made no sense. I rushed there to find you, and then the Beau guy himself tells me you're marrying some stuck-up asshole and came here to celebrate finding your gown."

"So, basically, you're a stalker," Ephraim said.

James threw his hands in the air. "Whitney, what the hell?"

I bit my lip, "I understand why you're upset. I'll explain everything soon. In the meantime, please try to recognize. I have my reasons."

"What reasons?" he snapped. "Money? I'll give you more. Freedom? I'll support you in your career. Whatever you want. What's marriage to you?"

"A vow," Ephraim bit back, looking about as dangerous as I'd ever seen him. "Marriage is a promise that no matter how terrible life's circumstances, no matter how uncertainty closes in, or how you think you feel, it's a promise that neither of you will face the world alone. Not ever."

My pulse raced in my veins and the room tilted at an odd angle. Had Ephraim meant what he said? Was that how he felt about marrying me? Or was he trying to get under James' skin?

I straightened, my heart pounding in my ears. I knew my face was flaming. What could I say to James after all of that?

James' lips curled, "Whitney, who is this?"

Ephraim chuckled, a dark, dangerous sound. "You know exactly who I am."

His handsome face beet-red, James clenched a fist, and for a second it looked like he might bring it down onto the table. "Something strange is going on here. And I'm going to get to the bottom of it."

He was right. Something strange was going on. I would give him that.

"The only place you need to get," Ephraim said, "is back to Charleston."

I nodded, unable to think of a time I'd ever felt more awkward. "He's right, James. I'm so sorry."

James stared at me for a long moment, a tumult of unanswered questions and unrequited feelings sparring behind his tortured gaze, then without another word, he turned on his heel and stalked out the door.

I gripped my teacup with trembling fingers and tamped down a sudden wave of nausea.

"Well, stick a fork in me. I haven't been this hot since Woodstock," Rose fanned herself with a dessert menu, her cheeks indeed a little rosy.

Mama rolled her shoulders. "It'll be a miracle if we get through this wedding with our reputation intact."

"Everything will be fine, Nora," Ephraim placed a comforting hand on her shoulder, his gaze holding mine. "What would life be without its little dramas?"

"Relaxing," Adele quipped.

"Whitney, what on earth was that about?" Mama asked. "Is there something between you and that man?"

"No," I said too quickly. "He wanted there to be. For a while. But I've always turned him down."

"Well, he hasn't digested the message," Adele said. "He acts like you cheated on him."

"Only if you count leaving my career without notice."

"You dated your boss, Whitney?" Mama said, taking a cue from Rose and fanning herself with a menu.

"No. I literally told you that I didn't." I tore my gaze from Ephraim's. "We went on two or three dates. Over a year ago. Nothing serious."

"I'm adding him to Officer Evans' watch list," Ephraim said.

I rolled my eyes, "That's completely unnecessary."

"You think he's dangerous?" Mama asked at the same time.

"I doubt he's anything more than a nuisance. But he did come here and make a scene." Ephraim slid into the empty seat across from me at the table and placed an unused linen napkin in his lap.

"I thought you weren't staying," I said.

He pulled an egg and olive finger sandwich from a four-tiered tray. "Oh, Whitney, darling." He popped the tiny sandwich into his mouth and swallowed it in one bite. "Someone's got to protect the bride. It appears we're under siege."

Chapter Ten

Whitney Darling

Rain battered my bedroom windows, falling in jagged teardrops down the glass. The storms this month had been legendary, strange for this season, and if the quick succession of lightning was any indication, Darling House was in for another epic night.

The clock on my mantle chimed midnight. I leaned a hip against the windowsill and gazed out over the endless marsh, my mind vacillating between thoughts of Ephraim and memories of the woman in the mirror at Beau's. She'd been so sad. Stricken. As if she were caught in a perpetual state of shock and despair.

Had it truly been Julia Darling? The ghost had certainly looked like her.

But Julia hadn't died a violent death. She'd lived to an old age with William, happy and surrounded by their children. At least that's what I'd always been told.

I stiffened as a shadow strode up the boat dock toward the house, steady and measured. It was Ephraim, returned from another evening brood on the water. The storm must have forced him back. I imagined the wind whipping in his dripping hair, the tense set of his square jaw.

The sorrow in his eyes that he almost never let loose.

Except in these shrouded moments of quiet, wild, solitude.

I released my breath.

My heart squeezed as little fissures of pleasure shot through my core at the memory of how he'd looked at me in the tearoom, powerful and possessive.

His shadow disappeared into the shade of the Live Oaks lining the gardens, and I stepped away from the window so he wouldn't see me as he approached the house.

"Good night, Ephraim."

My skin still warm from my late-night shower, I crossed to the open luggage at the end of my bed. I supposed it was past time I unpacked. I shuffled through my bag, selecting a long, white satin nightgown, and pulled it over my head.

I chewed my lip.

Tonight, I'd emailed my official resignation to James. After today, there was no way I could step back into that office. I cringed, pushing away the memory of the look on his face after Ephraim had put him in his place at the tearoom.

I felt bad for him. I knew James cared deeply for me.

He had been a comfort, a refuge of novelty and change after my flight from Darling House. But he didn't know me. Not really. He didn't know my story in detail, only the carefully curated bits I'd chosen to share with him. James loved the Charleston version of Whitney. But she was a façade. A paper doll cut perfectly to fit a make-believe world that I'd once hoped could be my home.

But I understood now.

There was no going back to Charleston.

Now, my body aching, my mental health in shambles, and desperate for the oblivion of melatonin-induced sleep, I pulled down my duvet and crawled into bed.

A knock on the door made me stiffen.

"Come in," I sighed.

Addison peeked into the room with a sweet smile, a hand resting on her belly. She wore a nightgown like mine, but also sported a blue and white striped bathrobe and a pair of fuzzy socks. "Got a minute?"

"Of course," I motioned for her to have a seat on the bed.

"I wanted to check on you. I could tell you were overwhelmed at dinner."

I bit the inside of my cheek. If she only knew.

She hoisted herself onto the mattress, her face scrunching with discomfort. Her blonde hair trailed over her right shoulder in a messy braid, and her skin glowed with perspiration. "You had a couple visitors today," she said, "while you were at Beau's."

"Visitors?" I straightened. "Was someone here with James?"

She shook her head. "Monica stopped by an hour after he did," she fluffed a pillow behind her head. "I think she wants to work for the studio again. I get the impression she misses it."

"I saw her at the funeral. But we didn't talk much," I said. "Isla told me the way Monica quit was pretty dramatic."

Addison pursed her lips. "It was hard on Monica after you left. Without you or Seth in the studio with Granddaddy, a lot of responsibility landed on her shoulders. Which I think she was okay with at first, but Granddaddy wasn't the easiest to work with. He was emotional toward the end. Almost like he was paranoid about something."

"Paranoid?" I thought of his letters, and their cryptic turns of phrase. What had he been looking for?

Addison nodded. "He spent more time alone, pouring over old family photo albums, and spending hours digging through old chests and things in the attic. It was strange. The more eccentric he became, the more agitated Monica seemed. I think after his accident, she finally snapped. It must've been incredibly traumatic for her to find him like that."

I sighed, imagining my beloved grandfather lying limp and lifeless at the bottom of the glass studio steps, his neck twisted at an unnatural angle. I swallowed hard and pushed the image away with a quick shake of my head. Should I tell my sister about the letters? I wanted to. But Solomon made it clear, Granddaddy had intended that I keep them secret.

"I think it's about time for this baby to arrive," Addison said, pointedly changing the subject. She pitched forward a little, her hand moving to her stomach. "You never answered my question. You seemed stressed at dinner. Was dress shopping difficult? I can only imagine what you're feeling."

I held up a calming hand, "I'm fine," I said. "Just tired. It's been a strange few days."

"Francis is impressed," she smiled.

"Oh, is he?"

She nodded, "He says any person who can endure what you have, is basically capable of anything."

"Well, he's a degree or two more complimentary than my therapist."

"I'm excited for you to get to know him better," she said.

"He's such a talented veterinarian. He's brilliant and kind. Strong. And he loves me and Percy so well."

"I'm sorry I haven't been here," I said, meaning it. "I've missed so much."

"We've been content to love you from a distance, Whit. But Alistair was right. It's time you were home." Addison tensed, and a deep flush crept over her face and neck.

"Addie, are you okay?"

She nodded, but her breath came fast. "I have a strange –" Her words cut short and she doubled over.

I lunged over to her, wrapping my arm around her shoulders.

"Get Francis."

I froze, barely registering her plea.

"Whitney," she moaned.

"Don't move." I darted from my room and down the hallway. "Francis!" My voice echoed, shrilly through the house. "Francis!"

Moments later heavy footsteps raced up the stairs. Francis was in front, Ephraim, still dripping wet, a couple of paces behind him.

Francis grabbed my arms. "What is it? Where's Addison."

"My bedroom."

He nodded and sprinted down the hall.

"Second babies often come early." Ephraim said, looking altogether too casual.

"A whole month early? There could be something wrong."

"Everything will be fine, wife," he soothed. "Francis is more than capable."

Before I could bite back, Mama and Adele's concerned voices chimed from where they rushed up the stairs. Francis already walked back toward us, Addison carefully tucked in his arms. "No time to get her to town."

"What?" Mama gasped from over my shoulder. She and Adele leaned against the banister, both of them panting and disheveled, "She can't have the baby here. We don't have any supplies."

"You don't need many supplies if things go the way they're supposed to."

"And how would you know?" Mama asked. "You're a veterinarian. Not a doctor."

"It's all the same," Francis said. "Bring towels, coconut water, and a shot of vodka."

"What's the vodka for?" Adele asked, sounding more amused than concerned.

"Me," Francis growled, turning the corner toward their bedroom.

"I'll be damned," Rose said, from her wheelchair at the bottom of the stairs. "I dreamed this would happen."

"Then we could've used a heads up," Adele quipped.

"You wouldn't have listened." Rose turned her gaze to my mother, who still stood frozen beside me. "Nora, do as Francis asked. Everything'll be fine."

"Do your dreams always come true?" Ephraim asked.

"Hardly ever," Rose replied with a shrug. "But when they do, it's awful neat."

A wail traveled from Addison's bedroom.

Adele's eyes widened. "Lord, I'll have a shot of that vodka."

* * *

I stumbled down a long, shadowed hallway, my feet moving one after the other in steady rhythm. I had to get away.

Away from the noise. Somewhere I couldn't hear my sister. It was the strangest thing, the idea that out of such pain something wonderful was going to happen. It was beautiful.

But my nerves were open wounds.

After two years of careful avoidance, the past few days had been entirely too much. The funeral. The marriage. Now this.

And I was here. At Darling House. Carrying a curse with me that systematically stole away the ones I loved. I needed to leave.

If anything happened to Addison or the baby, I would never forgive myself.

The air around me crackled with energy. Whatever unseen faces that liked to hide within the house, they were all awake, all aware of the changes happening. New life was coming into the world. And my sister was at the center of it.

Nearing the end of the hall, I swung to the right and stepped quickly through a large, familiar door, then slammed it shut behind me.

The grand conservatory.

A giant, four-story room of glass and vintage metal framing, a shining marble floor and hundreds of luscious, exotic green plants.

An elaborate marble staircase led all the way from the ground level, up to the fourth floor, then extended to a narrow staircase to the attic, effectively connecting each of the floors of the house to this single, magnificent space. The glass exterior walls allowed for sweeping, elevated views of the marsh outside. But the most eye-catching aspect of the atrium was the color. From top to bottom, anything that wasn't made of marble or glass was painted haint blue. Richer than sky blue, not as green as turquoise, but somewhere in the middle, the whole room was wrapped in blue.

The Gullah-Geechee believed spirits couldn't pass over water. And so, to keep evil spirits, things like boo hags and plat eyes away from their homes, many painted their porch roofs, their shutters, their doors, all haint blue. Over time the tradition had grown to include interior spaces, like primary bedrooms, and common spaces like this one.

But aside from the striking views and unique paint choices, there was something special about the conservatory. Something ephemeral and strange. When I'd been a child, I'd come here. Whether for time alone to think, or because I'd seen or heard something that had scared me, this place had been a refuge. Somewhere to rest. Somewhere quiet. Safe.

But all beautiful, safe places had their secrets.

I pictured the door at the bottom of the stairs.

It was always locked.

It had been for as long as anyone could remember. Lined on one side with eleven distinct brass locks and painted a deeper shade of blue than the rest of the space, it had been the source of generational speculation and childhood nightmares. No one had been brave enough to try to unlock it, or to open the door.

Thank God.

All we needed in this family was to let loose another curse.

Eyeing the pitch-black marsh outside the windows, I crossed the second-floor landing and took a seat on the top step, looking down to the first floor below. I held my breath and listened. I couldn't hear a thing.

Absolute quiet.

In here, it was as if nothing remarkable was happening at all.

I sighed and leaned against a stair rail.

Once the storm passed and the water levels went down, we could easily move Addison to a hospital, couldn't we? I didn't know enough about any of this. And that was my own fault. I hadn't had a meaningful conversation with my sister in far too long.

A flash of lightning illuminated the conservatory, followed closely by a boom of thunder. The windowpanes shook with it. The bridge would still be flooded for a while now.

My sister had gone to a place I couldn't follow, a wild place, where no one could stop what was happening. God willing, my little niece would thunder her way into the world on a wail, as suddenly as our loved ones had left it.

Lightning flashed again. Another, almost immediate crack of thunder.

Rain splashed now in horizontal fashion against the windows.

"*Whitney.*"

I stiffened.

"*Whiiitney, lovely girl.*"

An icy trickle slipped down my spine.

Since I'd turned twelve and the glass had started speaking to me, calling to me at all hours, I'd gotten used to the idea of voices in my head.

But this wasn't in my head.

And this was not the glass.

"*Whitney, let me out.*"

A numb sort of tingling crept over my scalp and down to the soles of my feet. My eyes darted to the ground level beneath me, where the locked door waited around the corner at the bottom of the stairs.

"*Let me out. I swear I'll be kind.*"

A strange, sudden compulsion washed over me.

I needed to see it. The door.

I stood, my hand grasping the railing like a lifeline, turning my fingers white as bone.

I wanted to leave. I tried to turn, but I couldn't.

Something forced me down the stairs.

One step. Then another.

Another.

Was this how it felt to lose your mind?

"It's in your head," I whispered, pushing away the panic threatening to take over. "It's only a door."

The house was getting to me. The events of the past few days were getting to me.

"*Whitney.*"

I reached the bottom step. A thick carpet muffled my footfalls as I let go of the railing and turned to the left, the windows and black marsh to my back.

And then there it was.

The sight was jarring, the ancient blue paint, the vertical lineup of decrepit locks and bolts lining the doorframe. It was nothing like the rest of the house. This small piece of history had been intentionally left to ruin. I'd never touched the door. Seth had warned me away from doing so, as had Alistair, and on one occasion, my father.

This place I stood now, had been one to avoid, like the oyster-run parts of the beach, or a broken bit of sidewalk. A place you didn't step, or you risked being hurt.

"*Let me out, Whitney.*"

I pressed my fingertips against the cool surface.

It was a door.

Only a door. In a moment I would turn, go back up the stairs, and find my mother. We'd make a cup of tea or bum a shot of vodka from Francis.

"Just a door," I whispered.

I released my breath and flattened my palm, spreading my fingers out like a star.

I studied the row of brass locks on the doorframe. There were eleven in total, each with differently shaped keyholes and mechanisms for releasing them.

Would it take eleven different keys to unlock them?

Or a sledgehammer.

That's what Seth would have said. I smiled a little at the thought and squeezed my eyes shut.

BANG.

The door shuddered beneath my hand, with a loud, stinging vibration.

I screamed, staggering back, as if I'd been pushed, then fell to my bottom on the hard floor.

Blood rushed through my ears, pumping in my head, urging me to run away.

But I couldn't move.

Something hit the door.

From the inside.

My mind begged me to run.

But I could only stare at the door, waiting for the moment it would burst open and some half-rotted monster would lurch forward and pull me into the dark.

I splayed my fingers and slid my feet beneath me, preparing to stand, when I froze.

Tap.

Against the door.

Tap.

Tap.

Tap.

A flutter of white skirts flashed in the corner of my vison, followed by the distinct sound of a woman's guttural wail.

I screamed again, adrenaline finally kicking my legs into motion, propelling me up and toward the stairs.

"Whitney!" Ephraim's voice echoed through the conservatory. He ran down the steps toward me, and I crashed into him, falling in a crumpled heap at his feet.

"What's happened?" he snapped. His eyes scanned the room as he lifted me to my feet.

I gripped his shirt, my eyes trained on the blue door, as I braced for it to swing open.

But moments passed.

And the door stayed shut.

Ephraim grabbed my chin, searching my face, "Did you see someone?"

Overcome with trembling, I swallowed, still grasping for words.

The legend was true.

The haint blue paint. Ghosts couldn't, wouldn't, pass through it.

The paint, and somehow, I imagined, the locks too, were keeping whatever that was, trapped behind the door. And had been day after day, year after year, for as long as anyone alive could remember.

So why had it waited until now to reveal itself?

"Whitney." Ephraim's voice held a gentler edge than I'd heard in a long, long time. "I've been looking for you."

"Addison?"

He shook his head, "She's alright." He guided me up the stairs, his steps measured, his grip gentle, as though I'd disintegrate if we moved too quickly. "Francis thinks the baby finally shifted. It's only a matter of time now."

"What about the curse?" The words ground from my lips on a ragged whisper. And I realized I'd been too afraid to say them out loud.

"The curse," Ephraim sighed. He led me out of the conservatory and down the hall, bringing us to Granddaddy's study, where he lowered me into a leather club chair and poured us each a tumbler of whiskey. He leaned against Granddaddy's desk, settling himself between me and the storm raging outside the window.

He narrowed his eyes, "What made you scream in the conservatory, wife?"

"Don't call me that."

"Why not? That's what you are."

"Ephraim, something was inside the locked door at the bottom of the stairs. Something, not normal. I heard it."

He didn't say anything for a long time, only sat studying me and rubbing the scruff along his jaw. Ephraim would tell you that he didn't believe in ghosts, but he knew better than to say something silly like that within the walls of Darling House. Still, I wanted him to react, to show some sort of emotion to the news that something . . . ugly . . . dare I say, evil, was hiding behind that door in the conservatory.

"Do you see that painting?" he asked, finally. He pointed at a framed oil painting across the room. "The one of William Darling looking at himself in the mirror?"

I nodded, remembering the countless times as a little girl I'd ambled around this large, cozy space, examining the art and curiosities Alistair had collected over the years.

"One morning after my parents died, I was in here," Ephraim continued. "At some point I'd wandered off alone. There was a fire crackling in the fireplace, and the room smelled like pipe tobacco and bourbon. I was desperate for distraction. But at the same time, I was desperate for solitude. To think. To try and feel something besides loss and anger."

Another crack of thunder. The windows vibrated violently.

Ephraim tapped a finger on the desk. "I wandered around, examining the glass and the paintings, opening books, and sitting in the leather chairs, imagining I was grown and far beyond the reach of everything bad that had happened. Alistair walked in as I was looking at that painting of William. He didn't chastise me for being in his office. He poured himself a drink and asked me what I thought the painting meant. I told him I didn't have any idea, and I'll never forget his words."

"What did he say?" I asked.

Ephraim's lips tilted into a half-smile. "Whatever happens to you has been waiting to happen since the beginning of time."

I stared at him blankly. "Is that supposed to make me feel better?"

He shrugged. "Ask Marcus Aurelius. He said it first."

I sighed, "So, we have no control over our fate?"

"That isn't what it means."

Calmer now, I crossed my arms, "Tell me, then, great philosopher."

He quirked an eyebrow, then took another sip of whiskey. The cut crystal at the bottom of his glass twinkled in the soft candlelight. "Cause and effect. Each time we act, we change the future. By the time we get there, the destination is the only logical explanation."

"Is this your round-about-way of saying you don't believe in curses?"

He eyed the last bit of amber liquid in his glass before swigging it down. "If I did, I wouldn't let myself feel powerless in the face of one."

Thunder boomed again, only now it sounded farther away.

"Something's going on at Darling House," I whispered. "Granddaddy was looking for something. And I have to figure out what."

"I know," Ephraim said, flatly.

I swallowed. "How much do you know?"

"Whitney!" Rose's cry echoed breathless and excited.

I stood fast, almost knocking the crystal glass from Ephraim's hand, and darted down the hallway, Ephraim behind me.

We topped the stairs and rounded the corner to Addison's bedroom.

The eager voices of my mother and my aunts grew louder as we neared.

"She's here." Francis laughed. "One more. One more, love, and you're through."

I rushed into the room to see Addison sigh and fall back onto her pillows.

There was a breath of silence, and then a wail, a skittering little cry that came on a boom of thunder. My eyes widened at the sight of the tiny, squirming bundle in Francis' arms.

It took me a moment to find my voice. "Is she alright? Are they both okay?"

"They're perfect," Francis grinned, his blue eyes glowing with pride.

Aunt Adele was beside me now, handing Francis a clean towel.

"I did it," Addison whispered.

I stepped to the bed and leaned down, pressing my lips to her salty forehead. "You did."

My fingers brushed something soft beneath her pillow.

The protection charm Solomon had gifted her the night before Granddaddy's funeral. My heart squeezed in my chest, and I mouthed a silent prayer of thanks. Addison was okay. The curse hadn't taken her.

"Stay with me?"

I nodded and looked back at Ephraim standing at the door.

He smiled at me, a genuine, handsome smile that brought out the dimple on his cheek, and a deep, lonely sadness in his eyes. With a nod of congratulations, he turned and disappeared down the hall.

Chapter Eleven

William Darling

Meeting Horace Leroux felt like being born. I suppose that was the day I was born into my life as a businessman.

Horace was unlike anyone I'd ever seen up close. His clothes were more than fine. They were exquisite, expertly tailored, a single piece worth more money than I'd made in my lifetime. Horace's thick blonde hair fell in waves down to his shoulders, framing an aquiline face that looked closer to a sculpted angel than a flesh and blood human.

"Mr. Darling. It's a pleasure to meet you." Horace held out a manicured hand, and I was surprised to find his shake firm and strong. "It's a shame the start of your American adventure was less than welcoming. But I hope my sister, Layla, and I can help remedy whatever false impressions you have of this place. It's a dream for those young artists brave enough to explore it."

"I appreciate your help," I said.

"Well worth the effort. Your Julia's enchanting. I'm better for knowing her."

Horace motioned for me to follow as he strolled down a

tabby path behind the Charleston hotel where he'd brought Julia and I to rest before our trip with he and his sister to Savannah.

"Your accent. Where are you from?" I asked.

"Louisiana. Though, Layla and I were originally born in France. We were on our way back from visiting family there when we met your lovely Julia on the ship." He smiled. "I grew up in New Orleans. Business brought me to Charleston. And now Savannah, as you know."

"What sort of business?"

"It's all very dull. I prefer to talk about more exciting things. Tell me about this glass. Julia made it sound like magic flows through your veins."

"I don't know it's anything that impressive," I lied.

"Well, we'll find out. When we get to Savannah, you'll have a studio equipped with everything you need, and I'll be your patron."

"Why?" I asked, nodding back at a pretty maid who brushed past us, her arms full of laundry.

"Without beauty, there is no life. And glass is the most beautiful. All the better if I can pull a handsome man from the gutter and make him a king. It's the least I can do. I have too much money. I will die with too much money." He twisted a manicured finger through a golden wave brushing his shoulder." Firstly, I'll commission a chandelier. And then another. And then something else. It hardly matters, if it steals my breath away."

"What do you want in return? Other than the glass. I know enough about business."

"My friend, you know nothing of business. That is why you are you, and I am I. It's hardly charity, though. My sister took a liking to Julia on the ship, and when we get to Savannah, she'll have no one. All I ask is that Julia come to visit us, at least once a week after we've established our residences. I don't want my Layla to be lonely."

"I'm not sure that sounds like a fair trade."

Horace's lips parted in a sly grin, his eyes gleaming, as if he'd tasted some mythical ambrosia. "Then you haven't been paying attention. Julia and Layla are pure sunlight in a dark world. Julia's company alone will pay your way in rent." He wrapped an arm over my shoulder and pulled me close to his side as we walked. "We shall be friends as well, William Darling. Which is why we go now to the tailor. You have a thing or two to learn about the garments of a gentleman artist."

* * *

The days turned to weeks and in a flurry of documents and satchels, trunks and trinkets, Julia and I found ourselves the tenants of a large townhouse in the center of the bustling southern city of Savannah. Horace and Layla seemed ever present, and invitations to social gatherings and private yard games quickly became part of daily life. It was a world not at all uncommon to Julia, but for me, the gilded culture of America's elite was overwhelming. Though Julia had spent most of the voyage over from Scotland instructing me on the gentler social graces, I was still too bold, too blunt, too brawny to fit easily into the genteel confines of parlors and sitting rooms. I found myself wishing for the ripe smell of the stables and the wild feeling of a horse's bare back between my thighs.

I indulged myself making love to Julia, atop tangled sheets, and velvet sofas, even marble floors, basking in a kind of primal luxury neither of us had ever encountered. I memorized her naked thighs, the curve of her back, her golden hair, the strawberry lips that had saved me so long ago, when I'd first told her my name was Darling. And now I'd made her a Darling too.

The glass ever called to me. I heard it in the early morning, in the moments between sleeping and waking, when dreams still held fast to my eyelids. The glass whispered of the things it would be, and of who I would become. As long as I listened, my success was secure.

"Tell me again how you came by the talent for glass," Horace asked me one day as we strolled through a boxwood lined garden in the courtyard of an imposing Savannah home. "You're not the kind of man born to a profession. If you don't mind me saying so."

"Julia's father apprenticed me."

"And that was why young Julia accompanied you? Because of your prospects?"

"A man in America can make himself whatever he can imagine. Julia liked the idea too."

Horace grimaced. "I'm afraid America isn't immune to the realities of life. It takes money to make money, my friend. No imagining of utopia can change that."

"Yet here I am."

Horace guffawed and slapped me on the back, his eyes twinkling.

"Were you born rich?"

"Yes, but with stipulations," Horace reached into his pocket and pulled out a glimmering stone caged in delicate gold and hanging from a chain secured to his jacket. "This trinket, as I like to call it, is a flawless, ten carat diamond." He smirked as I leaned closer. "That means, of course, that it's worth more than a small kingdom. But it's not the diamond itself, so much as its origin, that ties it to me. My father was an explorer of ancient Egypt. This stone once sat in the crown of a pharaoh." He tucked it away again. "The day my father pried this from the putrid, mummified remains of that old badger, our family's fortune increased exponentially. Egyptian treasure notwithstanding, we've become supremely auspicious. I intend to stay that way."

"You believe it's a magic stone, then?"

"My friend, all diamonds are magic stones. Depending on what you do with them."

* * *

The studio Horace presented me was everything I'd ever dreamed of and more. I stood at the poured glass windows and gazed down over River Street. The Savannah River slipped lazily by, bustling with tugboats and dinghies and barges all clamoring for space. Workmen strode down the edge of the street, their shoes and legs covered with mud and grime and splashed with water and coal. Their hands were full, and their faces hard and sour, their clothing ragtag blends of wool and worn-out cotton.

I turned to face the old warehouse-turned glass-blowing studio.

This was no small shop at the back of a manor house in Scotland. This was an industrial-sized glass production facility. This was big. This was new. This was American.

A team of assistants strode back and forth, carrying bags of sand, metal rods, pliers, and other tools, each of them busy at work duplicating the techniques they'd been taught to produce simpler items. A bottle. A vase. A paperweight. The kinds of things that could be easily stocked and sold across town and in more than one store on Broughton Street, the shopping district that had fast become Julia's favorite.

Meanwhile, I was free to work on my art. The complicated. The refined. Whatever the glass whispered it should be, I knew how to create – as though the pattern, the technique had been etched into my heart at birth.

My chandeliers were the item in vogue. Sold at an outlandish price because Mr. Leroux said that they should.

I woke each morning and knew exactly how many glimmering crystals I would make that day. And without fail an order would arrive that afternoon to match.

I was famous now, for my skill, for my timeliness, and my uncanny ability to deliver precisely what it was my customer imagined in their minds. Sometimes better.

Overnight, Darling Glass Company grew to be known within the most prestigious parlors and clubs on the American East Coast. And I, the little boy named Darling, had become a rich man.

"Investment. Compounding interest. That's the secret," Horace said to me one evening as we sat in his lamplit garden and smoked cigars. "Compounding interest is what takes a rich man and turns him into a wealthy one."

I went home that night, to my four-story townhouse on Jones Street, greeted the butler, and then ran upstairs and made love to Julia, her opera pearls still wrapped around her delicious neck. She grasped my face in her hands and kissed my lips and whispered to me that she loved me most in the world.

I held her when she fell asleep, and I thought of compounding interest.

Chapter Twelve

Whitney Darling

hitney Darling. Broken.

The glass whispered me awake, finding me buried deep beneath the blankets, surrounded by an ebbing dream of sparkling chandeliers and a boy with emerald green eyes, and for a moment, I couldn't remember why I was supposed to be sad.

The earthy scent of coffee brought me closer to consciousness.

Please not yet.

I hadn't slept this hard in weeks.

Addison had been desperately tired after delivering the baby, but not too tired to name the newest addition to the family. Alice Henrietta was a tiny thing, with blue eyes and a cry that could wake the dead. Fortunately, she settled quickly, content to snuggle on her mother's chest, all beneath the watchful eyes of Francis and her tearful Grandma Nora.

Around three in the morning, I'd crawled into my own bed, my mind buzzing. In the space of a few hours, I'd encountered an unknown entity behind the door at the bottom of the conservatory stairs, and then promptly become an aunt amid the most dramatic of circumstances. And I'd spoken with Ephraim. Not a word here and there, meted between waves of frustration, but really spoken with him. Granted, I'd been hopped up on adrenaline, and he'd been under the influence of several glasses of whiskey, but somehow, in the space of those minutes, we'd fallen into the easy cadence of long-ago.

My stomach fluttered traitorously at the memory of concern in his voice when he'd called my name in the conservatory, the way he'd rushed to me and pulled me to him, ready to ward off whatever danger.

And what had been the danger, really? My eyes and ears had played tricks on me. What had appeared as a flash of white skirts was only a flash of lightning, surely. And the bang on the door had been caused by a clanging pipe in the ceiling, or the settling of the house. And the voice?

I squeezed my eyes shut against the morning sun streaming in my window, and worried my lip again, harder this time.

A creaking floorboard by my bed made me stiffen.

The feeling of eyes on me.

I froze. My heart skipped a beat.

Clearly, I was freaking myself out. Not a difficult thing to do in Darling House.

A child's giggle beside my pillow turned my blood to ice.

On reflex alone, I lunged from the bed, one foot on the floor, the other tangled in the sheets and stared wide-eyed at the culprit.

Percy beamed back at me from behind a Batman mask.

I flopped back on the bed. "Percy, my goodness. You aged me ten years."

"You didn't hear me come in?" He grinned.

I rubbed my eyes. "Definitely not."

"I'm getting better!" He leaned against the mattress. "Did you know Batman was a ninja?"

"Is that so?"

He nodded. "Your hair's a mess."

"Is that so?" I pulled him into my arms, my fingers seeking out his most ticklish places.

He dissolved into instant breathless laughter. "You're beautiful! You're beautiful!"

"That's what I thought you said." I released him with a pat on the head. "Have you met your new sister yet?"

"Francis says Mommy needs more sleep. I get to meet her when they wake up."

"Francis is right. Your Mama worked hard to get Alice here."

"How?"

I hesitated, at a loss for words. "I think that's a question for your Mama and Francis."

Percy nodded and dashed from the room, the pounding of his little feet echoing down the hallway.

A few minutes later, I emerged from the bathroom. I'd skipped my usual routine in favor of loose, messy waves, a swipe of mascara, and a little lip-gloss. My favorite black leggings and long, ivory cable-knit sweater matched the mood of the cozy, cool morning outside my windows.

My phone chimed, and I picked it up as I strode to the door, my stomach rumbling loudly.

It was from Isla.

Checking on you! I know you need rest after last
night. But I could come over for a cup of coffee

later. We can sit and talk. Or simply sit. Either way, I'm here.

I shot her a quick reply that I'd love to see her and trotted down the stairs toward the kitchen.

I rounded the corner into the red parlor and froze.

Percy. He lay on the floor, perfectly still, his little arms sprawled out at his sides, his mouth slightly open, his eyes closed.

I collapsed to my knees beside him. "Percy?"

He didn't move.

"Percy."

Again, nothing. I reached out and shook him, but he didn't respond, his head lolling from side to side as though his muscles had turned to water.

"Percy!" I pressed my fingers to his neck, searching for a pulse.

His heart beat strong.

And fast.

His chest moved then.

Up and down.

Up and down, sporadic and heaving.

"Percy?"

A snicker escaped his lips and I nearly fainted.

I grabbed him by the shoulders, forcing him to a sitting position, and his eyes popped open.

"What are you doing? You scared me."

"I'm sorry, Aunt Whitney. I was practicing."

"Practicing?"

"For when the curse gets me." He motioned to the carpet. "I lay here and try not to breathe for a long time."

"Oh. Sweetie." I pulled him onto my lap. "The curse is not going to get you. Where did you get an idea like that?"

"It got my daddy. And mama tells me how strong he was. I'm not. I'm little. It'll get me next."

I pressed a kiss to his soft, round cheek. "No, it won't. I don't want you to say that ever again. There's no curse coming for you. You're going to grow up to be strong like your Daddy was. You're going to get married and have five babies and live to be an old, old man. Say it out loud, Percy. Say it."

"Say what?"

"I'm going to be an old, old happy man."

He shook his head.

"If you say it, it will come true. I promise."

"I'm going to be old."

"And happy," I insisted.

"And happy."

I patted him on the knee. "Good. Feel better?"

He nodded, "I'm sorry I scared you."

"It won't be my last scare of the day, I'm sure," I said, thinking again of my ghostly encounter in the conservatory.

He quirked a delicate eyebrow.

"Never mind."

He leapt up to speed from the room.

I stood and took a deep breath. If this house didn't give me a heart attack, that child certainly would.

Adele sat alone at the table by the kitchen windows, sipping from a pottery mug, her leather-bound Bible open in front of her. "Alice and Addison are both doing wonderfully," she said, without looking up at me.

I pulled a mug from a cabinet and poured a stream of steaming coffee, then topped it off with a splash of cream. "She's a gorgeous baby."

"The spitting image of you and Seth when you were born."

I joined my aunt, sliding into the seat across from her. I plucked a fat blueberry muffin from a platter in the center of the table. I'd missed these mornings with her when she and I were often the first ones awake. There were so many things on the tip of my tongue to say now, like how I'd been desperately lonely, or how living in the city was so different from here, or how I'd dreamed about the glass.

But somehow, I knew Adele already knew those things.

"I've missed our coffee chats," I whispered.

"Me too, Darling girl." She placed a wrinkled hand over mine, her elegant fingers warm and strong.

A familiar easiness settled between us.

The house still buzzed with energy, a kind of magic in the air that only sprang to life following something wonderful.

"Can I ask you a question?"

"Evidently," Adele chuckled, lifting her eyes from the Bible in front of her.

"A lot's happened since I arrived," I said. "Certain things have been brought to my attention."

"Yes?" The light behind her eyes dimmed, and I felt immediately guilty for saying anything.

"Last night, prior to the baby situation, Addison said something about Granddaddy seeming paranoid before he died. And that he'd seemed to be searching the house for something. Do you know about any of that?"

Adele didn't speak for a long minute, staring at me as she took a loud, leisurely sip of coffee. "Your sister's correct," she said, finally. "Alistair was unsettled in his final days. He didn't share much with me. The most that I can tell you, honey, is that he believed he was being haunted."

"Haunted?"

She nodded. "He claimed Julia Darling was here in the

house, trying to warn him about something." She pinched the bridge of her nose. "Your Granddaddy loved you and your brother more than life itself. When Seth passed in such a terrible, abrupt manner it about killed him too. Then you left. Then Percy's father died, hanging Christmas lights of all things, and then Rose's stroke, and – "

I held up a hand, my pulse skittering an unsteady pace. I forced away the memory of Julia, bloody and pleading, in my dressing room at Beau's. "I understand," I said. "Did he tell you what Julia was protecting him from? Was it the curse? What was he trying to find?"

Adele shook her head, straightening at the sound of Percy's little footsteps in the hallway.

We both plastered smiles on our faces as he peeked a cheery face around the corner and joined us in the kitchen.

Rose, sporting a smocked pink caftan, followed closely after him in her wheelchair. She smiled when she saw Adele and I, then held a band-aid out to me as if she presented The Ark of the Covenant. "Here you are, my dear. You're going to need this."

"Thank you," I said, taking the bandage from her. "I hope it's nothing serious."

"Oh, he'll be fine," said Rose, reaching for a china plate and a muffin. "Bring me my coffee, will you? And then get a move on. Head down the beach. Not the marshy river beach, I mean the ocean side of the island. To the east."

"She knows which side the ocean's on, Rose," Adele quipped.

I looked over at her. "Any idea what this is about?"

Adele shrugged. "You better get moving."

Percy giggled.

"Fine." I poured Rose a cup of coffee. "I'll go find my shoes."

Rose pointed at the door; her eyebrows raised to a severe height.

"Okay," I sighed. "I'll go barefoot."

* * *

The wet morning sand shifted beneath my feet as I made my way down the beach. I ran a fingertip over the edge of a small white shell I held in my hand, feeling its tiny ridges, and the course specks that clung to its underside.

Cold wind stung my nose and face.

It felt good. Though, with my luck, I'd catch a cold and end up in bed for days.

The man running down the beach in my direction was tall and lean, his stride long despite the layers of black athletic clothes covering him from head to toe.

Ephraim waved to me as the distance between us closed, and I noticed the handsome stubble on his cheeks and the sweat-drenched waves peeking out from beneath his knit beanie.

He slowed as he neared, his eyes studying me closely.

I crossed my arms in front of me. "Fancy seeing you here."

"I'm here every morning."

I nodded, trying not to read into his tone.

He pulled off his hat, and the breeze ruffled his damp hair, like wind on bird's feathers. He turned to face the water, stretching his arms out as if he meant to take the view into himself. "I've never run beside an ocean that had so much to say."

"Hearing voices?"

He rolled his eyes and chuckled. A deep, husky sound. "You'd know all about that."

"Touché."

He groaned and sat down on the sand, almost close enough for the surf to reach up and touch him. He pulled off his sneakers and socks, then rolled up his sweats, revealing strong, tanned calves and feet. He motioned for me to join him. "Sit."

I hesitated, then sighed and plopped down beside him. "You do realize it's like forty degrees out, right?"

"More like sixty." His smile broadened, "And you wouldn't be so cold if you'd bothered to put on some shoes."

I rolled my eyes, not bothering to explain as I leaned back onto my elbows and looked at him expectantly.

He ground his heels into the sand. "Now bury your feet."

I wiggled my toes into the course wetness. "Why are we doing this?"

"It's called grounding," he said. "Communing with nature."

I shivered and fought to keep my teeth from chattering. "Is the ocean going to speak to us?"

"Sure. But you can't hear it if you're talking."

"Fine."

Ephraim closed his eyes, letting his head loll between his shoulders. He splayed his arms out beside him and let his head come to rest on the sand. "Lie back."

"I'll get sand in my hair."

He glowered, clearly annoyed.

I clenched my jaw and laid back against the cold sand. I stared at the grey clouds and shivered. "Nothing's happening."

"Shut your eyes, take a deep breath, and listen."

I closed my eyes.

Whitney. Broken.

Ugh. I couldn't do this kind of thing. The glass.

Waves crashed just shy of our toes, reaching for us with bubbling, icy fingers. The wind whispered. A seagull cried.

Seconds passed into minutes, winding and bending with the ocean's steady rhythm. I could feel Ephraim's eyes on me, and I sensed him sitting up.

"What's it saying to you?" he asked.

Maybe it was the tender way he asked it, or the tone of his voice that reminded me of Alistair, and a hundred other tiny moments like this one, from the life I'd had before, but it was all suddenly too much.

All the sadness, the frustration, the guilt, the fear that I'd kept carefully under wraps since returning to Darling House rushed to the surface.

"It says I'm broken," I choked, standing fast. "It says everything that's happened is my fault. That I shouldn't have come back here." Tears welled in my eyes and my throat constricted painfully. "It says it should've been me the river swept away that day, not Seth. It should have been me." I turned on my heel.

"Whitney, wait."

"What, Ephraim?" I glared at him. "What do you want from me?"

"We're getting married in three days."

I sneered. "We're already married, remember?"

"You know what I mean."

"I know. And I don't care. This is a miraculously screwed up web of lies and secrets and tragedies. I don't know how you expect me to feel, but at the moment, pissed off seems like my best option."

Eyes flaming, he shot to his feet and pulled me hard against him. His lips crashed into to mine, wild as the ocean beside us. And he could sweep me away just as easily.

Blood roared in my ears, each beat of my heart a warning to tear away from him, but my traitorous arms looped around his neck.

"Ephraim, we can't," I gasped. "The curse."

"Damn the curse," his voice rumbled, ragged and breathless. "Be here. Be here. In this moment. With me."

I met his eyes, studying the flecks of gold in a sea of emerald. A rare vulnerability stared back at me. Cold wind whipped off the ocean, tossing my hair around my face.

"I know you'd like to imagine," he said, "that you can remain as detached and unaffected as you've been these past two years. But we are not ghosts, Whitney."

"No?" I did my best to match the intensity of his gaze. "Then what are we?"

His jaw ticked as he cradled my cheeks in his hands. "Before this year is up, you'll be well acquainted with how alive we are." He pressed a gentle kiss on my forehead, and then let me go.

So many words sat on the tip of my tongue. So many things I wanted to say.

I've missed you.

I've dreamed of you.

I still desperately love you.

"I found another letter," I whispered.

His eyes softened, and his lips tilted up in the corner, revealing a handsome dimple, "From Alistair?"

"No," I said, wrapping my arms tight against me. "This one is old. It was in the frame by my bedroom, tucked behind William and Julia's wedding portrait."

"I'll refrain from asking how you discovered it. What did it say?"

"It was an apology. From William to Julia. He'd done something unforgivable."

Ephraim shrugged. "We know things worked out for them. They had children and grew old and died days apart. What more could you ask for?"

"Someone, or something, wanted me to find the letter." My teeth started to chatter. "I think it's to do with the curse."

He shook his head. "Enough about that for now. Let's get you inside. You're freezing."

I placed my cold hand in his warm one.

"I can't believe, as cold-natured as you are, that you came out here without shoes or a jacket."

"Rose said there was no time."

Ephraim took a step, then leapt back as if he'd been stung.

I gasped as a bright red drop of blood splattered beneath him onto the sand.

He lifted his foot and craned to look, "It's a piece of glass," he said through gritted teeth.

Fumbling with the pocket in the back of my leggings, I pulled out the bandage Rose had given me. I held it out. "Rose sent this along with me."

He chuckled, "Of course, she did."

I knelt to study the injury. "The glass is still poking out. I don't think it's deep."

"Pull it out."

"Are you sure?"

"Indisputably."

I moved closer and gently grasped the shard between two fingers. Feeling a little queasy, I pulled on it firm and quick.

He winced.

"I'm sorry."

"No need."

"The cut's not too bad. You're lucky."

He smirked, then pushed up to limp toward the ocean. "Nothing a little saltwater can't fix," he said, plunging his foot into the cold water. "Got that bandage?"

"Right." I pulled the wrapper from the thin material, trying my best to keep the wind from whipping it all over. Ephraim sat back down next to me, placing his foot between my knees.

"I don't know how well this will stick," I said.

"It'll do until we get to the house."

I leaned forward and dried his foot with my sweater, then pressed the bandage into place.

"This constant bickering between us has to stop." Ephraim clenched his jaw, and I saw a flash of the young man from all those years ago, the one whose parents had gone down over the marsh and left him alone.

I was silent for a long moment. He was right, of course. "Fine." I tried my best to sound nonchalant. "But no more kissing. And stop bossing me around."

"Don't count on that." He pulled out his cell phone, looking at the screen as he stood. "We're needed at the house."

"What's happened? Addison?"

He shook his head. "Officer Evans is here. And he has questions."

Chapter Thirteen

Whitney Darling

Ephraim and I entered Darling House to heightened voices in the kitchen.

"We could have done with a little notice before being called on by the law." Mama's tone was terrifyingly pleasant.

"I apologize for the abrupt nature of my visit," drawled Officer Evans. "But there are certain time frames within which I must adhere when it comes to investigations."

"And what would your mother say if I told her, Reginald, that you arrived at my doorstep first thing on a Saturday morning. The night after my granddaughter was born, no less."

Ephraim and I stepped into the room in time to see Officer Evans wipe his forehead with a handkerchief. "Congratulations are in order then."

"Thank you," Mama said, pursing her lips.

Rose wheeled her chair into the room. "Why, what an unexpected surprise," she preened, her round, rosy cheeks glowing as she surveyed Officer Evans.

Adele put her hands on her hips. "You know when

Whitney's going to need a bandage, but you don't know when the law's coming?"

Rose pinkened, and waved a dismissive hand at her twin. "It's not an exact science."

Officer Evans cleared his throat. "Ladies, I have a few questions for you all." He adjusted the belt straining around his formidable middle. "Did anyone notice anything unusual in the days leading up to the break-in? Any strange cars in the drive? Unexpected visitors? Were there any packages delivered or service providers out to the house?"

Mama shook her head, her oversized pearl drop earrings tapping against her neck. "I suppose we can't be too sure. We were all in and out of the house quite a bit between visiting my father in the hospital, and then seeing to his," she pinched the bridge of her nose, "final affairs."

Officer Evans nodded. "The thing is, Mrs. Darling, this is a strange break-in. No outward sign of forced entry and the intruder didn't appear to take anything. Which leads me to believe this may have been an inside job."

"Excuse me?" she snapped.

"Is there anyone you can think of who has regular access to the house? Or someone who had bad blood with Mr. Darling?"

"Everyone loved my Daddy," Mama shook her head. "As far as access to the house, I can't think of a soul. I mean, we have a local lady who comes weekly to clean the house. But she's sweet. She brings her little son with her sometimes, and he plays with Percy. A polite young man. Good home training. I can't imagine his mother doing something like this."

"Anyone else?"

"There's a man who tends to the yard once a month.

General cleanup. I don't think he's ever been inside the house."

"We did have the dishwasher replaced recently," Adele said.

Officer Evans nodded, looking as though none of these revelations offered much of an impression. "Ma'am, may I ask why you don't have any cameras stationed around your property? With a place of this scope, relying on the alarm system alone isn't your safest option."

Mama pursed her lips again.

"I've been asking her the same thing for years," Ephraim said, drawing Officer Evans' attention over to where we stood in the doorway to the mudroom. "People like the Darlings value their privacy to a fault. They never give out their social security numbers. They don't use debit cards, online banking, or social media. And they absolutely don't allow third-party controlled technology in their homes, let alone cameras."

Officer Evans, who looked more tired by the passing second, shifted on his feet and released a deep sigh. "Good morning, Ephraim. Morning, Whitney. The thing is, Mrs. Darling, that no one is watching you through the cameras, the cameras are doing the watching and then you can go back and review the footage anytime."

"I don't believe it." Adele shook her head. "It's like with those smart phones. You can't tell me the government isn't listening to every word you say."

Officer Evans looked from Aunt Adele to us, his eyebrows in a sharp V.

"I've tried my best," Ephraim said, leaning casually against the doorframe. "This is a unique crew you've got here."

"I can see that," Evans said. "But outside of cameras, it's

going to be difficult to effectively monitor your property. Safety would dictate that you should at least have a couple of them installed at the gate, so we can try and keep up with the island's comings and goings."

"I'll think about it," Mama said.

The doorbell rang.

"I'll get it," I said. A little air and a moment of silence between the kitchen and the front door sounded like heaven.

I brushed past everyone, hurrying through the dining room, the rear and formal parlors, and crossed into the foyer where I could see the outline of a person through one of the windows that overlooked the porch.

I swung open the door.

"Monica!" I motioned for her to come in. "Addison told me you'd called yesterday. It's been a whirlwind since."

"I don't mean to intrude," Monica said, taking my arm as we stepped inside. "Before I forget, I saw a rather sizable alligator in your yard when I drove in. I almost didn't get out of my car, but I figured it'd be more afraid of me than I am of it. I swear, those creatures are adapting better to saltwater every day."

My blood went cold, and I thought of Percy.

"Where exactly?"

"Just inside the gate. Looked like he was crossing the driveway to get from one side of the marsh to the other." She waved her hand dismissively.

I nodded and led Monica to one of the chairs in the parlor. "Have a seat. I'm going to make sure Percy, or anyone else for that matter, isn't outside where they might come across the gator. Can I get you anything?"

"Just a glass of water, thank you. Or sweet tea if you have it. I promise not to take up much of your time. I'm here on business with the Southern Art and Culture Society."

"Of course," I said, noting the prim way she perched in the chair, the green and pink neon of her Lilly Pulitzer dress in stark contrast to the chic coastal pallet of the sitting room. "I'll be back in a moment."

"Who was at the door?" Mama asked, as I strode into the kitchen.

"Where's Percy?" I asked, unable to keep the worry from my voice.

Ephraim straightened. "What's wrong?"

"An alligator."

"A gator?" Officer Evans exclaimed, sounding unconvinced.

"Percy's here," Rose said, from where she'd pulled her wheelchair to the table.

Percy sat next to her on a cushioned chair, an old deck of cards between them. "We're playing Slap Jack. I'm winning."

"Percy," Ephraim said, "you're not to go outside without an adult until we say it's safe, do you understand?"

"Oh, I'm sure that old thing is already halfway down the May River." Monica's voice was sweet as keylime pie from over my shoulder.

I turned to see her standing in the doorway, her eyes gleaming with equal parts curiosity and politeness.

"I was about to come back with your tea," I said.

"I'm not interrupting, am I? I saw Officer Evan's patrol car parked out front when I arrived, I figured things must be a little hectic. We can skip over the pleasantries."

"Apparently," Mama said. She leaned close to Adele, and I heard her whisper something about the death of gentility.

"Mama, everyone," I said. "Monica's paid us a visit from the Southern Art and Culture Society."

"Good morning," Monica said.

"What can we do for you?" Mama asked, her usual pleasant tone restored.

Monica pulled a folder from the tote hanging from her shoulder. "I'll cut right to it. The society would like to co-sponsor a gala to be held here."

"A gala?" I asked.

"To honor the life and work of Alistair Darling, Savannah native and world-renown glassblower."

"We know who he was," Adele said. "What's your hope in hosting this party? Is it for charity?"

"Well, yes." Monica looked a little affronted. "The event would raise money for the society, which in turn would be used to fund up-and-coming artists of all backgrounds from around the region. Something we all agree Mr. Darling was exceptionally passionate about."

"He certainly was," Mama said. "Why don't you leave your folder here. We'll have a look at it and get back to you."

Monica's smile thinned.

"Miss Harding, where did you see the alligator when you arrived? I assume the gate was still open from my having entered before you." Officer Evan's cocked an eyebrow.

"It sure was," said Monica, her saccharine tone sweeter than the tea I still hadn't gotten for her. "The gator was just inside the gate. Like I told Whitney, I'm sure he's long gone by now."

Ephraim waved over his shoulder at Officer Evans. "We'll have a look anyway."

The two men strode from the room.

"I should be going too," Monica said.

No one protested.

"I'll see you out," I placed a gentle hand on her arm as we walked back to the front door. "We'll let you know what we think about the proposal. Thank you for thinking of my grandfather for the event."

"Oh, it was an easy decision."

We stepped onto the porch, within sight of Ephraim and Officer Evans walking the perimeter of the yard.

"Please excuse everyone in there," I said. "We had a long night, and obviously, we're juggling a lot."

"It's not their fault," Monica said. "I'm afraid I didn't leave Darling Glass on the best of terms before."

"No?" I already knew that, but I was curious to get her perspective.

She shook her head. "I was distraught after your brother passed, of course. You know how close we were." She sniffed and dabbed a delicate finger beneath her nose. "Then you left, and it was me and Alistair. Which was a dream at first, but then his health took a turn. And then when he died so shockingly – "

I pressed a comforting hand to her arm.

Monica forced a smile, her brow creased with pent up emotion. "I couldn't handle that much grief, you know?"

"I do, actually."

A few moments of quiet stretched between us before Monica stared up at the house, her eyes scanning the upper windows, not unlike how I had done when I'd first arrived and caught sight of the woman in white starting back at me. "This place is so hypnotic," she said. "A house this big and old, there's no telling how many people have died here. How many accidents there've been. Tragedy upon tragedy."

"There have been good times too," I said. "We can't

forget those. Speaking of, I hope you're able to make it to the wedding this weekend. You received your invitation, right?"

"Of course," she said, blotting her cheeks with the back of her hand. "I'll be there for sure. Thank you."

I motioned up at the sky, where sunlight struggled to burst through heavy grey clouds. "It looks like the rain's finally clearing out for a pretty Savannah day. Enjoy it."

"You too," she smiled, rolling her shoulders back with a decisive sniff of her nose. "Keep in mind, if you decide to let the society host the gala here, it would be great publicity for Darling Glass." She started down the stairs toward her car. "Just think about it."

Chapter Fourteen

Whitney Darling

When I was a little girl, and Seth a little boy, we would wake up early in the morning, when the sunlight spilled like honey through our bedroom windows, and the house smelled like stove-top coffee and fresh-cut flowers. The patter of feet downstairs, and the muffled easy drawl of conversation was the music we lived by. Alistair's deep voice, his handsome chuckle. Daddy's slow, sophisticated timber. And Mama's laughter, like a wind chime.

We'd roll out of our beds with sleepy almond eyes, our hair like fuzzy halos around our heads, and put on our matching robes as we walked over to the big window in our bedroom. The one that looked out over the gardens, the marsh, and the wide, wild river. We would measure the likelihood of finding treasure that day. Shark teeth, or old broken china half buried in the riverbank.

We'd race down the stairs and through the kitchen, out to Adele's parterre garden, where a little hidden path led to the stone statue of a bullfrog sat atop a pedestal, his lips puckered, as if waiting for a kiss. We'd drop a penny through the hole in his lips, and pat him on his cold, fat head and make a wish.

I sighed, not quite ready to let the dream go, the sweet memory that played at the edges of my mind.

I lay buried deep beneath my pretty white quilt and down comforter. Keeping my eyes squeezed shut, I curled and flexed my toes and lifted my hands over my head.

I'd wished for this day once. I'd given the frog a penny. Hundreds of pennies over the years, wishing for this day.

Today was my wedding day. And I was marrying Ephraim.

Again.

A loud knock on the door startled me awake, and I sat up as the door cracked open.

"Are you decent, dear?" Aunt Rose's voice peeped from the hallway.

"Still in bed."

The door opened and Rose wheeled her way over to me, Aunt Adele behind her carrying a steaming cup of coffee and a thin black velvet box tucked under her arm.

"Good morning, pretty lady," Rose said. "Time to get ready for the most beautiful day."

"Aside from the day she was born," Mama said, following them into my room. She came to sit on the edge of the mattress and grabbed my hand, placing a quick kiss to the back of it.

"Thank you, Mama."

Adele passed the coffee mug over to me, and I inhaled the cozy scent before relaxing back against my pillows and taking a sip. "There's no use resisting whatever ceremony you're all here to impose. What will it be? Weaving flower crowns or sewing century-old lace onto my garter?"

Adele snorted, "It's an honor you've inherited my sense of humor."

Mama shook her head. "We're here with the pearls."

I straightened. I'd forgotten about those.

One of our oldest family traditions.

Adele held out the box in her hands, opening it reverently, then lifted the shining strand, letting it spill over the side. "They've been in the family more than a hundred-years now."

I leaned close.

The necklace was at least three feet long, with perfectly proportioned round pearls that trailed in a pattern of smallest at the ends, then tapering to the largest in the center. Gold fasteners boasted a series of tiny, engraved charms, each of them marked with the initials of brides-past, including Mama and Addison. Three large diamonds hung nestled near the clasp. It was heavy. And gleaming.

And mine.

For today, anyway.

"Every Darling bride has worn these on their wedding day. Julia brought them over from Scotland."

"They're beautiful." I touched one of the smallest pearls, turning it gently so the light from the window danced in a swirling motion across its pale surface. They were darker in color than I remembered. Ivory, like preserved white flowers from long ago. The largest charm at the clasp glittered, the initials *WJP*, winking up at me from the warm metal.

William, Julia, and - what did the *P* stand for?

"Just take care of them. They're freshly strung and oiled, so they should hold up fine for the wedding," Mama said.

"We'll leave you alone to get moving. The makeup

artist, hairdresser, and photographer will all be here at eleven. There are already crews in the back setting up the tents and preparing for the florist. You know the drill. You've been to your fair share of parties at Darling House."

"And this will be the most beautiful of them all," Rose chimed dreamily.

The gaggle left as quickly as they'd come, shutting the door behind them with a flurry of checklists and reminders, as if they'd forgotten –

My marriage to Ephraim was a business arrangement, a consolation to the wishes of a dying man who may or may not have had all of his faculties.

I sighed and swung my legs over the side of the bed, touching my toes to the floor. For better, or worse, today was the start of something.

This wedding would either be the fulfillment of a dream, or the continuation of a curse.

And there was only one way to find out.

* * *

A little more than ten hours later, draped in Julia's ivory pearls and dressed in the satin gown from Beau's, I stood at the far end of the petal-strewn path that led from Adele's gardens to the marsh.

I'd walked this way so many times. As a small child with Mama holding my hand. Alongside Alistair on the way to the glass studio. With Seth to explore the river, and then to lose him there. With Ephraim. So many, many times.

I rolled my shoulders.

Surprisingly, it didn't matter to me that hundreds of curious Savannahians watched me now. I hardly noticed them.

Because with each step I drew nearer, Ephraim's eyes swept from the top of my head down to where the tips of my shoes peeked from beneath my gown.

A vow. To never leave. A vow to never be alone.

Was he also thinking about the words he'd spoken?

My mind swam with contradictions. I was entering into a false marriage with the man I'd loved for most of my life. The man who'd loved me back for a time.

Ephraim was gorgeous, the strong line of his jaw hard, his shoulders broad, his muscled legs planted as firmly as the Live Oaks at his back. He wore a black tuxedo with a black satin bowtie, and his wavy hair was loose and wild, the way he'd worn it when we were teenagers. Like when I'd first fallen in love with him.

When I finally arrived at the altar it was all I could do to look up into his eyes.

"Beloved, we are gathered here today," began the pastor. I entered a gossamer dream. Ephraim's warm, rugged hands wrapped around mine, and we repeated words to an eternal promise, a vow he'd made clear surpassed any other we could make.

And this time, Ephraim sealed the vow with a kiss, passionate and chaste all at once.

We were married beside the river, beneath moss-draped oak trees. A super moon hung bright white in the sky, so by the time the reception found flutes filled with champagne, the tide had crept halfway up the garden.

An orchestra played Frank Sinatra, Johnny Mercer, and Nat King Cole beneath a thousand strands of lights. My gown shined and twirled, and red rose petals and Spanish moss clung to the bustled train.

"You're exquisite," Ephraim said, as he swept me into an

effortless waltz. His hand slipped to my waist, pulling me close to him.

"You look dangerous."

His arm tightened around me. "Do you feel different, Whitney Callaghan-Darling?"

The sound of my taken name sounded musical on his tongue. "Should I?"

He cracked a knowing grin.

"Do you feel different?"

"No."

"No?" The word burst out a little too loudly, and I blushed.

He shook his head, "You've been mine much longer than you imagine."

"And how is that?"

"I made a promise a long time ago that you would never be rid of me. And I've kept it. I've always watched over you. Even when you didn't know it – or want it."

My lips moved, but I couldn't find words.

Watched over me?

Ephraim stiffened, halting our dance as a finger tapped my shoulder. "It's a beautiful wedding, Whit."

"Daddy?" I turned and flung my arms around him, breathing in his familiar scent. Vetiver and pine. I leaned back and looked up at his ruddy, proud face. He'd grown older, and rounder. "I thought you were stuck in Paris."

"I couldn't miss my Whitney's wedding." He pressed a kiss to my forehead before casting a censorious gaze at Ephraim. "Even if I only had a week's notice. I hear this is more of a business arrangement than a marriage." He lifted a brow. "I admire your sense of duty. Though, what this place has ever done for you is beyond me."

"How did you get here in time?" I asked. "Mama said you were still in Europe."

He shook his head. "Your mother says a lot of things. I caught the red-eye last night. And, unfortunately, I've got another to catch in a couple of hours. But I'm here for a dance with the bride. The band's waiting for my cue."

I grinned, tamping down my disappointment that he'd be leaving so soon. "I've missed you."

"I've missed you too, honey." He pulled me into his arms, sweeping me into an easy foxtrot. "Right now," he said, his voice a harsh whisper, "while it's you and me, tell me one thing."

"Yes?"

"Did they pressure you into this?"

"Who?"

"Any of them. The Darlings," he spat. "I know how they can be."

"Daddy, I'm a Darling."

He shook his head. "By name. But you're not like the rest of them. You had the guts and independence to get out, to move to another city and start a life for yourself."

"What are you getting at?"

"If you don't want this, Princess, say the word and I'll take you away with me, back to Paris. I brought an extra ticket for you."

"You're talking like I've been kidnapped. This is my home. Mama, the aunts, my sister, they all love me."

"And Ephraim?"

I swallowed.

Something smug flickered behind Daddy's eyes, but he replaced it quickly with cool indifference. "As long as you're happy."

I nodded.

Happy.

My gaze fell on Ephraim who stood speaking to Mama and Isla at the edge of the dance floor.

"I am happy," I whispered.

He grunted. "That's all I needed to know."

The music slowed, then faded into another tune.

Daddy led me back to Ephraim, eyeing him with stony calculation. "Take care," he said. "If she's anything like her mother, she'll drain you of more than your finances."

Ephraim scowled and pulled me to his side. "Watch yourself, Mr. Darling. Alistair wouldn't have stood for that talk. And I can assure you, I'm less gracious than he was."

Daddy straightened, a tinge of red staining his cheeks. Whether from anger or embarrassment, it didn't matter. "You're bold," he said, flatly.

"Disrespect my wife again, and you'll find out how bold."

I squeezed Ephraim's arm.

Daddy turned stiffly to my mother. "Nora."

"Husband." Mama shot the word at him like an accusation, the raw wound of their separation glimmering in her eyes.

Daddy placed a quick kiss on my forehead. "Love you, Whitney. Enjoy your wedding."

"You, too," I whispered, conflicted, angry tears pricking the backs of my eyes. I watched in silence as my father walked away, his tailored black suit disappearing into the crowd.

And then, like a boom of thunder, he was gone.

"Well, that was classic," Mama said. "Whitney, I'm so sorry. His insults were intended for me, not you."

Ephraim took me gently by the arm. "Come on," he said. "It's time to dance."

Several hours later, after much dancing, and talking and laughing with my not-so-new husband, I wove my way through the ballroom toward a row of linen covered tables and golden chairs. Ephraim and I had managed to slip away from Monica, who we'd happily informed her gala proposal was accepted. She'd gone on to hold us polite prisoners for twenty minutes as she regaled us with the upcoming hypothetical arrangements. It had been Isla, and her brother Asher, who had finally relieved us.

Now, I needed a tall glass of water and a break.

Solomon Potter raised a crystal flute and motioned flamboyantly for me to join him at a nearby table. "You look like a lady having a good time."

I collapsed onto a golden chair with an inelegant sigh. "You know? I am."

"And where's your husband?"

"He'll be along. He got sidelined by an acquaintance."

Solomon nodded, his brows furrowing over bloodshot eyes. "Your granddaddy would've loved this party."

"I know," I said, noticing the way Solomon swayed in his seat. Solomon Potter was drunk.

"I don't imagine there's been an affair this glitzy here since that one in the thirties," he said, his gaze narrowing pointedly. "When that rich fellow went missing."

"Missing?" I laughed, the effects of the champagne hitting my own equilibrium a little harder now that I'd sat down. "Is this another tall tale?"

"No, ma'am. The scandal was all the rage back in the thirties and forties. One of the true unsolved mysteries of the South." Solomon shook his head, adamant. "You're telling me Alistair didn't write in his letters to you about the man who disappeared here?" He clicked his tongue. "I suppose Ali worried his letters might end up in the wrong hands."

I shifted, suddenly uncomfortable. "What happened?"

"Not anyone knows. He was a young, handsome businessman. Friends with your William Darling. Can't quite remember his name. It'll come to me eventually."

My gaze dropped to the finger-bone necklace around Solomon's neck.

"It was an unusual name, I think. Exotic, almost."

I felt Ephraim's presence behind me before his fingers caressed my shoulder. The touch was light, but it rippled through me with seismic effect.

"Have you stolen my bride away, Mr. Potter?"

Solomon looked up at Ephraim with a lopsided, toothy grin. "I wouldn't dare. Though, I would enjoy a visit from time to time now that she's making her home back in Savannah."

I nodded, struggling to force my champagne-softened attention away from Ephraim's warm fingers. "It's a promise."

"Good." He rose on wobbly legs and tipped his chin. "Alistair sure would've enjoyed this party. For sure, he would. And I did too, my Darling. But I must retire. These old bones aren't what they used to be."

I stood to wrap Solomon in a long hug. My heart squeezed at the thought of him getting older. Like Granddaddy. We could never truly be certain of how much time we had left. "Darling House could spare a room for the night. Stay here."

He pulled away with a chuckle. "Aw, now, I'm not quite as old as all that. Your Mama's already called a town car to drive me home." He held his hand out to Ephraim, and they shook. "Y'all enjoy the rest of your special night. I'll be seeing you again real soon."

Solomon made his way through the ballroom for the exit.

"Come with me," Ephraim said.

"Where are we going?"

He chuckled as his thumb caressed my fingers, back and forth. "Just come."

He led me back outside and up a little garden path toward the main wing of the house.

I tried to focus through the soft haze that settled over my skin like warm feathers. "Where are we going?"

"We're retiring."

"But the reception's not over," I said, trying unsuccessfully to squelch a hiccup. "There are still so many guests here."

"It won't be over until we leave. That's how weddings work. It's nearing midnight, wife."

"Don't call me that." I hiccuped again. "I haven't said thank you to everyone. I've barely had a chance to speak with Isla."

"Mrs. Callaghan-Darling, are you drunk?"

"Certainly not." *Hiccup.* "That would be unladylike."

"What would you call it then?"

"Floating."

"Floating?" He laughed. "Floating with love?"

I stopped cold, pulling him to a halt.

He turned and smiled patiently down at me.

"Are you floating?" I whispered. Immediately mortified, I couldn't bring myself to look him in the eye, so I stared at his jaw, watching the little muscles clench and unclench.

His fingers trailed up my arm, feather-soft, sending fissures of anticipation shooting from my core to my toes.

"Is this all for show?" I asked.

He leaned down and brought his lips beneath my ear. "I've always liked the way you bite your lip when you're nervous." He caressed the curve of my waist, then drifted lower, cupping my hip in his palm. "Time to make our exit."

"Together?"

"It'd look strange if we went separate ways, don't you think?"

I didn't answer.

But I didn't pull away when he took me by the arm and walked me to the top of the landing where he turned and whistled.

A hush fell over the dance floor. The musicians stopped playing.

What was it like to command that kind of attention?

"Thank you all, for coming," Ephraim's voiced soared over the crowd. "I'm afraid I'll be whisking the bride away now."

Adele threw exasperated hands in the air. "I've got forty boxes of sparklers ready for your grand exit."

Ephraim laughed. "By all means, pass them around."

"A round of applause for the newlyweds!" My mother's cheer, and the sudden cacophony of clapping and whistles that followed, brought tears to my eyes.

"Are you looking, Whitney?" Ephraim's voice was husky. "You'll want to remember this."

The faces of the people I loved most in the world smiled up at us, ruddy with laughter and wine.

He was right.

This was the exact moment I'd been waiting for. All my life. Even after everything that had happened.

It didn't matter that it wasn't real. I'd had enough champagne to make me hope, in the quiet, delicate part of my heart, that maybe, Ephraim and I could find a way to make this go on forever.

The crowd of guests moved in unison toward the drive and our exit car.

"Time to go." Ephraim tucked my arm in his.

A delicious tension pooled in my belly as he helped me into the back of a black Mercedes, then lifted the bustled train of my gown so high that cool air kissed my thighs.

I settled in, seeing out the windshield that guests already lined the drive, golden sparklers waving. "It's a fairy tale."

Ephraim smiled wickedly as he slid onto the seat beside me. His long muscular leg brushed against mine as he placed a hand on my knee. "Now then, wife."

Chapter Fifteen

Whitney Darling

"Where are we going?" I asked, as the Mercedes turned down yet another oak-lined back road.

"I'm kidnapping you."

A delicious tension curled in my belly at the memory he alluded to. "Can you kidnap your wife?"

"It's becoming a trend."

"Where are we going, Ephraim?"

"It's a secret, I'm afraid."

"Tell me."

His fingers flexed over my knee. "Somewhere private."

Bright moonlight filtered in the through the car windows, casting the interior in cool silver. We'd been driving for half an hour now, mostly in silence. But the energy was deafening, overwhelming, making my chest rise and fall with anxious breath. And with each passing moment, the champagne buzz I'd been wrapped in slowly loosened its hold, until I was nothing but a bundle of raw nerves.

I knew we'd have to leave the wedding together. If only

for keeping up appearances. As far as anyone was concerned, he and I were married because we'd chosen to be. Not because we'd been blackmailed into it.

A forced marriage between two of Savannah's oldest families would be the scandal of the century. No one could know.

But this.

This tension was unbearable.

"Ephraim."

"Relax."

I nodded, my heart rate rising precipitously. "We've just waltzed through a faux wedding. And you're telling me to relax."

His lips curled into a lazy, amused smile. "There's nothing faux about what we did. Another trend you should get used to."

My lips parted but I couldn't form a word. Why did he look so smug?

Had he planned this from the beginning?

Had this truly all been Alistair's idea?

Had Ephraim tricked me? That would be so like him.

He chuckled. "Don't start weaving anxious stories in your head. I'm as trapped as you are. I just plan on taking full advantage of it."

"I wasn't weaving stories."

He lifted an eyebrow.

I rolled my eyes, "Ephraim, tell me where we're going."

"I'll tell you. But it'll come at a price."

"Excuse me?"

"You heard me."

"What price?"

His thigh pressed harder against mine a moment before

his hands wrapped around my waist, and he pulled me between his thick legs in one powerful motion.

I squealed and pushed at his chest, but then his fingers were in my hair, gripping the back of my head.

His lips crashed into mine with the hungry, savage energy of a man long deprived of water, and I was a cool spring in the desert. His tongue flicked past my lips, and he groaned deep in his chest, the rumble vibrating beneath my fingertips.

The sharp stubble of his beard rubbed painfully against my chin. But I didn't care.

He smelled of champagne and tasted like whiskey.

His heart pounded beneath my palms, in time with my own, and my eyes fluttered closed as I slid into the heady rhythm.

And then, abruptly, he pulled back.

Stunned speechless, I stared into his eyes, and touched a trembling finger to my lips.

"We're going to Ophelia," he said gruffly.

I gasped. "The tower?"

He nodded and lifted me gently to my seat.

"Ephraim."

"We'll have privacy there. You need time to process the past weeks. We won't be bothered. And it's beautiful."

"I'm sure it is," I whispered.

"My boat's waiting to take us over. We'll be at the dock in less than ten minutes."

Ophelia Island. The private retreat where Ephraim's parents had famously stolen away together. It had been a wedding gift from his father to his mother. Complete with a five-story stone tower only visible to outsiders by boat. Locals referred to the structure as *the castle*, and more than a few otherworldly legends surrounded the island.

But to Ephraim, it was real, and tremendously personal.

His parents' paradise.

And the last place they'd been seen alive together.

I stared out the window, willing my heartbeat to slow. My body buzzed in the afterglow of Ephraim's kiss. But my mind reeled with the implications.

Of all the places he could've arranged to take me.

Almost anywhere.

He'd chosen Ophelia.

Did Ephraim expect something to happen between us tonight?

Did I?

We would be alone. Besides whatever staff was there, of course.

Absolute privacy.

Absolute isolation.

Did he mean to seduce me?

I squeezed my thighs together and pressed my back against the leather seat. If that kiss was any indication, it would take every ounce of willpower to keep my head. But did I want to?

The car pulled to a stop in front of a long, private boat dock. A sleek white cruiser waited at the far end, neon blue lights glowing in the darkness. Several minutes later, I stepped from the wooden dock and onto the vessel. My eyes trained on the name *Constance* displayed in stately script across the back.

Constance. Ephraim's mother.

The yacht was too new for Ephraim's father to have bought and named it.

No, Ephraim had done that.

My heart ached for him.

His broad hand settled on the small of my back as he

guided me ahead of him up a narrow flight of stairs and onto the deck. "A short twenty minutes and we'll be there." His gaze softened. "You must be tired."

"No. I'm far too curious."

His lips twitched. "Curious."

"I've never been to Ophelia."

"I'm well aware."

"Is the inside of the tower as spectacular as they say?"

"You'll judge that for yourself. My mother certainly thought so."

I stared out over the small channel and the black, tossing ocean beyond.

"I'm not going to sleep with you, Ephraim. It would make this too complicated."

"You won't do anything you don't want to, wife."

"I wish you wouldn't call me that."

"That's what you are."

"This is a business arrangement."

"Aren't all marriages?"

"No." I looked up at him. "No, they aren't."

The boat rumbled beneath our feet as the engine kicked into motion. Silence settled between us as we eased away from the shore and into the endless black.

* * *

I didn't know quite what I expected to find there, but Ophelia Island was nothing like what I imagined. Granted, it was midnight, and moonlight cast long shadows across the palm-dotted landscape and the tall, ivy-laden stone tower.

Ephraim explained the structure was originally built by an eccentric Scottish immigrant who wished to feel like he was back at home, accounting for the overtly medieval vibes. It was once used as a civil war outpost, then functioned loosely as a lighthouse for a time, before being bought and renovated by the Carnegies in the early twentieth century. But when the Jekyll Island Club had opened, the family neglected the property in preference of the new social scene. The landmark sat empty for over fifty years until an architect revitalized it and sold it to Ephraim's father.

I stared up at Ophelia tower. The otherworldly place reminded me of the story of Rapunzel. An isolated round, stone tower, surrounded by gardens. And for the next handful of days, I would be the maiden trapped inside.

The interior and furnishings were surprisingly modern, more akin to a Miami resort than a cold museum. Oversized black and white portraits of Ephraim's parents hung in the common area. Sleek, champagne-colored sofas sectioned the room into cozy seating zones, divided by tall ivory columns and a recessed ceiling lit with warm ambient light. Gilded mirrors and long, linen draperies exuded luxury, and large pots housing exotic trees brought life to the space.

"It's stunning, Ephraim."

I spun in a slow circle, taking in all the little luxurious details. "It's like we're a thousand miles away from everything."

"Welcome back, Mr. Callaghan. Mrs. Callaghan, congratulations on your wedding." A woman in a tailored grey top and pencil skirt walked in from an adjoining hallway.

Thank you, Mrs. Smith," Ephraim said. "It's a delight to see you again. My wife has taken the name Callaghan-Darling. All the Darling women keep their name."

"It's an old tradition," I said quickly, noticing the splotches of red that bloomed on the woman's face.

"Pardon me, Mrs. Darling. I didn't realize. I'm Mrs. Smith, the housekeeper here at Ophelia. If you need anything at all, I or the staff will see to it." She motioned to my gown. "At the moment, I'm sure you'd like to see your room."

I nodded. "Yes, please."

Mrs. Smith turned on her heel, as if to lead us, but Ephraim cleared his throat, making her pause.

"We'll find our own way tonight, thank you."

The housekeeper blushed again. A little deeper this time. "Oh. Yes, of course, Mr. Callaghan. There are various refreshments stocked in your room. Everything you might need."

"Thank you. Good night." Ephraim took me by the arm and led me past the blushing woman toward the most imposing of three different alcoves branching out from the common room. We came to a little elevator, complete with brass doors and vintage moldings all around.

It was a tight space, big enough for six people standing close together. The interior was nothing but mirrors, even on the ceiling, and a pale marble floor with the Callaghan insignia in the center. Ephraim pressed the number five on the control panel and the elevator buzzed into motion.

"We're on top. On a clear night, you can see the lights from Darling House in the distance."

I nodded, not sure where to look. Our reflection glittered in every direction.

My white gown, bare shoulders. His black tuxedo, wind-tousled hair. He stared ahead, looking relaxed. But that muscle in his jaw.

I released a shaky breath as the elevator stopped and the doors opened, revealing a decadent, moonlit room. A bedroom.

We'd arrived straight at the bedroom suite.

His hand at my back pressed me forward, and I stepped onto a plush rug. Two sofas sat opposite each other in a cozy seating area near the door.

Across the room, a sleek black headboard crowned a large bed. Satin comforters and a fur blanket lent it a decadently plush look, and I realized how tired I was, and how wonderful it would feel to crawl between the sheets.

"It's been a long day," I said, hating the tremor in my voice.

Ephraim crossed to a built-in wardrobe. "I had some things ordered for you." He pulled a black lace nightgown from a row of clothes and draped it over the back of the sofa.

"That was kind of you. Thanks for seeing me settled in." My stomach flip flopped at the way his eyes narrowed with amusement.

"We're sharing the room, Whitney."

I straightened. "You're afraid the truth would get out if we didn't?"

He shook his head. "Our privacy on Ophelia is absolute." He took a step toward me, leaving the lace gown behind him. "We're sharing my room because we're married." He quirked a brow. "And because I know we both want to."

My cheeks burned so hot they stung. "You're an overconfident ass, Ephraim Callaghan."

"Maybe." He said, huskily. "But I'm not wrong."

I wanted to step back. To turn away from him as he came closer. But I couldn't. I was rooted to the spot.

"You're biting your lip, wife."

I crossed my arms. "Don't call me that."

And then his hands were on my waist, pressing me gently back, until my shoulders pressed against the cool stone wall. His gaze searched mine so intently, I couldn't look away.

"Whitney, be here. With me." His voice rumbled deep in his chest, like thunder over the marsh, making my heart skip. His lips crashed into mine, hard and demanding.

The room bottomed out beneath me, like a boat pitching on a wave. My knees went soft, and I clung to him as if he were the only solid thing in an ocean of night.

His fingers dug into my skin, and he deepened the kiss, his tongue pressing my lips apart, forcing entry. Pleasure snapped and spiraled down my limbs, making me tremble.

He brought his lips to my ear. "Tell me to stop."

I willed my lips to form the words. But they wouldn't.

I should.

But I couldn't say it.

My fists curled into the fabric of his shirt as another anxious tremor shook my core. I forced my gaze up to his.

"Don't."

He stiffened, and for a terrible moment I thought he meant to step away.

But then he growled and pulled me to him, one hand on the small of my back.

"Don't stop," I moaned.

He lifted me in his arms, cradling me tight against him as he carried me to the bed. He lowered me to my feet and twirled me around, his fingers moving to the laces that ran down the back of my gown.

His lips pressed to my shoulder, to my neck, tracing delectable kisses up and down as his fingers flew, and by the time my gown pooled in an ivory puddle on the floor, my chest rose and fell with anxious, unsteady breaths.

He caressed my shoulders, feather-soft, then moved to my back, trailing down my waist and over the thin fabric of my panties, and the curve of my bottom. He pulled me back against him, and his arms wrapped around me from behind, so that his large hands smoothed over my belly, and then higher, grasping my breasts as he dropped his lips to my neck.

Sparks shot white lightning beneath my skin, and I leaned into him on a moan.

"Whitney Darling."

I turned and pressed my hands to his chest. His heart raced, like he'd sprinted a mile, and a for a moment I thought of that day, so long ago on the beach when he'd chased me, and caught me, and kissed me for the first time.

But he wasn't that young man anymore.

He was my husband.

I shivered, and stared up at him, studying the outline of his perfect face, the one I'd dreamed of, and tried to forget. Beneath his tuxedo shirt he was all broad shoulders, muscled arms, and tapered waist, poised, still.

Waiting for my word.

Moonlight streamed in through the windows, bathing us in silver. His ebony waves framed his face, and his eyes glowed with passion and something darker. My gaze dropped to his swollen lips.

If I asked him to, he'd walk away.

If I said the word, all of this would stop.

"Make love to me," I whispered. "Please."

A dangerous light sparked behind his eyes.

"Ephraim, I'm yours."

* * *

My eyes fluttered open, barely focusing beyond the white sunlight that spilled over the hardwoods.

I was naked.

Little goosebumps peppered my skin, kissed awake by the cool morning air, bringing to mind a different type of shiver. I flicked my tongue over my bottom lip. A fresh tremor of pleasure skittered down to my toes at the flurry of erotic memory.

Ephraim's muscled arm lay slung over my waist, and his soft breath tickled the baby hairs at the nape of my neck.

Flashes of the night before danced through my memory, his hair between my fingers, the languid kisses he'd trailed down my neck, over the pearls and across my chest, trailing lower and lower, until he'd tasted and teased and punished every last inch of me with the most delicious, exquisite torture.

Until he'd finally released me. And for a moment I'd been freed of the longing that accompanied every day I'd known in his presence.

For a moment, I was complete. Sated.

Only this morning my desire was back. Stronger than before.

I knew now exactly what it meant to belong to Ephraim Callaghan, mind, soul, and body.

I touched the layered rows of pearls still wrapped around my neck. The necklace was the only thing he hadn't taken off me last night. Now the long strand draped languidly across my pillow, the golden clasp shining in the morning light. My gaze narrowed on the small charms there, the smallest engraved with the initials, *JWP*.

Julia. William. Who was P?

"You're awake." His whisper rumbled against my shoulder, and he tightened his hold, pulling me fully against him.

I twisted around to stare back at him.

His hair was wildly messy, and a thick layer of scruff covered his jaw.

"Wife."

"Husband." I splayed my fingers over his chest, feeling the solid, strong beat of his heart beneath my fingertips.

I studied the fine details of his rugged face, looking for the young man underneath, the one I'd grown up alongside, racing up and down the riverbank, carefree and happy. Until things had changed. "You know, I've watched you so many nights. I've seen you wander down to the boat dock, and disappear onto the marsh, alone. What are you searching for out there in the dark? A ghost?"

Ephraim didn't answer, only trailed a finger along the back of my hand, his touch so light and gentle I almost didn't feel it.

"What would you ask Seth if you found his ghost? What would you say to my brother?"

He sighed, looking resigned, then tucked a strand of hair behind my ear. "I would tell him that I kept my promise."

"Promise?"

"I swore, long after the tide carried him away, that I would protect you. That I would watch over you. Always."

"I suppose with or without my permission."

He grinned, relaxing a little, "Obviously."

"Quite the commitment, seeing as how I'm cursed and all."

"Oh, I've known long before any curse, Whitney Darling." He rolled on top of me, bracing on his forearms, and trapping me between his hard thighs. "I've always known that you will be both the death and the life of me."

He lifted my chin as his lips met mine, and a strong arm wrapped around me in a desperate, tight embrace. His kisses found my neck, the stubble of his beard painfully sweet against my chilled skin. Then he growled deep in his throat, dropping his mouth to my breast.

"I mean to save you back, Ephraim," I raked my fingers through his hair and down his muscled back, pulling him closer as renewed tension bloomed at my core. "I'm here. I'm here now."

He growled again, and buried his face in my soft belly, trailing hot kisses southward, the tender flick of his tongue sending ribbons of delight crisscrossing over and through me, wrapping around my consciousness until all that was left was the heat of him, the press of his big hands, and the delicious, careful work of his fingers.

Then finally, when my body trembled at the edge of oblivion, he met me there, his hips moving in time with my own, in urgent, desperate passion. Higher, faster, wilder. Our breath came fast and the bed groaned like the tossing ocean outside.

"I love you, Ephraim," I whispered, too softly for him to hear, and we crashed back down together, into the hazy, sun swept quiet.

* * *

Relaxed in a way I hadn't known was possible, I sat on the bed watching Ephraim pull on a pair of black joggers. The muscles of his back and arms rippled with the movements.

He winked at me, provoking a fresh blush.

"Solomon told me a story last night," I said. "Just before we left."

"I take it was an interesting one."

"Did you ever hear about a disappearance at Darling House? A long time ago."

"Disappearance?"

"Of a wealthy and powerful man. Not unlike yourself. It was a mystery for decades. I guess it still is. Only no one talks about it anymore."

He shook his head. "It seems unlikely a family as obsessed with the past as yours would forget a tale like that. Were there any other details? A name, for example?"

"Solomon said it happened at a party, and it was the last time the man was seen. He disappeared. No trace of him."

Ephraim was quiet for several moments. "Assuming Solomon wasn't drunk and pulling your leg, Darling House is on the river. Whoever it was had too much to drink, lost his faculties, and got swept away."

A picture of Seth flashed in my mind. How quickly he'd been dragged under. There one moment and gone the next. "I'm sure you're right."

Ephraim nodded and pulled on a black, fitted t-shirt.

"I can't shake the feeling, though, that there's something more to it."

"I've got connections at the Historical Society. I'll make an appointment, and you can play Nancy Drew to your heart's desire." He sauntered over to the bed. "All I know, is that last night," he paused, lifting my chin up so that I met his gaze, "last night was amazing. And I wouldn't change a thing."

"Floating," I whispered, with a coy smile.

He pressed a kiss to my forehead and straightened. "I'm going to check on things downstairs. Can I bring you back a latte?"

I nodded. "I'll be ready to explore Ophelia by the time you get back."

"Oh, wife. Don't assume I have any intention of you leaving this bed anytime soon."

I collapsed back onto the pillows, watching as Ephraim strode across the room, then disappeared into the elevator.

I stretched my arms and legs, letting life bloom in my fingers and toes.

Yesterday I'd woken up Whitney.

Today, I was Whitney Callaghan-Darling. Wife to Ephraim.

"Wife," I whispered, and reached up to touch the strands of pearls at my neck. I loosened the clasp and slid off the necklace, absent-mindedly examining it as my mind whirled around the implications of what I'd done.

Sleeping with Ephraim. No, making love to Ephraim took our situation from complicated, to insurmountable. No longer could I imagine that time and distance would ever be enough to dim the feelings I had for him, or the other-worldly magnetism that existed between us.

What was he thinking now? Were memories of last night making his breath come fast? Making the core of him hot? Did his heart race at the thought of our bodies moving together?

Did he mean to keep me?

He'd said last night, this marriage was nothing but a business-arrangement to him. This was a contract he'd agreed to. Did he mean to abide by the parameters of it?

Would this marriage last only a year?

And did he still plan to go to New York and leave me behind to run Darling Glass alone?

All questions that should have been answered before I let him take me to bed.

He'd done what he promised. He'd saved my family from losing everything. And he would always protect us. He would do whatever was necessary to keep the Darlings safe, and preserve our heritage, as long as he had breath in his body.

But I wasn't a legacy. I was not a grand house by the sea.

I was a woman. One person. One Darling.

Technically, he owed me nothing, promise to my brother or not.

Even after last night.

Sighing, I wrapped the pearls in my hand and slipped from bed, heading into the bathroom.

It was a pretty room, with a glassed-in white marble shower, a clawfoot tub in the corner, and a delicate sink set into the top of a converted antique sideboard. A large, gilded mirror hung over the sink, reflecting the sunlight that shined in the window over the tub.

I turned on the hot water and let the warm liquid run over my hands before bending down to splash my face.

I closed my eyes, releasing a deep, steadying breath.

My cellphone chimed from the bed. It was probably Isla. She'd told me at the wedding that she'd check in on me this morning.

I reached for a towel.

The room went frigid.

A sharp chill skittered down my back.

I pressed the towel to my eyes.

Don't look.

Don't look and it will go away.

Go away.

Go away.

Go away.

A delicate sigh tickled my ear. Ice cold.

I froze. Blood pounded in my ears.

Don't look. Don't look. Don't look.

A frozen fingertip trailed down the length of my bare neck.

I screamed, lurching away. My gaze fell on the mirror.

The woman in white stood behind me. Julia. The clearest I'd ever seen her.

Her eyes were empty, gaping black holes in her pale face. Blonde hair spilled over her shoulders in a mess of crushed curls. Her white satin gown was torn, and a red stain bloomed below her waist, trailing in a waterfall of crimson to her feet. Her long fingers curled into the fabric at her swollen belly.

Her mouth opened, as though she wanted to speak, but no words came.

She stepped toward me, reaching a quivering hand in my direction.

I screamed again and spun to face her.

But nothing was there.

I whirled back to the mirror.

Nothing.

Julia was gone as suddenly as she'd appeared.

My heart pounded a dizzying staccato, and I stumbled back to the bed, pulling my legs beneath me, far from the edge of the mattress.

What had happened? And why was Julia here now?

My gaze darted back to the bathroom and my breath caught in my throat.

There, on the marble floor, was a bright red drop of blood.

Chapter Sixteen

William Darling | 1927

Julia wore a dress of red satin the night I met Solomon Potter. Her sleeves, covered in tiny shining beads capped the edges of her silky shoulders, leaving the crown of her lovely chest and neck bare. Her décolletage, she said it was called. I didn't care what she called it. I wanted to trace the contours of it with my tongue, then trail warm kisses down to her breasts, and lower.

"William, are you listening?" Julia's voice pulled me from my erotic thoughts.

"He's conceptualizing the next great industrial revolution, no doubt," Horace smiled and leaned close to where Layla sat beside him. He whispered something softly in his sister's ear, sending a flush to her cheeks.

"I'm sorry, my love. What did you say?"

Julia shook her head. "I was telling you about the gentleman I met today in the park. He's the most brilliant inventor, here from Boston."

"And what's he invented?"

She gave me a coy smile, twisting a finger through one

of the blonde locks spilling over her shoulder. "Why don't you ask him yourself?" She rose and crossed to the double doors that led from the dining room to the foyer. "Come in, please, sir."

I straightened in my seat, mildly annoyed. I hadn't been prepared for company.

"William Darling, meet Professor Solomon Potter."

I stood and walked around the long table to greet our guest. Solomon was tall, dressed in a well-tailored suit. His honey eyes and midnight skin were highlighted behind a smart pair of tortoise shell glasses. He gave my hand a strong shake and smiled in a way that reminded me of Julia. The kind of smile that made it to a person's eyes.

"It's a pleasure, Mr. Darling. I've heard only good things."

"And I of you. If you've won Julia's endorsement, that makes you good people."

He nodded and grinned over at my beaming wife. "Mr. Darling, I'll get right to the point. I've got something of a new invention, and I think you and I would make a wonderful partnership."

I motioned for him to take a seat at the table. Horace and Layla made pleasant greetings and we all settled in to listen.

"I'm calling them sun spectacles. Now, I didn't invent the concept. People have been using all kinds of materials to shade their eyes for centuries. But the kind of darkened glass I'm picturing – it would revolutionize the accessory. I think everyone will be wearing them, from ladies and gentlemen, to children, to soldiers and sailors."

"Sun spectacles. So regular glasses, but with shaded lenses to block out light."

Solomon nodded. "I'd like you to supply the glass. I'll take care of the rest. We split the profits sixty-forty."

"Well, I'll need to see the product, of course, and test it out. My expenses would be considered, the labor and supplies."

"I've estimated most of it already." Solomon said, adjusting a stylish pair of glasses on the bridge of his nose. "Aside from the specifics of your particular operations, I think you'll find my offer is in the correct range."

"I'm excited to see more. In the meantime, we'd be honored if you'd join us for dinner. We're preparing to eat and there's plenty to go around."

Solomon Potter beamed, "Happy to."

By the end of the meal, I'd resolved to do business with my new acquaintance. Horace and Layla left early their farewells decidedly short, and Julia and I didn't hear from them for several days after.

The following weeks were a blur of prototypes and meetings. Solomon and I spent more and more time together and found that we both had quite a lot in common. We became fast friends and his appearance at our dinner table began to outpace that of even Horace.

"I don't know how to thank you for believing in this," Solomon said to me late one night as we ambled down Bull Street. "I didn't tell you this, but you were the final hope I had in a glass supplier. All the others turned me down."

"I see how it is," I said. "I was your last choice."

"Seriously. I put every dollar I had to my name into this idea. I would have been ruined."

I patted him on the back. "I'm glad the others told you no. As far as I'm concerned, this venture was destined to be. But your friendship means the most of all."

* * *

Horace reclined in one of the leather club chairs in the corner of my office, a glass of bourbon in his hand and a sour look pursing his lips.

"Your face will get stuck like that," I said. "Why the sulking?"

"You know exactly why. You have a new obsession." He tossed his long hair over his shoulder and toyed with the tie at his neck. "A new friend. And it isn't me."

I crossed my arms and leaned a hip against my desk. "You know that isn't true. A business relationship could hardly compete with the bond between you and I. Honestly, I've seen grammar-school girls look less petulant."

"Layla is dejected too. Julia's busier than ever these days."

"She's simply involved in the community. I'm sure Layla would be welcomed at all the same social affairs."

"You know my sister's delicate in nature. She's far too private for all of that." He stood and joined me beside the desk. "You've been working too much. I miss the early times, when we'd spend endless hours smoking cigars under the stars and drinking brandy until the sun rose. I need a party. A Darling party."

"I'm afraid that's out of the question for some time, my friend."

"Out of the question?"

"I've bought an island."

He quirked a pale brow. "Say that again."

"An island. I'm building an estate on it. Darling House. It's to be the most magnificent manor the East Coast has ever seen."

"Oh, William, that's a great waste of money."

"No, it's legacy. My family will pass this house down for generations."

"And who's the architect?"

"A young man Solomon referred me to from Boston. I doubt you've heard of him."

Horace pulled the palm-sized diamond from his pocket and rolled it on the chain back and forth across his hand. "Well, then. If Solomon recommends him, I'm sure he's the best. Who knew cloudy spectacles would amass a fortune to rival Midas?"

"I had a hunch."

"Yes. Hunches come by you quite naturally."

I motioned for Horace to follow me out the door. "I'm off to lunch with Julia. Join us."

"I think not," Horace said. "Layla isn't feeling well. I need to get back to regale her with the pages of a bawdy novel."

"Suit yourself," I said. I grabbed him by the arm as he walked past me, pulling him close. "I know you miss the way things were before. I promise when Darling House is done you and I will host the most extravagant party Savannah's ever seen."

His beautiful face broke into a grin. "Live orchestra and flapper girls with blushing knees and droopy stockings?"

"Julia won't approve of rouged knees."

"Oh, she's naughtier than she lets on."

I guffawed. "Flapper girls it is."

"I hate to wait. But I suppose the longing is half the fun. Don't take too long building your castle." He pressed a quick kiss to my cheek and strolled down the hall with the swagger of a dog who'd found a bone.

"What was that about?" Julia walked up behind me and wrapped her arms around my waist.

"The usual." I turned and pulled her against me. Her perfume tickled my nose, and I buried my face in her neck, tracing the rows of her pearl necklace with kisses.

"I've missed you today," she moaned into my hair.

I smiled and twisted my hand into her skirt, lifting it up past her silky thighs as I backed her into my desk.

"I've missed you too, angel. Why don't you take me to Heaven?"

Chapter Seventeen

Whitney Darling

The days on Ophelia Island, hidden away at the top of Ephraim's tower, passed in a decadent blur of satin sheets and discarded clothing. He never mentioned his plans or the contract that had finally brought us together. But when it came to the unspoken things, the physical manifestations of years behind us, there were no more secrets. I knew now, he had craved me as hopelessly as I had him. I could feel it in the way he touched me, in the reverent way his fingers trailed my length, and the ravenous way his lips captured mine.

I lay in his bed, on our sixth and final morning there, my eyes tracing the hard curves of his muscled chest and thighs. Thighs that had routinely parted my own so he could bury himself in the softest, most secret part of me, again and again and again.

"Will you leave for New York soon?"

He smirked, not bothering to lift his beautiful head from where it rested against the headboard. "Would you like me to?"

"No," I said, not hesitating.

He smiled a little at that, revealing the dimple in his cheek. "I'll go eventually. But they'll survive a while longer on their own."

I tried hard not to show how happy his words made me. Despite the walls I'd spent years building, Ephraim was making short work of them, one by one. And all it had taken was a week on this island. In Ephraim's bed.

"Do you have a large team there?"

He nodded.

"How large?"

"A few hundred people. But I mostly interact with the board. Which is more like twenty particularly entitled people."

"Do you enjoy it?"

"Enjoyment isn't the point. Many people and their families count on my ability to guide our company in the right direction."

"That's a lot of responsibility."

"I was born to it. Like you."

I thought that over for a moment. How often as a young woman had I bristled under my obligation to Darling Glass, the constant voice in my head, driving me toward some ephemeral form, made solid only in the heat of the glass-blower's furnace? But now, having experienced so much, the weight felt more welcome. Almost desirable in its familiarity.

Did Ephraim feel the same? Had New York become the place he went to escape the loss and chaos in Savannah? If so, I couldn't blame him, though, the ocean of skyscrapers and people could never compare to the wild marsh, or the grey Atlantic that kissed the shores of Darling House.

"Have you ever seen a ghost on Ophelia Island?"

He shook his head. "Not that I recall. But then, I've

never been one to see them as easily as the Darlings seem to. Why? Did you see my parents dancing on the beach?"

His words took me off guard and I sat up. "Have you?"

"No," he chuckled.

Despite coming close, I hadn't yet told Ephraim about my ghostly encounter in the bathroom.

"Ephraim, I think Julia followed me here."

"Julia Darling?" His eyebrows rose. "What makes you think that?"

"I saw her. In the bathroom mirror."

"Did you turn around three times first and chant? I've heard that's how that works."

I swatted his arm. "This isn't a joke. Blood was all over, and she kept grasping at her belly. I think she might've been pregnant."

His brows drew together. "Julia died an old woman."

"I know. You keep reminding me of that. But it's what I saw. What if she's trying to tell me something?"

He turned to look at me, his eyes serious, "I'm not good at these things, Whitney. You know I leave the dead to their death and dying. It's dangerous to do otherwise."

"I know. But what am I supposed to do?"

"Ignore her."

"It doesn't work that way."

"Then go to Solomon for more sage and cedar. Pray in the corners. Bathe in holy water. But I don't want you encouraging this."

"I didn't ask her to come."

"That doesn't change the fact that I don't want you following some paranormal rabbit trail. Things are complicated enough right now. Let Julia bother someone else. She's got nothing but time."

"Ephraim."

"That's it, Whitney. That's my answer. We'll stop by Solomon's place on our way back to Darling House."

I stiffened. "I'm sorry, did you think I was asking your permission?"

His gaze softened, and he tucked a strand of hair behind my ear. "I'm not trying to be short with you. But for a little longer, can we let the dead be dead?"

I wanted to argue. To explain to him that these things weren't as easy as bundles of herbs and the resolve to ignore them. But the earnest look in his eyes, the way the muscles in his neck tensed, this wasn't a subject he felt comfortable discussing. Not now.

And I understood. The past days had been a dream, an erotic, languid intermission from circumstances that only became more confusing, and more dangerous with each passing day. And if I was honest, neither was I ready to step out of the cozy sanctuary Ophelia offered.

I lay back down beside him, willing, for now, to let the topic rest. There were only a few more hours before we returned to Darling House.

Ephraim slid his fingers along the contour of my naked hip, pulling me away from the questions that whirred in the back of my mind. I turned on my back, wrapping my arms around his muscled waist as he shifted above me. His lips found my neck, then my ear. He groaned as he eased into me, stealing my breath.

But the little voice persisted.

Something was going on. Something bigger than either of us. And, if my intuition was right, it all had to do with the disappearance at Darling House. This wasn't all a coincidence. Solomon knew something. He'd brought up the story to me on purpose.

And if I was going to stop the curse, if I was going to

protect my family, and keep this man, I needed to find out why.

* * *

My boots sank into the mud with each step, as if the earth tried to wrestle me beneath the surface, ensuring I never discovered the answers to my questions.

The enormous Victorian house down the lane was painted from ground to roof in a pale shade of haint blue, reminding me of the grand conservatory and the mysterious locked door back at Darling House. But unlike the haunted door, with its eleven locks, Solomon's home appeared fresh and inviting, a beacon of bright color in the expanse of marsh all around. Like Darling House, it had been here for a long time. Since at least the turn of the twentieth century, cradling within it the many treasured generations of his family.

A pair of brown boots lay on the porch, next to a white wicker chair with an olive Barbour field jacket slung over its arm. Stacks of marshgrass baskets were strewn on the far end of the porch beside a cushioned swing. One of them overflowed with green and yellow palmetto flowers, each woven to look alike. A long fishing pole sat propped against the door frame. As I neared, I caught the distinct scent of Solomon's famous shrimp and grits wafting through the screen door. My stomach rumbled and my mouth watered. I should've had a bigger breakfast, but the prospect of leaving Ophelia Island this morning had stolen my appetite. Ephraim hadn't eaten much either, and after one last tryst in his giant bed atop the stone tower, we had stepped onto the *Constance* and returned to Savannah.

Ephraim had received a call from New York shortly

after climbing into the car, and so he'd motioned me to go ahead of him when we'd pulled up to Solomon's.

I reached for the heavy brass knocker on the door frame.

Today was about answers.

The origin of the curse. The break-ins at Darling House.

Alistair's letters. His death.

And an almost-forgotten unsolved disappearance.

I rapped the knocker three times, the sound reverberating off the porch ceiling and into the stately foyer.

A moment later Solomon appeared from around a corner and came toward me, a grin on his face. "My Whitney girl. Your Aunt Rose texted me you'd be coming by." He swung the screen door open and ushered me inside.

"I don't remember telling her," I said, as I followed him into the front parlor. "I don't think I told anyone."

"Well, you know Rose. She also reminded me that shrimp and grits is your favorite, and that you'd arrive hungry. Luckily, I had some bacon grease in the pan and a fresh catch of shrimp in the fridge. Oh, and my garden boy, Davy, brought some of the most delicious Vidalia onions I ever tasted. I sliced one open for us."

"Thank you," I said. "But you shouldn't have gone to all that trouble."

"You're hungry, aren't you?"

"Starving, actually."

He nodded and motioned for me to follow.

We walked through the front parlor and dining room, past an oak table, and through a narrow little hallway into the kitchen. It smelled like Heaven. And not only because of the shrimp and grits. This room had served up generations of mouthwatering southern food, and you could tell.

Solomon pointed to the butcher block table in the

middle of the room. "Have a seat. It won't be five minutes before we can dig in."

"I apologize for dropping in this way." I slid into an antique cane chair, letting my gaze drift over the many framed paintings and portraits covering the walls.

"Don't think twice about it."

"How have you been doing since the wedding?"

"Fine. Fine, child. I've been fine."

"One more fine and I'll think something's up."

"Nothing, aside from getting old," he said. "The real question is, how are you? I bet your nerves are as fluffed as a cat caught in a tumble dryer. Hopefully, your husband was able to remedy that a little."

"I tried my best." Ephraim's deep voice made me whirl. He stood, casually leaning against the door frame. He winked at me, sending an instant, embarrassing flush to my cheeks.

"Welcome, son." Solomon motioned to the table. "Have a seat."

"Thank you." Ephraim slid gracefully into the chair across from me.

"Whitney was about to tell me about the honeymoon. Savannah has been abuzz with speculation as to where you were headed."

"Ophelia Island," I said.

Solomon turned on his heel and pinned Ephraim with a surprised, if not approving stare. "I'm happy to hear it."

"We stopped by to see if you might be of assistance," Ephraim said. "Whitney's in need of some sage and cedar. Or something stronger if you have it."

"Got a ghost?"

"Something like that," I said.

"Julia, I imagine." Solomon set two steaming bowls in

front of Ephraim and me. "I've got some bundles. But I doubt it'll do any good. She's stubborn, that one. Desperate, if you ask me."

"What?" Ephraim growled the word more than spoke it.

"She gave Alistair a hell of time before he passed." He studied me as though gauging how much I already knew. "I suppose he didn't put that in his letters to you, either. What was the point of those letters, I wonder?"

"I need to know what you know," I said. "Granddaddy was convinced there was some detail from our family's past come back to haunt us. At first, I thought he simply meant the curse, but with the break-in, and then the disappearance you mentioned the other night, I'm wondering if there's something more."

Solomon sat down between Ephraim and I, his bowl of food casting a tall, winding trail of steam. "Your Granddaddy was a troubled man at the end, Whitney. I'll admit there were days I wondered if he was losing his faculties, as some older folks do."

"He was sharp as a tac," Ephraim said.

"He believed Julia was directing him toward a secret," Solomon said. "Something that happened before, but that somehow matters now. Sent him on a hell of a goose chase. Hours of research and digging through old books and albums."

"Did he find anything?" Ephraim and I asked at the same time.

"Well, he learned of the disappearance I told you about." He tapped his forehead. "At least, I think I told you about that. I was a little tipsy by the end of the wedding. But I could have sworn – "

"Yes, you told me," I said, trying to remain patient. "But you couldn't remember many details."

Solomon sighed, looking a little sheepish. "Well, here's what I know. It happened nearing on a hundred years ago now, 1932, I believe. After the Depression forced William and Julia Darling to the house on the island. They hid their troubles well. Not that the glass would've ever left them destitute. You know for yourself how well they did in time. There was a party one night at the house. A whole bunch of rich folks showed up to congratulate one another on having outmaneuvered the worst economic crisis in history."

"The night of the disappearance?"

Solomon nodded. "A wealthy businessman, well-known at the time, was in attendance. He was seen by all sorts of important people, schmoozing and flirting, and then he was gone." He tapped a finger on the table. "I do remember now. His name, I believe, was Horace Leroux. By all accounts, he was one of the first people your William Darling did business with here in the states."

"Were they friends?"

"So, it would seem. Though, on paper there isn't much account outside their financial relationship."

"And you think the Darlings had something to do with the disappearance?"

"All we know for sure, is William loved Julia more than life itself. A love like that makes a man dangerous. Makes a man capable of all manner of violent, secret things."

"You can't think he killed Horace?"

"I have no idea. It could've been one of the other guests. Or Horace got too drunk at the party and stumbled into the river. The last interesting detail your Granddaddy found before he died was that it was shortly after Horace disappeared, that Julia Darling had the conservatory painted haint blue. He wondered if there was some connection."

Solomon massaged the back of his neck. "Or Julia just liked blue. Who knows?""

I narrowed my eyes at him. "There has to be more."

"I'm sure there is. But it's beyond me. This is your family curse to break, Whitney Darling." He took a sip of tea. "That monstrosity of a house is full of undiscovered secrets. I imagine you'll learn a lot quickly if you follow your nose. Which room gives you the worst case of heebie-jeebies? That's a good place to start."

The blue door at the bottom of the conservatory stairs loomed tall in my mind's eye. I worried my lip. "Did Grand-daddy tell you if he believed in the curse?"

"Believed in it too much if you ask me," Solomon shook his head. "Something like that'll tear you up from the inside if you give it credence. That's the thing with curses. They have to be believed to work. Tell a man he's cursed, it's up to him if he believes you. He does, he's cursed."

"That's exactly what I told her," Ephraim said.

I narrowed my eyes at him.

Solomon crossed his arms. "I could be wrong."

I leaned back in my chair. "None of this is making me feel much better."

"Life ain't about feeling good, honey. Life's about doing good. Might never feel good at all. Learn that, and a whole host of troubles will pass you on by."

I avoided Ephraim's cocky grin. "Do you know anything else about Horace?"

"Afraid not."

"I told Whitney that I have an acquaintance at the Historical Society," Ephraim said. "She's a bit of a sleuth. Stubborn. Smart. She'd be able to find the information we're looking for."

Solomon gave the table an enthusiastic slap. "There

now. A viable direction." He motioned to the steaming bowls in front of us. "Now, dig in. I've got business in town this afternoon. And I know y'all are excited to get back to Darling House."

* * *

Less than an hour later, our car pulled up to the imposing, white mansion.

The sky was a deep grey and great billowing clouds, pregnant with rain, hovered above.

"You ready for this?" Ephraim teased.

"Not exactly."

I turned in the seat, meeting his gaze. I'd already sensed him step back into boss mode since we'd left Ophelia. Gone was the devil-may-care grin, replaced now with a cool and aloof seriousness. I supposed they were the traits that made so many women obsessed with him. But they didn't know Ephraim the way I did. They didn't know his brooding toughness was a mask he wore. One that allowed him to navigate a chaotic world.

"I know what it meant for you to take me to Ophelia." I rested my hand on his thigh. "Thank you."

He lifted my hand to his lips and pressed a lazy kiss there. "I'll take you back. I promise."

He slid out of the car and walked around to open my door.

Whitney. Whhiiitney.

I stiffened. The glass.

Even on Ophelia, I'd heard it. But here it was loud as ever.

My gaze flickered to Ephraim's as I stood. Of course, he hadn't heard it.

No one could anymore but me.

A lonely thought.

Ephraim took my hand and led me up the front stairs and toward the glossy black doors.

But before we took two steps across the porch, the doors flew wide.

Percy, followed by my mother, Adele, and Addison spilled from the threshold in a flurry of smiles and laughter.

Rose in her wheelchair brought up the rear, baby Alice cradled comfortably in her lap. "Well, if it isn't the newlyweds."

Ephraim chuckled. "Something tells me y'all were expecting us."

Rose's lips twisted into a cute, demure smile. "Solomon might've texted and let us know you'd left his place."

Francis appeared in the doorway over Rose's shoulder, looking markedly more serious. He wore a white linen button-down, his blonde hair brushed back from his handsome, stern face. "Welcome back."

"Thank you," I said.

"Ephraim, once you get settled, I need to speak with you," Francis said.

Ephraim nodded, "How about now?"

"Everything alright?" I asked.

"Everything's wonderful, dear." My mother wrapped an arm over my shoulders. "There's a fresh pot of coffee. I want to hear every detail about the mysterious Ophelia Island."

"Maybe not every detail," Addison snickered.

I gasped and swatted her arm as I allowed the little gaggle of women to steer me toward the parlor and the kitchen beyond. But not before I looked back to see Ephraim disappear with Francis into the study, shutting the door silently behind them.

Chapter Eighteen

Whitney Darling

Five days and four sleepless nights later, I listened to an audiobook as I ambled to the kitchen, the narrator's soothing tone helping to calm my nerves. I'd formed a habit of playing something any time I was alone somewhere in the house, even for short periods of time. The perception of constant company made it feel less likely something spooky would materialize. The more chipper the better.

Right now, I needed coffee. And lots of it. I couldn't blame all my lack of sleep since our return to Darling House on fear of things that went bump in the night. Ephraim had certainly played his role, keeping me occupied in bed late into the evenings, proving to me that the range of his passions extended far beyond anything I could've imagined.

But despite our time in the sheets, there were still mysteries between us. Like what he and Francis had been discussing the day we returned from Ophelia. I'd asked him more than once, but he refused to tell me. Saying only that he didn't want to worry me needlessly. An answer that irritated me to no end, and only made my curiosity that much stronger.

So, I'd kept busy, spending most of my time getting reacquainted with the glass studio, going over incoming orders, and familiarizing myself with the upcoming calendar of events. Not to mention, my responsibilities concerning *Darling & Potter*, with which Ephraim was proving to be a big help.

I hadn't yet blown any glass, despite the annoying insistence from the glass itself.

One day it asked to be a paperweight, the next a vase, tinkling chimes, blue bottles, a set of bowls – the list of things it wanted to be grew. And as usual, its desires lined up perfectly with the orders that rolled in.

I'd continued to let the managerial oversight of the *Darling & Potter* sunglass factory in town fall to Monica, as well as any basic orders to be fulfilled at the studio on the island. She was more than qualified. No one, besides Seth or I, had spent as much time training alongside Granddaddy over the years. And I knew she cared for the business as deeply as any of us. Her family had been with Darling Glass almost from the beginning, after all.

But there was coming a day, soon, when we would get a request for something custom Darling. A chandelier that would require my unique talents to complete.

Today, though, was not that day.

Today Ephraim and I had an appointment at the Historical Society downtown, and we weren't going to leave until we'd found some answers about Mr. Horace Leroux.

I removed my earbuds as I came to the bottom of the steps and into the foyer, then slowed at the sound of women's chatty voices coming from the kitchen. Aunt Rose, Isla, and Monica all sat around the breakfast table, a spread of notebooks and colorful catalogues between them. They looked up in unison as I entered.

"Well, hello, sunshine. Kind of you to join us." Rose cast me a wry grin.

"Oh, don't give her a hard time," said Isla. "She's a newly married woman. Imagine the delightful distractions vying for her attention."

Monica looked annoyed. "You didn't forget about our meeting, did you? The gala will be here before we know it, and there's a ton to do."

Realization dawned. I'd absolutely forgotten about the gala meeting this morning. I reached for an oversized coffee mug. "I remembered," I lied. "I needed a few extra minutes to get ready. I've got an appointment at the Historical Society once we're done here."

Monica cast me a side-eye, looking unconvinced, but she didn't press the issue.

"Well, come join us," said Rose. "There's a fresh cheese danish here, and some cinnamon rolls Monica's mother sent over."

I slid into a chair, avoiding Monica's censorious gaze. "What are we discussing today? Seating charts? Décor?"

"Floral arrangements," Monica said. "I'm thinking vases and vases of white lilies."

Naturally. I wrinkled my nose.

"White roses are a good compromise," Isla chimed. "Or white carnations. People write them off as a cheaper flower, but they do lend themselves to the most gorgeous bouquets."

"I like the idea of roses," Rose said with a sweet grin. "Classic and sophisticated like our Alistair."

I nodded and Monica made a notation in her notebook. "Roses it is." She pulled a fresh stack of papers from her satchel. "Now, I think it would be lovely if we could recruit some local sponsors to help pull the event together. I don't believe it will be hard to find several. I'm thinking Levy Jewelers, Genteel & Bard's history tour company, or one of the cultural heritage societies. Whitney, do you think you'd be up to approaching our sponsorship candidates in person? Certainly, now that you're not only a Darling, but a Callaghan-Darling, you'll have all of Savannah at your feet."

I took a bite of cheese danish, savoring the creamy flavor, as I tried to muster up a response other than a simple denial. I was terrible at networking. Outside of the kind of laid-back waterfront events we used to attend when I was little, the Savannah social scene was not my forte. It wasn't that I hadn't wanted it to be, but I was too shy and private, which usually presented as awkward. "I'm not the best person for that job. But I'm glad to help organize any of the behind-the-scenes details."

Monica looked peeved. "I suppose Isla can take on the sponsorship acquisitions." She turned to Isla. "Do you think your brother would like to sponsor?"

Isla shrugged her thin shoulders with an easy-going smile. "I'm sure Asher will be happy to."

"I need another cup of coffee," Monica said, getting up from her seat and walking over to the counter.

"What's this appointment you have with the Historical Society?" Isla asked. "Anything we'd find interesting?"

"A little Darling House research. My own curiosity."

Rose tapped the table in front of her. "Keep in mind, if you go searching for answers, you'll sometimes find them."

I nodded, scraping the last of the cream cheese from my plate, "In this case, I'm hoping so."

Monica sat down, steaming mug in hand. "I think it's

great how invested you are in your family history. Our legacies are the most valuable things we have in this world. Lose your heritage and lose your truest fortune."

"Well said, dear." Aunt Rose lifted her coffee mug in toast.

"Alright," I said, "let's get down to business."

* * *

The gala meeting wrapped in time for me to make a quick sandwich before joining Ephraim in front of the house, where he reminded me that in the professional realm, fifteen minutes early was considered punctual. And I reminded him that he was a pompous ass.

Which, of course, ended with us stumbling to the bedroom, ensuring we'd be delightfully late.

Now Ephraim navigated downtown Savannah traffic as I shuffled through the oldies tracks on his phone. The sight of the majestic Hostess City sprawled around us in all her stately, historic splendor.

Rain fell in intermittent torrents, leaving deep puddles along the old brick and flagstone sidewalks. Wet moss hung heavily from giant Live Oaks that lined the streets like wise and silent guardians. Curses aside, it had been a blessing growing up in Savannah, beneath the gaze of extraordinary architecture and manicured nature, bursting with creeping ivy and hidden intrigues.

Ephraim stopped at a crosswalk, letting a group of women cross the street in front of us. Each of them was dressed in matching t-shirts, while the woman in the center sported a sash over her shoulders emblazoned with *Bride* in sequined letters. They'd obviously been drinking, and they openly ogled Ephraim through the windshield as they passed, giggling, and calling out things to him that made me blush.

Ephraim chuckled. "What would Savannah be without our bachelorette parties?"

"Classier," I quipped.

He grinned. I raised my eyebrow. I'd seen the piece written about him in South Magazine. Savannah's Most Eligible Playboy, my ass. "I suppose half-dressed women staggering to brunch isn't something that bothers a man like you."

"More than you'd guess. But not as much as you'd like."

"And why would I care?"

He smirked. "Oh, you care."

I refused him the satisfaction of a reply.

We parked near the Kessler Mansion, less than a block from the Historical Society that stood tall and stately at the corner of Gaston and Whitaker Streets. It had been years since I'd been inside the illustrious building, the last time for research on a history paper in college. It had been an intimidating place then, with row after row of bookshelves crammed with books, cases of old letters, and artifacts.

It had been renovated since then, so, I wasn't sure what to expect other than the usual feeling of overwhelm, and the desperate sense that I was in over my head.

But I needed answers.

And this was the most obvious place to find them.

Ephraim took my hand as we approached the columned building that looked more like a gothic mansion than a glorified library. He reached for the door handle when his phone rang. He pulled it from his pocket, his eyes narrowing at the screen.

"I need to take this. You go ahead. I'll meet you inside."

I nodded, as he pushed the door open for me, then I

entered through a series of doors before coming to the main hall where a sweet-looking woman with hair like cotton and little wireless earbuds sticking out of her ears rounded the corner.

"Hello, there." Her Lowcountry accent was so strong she might as well have been singing.

"Hello." I smiled back. "How are you?"

"Enjoying this beautiful day. Forsyth Park is a sparkling diamond."

Was this woman Ephraim's acquaintance?

"I'm here to do some research," I said. "On my family home, and an event that happened there a long time ago. My husband arranged a meeting for me here today. I believe he's acquainted with the director."

"Certainly, dear." She motioned for me to follow, leading me past a few rows of bookshelves before coming to a wooden reference desk. My stomach sank as I spied a beautiful, but serious-looking woman standing there. She looked up at me with an intelligent, censorious gaze.

"Miss Walker," the older woman said. "This young lady's here to do some research on her family home. Her husband arranged an appointment for her."

"Thank you, Cornelia." The woman's eyes swept over me with unveiled contempt. "I'm happy to help. Darling House is quite the historical landmark."

"Oh, Darling House," Cornelia exclaimed, clasping her hands together. "What a blessed little bee you are. That place is positively magical. I don't think I've ever seen a prettier Georgian mansion. And I've toured old homes from Mobile to Winston-Salem."

"Thank you," I stammered. I could feel my cheeks heating, and I wasn't sure if it was more from Cornelia's gushing, or the darts flying at me from Evangeline's pupils.

Ephraim had arranged for us to meet with Evangeline. *Seriously?*

Studiously avoiding further notice of her lithe figure, I swallowed the burst of anger that welled up my throat and forced a pleasant smile. I smoothed a hand over the leather satchel slung over my shoulder. "I'm here because I heard about a disappearance at Darling House around a century ago. I was hoping I might find more information in an old newspaper, or police records."

Ephraim chose that moment to approach our little group from behind, his warm hand coming to rest on the small of my back.

I stiffened, though the perturbed look on Evangeline's face was a tiny victory.

"Ah," Cornelia said, putting her hands on her hips. "My grandmother told me all about that particular tragedy when I was a young girl."

"You've heard the story?" I tried, and instantly failed, to temper the enthusiasm in my voice.

Cornelia nodded. "My grandmother wasn't there, of course. My family wasn't fancy enough to be invited. But her employers were. It's a strange tale, let me tell you."

Evangeline raised a sculpted eyebrow. "As fascinating as that sounds, I'm afraid hearsay isn't the same as documentation." She turned to me. "I'll see what I can find. Wait here, please."

Cornelia smiled awkwardly.

"Is she always like that?" I asked.

"More often than not," Cornelia said. "Brilliant people can be difficult. Comes with the package."

Ephraim cleared his throat. Was this making him uncomfortable? I hoped so.

"I think there's often merit to hearsay," I murmured.

"Would you mind sharing what your grandmother told you?"

"Of course. It may not be official."

I nodded and leaned closer, as if we weren't the only three people standing in the big room.

"My grandmother had it on good authority that the event that night was the most extravagant the city had seen since the Great Depression. More than a few of the country's most influential people were in attendance. Think the men who started the Federal Reserve. It was the kind of party where a lot more than dancing happens, if you know what I mean. This gathering was about business as much as it was about pleasure."

"Do you know anything about Horace Leroux, the man who disappeared?" Ephraim asked.

She shook her head. "I'm afraid not. It's been a long time since I've heard talk of that mystery, and my mind's not what it used to be. I do know that he vanished with a priceless Egyptian diamond. And my grandmother swore up and down that her employer told her that she'd heard the distinct sound of a gunshot."

"A gunshot?"

"Yes. She'd gotten turned around looking for the bathroom. Heard the voices of men arguing, and then - gunshot."

"Did the police believe her?" I asked.

"Oh, honey." Cornelia looked at me like I'd misplaced my marbles. "That isn't the sort of thing you disclose to the law. Not in circles like that."

Cornelia straightened at the approaching click of Evangeline's heels, stepping away moments before the other woman appeared.

"Surprisingly enough, I found a newspaper article about the disappearance." She placed a thick, leather-bound notebook on the table, then flipped it open to a weathered, brown page, protected with a clear sheet of plastic."

"Thank you," I said, as Ephraim and I joined her. "We shouldn't be too long."

She nodded, not bothering to make eye contact, "Let me know when you're through."

I slid into a wooden chair, my gaze already sweeping the aged paper. Ephraim stood at my side, his hip against my shoulder.

A black and white photo graced the top of the article, featuring a group of young socialites at a black-tie affair. I tried to make out the background, to place where they were on the estate, but the photo was a close-up.

Two of the four individuals I recognized immediately.

Julia was stunning, dressed in a white gown, her neck dripping with pearls and diamonds. Her long hair was twisted in a chignon that spilled into curling tendrils over her shoulder. Even on the old paper, her happiness was plain to see. Her eyes gleamed and, despite her intimidating appearance, her wide, sweet smile made her look friendly and approachable. William stood beside her, handsome and proud. One arm wrapped around Julia's waist, highlighting a pregnant belly.

"Pregnant," Ephraim said. "And she looks like you, only blonde."

I nodded tightly as a vision of Julia's ghost in the bathroom, her fingers clenching her blood-soaked gown, flashed across my mind. I forced my gaze from hers to study the beautiful woman standing at her side.

Instead of Julia's coloring, this woman had long, mousy hair, and eyes that overpowered her face. And unlike Julia's happy expression, this woman looked tired - almost sad.

I traced a finger along her jawline. It was the face of someone who'd lost something. Or someone.

My gaze flicked to the man beside her. They had many of the same features, though his hair was pale like Julia's. They shared the same bone structure and stature, down to the way they stood, shoulders back, chins tilted upward.

Everything about the man screamed wealth, from his coat jacket to the large, glittering jewel that dangled from a chain in his hand. It seemed to glitter even here, on century-old paper.

My eyes dipped to the caption beneath the photo.

Horace Leroux. And his sister, Layla.

And there, above the photo, was the headline, in bold, black letters.

BUSINESSMAN LEROUX GOES MISSING.
LEAVES NO TRACE.

It was strange to see his face. He looked nothing like I'd imagined.

He was young.

And handsome.

Strikingly so. He rivaled William in that. But whereas William's features were square and aquiline, Horace's were fair, almost ethereal.

He was captivating.

I scanned the text of the article, my eyes dancing back and forth over mostly innocuous details, the kinds of things journalists wrote when they didn't have any substance to report.

Leroux was last seen the night of a party at the
Darling Estate. His automobile was discovered the

morning after, half-sunk in the marsh. No trace of Leroux has been found. Authorities do not suspect foul play. The investigation is ongoing.

That was it then.
Not much to go on.
Except one rather important fact.
Horace Leroux wasn't the only thing to go missing that night. So had his priceless Egyptian diamond.

Chapter Nineteen

Whitney Darling

When we arrived home following our meeting at the Historical Society, there were two things I knew for sure.

One. I had a clear direction in which to conduct my search - find out as much as I could about Horace Leroux, his connection with the Darlings, and the missing Egyptian diamond.

Two. I was royally pissed at Ephraim.

Which was something of a conundrum, because if it hadn't been for his help, however distastefully arranged, I would lack the clearest bit of information we'd found yet.

Dark clouds, black with unshed rain hung low as we parked in the circular front drive. The air sparked with energy, as if lightning would strike at any moment. I braced against the roar of wind tumbling like waves over the marsh and tossing Atlantic beyond.

The house stood tall and immovable at the edge of chaos. I scanned the upper floors, narrowing my eyes at the shadowed windows, looking for some sign of movement, a flicker of blonde hair or white fabric. But all was still.

"Y'all, get in here!" Adele stepped on the porch and motioned for us to hurry. "Heaven's about to open. You'll be soaked."

Ephraim and I sprinted across the drive and up the steps.

"You look like someone walked over your grave." She pursed her lips. "Bad luck finding what you wanted?"

Ephraim shook his head, "We're hungry. Whitney's on the edge of violence."

"Aw, well. There's fresh soup on the stove. Help yourself."

Though the storm headed for Charleston, offshoots of thunderstorms and heavy winds often reached farther south to Beaufort and Savannah. By dinner time, we'd received reports of a water spout off North Beach on nearby Tybee Island, but nothing conclusive. Several things we knew for sure, the tide would rise, the old leak in the attic would start up again, and the power would go out.

Fortunately, this time we were through with the meal and discussing what flavors of ice cream we had in the freezer to go with the cinnamon rolls Adele pulled out of the oven as the lights flickered out. There was nothing worse than a half-baked cinnamon roll.

Two dozen candles illuminated the parlor. I leaned back against Ephraim, who I'd temporarily decided to forgive once the lights went out. A fire crackled in the over-sized fireplace. I breathed deeply the smoky wood scent.

"Tell the story about the skeleton in the wall," Percy said.

When I'd been little that had been one of my favorites too.

Ephraim winked at Percy. "What about the ghost of Alice Riley stealing children in Wright Square?"

"Nope." Percy shook his head. "That one's too scary. The hidden skeleton. Tell that one."

"Alright." Ephraim scratched his chin. "I think I remember the details."

Percy scooted closer on the wool rug. His pale hair glowed warm in the light of the fire, and his little blue and white striped pajamas made him look cuddlier than usual.

"Once, there was a beautiful woman named Honoria Foley." Ephraim's deep voice filled the quiet parlor. "She lived in a striking home on Chippewa Square – one that she had converted into a boarding house after the death of her husband and daughter. Her son-in-law, James, and his small children lived there as well. James had been a bricklayer, turned businessman, and he worked hard to support and protect his family.

One day, I hear it was a rainy, gloomy day in October, a visitor arrived at the Foley House Inn. A well-to-do businessman named Wally. He was handsome and charismatic, the type of man that would've made a good husband to Honoria. He was boarding for several weeks, and over that time, he let it be known he was fascinated with his hostess. He complimented Honoria. He did her favors around the house. He brought her gifts. He asked her questions about her life. Lots of them. Until after a while, it started to bother her.

One evening, Wally declared his love for Honoria in the parlor, and asked her to marry him. But she refused and retreated upstairs for the night. She took her time getting ready, leisurely fastening the buttons of her long, white flowing nightgown, brushing her hair, arranging her pillows, all to the light of a candle standing in a brass candlestick by the bed."

Ephraim's voice took on a more serious timber.

"Soon, Honoria blew out the candle and climbed beneath the covers, closing her eyes to the inky black room, and slowly drifted to sleep. But after a few minutes she heard a sound. Almost like a footstep in the hall, or the soft creak of the door. She lay stone still, listening, ears straining. And then all at once, someone leapt from the darkness. Strong fingers wrapped around her throat, pushing her down into the pillows.

She couldn't breathe. She couldn't scream.

She struggled, her arms fighting and flailing, until her fingers brushed against the cool brass of the candlestick beside her. With one final, brave effort, she grasped the heavy tool and brought it down hard on the head of her attacker.

The hands at her neck spasmed then released her, followed by a loud thud.

After several moments, Honoria peeked over the edge of the mattress. And as her eyes adjusted to the darkness, she made out the form of a man."

"Wally!" Percy shouted.

Ephraim nodded solemnly. "Honoria leapt from the bed and lit another candle. Bright red blood pooled around Wally's head. He was dead.

Honoria's mind buzzed. She was a single woman. Wally was an important, well-known businessman. Who would believe that he'd attacked her? Would they call her act a crime of passion? Would she be tried for murder? Would she hang?

No. No one could know what had happened there that night.

She sat still, trying to think. Until a brilliant idea came to her." Ephraim lifted a brow. "And can you guess what she did?"

Percy nodded his little head, eyes wide.

"Fast forward over one-hundred years. Honoria is long dead. Forgotten is the disappearance of the famed business-man, Wally. Renovations are being done to the Inn. A wall in Honoria's bedroom had to come down.

"But as the workers broke through the brick, they found not the room on the other side of the wall, but a narrow gap and another wall of brick. One of them passed over a flashlight, and what did they find there in the space between the walls?"

"Wally's skeleton. Top hat and all!" Percy shouted.

"Okay, that's enough of that." Addison reached for Percy, but he laughed and darted away from her.

"Was his ghost there too?"

Ephraim nodded. "They say when the wall was busted through, it released his ghost for good. He can still be seen today, standing in the courtyard, staring up at the house, his top hat in his hand."

"Whoa," Percy said.

"Yes, *whoa*," Addison snickered. "Come on, sir. It's bedtime."

"Can I sleep in your room tonight?" Percy asked, as my sister pulled him into her arms.

"I don't imagine you'll take no for an answer." Addison rolled her eyes comically at Ephraim as she ushered Percy from the room.

"I think it's safe to say you're his favorite uncle." I grinned.

"Boys need to feel fear sometimes." Ephraim picked up the fireplace poker and stoked the pile of glowing coals. "How else will they become brave?"

It was on the tip of my tongue to say our family was brave enough. Instead, I rested back against Ephraim's legs and stared ahead into the dancing flames, letting the warmth on my face lull me into a waking sleep.

Missing, murdered businessmen.

Forgotten secrets.

Curses.

Was my life a gloomy fairytale? On par with legends that sent little boys to bed afraid?

After a long time, Ephraim's hand squeezed my shoulder. "It's late."

"The fire feels so good, though."

He leaned down, pressing his lips to the soft skin beneath my ear. And then he lifted me to my feet and walked behind me up the stairs, his hand at the small of my back. I pulled my sweater tight around me. The chill in the house grew stronger the farther we got from the parlor and cozy fireplace.

Ephraim stepped close and swung open our bedroom door, ushering me inside. The room was opulent. Having been William Darling's, it was well-appointed with masculine furniture and jeweled-toned upholsteries. When I'd been a little girl, I'd sneak away to this room to cuddle up on the window seat and read *Wuthering Heights*, *Jane Eyre*, and countless vintage romance novels. I'd stare outside over the endless marsh and imagine a man. My own brooding Heathcliff.

I imagined Ephraim.

I looked at my husband, attraction warring with the annoyance that still clung to me from our Evangeline encounter at the Historical Society.

"You were quiet this evening," he said, as he pulled his shirt over his head. "Going to tell me what you're angry about?"

My eyes arrowed at the tempting view of muscled chest and abs. "I'm not angry."

"Don't lie, Whitney. You're bad at it."

"Did you think it would be funny to arrange a meeting between us and your ex-girlfriend?" The words tumbled out before I could stop them, annoyance winning out over lust.

His eyes widened a little, but he recovered quickly. "Was she rude to you?"

"No, of course not," I rushed. "Not really."

"Did you find the answers you were looking for? Tell me, where else would you have found them? It would have been wrong of me to go on about my relationship with Evangeline, her accomplishments, her academic acumen. I spared you the details and simply brought you to the person I knew would give you what you wanted."

I winced at the sound of her name on his lips. "You could've gone without me."

He raised an eyebrow. "You'd rather I'd gone to see her on my own without your knowledge?"

I gritted my teeth, turning for the door.

"Not another step, Darling." He grabbed my arm and whirled me back to face him. "It flatters me you're jealous. But there's no need. Evangeline was someone to go to partics with. Someone I could trust to hold an intelligent conversation. That's all."

"You don't need to explain. Who you spent time with, and what you did with them is none of my business. I'm glad you weren't lonely."

"I never said I wasn't lonely."

"Actually, you did say that once."

I watched the memory of our encounter after the will-reading cross his mind.

"What are you looking for?" I demanded. "When you go out on the marsh at night?"

He stiffened. And then his hands were cradling my face, and his lips touched mine, as soft as feathers. Then harder, coaxing my mouth open to welcome him inside.

Thunder boomed, and a fresh wave of rain pounded against the windows.

He walked me backwards to the bed, as he lifted my sweater up and over my head.

I didn't resist.

For tonight, he would leave the marsh and the wild things behind, and spend himself on me.

An hour later, we lay beneath the bed's massive canopy, listening to the sound of the storm wailing outside.

I'd put on a pair of flannel pajamas that Ephraim teased looked like something his grandmother had once worn. But I didn't care. I was desperate for as much warmth as I could get against the persistent chill.

Even Ephraim had donned a pair of grey sweatpants.

His fingers twined with mine. "Horace Leroux," he said. "What will you do about him?"

"Learn how he was connected to the family. I can't help feeling his disappearance ties to the curse and all the strange things going on."

"And what if he has nothing to do with any of it?"

"I don't know how to explain it, but Julia's trying to tell me something. Something important. I'll follow the clues as best I can."

He brushed his fingers through my hair, twisting the tendrils that fell over my shoulder. "Let's say Julia is communicating with you. What could she need? She and William lived two long, fulfilled lives together. What more could either of them have wanted?"

"I keep thinking about the note I found in the back of their portrait. Something terrible happened. What if there's something they left undone? Or something happening now that she's trying to warn us about? Or what if she knows how to break the curse?"

Ephraim raised a skeptical brow, but I didn't miss the flash of curiosity in his eyes. "Alright. How can I help?"

I was quiet for a moment. I hadn't expected him to offer. "I'm not sure. But I'll let you know."

"Fine. In the meantime, I'll avoid telling any more ghost stories."

"I don't know if that's a feasible request around here."

He kissed me again. "Good night, wife."

"Good night, Ephraim."

Chapter Twenty

Whitney Darling

Something woke me.

I lay in bed listening, muscles tense, afraid to open my eyes.

I had the vague impression that there had been a noise, like the abrupt thud of a heavy object hitting the floor or a door shutting loudly. My ears strained against the silence, waiting for another sound, another tremor of chaos in my peace.

I held my breath and peeked, straining to see through a spiky, black curtain of lashes. A pair of round eyes stared back at me from the edge of the bed, inches from my face.

I thrust backward, half-rolling, half leaping across Ephraim.

Before I could right myself, his arms were around me, shielding me from the thing.

I peered over his massive shoulder. My eyes focused in the pale moonlight, and my scream dissolved into haggard laugh. "Percy."

My nephew stood next to the bed, his pajama shirt

rumpled, and a tawny, threadbare book tucked under his arm.

"Percy, are you okay?" I asked.

He nodded. "Are you?"

"Aside from the heart attack."

The little boy's bottom lip quivered.

Ephraim chuckled and held out his arms. I willed my pulse to slow as Percy crawled over Ephraim and into my lap. "Did you have a bad dream?"

He shook his head before holding a book out to me with both hands. "I went to the potty, and this was on the floor outside your room."

I took the worn leather volume. "That was sweet of you."

"Aunt Rose told me I'd find something, and that when I did, I should make sure to put it away, right away. Is this yours?"

I looked at the cover. It was a copy of *The Odyssey*.

No, it was *the* copy of *The Odyssey* that had fallen to the floor in Alistair's study all those nights ago. Only now a small piece of paper stuck out from the top of the pages like a bookmark. I opened it to the marked page and angled the book toward a bright streak of moonlight shining in from the window. A thin black line of ink underlined a single passage.

Ephraim leaned close. "You are asleep, Penelope; the gods who live at ease will not suffer you to weep and be so sad." The deep, solemn rumble of his voice made me wish he'd keep reading.

"Penelope." I traced my finger over the word.

"Is it yours?" Percy asked, half-yawning, and rubbing his eyes.

"I believe this belonged to Granddaddy Alistair. And

another Darling before that. Anyway, it's old. I'll make sure it gets back where it belongs."

I pulled him into a warm hug. "Go back to bed, sweetie. We'll talk more in the morning." I walked him to the door, then watched him amble down the hall to his bedroom.

As I turned back, a flicker of light outside the window caught my eye. The rain had stopped, and a distinct orange speck danced in the darkness. What could be casting a tiny light on the marsh at this time of night? I narrowed my gaze on the moonlit outline of the glass studio in the distance. The light was there.

A second light caught. And then another, each a singular orange flame in the blackness. Candles.

Someone was in the glass studio with candles.

"Ephraim."

"At your service, wife," he drawled suggestively.

"Someone's in the glass studio."

He sat up. "What?"

"They're lighting candles. What if they mean to set a fire?"

He threw back the covers and pulled on a sweater he'd left flung over a chair by the bed, then stepped into a pair of leather boat shoes. "Whitney, so help me. Stay in the house. There's a gas line running out there."

"You can't go out there. We need to call the police."

"Call them. But I'm not sitting around letting whoever's out there get away. They'll make a run for it if they see headlights coming down the drive." He glanced at his watch. "It's three-o-clock in the morning."

He opened the wardrobe and pressed several buttons on a safe before pulling out a handgun and tucking it in the back of his sweats.

"Ephraim. Please. At least wait until the police are closer."

He picked up his phone, and the glow of the blue light was too bright in the darkness. "I'm texting Francis to meet me by the garden door. We'll handle this."

I tried to think of something to say that he wouldn't argue with. But I knew it was no use.

He brushed past me, then paused and grabbed me by the arm. "Stay here. I'm serious." He pressed a kiss to my forehead and then strode into the hall.

I darted to the bed for my phone. My fingers trembled so violently I could barely dial any numbers. The call with the emergency operator was a bizarre feeling, as if I was listening to myself talk from outside my body. I sprinted down the stairs, my socks sliding on the polished hardwoods as I plowed straight into Addison.

"Lord, have mercy!" I doubled over, "You scared me."

"Francis took a gun. He's meeting Ephraim." Her voice shook, and her skin was stark white. "I told him to wait for the police, but he said no."

I took her by the arm. "Where's baby Alice?"

"Adele's with her. She took her the second half of the night so Francis and I could sleep."

"Come on." I raced down the hall to the back door, Addison on my heels.

"We're supposed to stay inside."

Moments later we crouched on the back veranda, a good distance from the men ahead of us. We crept, inches at a time, nearer the studio, pausing on the far side of Adele's parterre garden, where the men wouldn't be able to see us if they happened to look over their shoulders. They kept a low profile, their shadows barely distinguishable as they sidled closer to the stone cottage. The glow of candles still flickered in the windows, and every few seconds, the impression of a shadow seemed to move inside.

"We shouldn't be out here," Addison whispered.

"Go back, then."

"And leave you alone?" I felt her glare. "What if you run into trouble?"

"You'd like to be here for that?"

"Of course not!" She grasped my hand, her fingers squeezing my knuckles together until they hurt. "How long do you think it'll take the police to arrive?"

"Any time now," I murmured. "It's been ten minutes at least."

"We don't have ten minutes," Addison said as the men approached the wooden steps of the glass studio. Ephraim reached for the back of his waistband.

"He's taking out his gun."

"Whitney, if I hear gunshots, I think I'll faint."

"You'd better not. I'll leave you here in the grass."

All at once, the men bounded up the stairs and burst through the door.

My heart skipped a beat as we watched their outlines highlighted in the candlelight.

Long moments passed.

Silence.

A scream ripped through the dark, sending us reeling backwards.

I spun in the direction of the house.

Mama raced across the veranda, the baby in her arms. Percy ran beside her.

Addison darted toward them as a firm hand gripped my arm from behind.

"What are you doing out here?" Ephraim growled.

"What's happened?" Francis' voice was savage as he sprinted past me for Addison and the children.

"Someone's in the house," Mama said. "Dressed in black. Upstairs hallway. I grabbed the children."

"Where are the aunts?" Ephraim asked, releasing me, and already moving for the house.

"Locked in Rose's room with a shotgun. They couldn't move fast enough with the wheelchair."

Ephraim nodded grimly, then disappeared through the back door.

Francis pulled Addison and Percy into his arms. "Whoever it is must've snuck inside the house after we came out here."

Mama bounced Alice up and down to keep her from crying. "Would someone kindly tell me what the hell is going on?"

"Whitney woke up and saw candlelight in the studio," Addison's breathless voice was barely audible from where she buried her face in Percy's little neck. "Ephraim and Francis went to investigate."

Headlights illuminated the driveway.

The police.

I sprinted toward the cruiser, pulling my cell phone from my back pocket. I turned on the flashlight and waved it over my head like a beacon as the car pulled up.

Officer Evans stepped out of the car and ran to me. "What's going on?"

"There was someone in the house. Ephraim's inside. My aunts."

Another officer climbed from the car.

Officer Evans motioned me over to the others. "You ladies stay out here with Francis. Another patrol's on the way."

The uniformed men filed through the same door as Ephraim, only they were markedly less quiet about it – announcing their entrance in loud, booming voices.

Lights in the kitchen and mud room flickered on, as well as the chandeliers in the back parlor and dining room. I sighed. It would take all night for the police to go through the house, to make sure no one was hiding inside.

Mama drew me close, looping her arm through mine and passing the baby over to me. "I think I need to sit down."

"Of course, Mama." I helped her lower to the dewy grass.

Another police car arrived. Two more policemen leapt out, one walking quickly toward the house, the other over to us.

Ephraim stepped onto the veranda with a phone pressed to his ear. His eyes narrowed as he neared and pulled me into his arms. "We'll need four." He ended the call and slipped the phone in his back pocket. "Extra security is on the way."

"Did you see anyone? What's happening?"

He shook his head, a grim line creasing his forehead. "The front doors were open. It looks like someone ran straight through the house. As if they meant to hide inside and then thought better of it." He raked a hand through his hair. "A team of officers is combing the woods and the driveway onto the island. Whoever it was, won't get far."

"And the studio?"

"Just a lot of broken glass." His arm around me tightened as he pulled what looked like a folded piece of paper from his pocket. "And this."

I took the faded square in trembling fingers, opening it.

It was an old photograph. Black and white. And there in

the center was the image of Julia Darling. She sat in an ornate chair, dressed in an ebony gown that draped over her from chin to toes. And in her arms, bundled in lace, was an infant, its head covered in thick sprigs of pale hair, its eyes squeezed closed.

Julia's face was gaunt. Her spine ramrod straight.

And beneath the sole of Julia's shoe, as if intentionally highlighted, was a large, golf ball-sized stone. I looked closer.

Not a stone.

A diamond.

I flipped the photo over, and there, written in small dancing script, were four little words.

"You are asleep, Penelope."

Chapter Twenty-One

Whitney Darling

I*'m here.*

My phone lit with a text from Isla, who after hearing about the previous night's events, had insisted on driving over.

I'd taken my time getting ready this morning, adding an extra layer of concealer over the shadows beneath my eyes and running a curling iron through my hair. I listened to a podcast as I finished my makeup, praying to God that nothing terrifying showed up in the mirror.

All the while, four words repeated in my mind.

You are asleep, Penelope.

There were so many questions. Who had been in the studio last night? What had they been doing there? And where had they found that photo of Julia?

Had they left it behind intentionally?

Ephraim hadn't told the police about the photo. He'd slipped it into his pocket after showing it to me, then marched me inside to the parlor with the rest of the women while the officers and private security combed the house. After a few hours, once our island had been deemed safe, he'd escorted me to our room and dressed me down for following him outside. After which he'd literally undressed me and introduced me to the joys of angry sex.

I let out a shaky breath, flushing at the memory of the things he'd done to me. The places he'd kissed me. His body, hard, rippling muscle, tense and controlled, as he drove me higher and higher, closer and closer –

I willed my pulse to slow.

Lovemaking aside, last night had been terrifying. An obvious threat. Whoever was terrorizing Darling House, be they living or dead, was sending a message. And I needed to decode it.

I fingered the pendant I wore around my neck. I'd woken this morning with the strangest urge to put it on. I was worried that whoever had broken into the house might find it and steal it, and also, I had a feeling this journey included finding justice for little Penelope too. My eyes traced the intricate pattern of pale blonde hair, so delicately woven into the shape of a flower. The baby in the photo Ephraim had found was Penelope. And this was her hair. I knew it.

My stomach growled.

I needed food and coffee.

With a final cursory look in the mirror, I headed downstairs.

A white van was in the drive. The security company. After last night's events, Ephraim had put his foot down and insisted, not gently, that cameras would be installed. Not only outside the house, but inside as well.

Being the neurotically private individual she was, Mama had been madder than a hornet. But she'd acquiesced.

I watched as a rotund man in coveralls pulled a supply bin

from the back of the van. Ephraim stepped into sight then. He wore a pair of fitted black chinos and a white button down, untucked, the sleeves rolled halfway up his tanned forearms.

Even without sleep, the man was too handsome for his own good.

A text chimed again from my phone.

I brought you a pumpkin spice latte. It's getting cold.

I hurried toward the kitchen. Isla loved to sit at the breakfast table and look out over the water.

"Good morning, sorry it took me a second." I pulled her into a tight hug.

She slid a to-go cup over to me. "I'm sorry y'all had such a rough night. What in the world's going on around here?"

"We can't figure it out. Yet again, no sign of anything stolen. But I'm told they tore up the studio. Ephraim's called the gas company out to be sure the lines weren't tampered with."

Isla's eyes widened. "I can't believe Percy happened to wake you up like that, in time for you to see the candles." She leaned forward. "What are the chances?"

"I've tried not think too hard about that." I took a sip of my latte. "The police didn't find much. A few beeswax candles. They've got a crew out this morning looking for fingerprints."

"That's all they found? Candles?"

"Mmmmhhhmm."

Isla looked unconvinced.

"Should they have found something else?" I asked.

She sighed. "You'd think if the guys startled someone, they would've been taken off guard enough to leave more behind. A set of keys, a tool they used to break in, something."

A description of the photograph Ephraim had discovered on the studio floor sat on the edge of my tongue.

But for some reason, I kept it there.

"I guess whoever it was got lucky this time," I said. "We'll know more once the police finish."

"What about the book Percy found outside your door? Do you think it's connected?" Isla raised an eyebrow. "The biggest question, I suppose, is who keeps wanting you to see the book?"

I swallowed another warm sip of coffee. "In Darling House, happenings like that are usually chalked up to the typical suspects."

"You mean ghosts?"

Francis and Ephraim strode into the room.

"Good morning, ladies." Ephraim's eyes narrowed on me. "I've been looking for you."

I held up my mug with a sleepy, half-smile. "I've not gotten far, as you can see."

"And you'll keep it that way." He crossed his arms. "Francis and I discussed the situation. There's no more walking alone around the island, not even from here to the glass studio. Not without an escort."

"Ephraim." I looked from him to Francis, who only gazed back at me with the same handsome, stony stare. "This isn't reasonable."

"I know. That's why you and I are heading for my place in town. I need your input to get it ready for the family. We'll all be staying on Jones Street."

"Ephraim."

"It's only until we get this figured out, Whitney," Francis said.

"But leaving Darling House empty is an invitation to

whoever's doing all of this. Who knows what could happen?"

"The house won't be unattended." Ephraim's gaze dropped to the mourning pendant hanging around my neck. His brows drew together, but he didn't comment. "We'll discuss the particulars in the car."

Isla placed a comforting hand on my arm. "Whitney, the guys are right. This situation's getting dangerous. Downtown is safer. Besides, we've got so much planning to do for the gala, I'm sure you'll barely have time to miss this place."

* * *

By the time the sun sank beneath the rooftops on Jones Street and the last vestiges of orange sunset kissed the sky, I was still annoyed, but coming around to the idea of relocating to town.

Ephraim leaned forward on the antique sofa across from me, resting his forearms on his knees. He studied his hands, turning them palms up as he concentrated on the business call over his Bluetooth. An unexpected issue had come up in New York, and so our trip back to Darling House to collect my things had been delayed.

Despite my bad mood, we'd made quick work of prepping his townhouse for long-term company. The rest of the family were still on the Island with Francis and three of Ephraim's private security agents while the ladies gathered what they would need for themselves and the children for the stay in town. They planned to ride in tandem with us back here following one last dinner before deserting Darling House.

I stood by one of the tall parlor windows that looked out

over Jones Street. The house was silent, save for the ticking of the grandfather clock in the hallway, and the occasional smooth timber of Ephraim's voice.

A vase of dead flowers sat on the marble mantle, proof the housekeeper hadn't yet made her weekly rounds. White moonlight crept across the fifteen-foot ceiling.

Ephraim reclined back on the sofa, though the tension in his shoulders gave away a twisted combination of stress and something else.

I studied the elegant formal parlor as I waited, trying to picture it the way it must have been when he was a little boy, bursting with the love and security of his family. Ephraim's mother had been a talented homemaker with the skill of an interior designer, not in the professional sense, but in the innate way so many true southern ladies seemed to have. She'd made what could've felt like an intimidating museum of a house, feel like a chic and graceful refuge from the bustling city outside.

I knew Ephraim had gotten some incredible offers for the property. But in spite of the easy millions, he'd never sold. And I liked that.

I looked down at the lamp-lit street. A group of tourists on a ghost tour stood on the sidewalk, cell phone cameras flashing, as they tried to capture images of orbs or something more sinister floating around the house. The guide motioned in my direction. I moved back a little, despite knowing they couldn't see into the dark room.

Many a local claimed that Ephraim's home was haunted, and that was why he seldom stayed here.

Ephraim stepped behind me. "I'm sorry. That took longer than I thought. Ready to go get your things?"

"What if I say no?"

He chuckled. "I'd remind you that we didn't make this

decision lightly. It's for everyone's safety." He pressed his lips beneath my ear, sending little fissures of pleasure shooting straight to my core. "I promise the house, and the glass, will be safe."

"It wasn't so safe last night."

"We're better prepared now." His phone rang and he pulled it from his pocket with an annoyed growl. "Hey, Francis, what's up?"

I turned in his arms.

His face paled, then twisted with rage. "How bad?"

I leaned forward, trying to hear Francis' voice on the other line, but Ephraim had the cell pressed too close to his ear.

"I've got Whitney. We're coming." He ended the call, his shoulders rigid.

"What's happened?"

His expression softened. "She's going to be alright."

I reached for the pendant hanging around my neck. "Who?"

He motioned for me to sit down. "Adele's had a fall."

"Excuse me?"

"In the conservatory. She fell down the stairs."

* * *

Ambulance lights reflected dancing red prisms against Darling House, making it look like something out of a Halloween set.

My limbs shook as I half-stumbled, half-leapt out of the passenger's side door and ran for the porch. The front doors were open wide, and I could already hear voices from inside.

Ephraim caught up with me and we sprinted into the

front parlor where the family huddled around a cushioned cane settee. Adele lay sprawled across it, her nose red and swollen. Stains of purple flooded the skin beneath her eyes, and her bottom lip was split. She looked more like she'd been attacked than fallen down some stairs.

"What happened?"

"Stay calm," Mama said, pulling me into a pert side hug before directing me to a chair. "We're getting this sorted."

Ephraim pressed a warm hand on my shoulder. "Did anyone see what happened?"

Francis shook his head. "No, and Adele can't recall a thing about it."

"Would y'all stop talking about me as if I weren't here? It's like I've died and gone to Hades. I've told you multiple times. I remember walking in the hallway carrying my pink satin laundry bag. I stepped into the conservatory on the second floor and started down the stairs for the washroom. The next thing I knew I was lying here." She pressed a hand to her forehead and winced. "I must've tripped on my bathrobe tie or something."

"That's a possibility," Mama said, her voice a note too hopeful.

"Ma'am, we'd like you to come to the hospital with us. We need to be sure you've not sustained any internal injuries." The older of the two EMTs looked earnestly over at Ephraim and me.

"That's a good idea," I said. "We've got enough ghosts bumping around the house. I'll ride with you if you like."

Adele huffed, but I could see she was considering it.

"Ephraim will come too," I said.

"Fine. I'll go," she said. "But I'm not riding in any old ambulance. All that pomp and fuss. We'll take Ephraim's car."

"Ma'am," said one of the EMT's.

Adele held up a silencing hand. "You're welcome to ride with us, young man. You can bring your stethoscope and defibrillator if you like, but I'm not getting into the white box of death and zooming down President Street on a gurney."

"It's a deal," I said. "Let's go."

* * *

The waiting room was sterile and cold. My leg bounced rhythmically as I sat in a brown vinyl chair and stared at the clock hanging on the wall. The secondhand tic-tic-ticked its way around the stark circle of numbers, one dash at a time. Over and over.

It had been two hours, and while Adele had cooperated in riding here and tried to be chatty in the car, I knew she was nervous. My great aunt didn't like hospitals. And I couldn't blame her. I didn't like them either, with their harsh fluorescent lighting, long white hallways, and acrid scent of disinfectant.

"You're going to leave a hole in the tile if you keep bouncing your toe like that." Ephraim teased from where he sat flipping through a Halloween edition of *Southern Living Magazine.*

"I hate this."

"It'd be odd if you didn't."

"I don't know how you stay so calm."

"There's a difference between calm and composed." He set the magazine on the chair beside him. "Adele was lucid the whole way here. If there were serious injuries, I think we'd have started to see the result."

"Alright, doctor." I crossed my arms. "What do you think happened in the conservatory?"

Ephraim shook his head. "Adele's getting older. She misjudged a step and fell. It happens all the time."

"Like with Alistair?" I raised a brow. "What a coincidence."

Ephraim's lips thinned.

"What if something *made* them fall?" I whispered.

"You mean the curse? A ghost? Horace Leroux? Whitney, don't do this to yourself." He sighed, "It's natural for you to feel frustrated, especially after what happened to Alistair. It's hard to accept a misstep could take a life. A faulty fuel line. A rip current. It's devastating to see these things happen. But you can't allow it to get the best of you or your imagination."

The door to the waiting room swung open and a handsome man wearing pale blue scrubs came into the room. "Mrs. Darling?"

"Yes." I stood. "Is my aunt alright?"

"She's got a hairline fracture in her left tibia, and a host of bumps and bruises, but there doesn't appear to be any significant internal damage. We're going to keep her overnight for observation to be sure nothing comes up."

A wave of relief washed over me, leaving me light-headed. "Thank you," I whispered.

"I do have some questions for you," the doctor said.

"Sure." I took a seat next to Ephraim.

The doctor looked uncomfortable. "Several of your aunt's injuries aren't consistent with what we generally see in a fall."

"But they found her at the bottom of a stairwell."

"Yes, but she has quite a bash on the back of her head, inconsistent with the kind of blunt force trauma that would necessarily come with tripping." He hesitated. "Have there been any visitors staying at the house? Or could there have been cause for an argument between your aunt and anyone else?"

"Not a chance," I said.

"There's more," the doctor said. "After her scan she became unsettled. The machine can do that to some people, so we gave her sedatives to help her sleep. But before she dozed off, she said she remembered something."

"That's wonderful." A burst of hope bloomed in my chest.

"She said a locked door had been opened."

"A door?" The hope turned cold. I knew. I knew in an instant which door she meant.

The doctor nodded. "Does that mean anything to either of you?"

A chill skittered down my spine, and I looked over at Ephraim.

"There's been some strange activity at Darling House," Ephraim said. "The perpetrator hasn't been found."

The doctor straightened in his seat. "Let me be clear. I don't believe your aunt fell down the stairs. By all indications, she was pushed."

Chapter Twenty-Two

William Darling | 1929 | Black Tuesday

I stood on the roof of Savannah's towering Manger Building and looked over Johnson Square. People rushed and ambled in chaotic rhythm back and forth along Abercorn Street. A tall ship made her way up the Savannah River, sails peeking over the tops of the Live Oaks that lined the square beneath me.

I placed a toe over the roof's edge. A gush of wind pressed back against me, as if the sky herself tried to coax me back in the other direction. Back to safety.

How would it feel? To jump. Weightless? Like a dream?

Would the glass know I was gone?

I looked over at the man standing rigid beside me.

"Step back, Horace," I said, "You don't want this. Not really. What would Layla do without you?"

The question made me think of my Julia. "It's only money, my friend. We'll find a way past this together."

"That's easy for you to say." Horace grimaced. "You didn't lose two-hundred years of family legacy in the space of one morning."

"The market will come back. That's how it works. You, on the other hand, are not so simple to resurrect."

Horace dropped his chin, appearing to examine the ground several stories beneath us. "Someone like me. That's for the best."

"Stop this. Don't you think I've lost something too? Thousands have. Millions. They're calling this the collapse of a century." I turned and stepped off the ledge.

"That's not fair," Horace snapped. "He pulled his diamond from inside his jacket, cradling it in his hand. "You've not lost near what I have."

"I've lost twice as much, easily. And without the consolation of having had it that long. But by all means, sulk. Hurdle off the building and burst into a bloody heap at the bottom. You'll make the front-page tomorrow."

Horace shook his head, his thick golden curls blowing in the breeze like a lion's mane. He backed off the ledge, pinning me with a sour look. "You're a real ass, you know that?"

"I learned from the best."

He fell in step beside me as we made our way to the door that led back inside. "What are we going to do?"

"I'm taking Julia and retiring to Darling House. Simplifying things for a while will make all of this feel more manageable."

"You sound confident."

"I am."

"By tomorrow I won't have a home to retreat to. Besides some decrepit cottage my father left me on the coast of Louisiana."

"Don't leave Savannah. Layla won't take well to the change, and Julia would miss her too much." I rested a hand on his shoulder. "You're welcome at Darling House until you find your feet. God knows, we have plenty of room. We'll have more once construction is done."

"A refuge on your island." Horace kept his eyes trained on the floor. "I hear there's good fishing this time of year."

* * *

Solomon Potter strolled beside me, his eyes focused on the polished ebony cane he swung back and forth as we inspected the main foyer of my long-awaited Darling House. It had been two years in the making, the construction taking less time than expected, as there was an influx of men looking for work, and I'd the good blessing to provide it for them.

A pair of sun spectacles perched on the end of Solomon's nose, the original prototype that had turned into our best-selling design.

Our venture had found success beyond our dreams, leading to a wealth that had not only weathered the market crash, but had expanded during it. The discussion now was only the growing competition, as sun spectacles, coined sunglasses by a couple of other companies, had taken the culture by storm.

In this new age, it seemed, utility was the key to prosperity, establishing our wares among the likes of automobiles, lipstick, and liquor.

I glanced at the sparkling chandelier above our heads. A delicate, glimmering piece that whispered *good morning* to me as we passed beneath it. As of this week, its twin hung in the reception lobby of the Astor family's residence in New York City. A sale that had afforded a fresh and teeming influx of chandelier orders from the Northeast. We would need more assistants.

The bulk of *Darling & Potter* sunglasses were manufactured in our factory along the Savannah River downtown, but my chandeliers were an all-together more delicate matter. Which was why I'd built my stone-walled glass studio here by the sea, where the sounds of my interactions with the glass could be all but drowned out by the crash of the ocean, and the lilting moan of wind over the marsh.

"It's a marvel, William," Solomon said, his gaze caressing the panel work on the walls, the swirling moldings on the ceiling. "Vanderbilt would be jealous."

I laughed. "I doubt that. He's more about emphasizing the size of things, wouldn't you say? I prefer to bask in the details."

Solomon chuckled. "Don't let him hear you say that."

A sudden cry reverberated through the hall, bringing our progress up short.

"Was that – "

"Julia." I rushed forward toward the study where I'd left her sitting in the sunlight reading a book not ten minutes before.

Another cry, more muffled this time.

I broke into a run, my mind going to the number of men who still worked around the house. Some of them from far distances, and not the clearest of references. Had one of them spied Julia alone and forced their way in from the terrace?

Turning a corner, I burst into the study.

My blood went cold.

Julia struggled, pinned, and doubled over backwards on my desk, straining against a strong hand that gripped her jaw.

At the sight of me, she twisted, jerking her chin free. "William!"

At the same moment, I lunged forward, grabbing her attacker and flinging him across the room.

His body hit the floor, bouncing once like a rag doll.

I pulled Julia into my arms, unable to turn for several moments as I registered Solomon walking over to the debased man and taking him by the collar.

"William, my friend," Horace's words were stunted and slurred.

"Your hands on my wife," I growled, seeing red. Blood raced through my veins, screaming like a freight train. I couldn't form a complete sentence. Julia's arms around me were the only things holding me back from doing violence.

"It wasn't how it looked," Horace said, sounding as if he might sober quickly.

"How did it look, exactly?" Solomon quipped, giving Horace's arm a shake.

Horace's lips moved, but no sound came. He lifted glistening, bloodshot eyes to mine, icy blue and pleading.

Unlike my own, Horace's wealth hadn't bounced back. In fact, it had continued to dwindle, forcing him and Layla on the mercy of my hospitality. His lawyers and accountants had resigned one by one. His debts had defaulted. Collections had rolled in. His grand Louisiana mansion, remortgaged during better days, had reverted to the bank. His investments had dried up. His art had been sold. Much of Layla's jewelry.

I'd offered him money. I'd offered to help pay his bills, for a time. But he'd refused me.

In the end, Horace's pride meant more to him than all else.

His pride, and the Egyptian diamond that he still wore on a chain at his chest. Even now he pulled it loose, cradling it in his hand as if it were imbued with some magical ability to turn his world right-side up again.

I'd felt pity for Horace these past six months, as he'd ambled around my little island, offering up droll opinions on the architectural design of the house or the paint colors Julia chose for some interior room or another.

But that was before.

I cracked my neck as a fresh wave of rage threatened to boil over.

Julia shuddered in my arms and drew in a shaky, halted breath. "William," she whispered, "he's had too much to drink."

"Don't make excuses for him," I snapped.

Horace continued to stare up at me, his white cotton shirt stained and wrinkled, his linen suit pants a rumpled mess. His hair, a riot of tangles, was pulled back haphazardly from his unshaven face.

My fingernails bit into my palms.

Even in despair, he was striking, his fine, aquiline features, still noble. But the ice blue of his eyes had lost their haughty edge, instead rimmed with sadness and something that looked much like defeat.

I wanted to rail at him. I wanted to punch him in the jaw for touching my wife, for betraying me. I wanted to pick him up by his collar and shake him and remind him that he had generations of industrious success behind him.

But most of all, I wanted to rip that damned diamond from his grasp and force him to sell it, to start fresh, and save him and his sister from the ruin he was all too content to wallow in.

"Out of my house."

Solomon lifted Horace to his feet.

Horace glowered. "You've replaced me, William. For

good this time." He traced a trembling thumb along Solomon's jaw. "And with this one of all people."

Solomon cut his eyes toward me, no doubt waiting for the word to throw Horace out on his ass.

"You did this, Leroux," I said. "How could I allow you to remain?"

Horace nodded, his head lolling side to side with the motion. "And Layla?"

Julia squeezed my arm.

I bit the inside of my cheek, my head still reeling. "Your sister's welcome at Darling House for as long she needs."

Horace looked as broken as I'd ever seen him. "Thank you for that," he whispered.

"Take your things and go back to town. Stay in my apartment at the factory until you figure out a new situation. You have two weeks."

"My friend – "

"Don't." I ground out, my fingers balling into fists. "Go. Before I lose control and leave my lasting mark on you."

Horace winced and pressed his diamond tight against his chest.

The proud, successful man who'd pulled me from an impossible position and granted me a life – he was nowhere to be seen. And I had no idea how to find him again.

I nodded at Solomon, who jerked Horace to his feet, then ushered him through the study door and out of sight.

Chapter Twenty-Three

Whitney Darling

I stood outside the ground floor entrance of the conservatory, at the threshold of the house, so near the terraced gardens, I could turn and run. A few paces ahead of me, for the first time in as long as anyone alive could remember, the ancient, blue door hung open.

Ephraim and I had arrived back from the hospital not an hour ago, this time greeted by the flashing lights of police cruisers. Ephraim had called Officer Evans on the way home and told him what the doctor had said about Adele being pushed. And so, they'd sent yet another team out to investigate.

And investigate they had, each of them unknowingly venturing back and forth across a haunted room. They hadn't found anything, of course. This wasn't their curse.

But that hadn't prevented them from rushing past us as we entered the house, white-faced and visibly shaken. I'd heard them whisper about the Darlings, about our hauntings, and our ghosts, and the strange things that happened here in the old mansion by the sea.

I couldn't blame them.

Outside of the mysteriously opened door, there was no evidence of an intruder. No sign of anything on any of the cameras. The cameras that bothered to work, anyway.

Naturally, the ones in the conservatory were on the fritz. And we all knew it would stay that way.

Until we got rid of it.

Whatever mad, sinister thing had brought the curse down on us to begin with.

The scent of must and age, the aroma of long-forgotten things, drifted from the open blue door, filling the space ahead of me, making my nose twitch and my throat tighten. All eleven locks dangled from the doorframe, broken, and wrenched from their home. I studied their shapes, the tarnished brass that had held fast for decades.

I no longer intended to leave.

I was angry now. Furious, at whatever had done this to Adele. Whatever it was, I was going to find it, and I was going to get rid of it. I wouldn't be scared away. I refused.

My pulse thrummed in my fingertips as I squeezed the bundle of sage and cedar Solomon had given me.

Even here, barely a foot into the conservatory, I could feel it smiling at me, the invisible dead thing in the corner.

In the corner of the long-shut room.

Hidden skeletons were always found eventually.

"Free," it whispered.

Free.

What was free now that the locks were broken? And who had broken them?

Something stronger than the blue.

Meanwhile, this ghost didn't care about blue paint. It wasn't afraid of water.

Had it tried to kill Adele? Had it pushed her down the stairs?

"Why?" I inched closer to the shadowed room. "What do you want?"

So many years I'd rushed past, avoiding this place altogether. Seth used to tease me about it, but I'd never seen him come close either.

But I had to know. I had to know so that I could fix what I'd done all those months ago. That damned vial of grave dirt had found its way from beneath the house, and I'd been stupid enough to lift it from the ground.

"Why are you doing this?"

No answer.

But I felt it smile.

I didn't care. I was done being afraid.

Standing inside the gaping door was like wading at the edge of a tossing, black ocean, where all manner of mysteries lurked out of sight. Some of them lovely. Some of them terrible with soulless eyes and sharp teeth that could tear me apart.

I took a step closer, holding my breath at the expectation of pale, slender fingers curling around the door frame, before they dragged me inside.

But nothing. Only acrid must and age. And silence.

Dim light from the conservatory windows flooded the space. It was a simple mudroom, no bigger than six by six feet. Perfectly normal. What you'd expect to find at the bottom of the stairs near a garden door.

But there, arranged together in the center of the room, sat a faded parlor chair and an antique baby bassinet.

I pulled my cellphone from my back pocket and flicked on the flashlight and then I stepped inside.

Inside with the dead thing.

The room was cold. Colder than the dressing room at Beau's. My breath came in bright white puffs, reflected in the harsh light from my phone. I reached out and ran my finger along the edge of the bassinet, proving to myself it was truly there. Cobwebs draped over the old, polished wood, like forgotten muslin. A tiny, faded pink satin pillow, like a doll's, was laid at the head of the mattress, an elegant letter P stitched into the center. The parlor chair was upholstered in matching pink fabric. A set. One for a mother. The other for her child.

I swept the trembling beam of light beyond the bassinet, casting it into each of the corners. But there was nothing but peeling paint and old floors, warped and dull with age.

My fingers went to the mourning pendant at my neck, my thumb rubbing gently over the transparent glass and the carefully preserved golden hair beneath.

"What happened?"

A frozen breeze kissed my cheek.

Tap.

Tap.

Tap.

Bile rose in my throat and my spine tingled, begging me to run. But I held my ground.

I pictured Adele in her hospital bed, her face blue and purple and green with bruises. I pictured Seth, struggling against the water that dragged him away. Alistair, and the smile I would never see again.

I wouldn't let anyone else die.

"What do you want?" My voice trembled, not with fear, but anger. "Tell us what you want, and we'll try. Please. Go away. Leave us alone."

A sound, like a fingernail scraping, rough over wood made my skin crawl.

Behind me. Between me and the conservatory.

I whirled around.

My toe caught on the edge of the basinet with a sickening thud, and I pitched forward with a scream, landing hard on my knees.

My eyes widened. There, scrawled on the floor between my hands, in skittering, uneven letters, was a helter-skelter inscription.

Diamond. I want it back.

I squeezed my eyes closed.

Against the invisible dead thing crouching beside me. Watching me.

I froze, and a strange, tingling numbness crept over my skin.

The diamond.

"Horace?" I whispered.

"Whitney!" Ephraim's voice boomed off the walls, jolting life into my limbs, and I belly crawled the small distance back out of the room.

Strong arms jerked me up and away. "Oh, for fuck's sake," Ephraim growled. "A crib? Seriously?"

"Stop it, Ephraim. There's something –

"What? Listening?" The vein in his forehead threatened to pop as he pulled me tighter against him. "I'll talk louder, then." He turned to the room, "Leave us the hell alone!"

"Can we please get outside?"

Shaking with anger, he lifted me into his arms and carried me to the garden, then collapsed with me onto the cool grass. "Have you lost your mind?"

I buried my face in his shoulder, struggling to catch my breath, bathing in his spicy scent, reveling in the pounding of his heart, his solid strength beneath my fingers, "I had to see for myself."

He shook his head. "Satisfied?"

"Not exactly."

"Darling House isn't safe, Whitney." He sighed, looking genuinely sorry.

"I know," I said, fighting a sudden onslaught of tears. "Darling House was never safe."

He raked a hand through his hair. "We're leaving. Now. Francis and the rest of the family are already on the road into town."

"No."

He laughed, but his eyes were hard as stone. "No?"

"I'm not going. Whatever's happening here can't be solved from downtown. I need to be here."

"Not long ago escaping Darling House was your primary goal in life."

I stood, brushing away the sting of his words. "Things change."

His jaw ticked and he stared at me for what felt like forever. "If I make you leave, you'll come back here, won't you?"

It was my turn to laugh. "You can't make me do anything, Ephraim."

He quirked a brow, looking tempted to prove me wrong. "Listen closely. We'll try this your way. But there are two conditions."

"Such as?"

"One. No wandering around the house alone. You're with me. At my side, twenty-four-seven. If you'll remember, this is the same request I've made of you several times now."

I took a step back. "And two?"

He reached out and grasped the mourning pendant at my neck, then gently snapped the delicate chain. He held it out to me. "Stop wearing this. It freaks me out."

Annoyed, I took the necklace and slipped it into my pocket, "I suppose that's fair."

"More than fair." He motioned toward the slate path that led around to the kitchen. "Come on. If we're going to fling ourselves into an Agatha Christie novel, I need a cup of coffee."

* * *

An hour later, after copious amounts of caffeine, donuts, and a tense call with Francis, explaining that we wouldn't yet be joining them on Jones Street, Ephraim and I stepped into Alistair's study. I smiled, mildly comforted by the roaming beams of flashlights outside the glass veranda doors, evidence of Ephraim's security detail hard at work.

I clicked on a floor lamp, flooding the room with warm light. I approached a wall of bookcases, scanning the vast collection of old leather spines.

"Here's what we know," I said. "There have been two break-ins in as many months. Nothing taken. We have in our possession a presumably cursed vile of graveyard dirt, an antique mourning pendant, and an old photograph of Julia and her lost baby, Penelope. In the photo Julia's foot is resting on what looks like a huge diamond." I pinned Ephraim with a pointed look. "We also have an article about a missing businessman and his diamond. And finally, we have a vindictive ghost who would apparently like the jewel back."

Ephraim sighed heavily. "I can't believe how well I followed that."

"If it is Horace's Egyptian diamond under Julia's foot, that would mean the Darlings had possession of it after the disappearance took place, because Julia's holding a baby, and she was still pregnant when Horace went missing."

Ephraim quirked a brow. "Which begs the question – "

"What were William and Julia doing with Horace's diamond?"

"I'm willing to bet the answer to that is why the Darlings find themselves royally cursed." Ephraim motioned to the shelves of books behind me. "So, what are we looking for in here?"

"A family tree," I said. "Some record of the genealogy dating back to William and Julia. Assuming the baby in the photo is Penelope, then we need to confirm her date of birth," I cleared my throat, "or death, to be certain we're on the right track."

"Alright, then." Ephraim strode toward the bookshelves. "Search for Bibles."

"Bibles?"

"It's the first place I'd look for old family birth and death records."

"Clever."

"I have my moments."

Within minutes we'd amassed a collection of old Bibles on Alistair's desk.

The warmth of the quiet study had grown cozy, and I dug in the top drawer for a lighter, then lit a fat orange candle that sat in the middle of the desk.

Ephraim cocked a questioning brow.

I shrugged. "It's pumpkin spice."

"Of course. How silly of me." He chuckled and opened a leather Bible as I settled into a chair beside him.

I stared at him a moment, watching the way the flickering light played along his handsome profile. My heart squeezed in my chest.

He was mine.

And I meant to keep it that way.

I forced my focus back to the book in front of me.

An hour passed. We poured over Bibles and old journals, finding nothing.

Until my fingers trembled over an old leather volume whose pages were so wispy, thin, and aged, that they stuck together in the corners. I pulled them apart gently.

Ephraim had been right. The opening and back pages were covered in little handwritten notations.

My eyes scanned over the multitude of genealogies written in the far edges of the paper, a flurry of recorded births, weddings, tragedies, and deaths.

I flipped through the thin pages, one by one, pausing near the front of the Bible on a page structured like a traditional family tree. And there, at the top, finally, were printed the names of William and Julia Darling.

Beneath them, denoted by their own little branches, were the names of their children and the dates they'd been born. Banner, Tara, Bronwyn, Agatha, Cornelia, James.

Ephraim stepped over to me. "What's this?"

I pointed to what I'd found. "The photo Evangeline gave us at the Historical Society, which showed Julia and William at the infamous party with Horace Leroux and his sister. That was 1930. Julia was pregnant in the photo. Very pregnant."

"Okay," Ephraim prompted.

"The oldest child listed here is Banner. Born in November 1931. There had to have been another baby before him." I ran a finger over the fine paper, my eyes narrowing on a small, faded line off to the side, near Julia's name. A tiny name sat atop it, beside a date, sad in its simplicity. "Penelope. Born and Lost 1930."

The candle on the desk flickered hard, as if someone had blown a puff of air into it.

"We're on the right track," I whispered, only partially to Ephraim.

I looked back down at the Bible, remembering the newspaper photo of Julia at the party, the gentle way her hand rested on her belly, serene and happy. So unlike the way she'd shown herself to me these past weeks.

"We're going to figure out what happened," I said. "We're going to find out how all of this started. And we're going to end it."

The candle flickered again.

Then blew out.

"You know, I've been meaning to mention," Ephraim said, his lips twisting in an amused smile. "I think your house may be haunted."

"Come on." I motioned for him to follow.

"Where are we going now?"

"The cemetery."

He stopped. "Are you serious?"

"Deathly."

"First, that's a bad joke," he said. "Second, absolutely not. Whatever's going on in your head can wait until morning."

"Why?" I paused at the study door. "Are you afraid?"

Ephraim grinned. "The cemetery gates are closed."

"Then we'll park outside the gates and sneak in through the woods."

"Whitney, no."

"There's a gravestone I need to see. A tiny one. I noticed it the day of Alistair's funeral. I think it might be Penelope's."

He crossed his arms over his chest. "And what if it is?

What new clues do you expect to uncover there tonight, Miss Agatha?"

I ignored the gibe. "I don't know. But it's the next best place to find something. Some kind of clue, some message. What does it hurt, really? It's not actually that late. Not to mention, it's safer there than it is here."

Ephraim shook his head, looking more amused than annoyed.

"I know you're curious," I prodded. "How will either of us sleep tonight, anyway?"

"I had plans for keeping you awake tonight," he said, his gaze dropping to my chest. "You're so sexy when you talk genealogies."

"Ephraim!"

"Fine," he chuckled. "To Bonaventure."

Chapter Twenty-Four

Whitney Darling

We arrived at Bonaventure Cemetery at a quarter past eleven.

I set an alarm on my phone for ten minutes to the hour. No matter what, we had to be back outside the grounds by midnight.

Every Savannahian worth their salt knew that nothing good happened in cemeteries after midnight.

I looked over at Ephraim as he pulled his car into a little alcove near the entrance, reminding me of another night, years ago, when the two of us and Seth had snuck into Laurel Grove Cemetery, and been promptly discovered by a bone collector. Somehow now, the idea of being handed a human rib and burying it in the back yard, which was exactly what we'd done, felt like a simple child's story. Hardly a blip in a life spent on the gothic marsh beside the most haunted city in the world.

Ephraim raked a hand through his shaggy waves and looked over at me with quick, black eyes. "You ready?"

I nodded, though my limbs shook as I reached for the

door handle. "We'll be in and out. It's not like we don't know where we're going."

Ephraim grabbed my hand and led me to the edge of thick trees that flanked the far end of the property.

"We'll stick to the woods, like you said, then cross over to the Darling plot when we get nearer. Stay close and don't make a sound."

"I don't think security would give us trouble, Ephraim. Aren't they used to ignoring midnight visitors?"

"It's not security I'm worried about."

I thought of the bone collectors again, and a chill skittered down my spine. I didn't think there was anything to fear from them. We'd simply leave them peacefully to their work.

I glanced back at the car one last time as Ephraim pulled me fully into the tree line. I clung to his hand, walking as quietly as I could behind his steady progress.

Fog kissed the moonlit ground, tucked in close, as if the ephemeral blanket might protect the slumbering residents from the cold. Moss trailed in soft procession over sunken graves and old, twisted iron gates, ringing finally, around the base of towering oaks, whose long branches stretched in wide, gnarled repose.

I shivered against a damp chill, feeling my bones cool. My hair was a frizzy halo, and my nose, I was sure, was already bright red with cold. I zipped my jacket all the way beneath my chin and tried not to trip over loose sticks and gravel as I struggled to match Ephraim's pace.

He didn't care for it here. He never had.

Though his parents lay to rest farther from our path, I knew he thought of them. Of flying things that fell from the sky. Of fiery crashes, and of lost days and empty rooms that would never be quite the same again. How could he not?

I was thinking the same.

I was thinking of cruel water, and of the brother who'd shared my face. And my heart.

I was thinking of Granddaddy. And Percy's father, Caleb.

But that was what one did in a cemetery.

You thought of the dead, and how one day soon, sooner than was fair, you'd join them there beneath the ground.

But what a place to rest.

Bonaventure was a melancholy fairytale. A sudden, gothic spit of poetry and slumbering, dusty epitaphs.

Once, a long time before, it had been the site of a beautiful manor house. One night, the owner threw a grand party. All the most important Savannahians were in attendance. But when a lantern was dropped upstairs, a fire broke out, and spread and spread, until the host was informed there was no stopping the inferno. And so, they brought the entirety of the congregation outside, each of them laden with tables and chairs, and every bit of silver, and crystal, and art they could carry. Even the musicians moved their instruments to the lawn, and the congregation continued to dance and play to the brutal splendor of the gorgeous, burning manor.

Ashes to ashes.

My gaze searched from one white, gleaming obelisk to the next, over wizened marble and granite tombs, to the upturned cheeks of cherubs and the grief-torn visages of weeping seraphim, until finally, my eyes leveled on the face of our own Darling angel.

She lay staring back at me in languid mourning atop the oversized monument to William and Julia.

"Make this quick, wife," Ephraim said. "We don't know who else is out here."

The stone angel watched our progress, as we stepped from the trees, past Seth, and Alistair, then past thirty or so tombstones of family members forgotten, and beyond, to the far corner of the plot, where an unassuming stone sat at the border of sleeping Darlings.

I squatted to study it. Emerald moss grew along the bottom edge, and the white marble corners were worn so smooth they looked almost soft to the touch. It was small, easily confused for a footstone, or a separate sort of marker. But there, in the center, was a shallow impression, a tiny epitaph.

You are asleep, Penelope. 1930.

I ran numb, trembling fingers over the words.

"Anything interesting?" Ephraim whispered.

"It's her," I said. "Give me a second."

"There's not much time to midnight," Ephraim said. "Now that your curiosity's sated, I suggest we come back in the daylight."

"Just a minute. Let me soak in the fact that I was right. Ephraim, we're getting somewhere now."

"Oh, yes. If I could only bottle this moment."

"Sarcasm is beneath you."

"On the contrary."

I sighed and ran a fingertip along the delicate outline of Penelope's name.

Strange that she was buried here, at the edge of the plot, so far from her parents. So far from everyone, really. I looked to my left. Her brothers, Banner and James, were buried on the opposite end of the plot with their families. She was nowhere near anyone who would've been close to her in life.

"Poor little girl," I whispered.

"It's sad when you see the small ones, isn't it?" A deep,

unfamiliar voice called from the main cemetery path to our backs.

I came out of my skin, half-leaping, half-falling backward into Ephraim's firm legs at the loud, unexpected sound.

Ephraim whirled toward the visitor, his hand flying to the back of his jeans.

He'd brought a gun.

He looked down at me in clear warning to be quiet and follow his lead.

"How's it going, friend?" Ephraim's voice was dangerously steady.

The man pointed a finger at the little tombstone beside me. "The stones. The small stones." His opaque eyes glowed against his midnight skin. He smiled casually from the edge of the little dirt path and tucked a pair of sunglasses into the front pocket of his shirt.

I straightened in recognition. "Solomon?"

The man's eyes widened, but he didn't respond. I realized belatedly, that though they could've been brothers, this man was not my long-time friend.

"The small stones are the saddest," he said again.

"Yes." I stood, willing my legs to stop shaking. "I agree."

Ephraim shot me a warning look.

The man shifted on his feet and pointed toward the Darling angel. "I was at the funeral, you know? I passed out the roses."

"It's late for a walk," Ephraim snapped, not acknowledging the man's story.

"I could say the same to you," he raised a bushy white brow.

"Were you friends with him?" I asked, assuming he

meant Granddaddy's funeral, though I didn't remember seeing him there.

The man nodded, "More than friends. Sworn brothers. A long, long time."

"You're here visiting, then?"

A smile creased his dark cheeks. "You could say that." He motioned over his shoulder. "My family's resting across the way. The Potters, we are. Your eternal neighbors." He chuckled. "Mr. Darling used to laugh and laugh at that."

Potter. That was my Solomon's last name. And his family's burial plot was indeed across the way. My scalp crawled. Was this some kind of joke? I narrowed my eyes, trying to better study the man's face through the darkness. But the moonlight cast strange shadows over each of us. Even Ephraim looked like a sharp-lined caricature of himself.

Mr. Potter motioned to the stone at my feet. "You're wondering who that is under there."

I shook my head. "This is Penelope."

He looked amused. "You know, Whitney, they say your Darling House is haunted."

Ephraim grabbed my arm, angling me back toward the way we'd come. "Alright. We're done here. We'll leave you to your visit, Mr. Potter."

"There's a blood stain on the marble, at the bottom of the conservatory stairs. That's why they keep a rug there. The spot'll never come clean," The man's smile widened, growing wild, and too wide for his face. "Not for lack of trying."

Ephraim guided me away from the plot, putting himself firmly between me and Mr. Potter. "A Savannah ghost story, sir."

"You ever looked there? Beneath the rug?" he shouted after us.

I began to answer that, of course, I'd seen the floor under the rug, but I paused, my lips half-open because now that I thought of it, I supposed I never had.

"Ask me how the bloodstain got there." The old man yelled after us, his gait widening with each halting step in our direction. He pointed a thin, gnarled finger toward the sky. "Ask William's chandelier. The glass remembers."

Ephraim's grip tightened painfully on my arm as we sprinted through the woods back to the car.

I glanced over my shoulder, expecting to see the stranger's too-wide grin following us.

But there was nothing.

For as far as I could see, there was no sign of Mr. Potter.

Sunlight sparkled in kaleidoscope rainbows across the breakfast room floor, tiny spiral bursts of color against the white marble. I sat cross-legged in a cushioned cane-back chair, my hands wrapped tight around my coffee mug, breathing in the warm, calming scent.

There had indeed been a bloodstain on the conservatory floor. A large one, faded and dark, hidden beneath the thick carpet. I'd hardly been surprised. Sadly, nothing much surprised me anymore. But Ephraim's eyes had been wide as saucers when I'd dragged him down after sunrise to see if Mr. Potter's claims were true.

It's sad when you see the small ones.

My mind chewed on the old man's words for the thousandth time.

Ask William's chandelier. The glass remembers.

They were so like the ones Alistair had written to me in his letters. But how was that possible? Of course, if my suspicions were correct, nothing about meeting Mr. Potter last night fell within the realm of the explainable.

I took another sip of coffee, absent-mindedly getting up and walking to where Ephraim had left out a bag of powdered donuts. My mouth watered as I opened the bag and took a deep sniff. I raised a small confection to my lips and spun around at the sound of approaching footsteps.

Ephraim came into the room, looking rugged in a black fisherman's sweater and faded jeans that were snug in all the right places. "I see you found a clue."

I smiled primly and took another mouthwatering bite. "Where'd you get these? I thought we'd finished off the donuts last night."

"I had groceries delivered early." He crossed his arms and leaned against the doorframe, looking satisfied with himself. "Who has time for things like shopping when there are ghosts to contend with?"

"You mean Mr. Potter."

He nodded. "Our other creepy friends, notwithstanding." Ephraim stepped closer, a sly smile playing at his lips. "I think for the foreseeable future, you and I should avoid all graveyards, cemeteries, and otherwise burial-oriented spaces."

"What about going back in the daylight?"

He took a deep breath, studying my face like he thought of something quite apart from diamonds. "I remember. Though, after last night, I might need some persuading." He wiped my chin with his thumb. "You've got a bit of sugar."

I licked my bottom lip.

"Let me help you with that." He lifted my chin and pressed his lips to mine, then groaned and pulled me closer.

I relaxed into him. He smelled like sandalwood, and the ocean, a heady cocktail of masculine grace and expensive bodywash. I melted into the kiss, enjoying the feel of his rising heart rate beneath my fingertips.

"You taste like breakfast," he whispered against my cheek, pulling back to trail kisses along my ear and down the crook of my neck.

A feminine laugh from the parlor room made me freeze. "Did you hear that?"

He chuckled. "Glutton for punishment that I am, groceries aren't the only thing I had brought in from town."

"What?" Before I could ask more, the sound of Isla's voice brought me up short. "What's she doing here? I thought it was too dangerous."

Ephraim grinned and traced a finger along my jaw. "It's 7:30 in the morning. A fresh security detail's arrived. I'm not convinced the gala should take place at Darling House, but I don't think it'll hurt anything for you and the ladies to work here on the details." He crossed his arms. "I'll take you back to the cemetery later today, once we've both had more time to recover from last night's adventure."

"I don't think you realize how late in the game it is to change venues," I said.

"And I don't think you realize," he said, "how many armed security guards it would take to secure your little event here on the island."

"As long as they're wearing black ties and tails, I don't care how many of them you ship in." I narrowed my eyes as I wrapped my arms around his neck and pulled him in for another kiss. "But thank you for this morning."

"There's nothing like the honeymoon phase," Isla said cheerfully, pulling a café chair away from the breakfast table. She unwound a thick, blue linen scarf from her neck, then shivered dramatically. "I feel bad for the poor trick-or-treaters going out this weekend. There's no sign it's going to warm up in time for Halloween."

"Which means it won't be warmed up for the gala, either, seeing as how it's the day *before* Halloween, and a *bit* more important," Monica quipped. Bundled in a sweater and fingerless gloves, she looked like she hadn't yet enjoyed a sip of caffeine. She joined Isla at the table. "I don't remember an October ever being this frigid."

"Guess we're nixing the outdoor seating and keeping to the ballroom," I said, thinking how much easier that would be on Ephraim's security team. I set three empty mugs on the table.

"We can place a few cocktail tables on the veranda," said Monica, who reached for a mug with a glance toward the gurgling coffeemaker. "We'll need something to put a drink on if anyone steps out for air. We could have torches lit and the fountain illuminated, but I don't foresee the party spilling out into the garden."

"Such a shame," Isla sighed. "Your wedding was so stunning out there."

"Okay, this is my cue," Ephraim said, sweeping in behind me to press a scruffy kiss on my cheek. "I'll be in the study working. There are security details peppered all over the island. They've all been told you're here, so you ladies stick to the pertinent parts of the house, please. Here in the kitchen, the foyer, the ballroom." He narrowed his gaze at me. "No conservatory."

"Yes, Daddy," Isla teased, her eyes dancing.

"I'm serious." Ephraim wrestled away a smirk and crossed his arms. "Maybe I should take my calls in here and accompany y'all around the house."

"Oh, goodness, no," I said, crossing to the counter to

retrieve the coffee pot. "Ephraim, we'll be fine. Go," I motioned toward the door the way I'd seen Addison do with Percy, "go work."

He chuckled as he stepped down the hall, turning to point once more at me. "No conservatory."

"He's wound tight," Isla said, after Ephraim was out of earshot.

A vision of me and him in the cemetery the night before flashed across my mind. The tiny tombstone. Mr. Potter with his wild, too-wide grin.

"He's worried," I said. "He's not used to dealing with loose ends, and these break-ins have thrown us for a loop. Especially this last one. Whoever it is isn't leaving a trace. Like a – "

"Ghost?" Isla finished my sentence. "Tell me you're not going to be at Darling House on Halloween."

"You and your obsession with Halloween," Monica said.

"Oh, I'm nothing compared to my friend Marin," Isla beamed. "She works for a ghost tour company in town."

"Not one of those," Monica interrupted, her face twisting up distastefully.

"Well, what's wrong with them?" Isla asked.

"They're so cheesy," Monica said. "You know most of the stories are made up."

Isla shook her head. "Not Marin's company. They do a lot of research. It's more dark history, than anything. Regardless, Marin knows all the best stories."

"I'm surprised you'd be friends with a tour guide," Monica said, pointedly.

Isla's brows drew together, "Why ever wouldn't I?"

"Usually, people like you stick to your own."

"People like me?"

Monica nodded. "Wealthy and privileged."

"Okay," I said, grabbing the bag of donuts and tossing it onto the table. "Monica, eat something." I turned to Isla, smiling at her soothingly. "Bring Marin by sometime. I'm sure Darling House would be her new haunted obsession."

Isla pinning Monica with an affronted glare. "She'll be at the gala. I'll introduce you."

"Speaking of the gala." Monica cleared her throat and tapped her notebook with a pink highlighter. "We need to finalize some details and do a final walkthrough of the ballroom."

I poured coffee into each of our mugs and joined them at the table as Ephraim strode back into the room, his phone pressed to his ear and a scowl on his face.

"I suppose when you're the boss, the problems never cease," Monica quipped.

Ephraim's eyes met mine, anger and concern knitted on his brow.

My stomach dropped, "What's happened now?"

He pulled the phone away and hit the speaker button. "I have her, go ahead."

"Good morning, Miss Callaghan-Darling," Officer Evans' familiar drawl echoed in the kitchen. "I'm afraid I'm gonna need y'all to meet me in Bonaventure Cemetery, as soon as you can."

* * *

Uniformed officers milled around the Darling family plot as Ephraim's black SUV pulled up behind a small grouping of police cruisers. Several white tarps lay across multiple graves, including Penelope's.

I clutched Ephraim's arm as we crossed the grass.

"I'm glad y'all could make it out so quick," Officer

Evans said, a steaming coffee cup poised halfway to his lips. "It's been a wild morning, and I'm hoping one or both of you might help shine some light on the situation."

"What's happened?" I asked, my eyes drawn back to the tarps.

"I'm sorry to say, Miss Whitney, but someone came here last night and desecrated the grave of one of your kin."

"What do you mean, desecrated?" Ephraim demanded.

Evans bowed his head, his brow furrowed. "We got a frantic call from a sweet old lady this morning. She was here early, leaving fresh flowers over yonder, when she noticed something strange strewn across the Darling plot."

"Which was?" Ephraim prompted, clearly irritated at Evans' lack of expediency.

"Bones. Parts of a skeleton scattered all around several of the graves." He motioned behind him. "We can't move anything until certain procedures have been completed."

"Show me," Ephraim said.

The officer balked. "I'm afraid that's not policy, Mr. Callaghan."

"Hell," Ephraim shouldered past him, striding for the open grave.

Officer Evans hesitated but stepped to the side. "Don't go beyond the yellow tape. You'll be able to see well enough."

I followed closely after them, but Ephraim paused, halting my progress.

"I don't want you seeing anything gruesome."

"I'll be fine," I said, hating the tremor in my voice. It was my turn to brush past. "I'm more than capable."

My heart skipped as Evans ushered us around the side of the white tarp near Penelope's little tombstone.

I held my breath. Penelope had been an infant when she died.

Maybe I couldn't do this. I didn't want to see.

"We'll need an official confirmation," Evans said, "but our specialist estimates the bones belonged to a male in his thirties or forties."

I gasped, my gaze snapping to Ephraim, who looked equally stunned.

"It's an odd thing," Evans continued, "the marker indicates this is the grave of a child. Course, things happen over the years. Stones get bumped over and moved around. But I assure you, Miss Whitney, we'll do all in our power to positively identify your relation and see him properly returned to rest."

I swallowed, my throat convulsing.

What was going on? I thought of the bloodstain on the marble floor, and the strange spark in Mr. Potter's eye. Had he known last night who was buried here beneath the grass? I shivered.

Ephraim took my arm again, offering his support as the white bones of a skeleton came into view.

"There's one other thing, Miss Whitney," Officer Evans said, his tone gentling. "This is a delicate topic, I'm aware. But do you know of any past relations who died of a gunshot to the head? Perhaps a soldier?"

I gasped, seeing for myself the clean, round hole in the skeleton's forehead.

And suddenly, I knew exactly who this was.

Ephraim squeezed my hand, a clear message to keep my thoughts to myself.

My mind buzzed with the possible implications of what I was seeing, "I'm afraid I don't know. My aunts, or Mama might be able to help with that. We'll ask them."

Voices behind us on the gravel path made us all turn. A small group of journalists approached, flashing their badges.

"Mrs. Darling," one of them pointed at me, then motioned for me to come closer. "I have a few questions for you."

Another called out for a comment.

Another snapped a picture with their phone, the flash sparkling obnoxiously despite the morning sunlight.

"Great," Ephraim scowled. "This is all we need."

"Y'all are free to go," Officer Evans said. "I needed someone from the family to lay eyes on the situation. We'll keep you updated on any developments."

"Thank you," I said, as Ephraim took my arm and marched us past the still-chattering journalists.

We didn't speak when we got into the car and pulled back down the gravel drive toward the cemetery gates. We didn't speak when we neared the island, or when Ephraim parked in front of Darling House, or when we stepped inside the foyer.

We didn't speak until we'd both climbed the stairs and stepped into William Darling's bedroom, our bedroom, and shut the door behind us.

"I'm taking you to New York. Now." Ephraim's voice was steel.

"Absolutely not."

"Whitney, we're leaving. Until whoever's responsible for all of this is caught."

I sank to the edge of the bed. "Ephraim, no. I can't leave. I won't. The gala is in three days. And if you think I'm getting onto an airplane with you – "

"Damn it, Whitney, I'm not afraid of a stupid curse!" Ephraim's eyes flashed with anger. "I'll do anything. I'll fly anywhere to keep you safe. Whoever's doing this has been able to evade our every precaution."

"Ephraim."

"That's enough. The gala can wait."

"Oh, can it? Ephraim, that means whoever's doing this wins."

"Let them win. Let them win their way all the way to prison. In the meantime, we'll be in New York."

"And what makes you think whoever it is won't follow us there?"

"What they want can't be found in New York."

I sighed. He was right. "Three days. Give me three days. We'll hold the gala, and then we can leave."

He crossed his arms.

"You've got this entire island locked down with security. Nothing strange has happened since Adele had her fall."

He quirked a brow, and I knew he was thinking of my encounter inside the room at the bottom of the conservatory stairs.

"Nothing non-ghost related has happened here since Adele's fall," I amended. "Let us put on the gala, and then I promise, I'll go with you to New York."

He lifted his chin. "And are we going to discuss how the skeleton splayed out over Penelope's open grave ties into all of this?"

I narrowed my eyes. "Obviously, someone was looking for the diamond. Let's assume they didn't find it, since Horace's ghost seems pretty obsessed with it being missing."

"No," Ephraim shook his head. "I mean, how did Horace get there? Why do you think Horace Leroux has been lying in the Darling burial plot with a bullet hole in his skull?"

I looked down at my feet. The dread I'd been holding

back since we left the cemetery rising quickly to the surface. I already knew what Ephraim was going to say.

The clock ticked twice. Three times. Four.

"Someone in your family killed him, Whitney. And they stole his Egyptian diamond."

"I know that," I said, wrestling with the implications. About William and Julia. About all the Darlings. About me. I met Ephraim's gaze. "They must have had a good reason."

I gasped, remembering the letter I'd found. The apology letter from William to Julia. About what they'd lost, and how he'd make it up to her.

"Williams's letter," I whispered.

Ephraim nodded. "I thought of that. What's important right now is that clearly, we aren't the only ones who know about this. And that makes everything exponentially more dangerous."

"Ephraim, we can't cancel the gala. If any of this gets out somehow, a cancelled event will only make things look worse. We should go on as if nothing is wrong."

He stared at me a long time, temper flashing in his eyes. "Fine. We'll stay for the gala, and then we're getting the hell away from here."

I glared at him. "Don't be an ass about it."

He scowled, the muscles in his jaw ticking rhythmically. "You're my wife, Whitney. You're my responsibility. As is this house, and that damned magical fairy dust glass studio, all of it. You're mine to protect. So yes, if you're being threatened, it's my job to be an ass. It's my job to be a damn savage."

He turned and stormed through the door, slamming it shut behind him.

I fell backward onto the bed and squeezed my eyes

closed, a thousand questions and hypothetical situations all clamoring for agency.

At least now, one thing was crystal clear.

A century after his disappearance, we had found the missing, unhallowed remains of Horace Leroux.

Chapter Twenty-Five

Whitney Darling

Moonlight filtered, soft and silver, through the bedroom window. I cracked my eyes open, not bothering to focus past my lashes, and breathed in the musky scent of Ephraim on the sheets beneath my cheek. I reached out for him, my fingertips seeking the warmth of his skin, the strong swell of his muscled back, but there was only cold emptiness beside me.

Still fuzzy with sleep, I sat up. His side of the bed was still perfectly smooth. I looked down at my watch, straining to see the tiny gold hands. After midnight. My heart fell. He was still angry.

I swung my legs over the side of the bed and walked to the window, half-expecting to see his shadow stalking down the boat dock and the glistening, delicate marsh. But there was nothing.

Turning for the door, I wrapped my white silk robe around me, and stepped into the dim hallway. The house was still and quiet. Too quiet.

I paused, listening for the sound of rustling skirts. But

there was nothing, no chatter of Ephraim's security detail, not even the soft ticking of the grandfather clock.

I was alone.

I floated down the stairs, my fingers grazing the cool wood of the banister. Surely, Ephraim was in the study working.

I turned and walked slowly down the candlelit hall, my gaze bouncing between closed doors, my heart sinking with each step.

No warm light came from the study.

No Ephraim.

Where was he? Had he left me here?

A sharp, startling clatter, like the sound of a champagne flute hitting the floor, echoed from another corridor far ahead. I hurried forward, my white robe fluttering around my bare feet, until I rounded the corner and found myself standing in front of the heavy oak doors to the ballroom.

One of them was cracked open, and the soft patter of footsteps, stilted and moving at odd intervals, lilted out into the hall.

I crouched low and peeked through the crack between the doors, pressing my face carefully against the wood and swallowed a gasp.

A tall figure moved in the middle of the cavernous, chandelier-draped room.

A man dressed impeccably in an old-fashioned white tuxedo, turned on his heels, gliding across the center of the dance floor in the most rhythmic way. His arms extended gently in front of him, as if he were holding an invisible, beloved partner.

It was hypnotizing, the elegant flex of his shoulders, the steady, alluring sweep of his thighs. Golden hair, awash with waves and thick curls brushed his collar, a stark contrast to the sculpted angles of his shadowed profile.

He swayed in the moonlight, his cadence so clear I could almost hear the tempo of the waltz he danced to, the heady, tinny melody of a big brass band. Gradually, his pace increased, one two three, one two three. One, two –

My eyes widened as, one by one, the candles in the Darling chandeliers above his head began to glow, soft orange at first, and then golden, reflecting light off the delicately molded ceiling.

A quickening, a strange, gentle whisper in my head, made me straighten. As if in a trance, I pushed gently against the door and stepped inside.

The waltzing man came to an abrupt, flourishing stop, his back to me.

"Whitney, lovely girl."

His breaths came slow, as though turning would take energy and, somehow, deep emotion.

The voice from the conservatory, the same one that had begged me to free him while I sat on the stairs.

My blood went cold, but I wasn't afraid. This was meant to be.

I had unleashed the curse. And it had led me here.

To this moment.

I took a single step forward and he turned. Vacant, black eyes rooted me to the floor. Though there was no expression in them, the pent-up anger behind his vacuous gaze was palpable, contorting his otherwise angelic face with pained rage.

He came toward me, his stature suddenly slack. Then he was limping, one of his legs giving out until he dragged it awkwardly beside him. His shoulders slumped and twisted, his golden hair faded to a mess of dull, matted tangles, and his cheeks sunk hollow, and a sallow shade of green crept over his skin.

His neck snapped audibly, canting his head to an odd angle, and his full lips turned blue and cracked open in a grimace of frustration as he struggled toward me.

And then, ever so slowly, a purple wound opened above his left brow, blistering, then caving into his skull until only a red, oozing bullet hole remained.

I stood glued to the cold marble floor, hypnotized by a mixture of fear and morbid fascination.

"Whitney Darling," he whispered through split lips. *"I've been waiting for you."* He lurched forward.

The movement snapped the frozen tether inside me, and I darted backward, a shrill scream ripping from my throat. My ankles tangled around my robe, and I tripped, landing hard on my bottom.

He crouched low beside me.

"You're so like our Julia." A bony fingertip brushed my thigh. *"And you have something that's mine."*

All at once, the heavy scent of rotting marsh and dirt stung my nostrils, rancid and suffocating. I squeezed my eyes shut against the gaze of the now-putrid corpse crouching in front of me. I screamed again, kicking wildly.

"Whitney."

"I don't have it!" My voice cracked, my chest constricting on the rotten air. "I don't have your diamond."

"Whitney!"

My eyes flew open and on instinct, I wrapped myself around Ephraim, latching to his naked waist like a vice.

His heart pounded under my cheek. I drank in his spicy, familiar scent as I struggled to breathe, my mind and body slowly waking to reality, and the fact that I wasn't about to die.

He pulled me upright and into his lap. "I'm here," he soothed, his fingers brushing through my hair. "It was only a nightmare."

My breath came fast now as I fought tears. "Horace."

"I gathered that when you wailed about not having his diamond. You almost kicked me in the face."

"I'm sorry," I whispered on a halting laugh.

He wiped a tear from my cheek. "It's okay," he smiled. "I'm unscathed."

I sat back in his arms. "You're here."

"This is our bed, and it's the middle of the night. Where else would I be?"

The last paper-thin vestiges of my dream fell away. "I woke up and you were gone. I went looking for you and I found Horace in the ballroom."

"I take it he wasn't happy to see you."

I pursed my lips. "I suppose, in a strange way, that's up for debate."

Ephraim's brow furrowed.

"Never mind."

I jumped at the sound of a loud bang from downstairs, followed in quick succession by another.

"What now?" he growled, setting me gently on the pillows.

I watched his naked outline as he stood from the bed and pulled on a pair of jeans.

"Stay here," he said. "I'll go see what that's about."

I lunged after him. "If you think you're leaving me alone in the dark, you've lost your mind."

"Fine," he chuckled.

He tossed me my robe, and I wrapped the white silk tight around me.

Ephraim unlocked the bedroom door and stepped into the hallway.

I followed him, happy to see that unlike in my dream, the house appeared well-lit and there was a distinct chatter of security personnel downstairs.

One of them, a young handsome man named Blake met us at the top step. He nodded to me in greeting. "Everything's clear, Mr. Callaghan. The banging you heard was Mr. Darling at the door. He's on the approved list of visitors, so we escorted him to the parlor. I was on my way up to let you know."

"Mr. Darling?" I said.

Ephraim looked down at me. "Did you know your father was coming?"

"He never said a word to me. Not even a text."

Ephraim thanked and dismissed Blake, then ran a jerky hand through his hair. "Alright. Let's see what's brought your father to Darling House at three in the morning."

* * *

Daddy greeted us in a fury. He radiated annoyance as he stood from a leather club chair, rain dripping from the sleeves of his black coat.

He glared at Ephraim and I as we came down the stairs to greet him, bringing us up short.

"What the hell's going on around here? And why doesn't there seem to be anyone present who can handle it?"

Ephraim made a sweeping motion across the room. "Make yourself comfortable, sir. Can I offer you wine? Whiskey? Melatonin?"

Daddy scowled and tore off his coat, revealing a mud-stained white shirt, slacks, and a set of gold cufflinks that winked at his wrists. A trail of muddy footprints traced a path from the marble floor in the foyer over to the carpet where he stood. His shoes were covered with mud. And the bottoms of his pants too.

"Did you take a hike in the marsh before coming inside?" Ephraim quipped.

Daddy glanced at the floor then gritted his teeth. "I stopped at Bonaventure on the way in. To see the disaster for myself."

"Bonaventure isn't on the way in from the airport," I said.

"I didn't come from the airport."

I crossed my arms, suddenly cold. "I don't understand."

"I've been on Isle of Hope the past few days. On business. I turned on the news this evening, and what do I see? A dearly departed Darling family member splashed all over the headlines. It's the scandal of the year. The decade. Not only are literal old skeletons coming to light, but the fact that my daughter was married under duress." He emphasized that last part with air quotes. "Are the elites going back to the tradition of arranged marriage? The Savannah public is enthralled to know."

My cheeks burned, and I felt Ephraim stiffen beside me.

"I don't understand," I whispered.

"I'm telling you the gig is up. The details of your ridiculous marriage, your grandfather's will, and the shame of a desecrated family grave are all over the local news." Daddy's eyes softened a degree, but his tone dripped with derision. "You should've come to Paris with me when you had the chance. As it stands, your mother can hardly contain her horror."

"We'll handle it," I said.

"It's no one's business but ours," Ephraim continued, pulling me close to him. "Gossip never keeps. This will blow over."

Daddy snickered and shook his head. "And what about these break-ins? Is there a reason why in this day and age no one under this roof, security or otherwise, can tell me what the hell is going on? How hard is it to catch a vandal and a thief?"

The way he looked at me made me feel like a little girl again, but I didn't care. "We're figuring it out. Admittedly, the police haven't been much help."

"Well, they wouldn't, would they?"

"There aren't many clues to go on," I said. "Whoever's behind it seems to know exactly where to go, and when, in order to not get caught."

Daddy grunted, then slid off his muddy shoes and kicked them into the corner of the foyer. "I was days from closing a new contract. I had to reschedule three weeks out to come here and take control. Hell, your Aunt Adele looks like she met the wrong side of a donkey. And your mother is more neurotic than ever. And that's saying something. No, this situation is going to take more than additional security."

"Daddy, we – "

"Shut it, Whitney."

Ephraim released me, stepping forward. "That's enough. You come here in the middle of the night, you disrupt our rest, and you insult me. I can excuse all of that, but you disrespect my wife, and we have nothing more to say to each other." He pointed to the door. "Leave."

Daddy stared blankly, visibly warring between surprise and fury. "This is my house."

Ephraim shook his head, smiling wickedly. "This house belongs to Whitney. It was left to her. No one else."

"Well, she's doing a shit job of managing it."

Ephraim's face turned a shade of red I'd never seen. He stalked toward my father, towering over the significantly shorter, softer man. "Leave, now."

"Do you have any idea the liability of this place?" Daddy asked, his tone milder now. "The way things work these days, a burglar falls down the steps and breaks a leg, he ends up suing you. Chances are he wins." He raked a hand through his grey hair. "Stupidity."

I took a deep breath and squared my shoulders. I loved my father. But I would never understand him. He'd always been disappointed with his life at Darling House. He was a man born to be king of his own castle. And then he'd married my mother and become another Darling living under Granddaddy Alistair's roof.

It was how things were done with the Darlings.

Mama told me once, that he'd sworn to her he wanted this life. But not long after they'd married he seemed to change his mind. He was all bluster. Granddaddy Alistair had helped to keep it restrained. But he wasn't here now.

My father's stomping reverberated through the foyer as he retrieved his coat and shoes, punctuated only by a flurry of curses as he stalked past me. He swung open the front doors, pausing to stare down Ephraim's security detail on the porch. "I love you, Whit," he said, and then he left.

I turned to Ephraim.

He stood in the middle of the foyer, his hands in his jeans pockets. "I'm sorry that happened, sweetheart."

He held out his arms, and I stepped into them, burying my face in his bare chest.

"Do you think it's true?" I asked. "What he said about the headlines?"

Ephraim sighed and pulled his phone from his back pocket.

I turned in his arms to watch him tap a few buttons, pulling up the local news app and scrolling down to the most recent top articles. And there, dead center, beneath a headline that read, *"DARLING DOWNFALL?"*, was a photo of us, standing next to Officer Evans in Bonaventure Cemetery, the bright white tarp draped over Penelope's tombstone.

He clicked on the link, and we stood reading together in silence.

The article laid out our family's difficulties with startling detail. From the unusual stipulations of Granddaddy's will, to the repeated break-ins and heavy security at Darling House. It was all there, all of it. Including the desecrated grave.

And the primary reference? Miss Evangeline Walker.

I let out a long sigh. "Looks like your ex-girlfriend has gotten her revenge."

"Let's forget about that for the moment." Ephraim clicked off his phone and turned me back around to face him, "Whitney, Evans still thinks all of this is an inside job. If that's true, then someone in your family, or someone close to them, snuck out to Bonaventure Cemetery and dug up a one-hundred-year-old grave the other night. The same night we were there. And I don't believe in coincidences. Whoever it was, followed us out there. Or at least, knew where we'd gone."

I groaned.

"Your father's the only one with the resources. I don't know how he's doing this. But I'm going to figure it out."

I looked down, unable to meet Ephraim's gaze. He was right. Outside of Francis, I didn't know of anyone else in the house who could've managed to unearth a grave in a matter of hours. Assuming they hadn't hired someone.

"It could've been Francis."

Ephraim shook his head. "You and I both know that's not it."

"What do we truly know about him?"

"Besides the fact that he's my close friend? Francis loves your sister. He'd never do something to hurt her."

I looked up at him, tired, confused, and done with every bit of the drama at Darling House. "People in love hurt each other all the time."

His gaze softened, and he caressed my cheek with his thumb. "I've got to tell Evans about your father's visit tonight."

"I know," I sighed, and something deep inside me broke a little. "I need some time alone."

Ephraim nodded, then pressed a kiss to my forehead. "Don't go far."

* * *

A persistent, moaning wind blew in from over the ocean, slamming against the stone walls of the glass studio, making the windows vibrate and tremble. On the table in front of me lay a menagerie of memory, a collection of seemingly unrelated artifacts that I knew pointed to a common reality, only partially revealed.

I sighed. And it was on that reality all my hopes depended.

I had no idea what my father had been up to in the cemetery. Or if he had anything to do with the skeleton that had been unearthed there. I could hardly let myself consider it, regardless of what Ephraim said. Because if I did, that implicated him in quite a bit more than disturbing a grave. It would mean he'd had something to do with all the trouble at Darling House. And while I knew he truly hated this place for his own reasons, I couldn't believe he would subject our family to that kind of distress.

As for how the Darlings had ended up cursed?

It looked very much like William had murdered Horace Leroux and Julia had known.

It was the only explanation I could think of for why Horace's body had been buried in a mismarked grave. Penelope's grave. But then, where was Penelope?

And where was the diamond?

I gazed down at the photo of her cradled lovingly in Julia's heartbroken embrace.

What did Horace Leroux's disappearance have to do with Penelope's death?

A flurry of vivid possibilities clambered for agency in my mind's eye. None of them pleasant. And none of them all that viable.

I stared down at the delicate letter in my hands, William's chandelier above me casting the old paper in a golden glow.

> My Julia,
> No words can undo the grave happenings that have befallen our household. What we've lost – I cannot write it. The pain is too great.
> I would not undo what I did. These hands alone will bear the responsibility. I didn't protect you as I should have, my love. For that, I am eternally sorry.
> You are the center of my world, and we will persevere in the face of this chaos. I have seen to it that a quiet and blessed life will make up the days ahead, for

us, and for the generations to come here at Darling House.

Forgive me, my love.

To new and charmed beginnings,

Your Darling William

I set the letter down on the table and let my gaze travel over the items I'd carefully placed there, hoping that seeing them gathered that way might spark some epiphany.

William's letter, the mourning pendant with Penelope's hair, a copy of the photo from the newspaper article showing William and Julia alongside Horace and his sister, Layla, on the night he disappeared. The photo that had been left on the floor of the glass studio after the break-in with Julia holding Penelope, her foot atop the golf ball sized diamond.

I stared at the photo of the four of them together, all of them young, beautiful, and happy. How was it that hours later Horace would go missing forever?

Had they plotted to kill him? Was my ancestry nothing like what I'd been raised to believe? Was the sparkling Darling legacy a lie?

William's letter suggested his actions had been a necessity. A point of protection.

And what about the glass? What exactly did Granddaddy, or the ghostly Mr. Potter for that matter, think it remembered?

And if the glass did remember something, why wasn't it talking?

A note chimed on the piano behind me.

Julia was watching. Waiting for me to figure out what must be so desperately obvious.

I sighed and sank onto Alistair's old polishing bench.

"What are you doing here alone?"

I spun around.

Ephraim leaning against the doorframe. He held a long black umbrella, at his side like a cane.

"How long have you been standing there?"

"I'm the one asking the questions." His green eyes sparked with anger. He was dressed all in black. Black tailored shirt. Black jeans.

Black mood.

"Ephraim, I don't have the energy for your temper. I told Blake I was coming to the studio. Your crew of special agents are keeping a close eye, I'm sure."

"And yet," he stepped inside and shut the door behind him, "I find you here alone."

"I'm not alone," I said, matter-of-factly.

"Ghosts don't count," he snapped. "The glass doesn't count, either."

I pointed at William's chandelier, heavy and dripping with glimmering glass and crystals. "Haven't you heard? The glass sees everything."

"I've heard." He stepped closer, his approach punctuated by a flash of lightning and an immediate boom that shook the rafters. "What could the glass have watched here tonight, I wonder?" he growled. "Could it have seen you followed? Hurt? Taken? The possibilities are endless."

My stomach twisted with each abrupt and horrible word.

"I told you, security knows I'm here." I knew that wasn't the point. I'd broken my promise to stay near Ephraim. He had a right to be angry.

But he didn't understand. I was with the glass. And somehow, that made me feel safe. Even if I couldn't explain exactly why. "I needed to be out here. It's the only place I can think clearly."

"If you would've asked, I'd have brought you."

"I wanted to come alone."

"Then you don't come! Don't you get that you're in danger?"

"I must figure this out. I don't have a choice."

His gaze fell to the photographs on the table, pausing a moment on the one of Penelope and Julia, "I told you, when Darling House is safe again, we'll find the diamond and be done with this. Let the dead be dead, Whitney."

I laughed out loud. "That's something coming from you."

He scowled, "What's that supposed to mean?"

"Your moonlight jaunts on the marsh, skulking around in the darkness, like some maudlin Bronte-inspired anti-hero, castigating yourself over Seth. You relive that day as often as I do." My chest burned, all the tension and overwhelm from the past days welling up in my throat. "You're as broken as I am."

He stepped closer, crowding me back against the polishing bench. "You're infuriating."

"And you're a hypocritical ass."

He grabbed my chin, his lips crashing down on mine before I could turn away.

The backs of my thighs pressed into the bench, knocking me off balance so that I had no choice but to wrap my arms around his neck to keep from falling.

His lips slanted hard and demanding, his tongue dancing with mine, as his hands moved to my waist. He lifted me up, guiding my legs around his hips as he carried me over to the baby grand in the corner, then set me roughly on the edge.

"We'll always be cursed," I whispered against his neck.

"We won't," he snapped.

"Ephraim."

"Enough!" His fingers went to my jeans, unfastening, then lowering the denim from my hips with practiced ease. My lace panties followed. And then he was pressing me back, until I lay across the top of the piano.

His lips found the sensitive flesh of my inner thigh.

Sparks flashed behind my eyelids.

"William's love protected Julia," he growled, his fingers digging into my skin.

"Let the dead be dead."

He chuckled, "Good thing we're not ghosts, Whitney Darling."

And then he set to work reminding me how alive we were.

Chapter Twenty-Six

Whitney Darling

"Ephraim and I met a relative of yours the other night." I poured a glass of whiskey from a crystal decanter on Granddaddy's desk.

The night of the gala had finally arrived. The ballroom officially opened in fifteen minutes, and guests were already being greeted in the foyer, attended to by the staff Monica had vetted and brought in for the event. Alongside Ephraim's additional security team, of course.

Solomon Potter, dressed in a chic black tuxedo, stood across from me beside the doors to the veranda. The scene reminded me so much of the first night I'd spent back at Darling House, when he'd given me Alistair's cryptic letter, and put this whole adventure into motion. "I have quite a few relatives," he said.

"I have a feeling you may not have met this one before."

He raised a bushy, white eyebrow "I see. I take it this wasn't a traditional run-in at the park."

"Not exactly," I said. "This one claimed to have been friends with William Darling. He resides in Bonaventure

Cemetery and seems to know an awful lot about Darling House."

Solomon nodded, looking amused. "My family's been tied to yours for as long as yours has existed, you understand. There are some ties that last forever."

"And secrets? Do those last forever too?"

His eyes crinkled up at the edges and he shook his head patiently, "Sometimes. But I swear to you, if I knew anything more about how to solve all of this, I'd have told you at the first."

I smoothed a hand down the front of my vintage, Gatsby-era gown. I'd known that, of course. But it felt good to hear him say it. It felt safe. I tilted my head back to study the glimmering chandelier above his head. "I need another protection charm," I said. "Something stronger than sage. Another mojo. It can be anything. I don't care. I'll pay whatever it costs." I straightened, reining back a flood of tears.

"Whitney."

"I didn't want to come back here. But I did. And now things are more dangerous and more complicated than ever. I can't let anyone else get hurt. I can't lose," my voice trembled, "I can't lose – "

"Ephraim?"

I nodded.

"Honey, I understand. I swear I do." Solomon lowered himself into Granddaddy's chair, crossing one leg over the other, and twirling his finger around the bone necklace at his neck. "I'm afraid another charm isn't going to put this matter to rest."

"Then what will? What if we never find the diamond? What if Horace never leaves us alone?"

"What has the glass told you?"

I glared up at the chandelier. "The glass won't speak to me. Not clearly. It's been weeks. I've asked it. I've begged it."

Solomon shook his head. "It's because you don't want it."

"Excuse me?" I barked.

He held out his arms, motioning to the cozy study around us. "You want what you know. You want back what you remember, the life you had before. But you can't move forward looking over your shoulder, sweet girl. The glass speaks to those who want it, the mystery, the risk. Ever onward, that's the way of the glass."

"I don't understand," I said, through gritted teeth.

"Yes, you do. You simply don't like it," he said, gently. "To truly hear the glass, you must become like the glass, my love. Unafraid to be broken."

A long silence settled between us.

"Why was Horace Leroux buried in Penelope's grave? Tell me that much."

Solomon shook his head. "Some secrets are buried so carefully it's impossible to uncover them. What my ancestors may or may not have been privy to, went to the grave with them. The Potter's are nothing if not loyal friends. If you're looking for those sorts of answers, I suggest you return to Bonaventure and see if you can't run into my grandfather again. I hear he was quite the gentleman."

I laughed and dabbed my eyes with the back of my hand, "I'll consider it."

He rose, crossing the carpet to pull me into a warm hug. "For tonight, let's you and I trust that all secrets will be revealed in time." He motioned to the door. "Come on. You don't want to be late to your own party."

"Thank you for always watching over me," I whispered, and then I leaned up on my toes, and kissed Solomon Potter on the cheek.

* * *

I descended the wide, curved staircase into the century-old ballroom, markedly free of Horace Leroux's dancing ghost, handsomely attired or otherwise. The elegant room was draped in glittering strands of golden lights. Delicate tables covered in black satin were decked with vases upon vases of white roses. Ivory lanterns and candlelit chandeliers hung low from the vaulted ceiling, playing court to the grand centerpiece sparkling down over the crowd, a massive, decadent Darling crystal chandelier. One of Alistair's greatest works. If someone bought it tonight, it would bring half a million to charity.

My eyes drifted lovingly over more pieces of Granddaddy's art, each placed strategically atop marble tables and columned pedestals, all of them up for silent auction.

A myriad of black and white photographs of Alistair with his glass, or posed inside the studio, or with his family and friends, hung from the ceiling from thick black ribbons draped low over the dining tables, a canopy of candlelit memories.

More than two hundred of the Lowcountry's most-notable were in attendance, all of them dressed exclusively in art-deco-inspired white tie attire. They crowded the room, swaying to music played by a live orchestra from atop a dais near the dance floor. Chimes of laughter rang out from every corner. Towers of sparkling champagne glasses stood sentinel at each end of the ballroom, while well-appointed staff bore trays of delectable gourmet bites, gold-leaf garnished caviar, juicy pomegranates, and enough sweets to satisfy a chocolate lover's darkest desires.

It was a dream.

I braced against the butterflies in my stomach. Once we saw the auction finished without any hitches, then Monica, Isla, and I would be cleared to celebrate a job expertly done.

I smoothed a hand over my vintage silver gown. It had been Julia's. The fine material was covered in tiny, sparkling crystals, complete with draping crystal cap sleeves, and secured at the back with a series of aquamarines. Matching earrings hung from my ears and my hair was swept in an elegant chignon fortified with an aquamarine pendant. The gown was a decadent piece of history, something that would certainly never be produced today. When we'd settled on the art deco theme for tonight in honor of the Darling family's origins, I'd known it was perfect.

Ephraim stared up at me from the bottom of the stairs.

"You're magnificent, Mrs. Callaghan-Darling," his easy drawl slid over my skin like warm velvet as he extended his arm.

He was devastating in his fitted, white tuxedo, at once the elegant gentleman and the dark, mysterious man who tamed the night marsh. I smiled and let him escort me into the crowd, noticing how more than a few women cast longing glances in his direction.

"How many people do you think are discussing our scandalous arranged marriage right this moment?" I asked, too caught up in the way he was looking at me to care what anyone else was saying.

A dimple flashed on his cheek, and he pulled me into his arms, stepping into the flow of a waltz that wound its way around the dance floor. Our bodies moved in perfect, fluid unison as he controlled our progress. "Let them talk," he said. "They'll get themselves so riled up they'll lose control of their auction paddles. It could lead to a smashing success for the arts."

"I like how you think." I laughed, my thoughts turning to Granddaddy as we swayed beneath ribbon-tethered photographs, an ocean of black and white memory. "This is an amazing turn-out."

"Your grandfather had an impact on a lot of people," Ephraim said. "Though, I think he'd be a little overwhelmed by all this fanfare."

"Wouldn't anyone at their own memorial ball?"

He chuckled, and the deep, easy sound made me smile.

I'd found in the past weeks that I loved to make Ephraim laugh, to see the little lines creep up at the edges of his eyes, and mirth light up the green. It was my favorite sight in the world.

I tightened my grip on his shoulder.

"Out of everyone here," he said, "I undoubtedly owe your grandfather the most. I suppose I should pledge the largest donation."

"Is that so?"

He bent low and pressed a kiss to my lips, lingering a beat longer than was proper, "Quite."

"Ephraim?"

"Yes?"

My heart swelled in my throat. "What if I decided . . . what if, after everything, and this year of marriage is through, what if I didn't want to leave?"

His expression became serious, and he pulled me closer. "I think it wouldn't matter if you did, wife. Because I'd come after you. And I'd bring you back to me."

My eyes pricked with tears. I tore my gaze from his, suddenly aware that if I didn't distract myself, I'd lose all control. "Mama and the aunts seem to be having a good time." I motioned over to where Rose and Adele stood regaling guests near one of the dessert bars. Adele was beautiful, her bruises carefully hidden beneath makeup. Mama stood beside them watching the party, beaming with more pride than I'd seen on her face in a long time. "I think as much as I resisted it, it's been good for them to be in town. Addison and Francis too. I forget that I had a two-year reprieve from Darling House. They've been here all along, taking the hits as they came."

"It's true," Ephraim said. "But none of them carried the burden you did. I think their happiness is due to your being home. You've brought Darling House back to life. Curse or no curse." He caressed my cheek with his thumb, "And that was brave."

"I didn't have much choice."

"There's always a choice, love." His eyes narrowed at something over my shoulder. He veered closer to the edge of the dance floor, bringing our waltz to a sudden stop.

A tender hand on my arm made me turn, and just as during our wedding, my father waited to steal me for a dance.

He smiled sheepishly down at me. "Good evening, Whitney."

"Daddy, what are you doing here?"

"It's a stunning party, sweetheart. You've outdone yourself."

"Thank you," I said, blinking away the shock of him standing there. Had my mother and aunts noticed yet? "I thought you were back in Paris."

"I couldn't miss the most talked-about social event of the season."

I narrowed my eyes. My father didn't give two cents about social seasons.

"Also, I've been worried about how we left things the other night. I was angry," he said. "I shouldn't have taken it out on you."

The orchestra started up again, and my father stepped forward, nodding dismissively at Ephraim as he spun us onto the dance floor.

We were both silent for a long time, moving with mechanical ease through the crowd as the music lilted, bringing the song near its close. I didn't miss the looks we garnered, accompanied by whispers out of earshot. Mama stood next to Solomon now, and I couldn't help noticing when he lent her his arm for support.

My father was a divisive man. People either loved him or hated him.

But no one wanted to end up on his bad side.

"You don't need to worry, Daddy," I said. "Ephraim and I are getting closer to figuring all of this out. The things that have happened in this house. You wouldn't believe it."

"Oh, I would. I believe it all. That's why I curse the day you married that man and tied yourself here all over again. You were so close to escape. I would've made a place for you in Paris, you know that." He tightened his grip on me, his face impassive. "Everyone judges me harshly for how I left your mother after Seth died. But death does different things to each of us, Whitney. Some of us it breaks, some of us it embitters, and some of us, in a strange sort of way, it strengthens." He twirled me in a final flourish as the music softened and faded into silence. "You, my dear, have become strong."

My father walked with me across the dance floor, back in the direction of where Ephraim stood watching us. Evangeline stood with him now, leaning close and whispering something in his ear.

I took a deep breath, reminding myself that Ephraim's time with her had been a fleeting thing. But seeing her stand so near to him, her luscious waves falling down her slim back, left bare by the black dress that clung to her svelte curves, made my nerves sharpen.

Had I ever looked that effortlessly put together?

I didn't miss my father's appraisal of the slender woman as we approached.

"Evangeline," I said. "How lovely to see you here."

She cast me a faint smile. "Whitney. Lovely to see you as well. What a demure gown."

"Thank you," I said, smoothing my hand down the priceless fabric that was anything but.

"It's vintage Chanel," Ephraim said, with a wry smile. "A gift from Coco to Julia Darling herself." Ephraim took my arm and drew me close to his side. "As a historian you must find that sort of thing fascinating."

"Quite," Evangeline blanched, then arched a well-shaped brow. "That's amazing."

My father cleared his throat. "Whitney, introduce me to your lovely friend."

"Daddy, this is Evangeline Walker. Evangeline, this is my father, Mr. – "

"Whitney, oh my goodness, can you believe it? Have you ever seen a gala this spectacular?" Monica's voice broke through all introductions as she grasped me by the arm and dragged me away from Ephraim. "We pulled it off."

I cast a look of silent apology back at my father, who

was already acquainting himself better with Ephraim's ex-girlfriend.

Ephraim's eyes danced with ill-concealed humor.

I swallowed my discomfort and let Monica, who wore a black flapper dress and elbow-length satin gloves, drag me to one of the champagne towers, where she plucked two crystal glasses free and handed one over to me.

"Just imagine all the money being raised. So many children will be blessed because of your grandfather's death. It's so poetic, wouldn't you say?"

I half-choked on my sip of champagne. I wouldn't have put it that way, but in an odd fashion, she was right. "Thank you for all your efforts, Monica. Alistair Darling's legacy will certainly live on through the artists funded tonight."

Her eyes flashed with an emotion I couldn't place. "Our legacies are truly all we have in the end, aren't they?"

"Whit, this champagne is to die for," Isla's excited voice made me turn. She was radiant in a green evening dress, her long blonde hair twisted in cascading curls over her shoulder.

"Well, it should be, seeing as how your brother supplied it."

She grinned. "He wanted to attend. But he wasn't able to put off his trip to Italy."

"You can't blame him," Monica said. "There's a lot of pressure on his shoulders running the family dynasty all on his own."

Isla shrugged. "Hardly."

"Oh, I bet he feels it more than you, being the firstborn." She took a long sip of her drink. "Y'all, excuse me. It looks like one of my museum contacts has arrived."

"Of course," I said, stepping aside.

Monica walked away, a professional, pleasant smile on her red lips.

"Well, that was awkward," Isla placed a reassuring hand on my arm. "I can never decide if she likes me or not. She's got to be one of the most uptight conversationalists I've ever met."

"I think she likes you fine," I assured her. "She's overwhelmed."

Isla raised a delicate brow but didn't argue.

Ephraim's hand settled on the small of my back and I relaxed against him.

"Come on," he whispered in my ear. The scruff of his beard on my skin sent little sparks of pleasure shooting straight to my toes. "I'm not done dancing with you, Mrs. Callaghan-Darling."

Isla giggled and I wasn't sure if the pink splotches on her cheeks were from embarrassment or the champagne.

"If you'll excuse us," Ephraim said, and led me back to the dance floor.

We danced forever.

I reveled in the steady pressure of his hand on my back, the way he moved us, like we were floating, effortless and ethereal over the black and white marble. The chandeliers above us sparkled like golden starbursts, mesmerizing in their beauty. They whispered to me, beautiful things, promises of destiny and children. Around and around we spun, one song after another, the wistful tones of cellos and violins, harps and pianos settling over the scene in a hypnotic evening rhythm.

"It feels good to enjoy a night with you," he said. "I mean without all the curses and ghosts and mystery business."

"Don't speak too soon," I warned.

He laughed and escorted me to the edge of the dance floor, before shrugging off his jacket and draping it over the back of a chair. "It's gotten warm in here. Join me for a walk on the terrace?"

"I'll meet you out there," I said, motioning to the powder room.

He nodded and stepped toward the wall of glass doors that opened to the gardens. "Don't be long."

A few minutes later I emerged from the powder room.

"Whitney." Evangeline took me by the elbow.

"Enjoying the evening?" I asked.

She twirled a slender finger around a chestnut curl. "As much as can be expected. I confess, it's strange to watch someone I was so recently intimate with married to another woman." She glowered down at me, the delicate lines of her face drawn. "Savannah may appear to be a city, but at its heart, it's a small town. A town of talkers."

"Are you trying to get at something?"

"The rumors. The news articles." A sly smile parted her red lips. "It makes sense that your marriage to Ephraim is only a business arrangement. In all the months your husband and I spent together, he never mentioned you."

I felt my cheeks flush, but I rolled my shoulders back anyway and pinned her with my most condescending smirk. "In all the time we've been married, he's never mentioned you, either."

"Trust me, Whitney, I'm not jealous. As far as I'm concerned, the two of you are made for each other."

A lie. I'd never seen a woman so green.

"Thank you," I said. "For the compliment". My phone vibrated in my clutch, and I silently thanked God for the interruption. I pulled the cell from my bag. "If you'll excuse me. It's Ephraim."

Evangeline smiled stiffly and turned on her heel.

Exhaling a long breath, I studied the glowing screen in my hand.

A text from Ephraim.

> *Meet me now. In the glass studio.*
> *It's about the diamond.*

Chapter Twenty-Seven

William Darling | 1930

Julia's white gown gleamed in the warm light of the dozen Darling chandeliers hanging above the ballroom, each of them whispering to me, a cacophony of joyous celebration. The room buzzed with the raucous chatter of our illustrious guests, while the orchestra carried the revelers in wave upon wave of dancing frenzy. It was a mass of glistening, champagne-happy bodies, too elated to remember anything of the hard years that had come before.

The first big party since everything had gone black, sad, and hopeless. This was the golden catalyst, the moment everyone had been waiting for, though they hadn't known it at the time. A new dawn was rising, and I was the Sun King himself, dancing the night away in my own Versailles by the sea.

"You look beautiful in your pearls, love."

Julia smiled coyly up at me. "I think it must be all the dancing."

I let my gaze fall to the swell of her belly, the exquisite

evidence of our passion and the chapter opening before us. "You've never been more lovely."

"Promise me life will never be uncertain again."

I leaned down and kissed her lips. "I'll do whatever it takes to make it so."

Her eyes glowed. "I suppose that's enough."

A commotion at the entrance of the ballroom stole our attention. A man in an ivory suit staggered through the door, his golden hair a torrent of tangled waves around his head.

"What's he doing here?" Julia gasped.

"He must've heard about the party."

She smoothed a delicate hand over her belly. "William, he'll only cause trouble."

"Go get something cool to drink. I'll take Horace to the conservatory and escort him out the back where his pride won't be too wounded."

"Pride? What pride could he have left at this point?"

I grimaced. "He's alive, so there's bound to be some in there somewhere."

Julia started to walk away, but Horace called out to her as he drew closer, forcing her to pause and take my hand.

I smiled tightly at him as he came to stand unsteadily in front of us, reeking of bourbon.

"You don't wish to welcome me to your party, Julia?"

"You and I both know she has nothing to say to you," I snapped under my breath, taking note of the curious attention we already attracted.

"She shouldn't take things so seriously. It was only a moment of passion."

Julia tensed, and I licked my lips, bracing against a wave of rising temper. "Horace, why are you here?"

He waved a dismissive hand in the air, "Surely, we've

moved past all this. We're brothers, William. Look at the gleaming spectacle around you. Not a square inch of this would exist, if not for me."

"That's up for debate, I'm afraid."

Horace gaped at me, looking genuinely insulted. "Perhaps, we should share the story about and take opinions on the matter." He motioned toward a group of ladies whose attention he'd drawn upon his arrival.

I grabbed him by the sleeve.

"Brother," Layla approached, her face carefully serene, but the look in her eyes told me she'd read the delicate situation perfectly. She looped her arm into her brother's and smiled up at him with a mixture of apprehension and deep affection. "What a pleasant surprise to see you here this evening."

Horace grinned, and pulled Layla close to his side, "I wouldn't have missed seeing you tonight for the world," he beamed. "You're a vision, my love."

Layla blushed, her eyes darting to the women who still studied our interaction with Horace. "We should step onto the veranda for some air."

"Excuse me, Mr. Darling." A young man in a black suit approached us, a camera hanging from a loop around his neck. "May I get a photo of your group, sir? I'm snapping shots for *The Daily Morning*."

Julia smiled at him and squeezed my arm.

I nodded stiffly.

"Wonderful. All of you get really close, now," the young man instructed, herding us so that we all stood side-to-side, Horace and I in the center. "Oh, yes, that's fine. Front-page-worthy stuff."

"Thank you, son," I said, as the young man shook my hand and walked away.

I turned to Horace, whose bloodshot eyes were studying Julia's swollen belly. I took him politely by the elbow. "You and me in the conservatory. Now."

* * *

Julia's white gown billowed around her legs as she ran onto the chandelier-lit landing of the grand conservatory's second floor. The flicker of ten-thousand glass crystals cast dancing shadows across her face as she stared at me and Horace.

I grit my teeth in frustration. I'd taken too long returning to the ballroom.

I'd tried to be patient with Horace, allowing him to regale me with his comings and goings, and his new business venture he meant to launch in an open warehouse he'd discovered on River Street.

Only he needed more funds.

In addition to the thousands of dollars he'd been given and promptly squandered since I'd allowed him the use of my apartments in town.

I'd told him no.

And now he wasn't only drunk.

He was angry.

"My love," Horace chimed, "come, join our little meeting. You must tell your husband. Make him understand."

"There's nothing more to say, Horace," Julia said gently. "We've helped you more than we should have already. It's time for the bird to fly the nest. Go and make something of yourself again. Do it for Layla."

Horace held up a shaking finger, his ruddy cheeks flaming, "You owe me. I released you from our deal, Julia, and you owe me."

"Deal?" A wave of dread washed over me. "Julia?"

Horace whirled to look at me. "My poor William, you don't know, do you? You truly haven't figured it out," a Cheshire grin spread across his face. "In return for your release from prison these eight years ago, your delectable wife agreed to give herself to me. Once a week when we first came to Savannah. As she did that first night off the ship. I'm nothing if not a man who appreciates beauty."

My heart pounded against my ribs. "You lie."

Horace kept smiling. "Tell yourself what you will."

I looked to Julia, expecting to see indignance, but her cheeks were flaming.

It was true.

Oh, God. It was true.

My vision narrowed and I staggered a step toward her, then doubled over.

"I went to them for help," Julia pleaded. "I didn't know anyone else. There was no other way to save you," she sobbed. "Darling, he gave me no choice."

"Your wife's indeed a loyal woman. She cried quite unattractively the first few times I took her," Horace leered, his eyes gleaming. "But neither was it unenjoyable."

"I'll kill you," I growled, my fists curling.

"I'm afraid, despite my compromised state, I'm too well-known to be murdered. You wouldn't leave your wife and child ruined and alone. Much better to settle this like civilized men. Give me what I'm due. Pay me back for giving you this life, and you'll never see me again."

"You forget where you found me. I'm far from civilized." I reached for the gun at my back.

"William!" Julia screamed.

Horace lunged and grabbed her by the arm, pulling her close to him near the top of the stairs. He gripped her face and pressed a hard kiss to her lips before scowling back at me. "You won't shoot toward your pregnant wife. Put the gun away."

"Release her." Sweat poured down my back. Blood whirred in my ears, turning the world at an odd angle. "You and I will settle this outside."

Horace stared at me, as if he considered the challenge, but then he pulled Julia closer, grasping her intimately around her waist.

"I promise you this," I growled. "You're a ruined man. You've gotten all you'll ever get from me."

Horace stiffened. "I'm not here for myself, William. It's Layla. She's ailing, she's," he hesitated, looking suddenly vulnerable. "She's pregnant, and none of this is her fault. William, you're a reasonable man."

"Reason leaves a man when he learns his friend violated his wife."

Horace shifted awkwardly. "Honesty is the purest form of flattery, Darling."

I shook my head. "You've got that phrase wrong. It's imitation." I took a step toward him, my fingers flexing over the trigger. "Imitation is the purest form of flattery. And I've imitated you, haven't I? I've done it so well, I've become you. I've replaced you."

Horace's face turned to stone. He twisted Julia's arm, making her cry out.

I took a step closer. "You think you're too important to disappear? No one is more important in this town than I am. And you made me that way."

"Give me what you owe me. Now, damnit, or I swear I'll ruin you," Horace snarled. "I'll tell them all where I found you. In a prison covered in dirt and shit. I'll tell them your wife is a whore."

"You'll tell them nothing."

I fired the gun.

It went off like a cannon, shaking the glass walls of the conservatory and setting the chandeliers trembling.

Horace staggered back, releasing Julia. A bright welt of red bloomed on his left shoulder.

Julia lunged for me, but despite his shock, Horace darted forward, grabbing her back by the arm, and in one fluid furious motion, he threw her down the stairs.

Her startled cry echoed shrill and horrible, followed by the sharp, sickening sound of her cracking against marble before tumbling down the steps.

I raced after her, faster than my feet could move, half-sliding, half-tripping in my descent. I reached her as she rolled to the floor.

Solomon already knelt beside her, his eyes aflame, "I saw everything, William."

I wrapped Julia's trembling form in my arms.

An agonized wail ripped from her lips. She curled into herself, clenching her hands around her swollen belly. "Our baby," she sobbed. A pool of red blood spread out on the marble floor beneath her, staining her white gown.

"What do I do?" I brushed her golden hair from her face. "Julia?"

"I'm so sorry, Darling," A tear traced a jagged path down her cheek, and her lips trembled, pausing, and hitching over some half-formed word before her eyes fluttered gently closed.

"Julia." My voice broke on her name as her body went limp in my arms. "Julia!"

Horace's halted breathing reached my ears. As if in a trance, I turned to see him staggering toward us, his face ashen. "Darling, is she –"

I lifted the gun at my side, and I shot Horace Leroux square in the forehead.

A stunned look crossed his face, a breath of a moment, before he crumpled to his knees, and fell lifeless down the stairs.

"Damn it, William," Solomon grunted, rising to his feet. "I mean, I don't blame you."

I watched, frozen, as Solomon grabbed Horace under the shoulders and dragged his limp body down the final two steps and across the conservatory floor. I tried not to look at the gaping hole in Horace's head. But my eyes returned to it again and again, making the seconds it took Solomon to drag him to the nearby garden supply closet last an eternity.

"*Darling, broken,*" the glass whispered, its ethereal voice, solemn and trembling in my mind. "*Broken.*" The chandeliers swayed back and forth, above me. The largest, my most beautiful creation, shuddered, sending thousands of tiny glass beads and shimmering crystals into timorous frenzy.

Dazed, I lifted Julia in my arms.

Solomon and I raced up two flights of stairs, bursting into the hallway. The sounds of the ballroom, not twenty feet away, echoed hollow in my ears.

"She's losing the child," Solomon said. "Doctor Sorrel is here. I'll get him. Discreetly. Take Julia to your bedroom. If anyone sees you, she tripped and fell down the stairs."

I nodded, steeling myself against a surge of panic that threatened to bubble to the surface.

"Once the doctor is on his way, I'll go clean the blood, find a padlock, and lock the garden closet. William, whatever happens, no one is to go in there."

"Solomon," I whispered, my voice quaking. "Solomon, please, if you've ever loved me at all – "

"No one will ever know." He squeezed my shoulder, turning me in the direction of mine and Julia's bedroom. "I swear it. Now, wake up, William. Time is of the essence."

Nodding my gratitude, I turned and raced down the hall, Julia's blood flowing in crimson streams down my forearm.

* * *

Our daughter, Penelope Julia Darling, was born to Heaven at two-thirty in the morning to the sound of booming thunder. Her sweet head was covered in blonde hair, like her mother's.

I cut three locks of it to keep forever.

Julia awoke not long after, her arms reaching out for the child.

I couldn't say no.

She cradled the tiny infant and she wept. Until I thought she might die from weeping. And then she looked at me with aching love, and grief, and something else that reminded me too much of shame. "Bring me his diamond," she whispered.

"What?"

"He's dead, isn't he?" Her eyes were vacant. "You killed him?"

"Yes, my love. I killed him."

Julia nodded. "Bring me the diamond. He took what meant most in this world from us. I'll take the same from him. And I'll tread over it, as if it were no more than a bit of coal."

"Julia."

"Bring it here, William. And I'll have my picture done with Penelope, before we – "

I rushed to her side as her words crumpled, and her breath halted with fresh waves of anguish.

"I would give up all of this. Everything we've built, to bring her back to you," I whispered. "All of it. For you." The muscles in my chest ached, and a rapid tap in my temple matched the beat of my heart. "But now is not the time for more vengeance. If someone saw we had the diamond it would be the end of us."

"When is the time, then?" A sob ripped from her lips as she rested her cheek against Penelope's tiny, feather-soft head.

Overcome, I twisted my hands into the fabric of my shirt, until the thin summer material strained, and my teeth ground together so hard they shot spikes of pain to my temples.

"I'm so sorry, Darling," she rasped between ragged sobs. "I'm so sorry."

I wrapped her gently in my arms. "This wasn't your fault," I soothed. "It was mine. This is mine to carry. Not yours. Never yours."

She bowed her head. Fresh tears raced down her cheeks now. "Where's Solomon?"

"He's fetching a boat." A boat bound for Bonaventure Cemetery. "He and I are taking care of loose ends tonight while the storm rages and no one will see."

She nodded, "And Horace?"

"In the closet at the bottom of the conservatory stairs. For now."

"There's nowhere they won't look. Once it's discovered he's missing, the police will tear this island, and all of Savannah apart."

She was right.

But Horace had been right once too. If I had been born good at anything, it was following a hunch.

Our precious, forever-sleeping Penelope. Hers would be a private funeral. Her mother and I would keep her close. Near to the undying love of her parents, and the watchful gaze of the glass that bore witness to her story.

I pressed a gentle kiss to the top of Julia's exquisite golden head. "Solomon and I have a plan, my darling. You can be certain, there's one place no one will ever dare look for Horace Leroux."

Chapter Twenty-Eight

Whitney Darling

The gala lights dimmed behind me as I strode away from Darling House. Strong, frigid wind howled over the marsh, whistling, and roaring in haphazard frenzy, like a banshee sailing the endless black.

I brushed my hands over my bare arms, wishing I'd taken the extra few minutes to grab a jacket from the mudroom. But the weather had hardly been a thought the moment I'd stepped from the ballroom and rushed across the lawn, beyond the parterre garden to where the manicured splendor ended, and wild earth gave way to Spartina grass and water.

Now, cutting an impression against the moonlight ahead of me, was the glass studio, and the warmth of a single candle flickering in a window.

I half tripped, half-ran up the wooden front steps, the material of Julia's gown catching and clawing, wrapping around my ankles in the wind, as if she herself tried to slow my progress.

My heart skipped a beat as I grasped the door handle, Ephraim's text playing in my mind.

Meet me now. In the glass studio. It's about the diamond.

Had he found it?

Excitement fueled my steps.

A shadow passed by the window, a flash of white and pale hair.

Julia. She was here too.

I swung the door wide, "Ephraim, why – "

My words died, greeted by the grey stillness of an empty room.

Only the flickering candle flame spoke to anyone else having recently been here.

"Ephraim?"

Silence.

"Hello?" I stepped into the dark studio and over to the center table, pulling my phone from my clutch to dial Ephraim's cell. The call went immediately to voicemail.

I looked down at the candlelit table in front of me. The photographs I'd been studying the other night lay there on the table, only they were arranged differently now. The photo of William and Julia alongside Horace Leroux and his sister lay in the center. I gasped as I neared, dropping my phone. Someone had scribbled over Julia and William's faces with black ink, the pen marks deep and furious.

I stared at the photo a long, paralyzed moment, icy fingertips of dread creeping down my spine.

"My great-great grandmother's name was Layla."

I whirled around at the voice. "Monica."

"The pretty woman in that photo. Her name was Layla." Monica stepped from the shadows beside the piano.

"Why aren't you at the party?" I asked, feigning calm.

An explosion outside made me tense.

The gala's grand finale. A fifteen-minute fireworks show.

Monica had insisted we end with a bang.

"Just in time," she said, pointing to the now glittering sky outside. "I've been so worried about how I'd get you out here, away from your arrogant husband. But then he went and left his jacket unattended. With his phone in the pocket, no less." She shook her head. "He made it too easy. I almost feel bad. Do you think he's figured out you're gone yet?" She lifted Ephraim's phone from the piano, then dropped it to the ground and stomped on it.

She took a step toward me, her smile not reaching her eyes. Her hair was a tangled halo, and her sophisticated dress had been splashed with pluff mud and ripped at the hem. She'd removed her elegant satin gloves, and now worried at a dirty bandage on her arm, twisting her wrist at odd angles.

She saw me notice and her smile morphed into a grimace. "I scratched myself badly digging up that grave. Come to learn, it wasn't worth the trouble." She shrugged. "No diamond. But you knew that, didn't you, Whit?"

"Monica, this isn't what you think," I said.

"No, it's not what *you* think!" Her face bloomed bright red, but she smoothed a hand over her hair and forced a composed smile. "I must admit it was a surprise to find my missing ancestor's remains beneath Penelope's marker. I might've claimed the discovery of Horace Leroux if I hadn't been committing a crime."

I shifted on my heels, trying to gauge how many steps lay between me and escape, when the door slammed open, hitting the wall with a reverberating bang that made the glass pieces on display tremble. Isla stumbled inside; her face ashen. Her eyes found mine, and in an instant, I knew that she'd followed me here. She'd been outside listening. And she'd heard every bit of Monica's admission. It was written all over her face. "Whitney, here you are! Everyone's looking for you," she smiled awkwardly and extended a hand toward me. "Come on, you're needed at the house."

"Welcome to our private party," Monica drawled, as though she was indeed the hostess of an exclusive affair. She bent with a flourish and pulled a gun from a holster on her thigh. "I was hoping you'd show up."

Isla blatantly ignored her, motioning for me to join her at the door. "Ephraim's here. Come meet him outside with me."

I stared at my friend. Had she not noticed the gun Monica waved in her direction? Was Isla in shock?

Was I in shock?

I stiffened, fighting to still the trembling that would make my teeth chatter if I gave into it.

Isla took another step toward me.

BANG.

I screamed. My ears rang, and my body shuddered, bringing my knees to the stone floor as Isla crumpled to the ground beside me.

Her hands clenched over her hip. Thick rivulets of blood oozed from between her fingers. Her eyes locked with mine, wide, and blue, and full of pain.

Monica sighed. "Ugh, sorry about that. I'm a terrible shot. Not fifteen feet away and I missed anything important." She lifted the gun again.

"Monica, no!"

Isla raised a helpless, bloody hand in the air as another shot rang out, this one in time with the explosion of more fireworks outside. A guttural wail left Isla's lips and she collapsed, motionless, to the floor, a fresh splotch of blood blooming over her shoulder.

"Damn," Monica said. "I promise I've been practicing. Third time's the charm."

I lunged at her with a shriek, but Monica skirted away, swinging the gun in my direction. "She'll bleed out before help arrives. The merciful thing would be to put her out of her misery."

"Monica!" Ephraim's shout boomed from the door.

We both turned to look at him.

My heart leapt in my throat.

He too held a gun in his hand, leveled steadily at Monica.

"Ephraim, we've been waiting on you," Monica motioned for him to enter.

"Drop the gun and I'll make sure you get the help you need," Ephraim said, deadly calm.

Monica cackled, her eyes widening with delight. "I'm not going anywhere until I'm given what I'm owed."

"What do you mean?" I asked, hating the desperate tremor in my voice.

"Oh, Whitney. Don't pretend you don't know."

"The diamond?"

"Yes, the diamond," she spat the words. "But it's so much more than that, isn't it? It's what your family took from mine. It's the life I should've had. The life you stole from me."

Ephraim stepped into the room, squatting down beside Isla to press his fingers to her throat. He grimaced.

God, let her be alive.

"It's been you this whole time," I snapped. "You broke into the house during the funeral. And it was you who tore apart the glass studio that night."

"Of course," she smiled. "But don't sell me short, Whitney. I've done so much more. You all believed Alistair broke his neck tripping. His neck was broken before I pushed him down those stairs. Like how I pushed Caleb's ladder from beneath him the day he found me snooping in Alistair's office. And Adele. She's too observant for her own good, and too stubborn to die. A true steel magnolia, I'll give her that."

I doubled over, suddenly nauseous. Murdered. She'd murdered my brother-in-law. And Granddaddy. The man who'd helped raise her, taught her glassblowing and the business, and welcomed her into our lives, as he had her mother before. "Granddaddy loved you," I whispered. "Our families have loved each other for generations."

Her eye twitched. "No. My family has worked for your family for generations. We've been the damn help, Whitney."

"How did you get in and out of the house?" Ephraim snapped. "On and off the island?"

"I never left," she said proudly. "Do you know how many crawlspaces there are between the walls in Darling House? How many little hidden crevices? I could come and go as I pleased, and none of you stupid superstitious idiots were ever the wiser. I had run of the entire house."

"Monica," Ephraim growled. "Put down the gun. We'll work this out like civilized people."

A maniacal grin contorted her prim features into strange angles, terrifying in the flickering candlelight. "I'm entitled," she whispered, wrapping a finger around a lock of hair, twisting it until I thought for sure she'd rip it out.

Ephraim stepped toward me, as though he meant to take me by the arm, but Monica rushed forward, pressing her gun against my forehead.

My heart stopped.

Ephraim froze, his gaze not leaving mine.

Tears pooled in my eyes, clouding my vision. I'd known

that if I came here, back to Darling House, that I would die. But I'd never imagined it would be like this.

"Drop your gun, Ephraim," Monica barked. "I didn't come this far for nothing."

Ephraim slowly knelt and set his gun at his feet.

"Kick it to me," Monica snapped.

Ephraim did as she asked, his scowl murderous. "You realize you fired two shots already. Chances are you've got about five security guards outside those windows, each with their gun aimed at your head."

"I doubt it, with all the fireworks going off, but if that's the case, let's hope they have some brains. They shoot me, and Whitney dies," Monica snickered. "Now, which of you is going to tell me where that damned diamond is hidden?"

"Monica," I whispered. "We don't have it. If you've been watching us so closely, you should know that."

"You, stupid fool!" she stomped her foot. "All of this was supposed to be mine. Julia loved Horace. And he loved her. It was William who kept them apart. It was William who committed murder and stole my family's legacy." She waved the gun above her head, motioning to William's magnificent, glittering chandelier. "Either Layla never figured it out, or she didn't care. But I care, and I'm taking it back."

I caught the flash of a white gown behind the piano.

Julia.

A low moan, the sound of a woman in pain echoed through the studio.

I looked over at Isla. She still lay unconscious.

The moan sounded again, but neither Monica nor Ephraim heard it.

William's grand chandelier rocked gently on its chain.

Back and forth, back and forth, hundreds of pounds of blown glass and crystals glinting in the candlelight.

Look to the chandelier.

The glass remembers.

The soft sound of a baby crying sailed on the wind outside.

Look to the chandelier.

Suddenly dizzy, I pressed my hands to the cold floor. I stilled, gasping as my finger grazed the tiny, familiar letter P carved into the stone.

"*Whitney,*" the glass whispered.

A tear traced a gentle path down my cheek as I ran my fingers over the inscription as my mind's eye watched all the details fall smoothly into place. How many times had I been in this exact spot?

"*P is for patience.*"

"*P is for passion,*" William's chandelier recited my grandfather's words, the ones he'd used to teach Seth and I countless lessons here, in this studio, the true bedrock of the Darling family legacy.

I stiffened, bracing for the revelation I knew was coming.

"*P is for Penelope.*"

All this time.

Here was where William and Julia had hidden their secret. Where they'd laid Penelope to rest, alongside Horace's treasured diamond. The one piece of evidence that could've been their undoing.

My gaze flew to Ephraim, but his sights were pinned on Monica. "How did you learn about all of this?" he asked, clearly trying to distract her as he inched closer to me.

"Her stupid brother died," she snarled. "Whitney was too torn up to help her poor mother prepare for the funeral.

So, like always, I stepped up. One day we were going through old albums, and there was the photo with Julia and her little brat, her foot propped on top of my family's diamond. I knew it the moment I saw it. The legend I was never allowed to talk about. So as not to insult the Darlings." She turned, stalking back and forth between us and the polishing bench behind her. "I started researching. Always so many steps ahead of you, Whit."

I inched forward, so close to Ephraim's gun that if I moved fast enough, I could reach out and take it.

Ephraim cast an eager glance in my direction, his eyes dark, the green depths telling me a thousand things at once.

That we would be okay.

That I shouldn't be afraid.

That he loved me.

"Alistair was on to me. I had to get rid of him," Monica sighed, turning to pin me with a look of feigned remorse. "It hurt me to do that. I want you to know." She raised her gun again, aimed at Ephraim's head. "Just like this will pain me too."

The gunshot shook the rafters.

I screamed but I was too late.

Ephraim reeled back, slamming to the ground. He glared up at Monica, blood pooling down his arm from his shoulder.

Ephraim, no. The world around me narrowed, caving in on itself, then cutting through me like a dull knife until I couldn't breathe. Tears burned behind my eyes. The curse. This moment. This was why I'd left. To never see him hurt. To never feel this pain.

"Damn, it," Monica rasped.

Her voice was muffled and far away, as if I were somehow underwater.

But the cocking of her gun was an electric jolt.

I lunged forward with a savage growl, scooping up Ephraim's pistol.

I crouched in front of my husband and pointed the gun back at a stunned Monica, who now stood directly beneath William Darling's grandest chandelier.

The chandelier that had asked to be moved here from the conservatory.

Because it had a destiny.

Even now, it swayed gently, back and forth, witnessing, remembering. *William's Pride.*

"*Broken,*" it whispered to me.

I centered my aim on the rafters, high above Monica's head, on the mess of cables and aged hardware that secured the chandelier to its mount.

A single note chimed from the piano in the corner. Julia stealing Monica's attention.

"*Be like the glass,*" Solomon had said. "*Unafraid to be broken.*"

I fired the gun. Three times fast.

With a splendorous groan, the massive chandelier came crashing down, all four hundred glimmering pounds of William Darling's finest work, right onto Monica's head.

Chapter Twenty-Nine

Whitney Darling

For the one who finds this,

My name is Solomon Potter, friend to William Darling.

I am not a humble man, but I am an honest one.

I was there the night Horace Leroux was killed.

I helped bury his body. He lies in Bonaventure Cemetery, where no one would ever look to find him, in the plot the Darlings purchased for their own eternal rest. His death is marked only by a tiny stone. A marker placed in remembrance of a lost baby girl, Penelope Darling, who died the same night at the hands of Leroux.

I leave this message here as testimony, that William and Julia Darling have committed no wrong, but have met out only justice, and atoned heartily since. Not only by nature of their abiding grief, but in the loyal care and support they have shown to Leroux's sister, Layla, and her offspring.

Here, in this humble, secret grave, lies the body of

beloved Penelope. An angel to guard over a priceless diamond. And she in turn, is watched over by William's glass. The glass that will always remember.

For my part, I have done all I can to ensure my faithful friends, the Darlings, are safe from wrath, supernatural or otherwise. I pray the marsh magic will suffice, and that the root doctor's mojo bestowed on the family will always endure.

Should something happen to me, this written account, and the truth, will live on.

- Solomon Potter

Pale sunrise sparkled on the river, shimmering like a thousand tiny diamonds winking out of time. The earthy scent of pluff mud was strong on the morning breeze. Black driftwood scattered the marsh beach alongside a variety of shells and a few stubborn oysters that poked up from the sand. The coolness made me sink deeper into the thick cashmere throw draped over my shoulders. I carefully folded Solomon Potter's delicate letter and slipped it into my pocket. I'd read it so many times now, I knew the words by heart. But each time my eyes traced them, I reveled in a comfort I hadn't felt in a long, long time. Certainty. Answers. Peace.

Ephraim stood silently beside me, his green eyes focused hard on the tossing water. My gaze traveled over his broad, strong shoulders. The bandage he wore over his wound was imperceptible beneath his thick, cabled sweater.

My heart clenched, and I slipped my hand into his big one, smiling as his warm fingers curled tight around mine.

"Looking for ghosts?" I teased.

He shook his head, a sly smile tugging at the corner of his lips. "The dead and I have come to terms."

A white heron swooped low and graceful over the water.

"How's Isla?" Ephraim asked.

"Doing great," I said. "Healing faster than expected. Her brother said she needs to lay off the true crime documentaries, though."

Ephraim chuckled. "Asher's always been a chicken about those things."

"Yeah, well, I'd say he has a right to be at this point."

The events the night of the gala had rocked Savannah like nothing else I could remember. Darling House remained the center of the region's media attention. So much so, that Mama and the aunts had elected to stay an extended period in Ephraim's house on Jones Street, while Francis took Addison and the kids to visit my father in Paris. I missed having them all around me, but at the same time, the circumstances allowed Ephraim and I a decadent amount of privacy. Though, he still retained heightened security across the island.

Ephraim's thumb rubbed back and forth across my fingers.

I took a deep breath. "Did you bring it?"

He nodded. "You sure you're ready to part with it?"

"Oh, I think I'm more than ready."

He chuckled and dug into his jacket pocket, careful not to jostle his bandage. He pulled out a glass vial, then held it up, studying it against the pale sky before handing it over to me.

I tested the weight of it in my fingers. Such a tiny thing.

Had it ever possessed the power to protect us from the wrath of Leroux and his missing diamond? Or as Ephraim believed, had everything that happened simply been the pattern of life, playing out in fine, interwoven detail?

Either way, after the night of the gala, we'd ensured that Horace was buried next to his sister in Louisiana, his long-lost diamond wrapped tight beside him.

No sense in taking any chances.

Penelope too, had been given a proper burial, moved to rest inside the Darling tomb with William and Julia. As I'd suspected it would, the piano in the glass studio had gone markedly silent, and not a glimpse of blonde hair or white gown was to be seen. Reunited with Penelope, Julia was at peace.

The glass seemed satisfied, finally speaking to me the way I'd always imagined it might. Darling Glass Company would remain alive and well. And if my suspicions proved correct, I'd be instructing Percy on the art of glassblowing in the next few years.

I took a step closer to the water, raised my arm, and threw the tiny, dirt-filled bottle into the river.

I released a breath I hadn't realized I'd been holding.

Ephraim pulled me into his arms, and his whiskered cheek caressed mine before he kissed the tip of my nose. I shivered as heat flickered to life inside me, and I pressed into him, breathing deep the scent of the ocean, and the river, and the Lowcountry air that had sustained me all my life.

My husband, Ephraim Callaghan, was deliciously dangerous, just as he'd been all those years ago, when he'd chased me, and caught me, and made me his.

On the horizon, the grey morning turned to gold and sang awake the trembling marsh and all the wild things.

Ephraim pulled me into his arms, "Have I told you that you'll be the death and the life of me, wife?"

"A time or two, I think."

He grinned and drew me closer. "I'll love you forever, Whitney Darling."

"Prove it," I whispered as he pressed his lips to mine.

And I knew that he would.

Epilogue

One year later.

Whitney, how are Ephraim and the baby?
You're never going to believe this. That haunted house on Liberty Street, the yellow one we always admired, it's finally been purchased, and the new landlord's renting out two rooms. No one can tell me much about her, but she's around our age. I'm going for it. Asher will be all right without me. Keep your fingers crossed. I sense an adventure on the horizon.
   -Isla

Return to Ophelia

A Gilded Gothic Romance Novella
Spring 2025

A wounded sea captain, dark and dangerous. A beautiful healer, trapped on a remote island off the Lowcountry coast. The year is 1750. And nothing is what it seems.

Enter Whitney & Ephraim Darling, the modern day Savannah power couple with a knack for attracting ghosts - and curses.

Once again, a tragedy from the past threatens their future, and on the haunted, beautiful shores of Ophelia Island, they must see an old injustice set to right. Or die trying.

* * *

Ophelia Island, 1750

Prologue

Pale lips.
Bloody hands.
Heart split wide

with rage.
Strangled. Boundless, reckless.
My heels in black, wet ground.
Above your cold skin.
Your perfect face.
Still heart. My heart.
Frozen fingers twist around the box. The last
    of you. The only piece.
A wild, ruckus, desperate plea. To marsh
    magic.
To bring you back.
Back, my love, to me.

Reviews are Like Love Letters...

If you enjoyed your time within the haunted halls of Darling House, a review would be so appreciated. Not only do kind and thoughtful reviews mean the world to authors like me, they also help others to find my book and enjoy the adventure.

Amazon Reviews | Goodreads

* * *

The Romance Continues...

For exclusive, members-only access to deleted scenes from **The Memory of Glass**, sneak peeks at upcoming books, my Savannah old money adventures, & more - join my Substack, *House of Darlings*.

Acknowledgments

If you're reading this, you're a part of a lifelong dream come true. Thank you from the bottom of my heart for spending a bit of your time here with me and the Darlings.

A book, much like a child, requires a village to thrive.

Timothy, I could write a thousand novels and never pen a romance that compares to ours. Your encouragement and unending support has made this journey a wonderful adventure. I love you more than words. Thank you, OBF. And Rhett, my little bunny, I hope I make you proud, my love.

Mama, there are truly no words. You introduced me to the craft of writing. You've read, you've critiqued, you've brainstormed - you've walked this journey with me from the start. Some of my fondest ever memories are of our times together at writer's conferences. Most of all, you've shown me what it looks like to be truly brave - valiantly vulnerable. You are, without a doubt, the best kind of person. Our family's very own curse-breaker. I love you. Thank you.

Daddy, thank you for always being there, and for always listening to my stories. I love you so much. Wil, Amber, Josh, Nicole, Steve - thank you for all the love and support. Zoe, Georgie, & Daisy - y'all are the sweetest. Our family is small, but mighty.

Chris & Cal - y'all's happy enthusiasm toward this dream has meant more to me than you know. I love you two.

Thank you to my copyeditor extraordinaire, Jean

Willett. It's so much fun when your great friend is also a professional punctuation wizard.

To my breakfast club gals - Alyssa, Wendy, Sarah, Yensy - y'all have been the best friends and most vibrant cheerleaders a girl could ask for. There's never been a better marketing team.

Miss Avery Ross, thank you for not only being one of the most exuberantly positive people I know - but for lending your heart and knowledge as my cultural sensitivity reader. I'm so lucky to know you.

Thank you to my many professional contacts in and around Savannah, Georgia who have contributed their knowledge and love for the Lowcountry toward this book. You know who you are.

To all of my fellow Seton Hill MFA grads - what a ride. Thank you for all the red ink.

And to Jeffrey Stepakoff - this idea took its first breath under your mentorship. Your encouragement fueled my art long after it was given. Thank you for believing in me.

Brenna Lauren, holds an MFA in Writing Popular Fiction from Seton Hill University, where she honed her talent for weaving sensual love stories set against the backdrop of haunted history and modern old money luxury. She's spent her career immersed in storytelling, whether through the pages of her novels or in building her luxury lifestyle & touring brands.

She resides in a historic Savannah townhouse with her husband and family. Together they indulge in a world of travel, fashion, and chandelier-lit parties in their neighborhood's haunted mansions. When she isn't writing, she can be found curating beautiful interiors, brunching with friends, or on her husband's well-muscled arm, seeking inspiration in the places where history and romance collide.

Find her on Instagram *@brennalauren* for behind the scenes updates, on her website (bren nalaurenbooks.com), and on her Substack, *House of Darlings*.